Praise for *Sweet Dreams*

"Carla Stewart has a knack for bringing to life the not-so-distant past of the 1950s and '60s. *Sweet Dreams* is no exception. Rich in detail and relationship, this story of two cousins seeking their own dreams amidst a tangle of relationships and secrets tugs the heartstrings in every direction. A lovely journey to self-discovery, truth, and freedom."

—Anne Mateer, author of *At Every Turn*

"*Sweet Dreams* is an inspiring novel and one that is heartfelt. Readers are sure to savor every page of this wonderful story."

—Michael Morris, author of *A Place Called Wiregrass*

"Pick up one of Carla Stewart's books and prepare to be enchanted by endearing characters, nostalgic settings, and lyrical prose. Capturing the angst of the '60s in the struggles of two determined women, *Sweet Dreams* is another outstanding novel from one of the best!"

—Myra Johnson, award-winning author of
Autumn Rains and *A Horseman's Heart*

"Carla Stewart writes about friendship, love, family, and what it is to dream. This is a book that takes you back in time, one that makes you laugh, and most of all, one that causes you to consider the importance of family. Like the best of Patsy Cline's music, *Sweet Dreams* is a book to be savored and enjoyed. What a funny and touching read!"

—William Torgerson, author of
Love on the Big Screen and *Horseshoe*

Praise for *Stardust*

"[An] enjoyable, worthwhile read."

—*RT Book Reviews*

"*Stardust* is told with heart and skill and obvious love for her characters. A gripping storyline that is inspiring and unforgettable."

—Julie L. Cannon, bestselling author of
I'll Be Home for Christmas and *Twang*

"A reverence for the past and a keen eye for interesting characters make *Stardust* as bright and magical as a twinkling neon sign on a dark, lonely two-lane. You'll love the journey as much as the final destination. Another winner from an author with a uniquely beautiful talent!"

—Lisa Wingate, national bestselling and award-winning
author of *Dandelion Summer* and *Blue Moon Bay*

Praise for *Broken Wings*

"While the story is heartbreaking, there is much more to this book...Stewart skillfully entertains and engages the reader with each character's private pain and survival skills."

—*RT Book Reviews*

"With apt descriptions and artful prose, Stewart delves into the vibrant, jazzy 1940s, at the same time creating a true-to-life present. Moving between the two time periods, readers discover what everlasting love is, and how strong a woman must be to recognize it."

—Christina Berry, award-winning author of *The Familiar Stranger*

"Carla Stewart writes powerful, beautiful, emotionally evocative stories that touch my heart. *Broken Wings* is no exception. I couldn't put it down."

—Susan May Warren, award-winning,
bestselling author of *Nightingale*

Praise for Chasing Lilacs

"Stewart writes about powerful and basic emotions with a restraint that suggests depth and authenticity; the relationship between Sammie and her mother Rita, the engine that drives the plot, is beautifully and delicately rendered. Coming-of-age stories are a fiction staple, but well-done ones much rarer. This emotionally acute novel is one of the rare ones."

—*Publishers Weekly*, starred review

"A warm, compelling tale with characters who will stay with you for quite a while…Those who lived during the 1950s will have delightful flashbacks, and those who didn't will get a true glimpse into that era. All will identify with Sammie and the friends and family who deeply influence her search for the truth about her family—and herself."

—*BookPage*

"Endearing characters, twists that propel the story ever forward, and soul-searching questions combine to create a heart-tugging tale of self-reflection and inward growth. Carla Stewart's *Chasing Lilacs* carried me away to 1950s small-town Texas…and I wanted to stay. I highly recommend this insightful, mesmerizing coming-of-age tale."

—Kim Vogel Sawyer, bestselling author of *My Heart Remembers*

Sweet Dreams

Heartfelt Fiction from Carla Stewart:

Sweet Dreams

Stardust

Broken Wings

Chasing Lilacs

Sweet Dreams

a novel

Carla Stewart

New York Boston Nashville

FaithWords

Hachette Book Group

237 Park Avenue

New York, NY 10017

www.faithwords.com

Printed in the United States of America

RRD-C

First Edition: May 2013

10 9 8 7 6 5 4 3 2 1

FaithWords is a division of Hachette Book Group, Inc.
The FaithWords name and logo are trademarks of Hachette Book Group, Inc.

The Hachette Speakers Bureau provides a wide range of authors for speaking events. To find out more, go to www.hachettespeakersbureau.com or call (866) 376-6591.

The publisher is not responsible for websites (or their content) that are not owned by the publisher.

Library of Congress Cataloging-in-Publication Data

Stewart, Carla.
Sweet dreams : a novel / Carla Stewart. — 1st ed.
p. cm.
ISBN 978-1-4555-0427-5 (trade pbk.) — ISBN 978-1-4555-0426-8 (ebook)
1. Cousins—Fiction. 2. Private schools—Fiction. 3. Brothers and sisters—Fiction. 4. Mothers and daughters—Fiction. 5. Communication in families—Fiction. 6. Forgiveness—Fiction. 7. Self-realization—Fiction. 8. Texas—Fiction. I. Title.
PS3619.T4937S94 2013
813'.6—dc22

2012033725

For Donna and Marsha
God made us sisters. Life made us friends.

ACKNOWLEDGMENTS

This book is dedicated to my sisters, not only because they are amazing, but also because they were there! Yes, in the glorious sixties with its miniskirts and bell-bottom pants, hairspray and hot rollers, cool cars and rock and roll. And now that we've grown up, their love and friendship mean more to me than ever. Thanks, Donna and Marsha, for sharing laughter, memories, and your hearts with me.

When the idea for *Sweet Dreams* came to me, I had grandiose visions of how easy it would be to plot and write. It was, after all, set in the era of my teens. I can only say that by the time I'd written the first three chapters for the tenth time, I wondered whose idea this book was anyhow. Thank goodness for critique partners, writing groups, and praying friends. Which brings me to the delightful task of thanking some key people.

Christina Boys. Your mad brainstorming skills and editorial insights defy description. You've made this a much better book in every way. Lauren Rohrig, Laini Brown, Shanon Stowe, and all of the FaithWords team—thank you for all you do behind the scenes creating marketing plans, cover art, and catalog copy and giving support to me, a grateful author. Sarah Reck, your excellent work and personal touches are above and beyond. You bless me more than you can imagine.

To Sandra Bishop who has my back and my heart. Thanks for everything you do!

An incident twelve years ago provided the seeds of imagination for the geological thread in *Sweet Dreams*. Craig Meyer, an enthusiastic geology student, rode with Max and me one day through the Canadian Rockies, ending at the Columbian Icefields. Craig gave us insider knowledge about the wonders we beheld. Now an accomplished geologist, Craig guided me through the "rock" scenes and had splendid ideas for adding authenticity. Thanks, Craig! A nod also to Dan Pettit who read the geology-related scenes and gave his stamp of approval. Any mistakes are mine alone.

In memory of the late Patsy Cline whose music has stood the test of time, I'll be forever in awe of her marvelous talent and innate ability to touch the lives of her fans.

Four special writing friends have, at various times, given me invaluable critique, advice, and a shoulder to cry on. Thanks Camille Eide, Myra Johnson, Courtney Walsh, and Carolyn Steele for every prayer, note of encouragement, and tweet. You know I'm in your corner, too.

I'm blessed by the friendships and encouragement of so many sojourners on this literary road: Julie Garmon, Judy Christie, Lisa Wingate, Marybeth Whalen, Ane Mulligan, Anne Mateer, Kathy Patrick (and ALL of the Pulpwood Queens!), Jenny Wingfield, Sarah Sundin, Julie Cannon, Joanne Bischof, Matt and Tracy Jones, and all of you in Sandra's online "support group." I appreciate you more than you know.

Thank you, Max, for being a willing participant on the journey. I'm grateful for your listening ear, for your love of great books, for every bookmark you've handed out at the golf course, and most of all, for your love.

Hey, kids—thanks for not calling me crazy even though you might think it. I'm proud of each one of you. Dream big!

To my dad, Mike Brune—thanks for sharing your stories with me and asking about mine.

Stories. That's what it's all about. Thank you, readers, for taking a chance on me, for your notes that thrill my soul, and for sharing my books with others. I write for you and my savior, Jesus, who makes it all possible and never fails even when I do.

Sweet Dreams

Two Forks, Texas, 1947

She found the stones the day they buried her mama. Three of them catching the sunlight, twinkling beyond the grave site. Her daddy clamped her small hand in his beefy, calloused one while she busied herself with sniffing the air, the smell of fresh earth tickling and sweet, mixed with the heavy perfume of roses. She itched to break free, to muster her way through the skirts that swished this way and that, to run past the stiff black britches of the men who stood like wooden soldiers at the ends of the box they said held her mama.

She craned her neck, keeping watch on the shiny stones. They winked back from their nesting place along the fence row.

When her daddy's hand went slack, she dashed for it and dropped to her knees on the grass, the scent of sage sharp from the field next to the graveyard. With plump fingers, she reached out shyly and touched the stones. They were warm like the summer sun, one of them full of sparkle with rough edges that bit into her fingers, another smooth, the size and shape of a pecan, black on the top and bottom with a ribbon of white through the middle. And the last one, dull brown and rough to her fingertips but flecked with a million black dots. When curled in her palm, it had a perfect indentation to rest her thumb.

"Whatcha got?"

She jerked her head around, then smiled. Her cousin, Paisley, stood with her hands planted firmly on her narrow waist, the taffeta of her dress noisy.

"Nothing." The spiny stone, the prettiest one, bit into the palm of her balled fist.

"Yes, you do. Show me."

One by one, she uncurled her fingers. "Here, you can have it."

"Really? Oh, look, it's covered with diamonds."

They plopped their bottoms on the grass and had just gotten settled when a shadow crept over them. Aunt Edith reached down and snatched Paisley up by the arm. "Come on. You're getting your dress dirty. It's time to go. Tell Dusty good-bye now."

When Paisley offered the stone in her open hand, Dusty shook her head. "You can have it and bring it tomorrow when we play."

Aunt Edith had already started toward the iron gate, pulling Paisley with her. Just one quick wave, and they were gone.

Paisley didn't come over the next day. Or the day after. Dusty's daddy said it was good riddance, and the way he spit the words out, she knew Paisley was gone for good. She squeezed her eyes to shut out the tears. Daddy didn't like crying. No tears for her mama. None for her cousin. All she had left was two stones—one with a skunk stripe, the other dull brown. She carried them everywhere in her pocket, the lumps as familiar as the dimple in her chin and the blue of her eyes when she stood on the bathroom sink and looked in the mirror.

She knew as sure as her name was Dusty Agnes Fairchild that the earth that swallowed her mama had given the stones in exchange. There was no other explanation. Later, when she told her daddy about them, he said she was mistaken about when she got them, that no three-year-old child could remember such a thing. He said there were a dozen places on the ranch she could've picked them up and that her imagination would get her in a heap of trouble.

She left him to his opinions and didn't mention that she also knew someday Paisley would return. She didn't know how or when, but the feeling never left her, like a tiny suitcase packed by the door, waiting for the day when the door would burst open and life would return to normal.

Then the summer after fourth grade, a fancy red Buick pulled into the drive and Aunt Edith stepped out dressed in a smart two-piece suit with a Peter Pan collar and high heels. She looked like a movie star with her painted lips and wore a cute little hat with a rosebud for decoration. Dusty could hardly catch her breath taking in the vision of her aunt and praying like mad that she wasn't alone. The back door of the car opened. Out stepped her cousin, but she wasn't the pixie-faced girl she remembered. Paisley kicked a rock, then stood in the drive, skinny as a stick, arms crossed.

"Now, sweetheart, remember it's just for the summer." Aunt Edith coaxed the unsmiling Paisley along toward the sidewalk and chattered. "My goodness gracious, Dusty, haven't you just turned into the most darling creature? All tanned and not awkward at all. I keep telling Paisley here that it's just a stage, that before you know it, she'll be as pretty as a picture."

Dusty pinched herself. Yes. Paisley had come, just as she'd always known. And Aunt Edith wasn't nearly what she remembered, either. She was elegant and shimmering. Like a mirage that rose from the blacktop in the heat of summer.

Trying to figure out what to do was impossible. Hugs? Handshake? She swallowed the boulder in her throat. "Daddy's not here, but he'll be back by supper if y'all want to come in."

Aunt Edith laughed, the sound carrying on the wind. "Won't

ole Flint be surprised? His baby sister showing up at the Fairchild ranch? I knew this was a good idea from the start. That's what I told Leonard, that there was nothing to worry about."

"Leonard?" Dusty's voice squeaked out the name. Of course. The driver of the car. She looked over and got a glimpse of the man driving. Big. Burly. Wearing a ten-gallon hat. He gave a tiny wave with just two fingers.

Paisley stepped up, her lips in a tight line. "Leonard. Mother's new husband. They're dumping me here while they go to Old Mexico on their honeymoon."

"Now, sweetie, we talked about this. You'll have a marvelous time. I bet Uncle Flint will let you ride the horses, and..." She looked at her wristwatch. "My goodness, look at the time. It's later than I thought. We can't stay. Come on now. Get your suitcase from the backseat."

Dusty thought she'd been punched in the belly. "You're leaving already? Without seeing Daddy?"

"We'll have worlds of time when we get back. Leonard's anxious to get on the road. Oh, you girls are going to have such fun."

The next thing Dusty knew, a cardboard suitcase sat on the driveway, and Aunt Edith was in the car. Leonard roared off, leaving a thundercloud of dust behind.

Paisley lifted her bowed head, her eyes the color of emeralds. The frown had turned into a half smile. She pulled something from her skirt pocket and opened her hand. A rock the size of a shooter marble glistened like a thousand diamonds in the sun.

Dusty's heart hammered in her chest, but she didn't let on. Instead, she gripped the broken handle of the suitcase with one hand and put her free arm around her cousin's shoulders. "I knew someday you'd come back."

CHAPTER I

Two Forks, Texas, 1962

The night of the party, Dusty wore a mango sundress with a swirling skirt, dangling turquoise earrings, and a matching turquoise necklace. A hot Texas wind blew across the mesquite and late summer alfalfa sending a playful ripple through her hair. Jack's dark eyes held hers as he twirled her on the sawdust floor of the outdoor pavilion, his lopsided grin holding promises of moonlight kisses when the dancing stopped.

Dusty lifted a bare shoulder and widened her eyes, feeling daring and flirty. A flutter in her stomach reminded her to be cautious and not take too much for granted. Just because she'd enjoyed Jack's attention the past two months didn't mean a lot with her leaving Two Forks in three days.

Miss Fontaine's was her daddy's idea. Not hers. Mentally she scoffed and let Jack spin her around, their fingertips barely touching. She dipped her chin and gave Jack a playful grin. At least she had tonight.

The party, on the south lawn of the ranch house, was in her honor—a late eighteenth birthday and going-away celebration all rolled into one. Her dad, Flint Fairchild, was considerate to put it together since he'd been gallivanting all over Texas the whole summer, whooping it up because three of his new wildcat ventures had paid off, gushing oil to kingdom come. He didn't fool Dusty for a minute. The party was a celebration for him, too, and there was nothing her daddy liked more than a good old-fashioned lawn party. With him the center of the attention, of course.

As Little Earl and the Wranglers played a lively version of "San Antonio Rose" from the bandstand, Dusty caught sight of her dad. Dressed in his customary starched white shirt, he wove his way through the crowd, dancing a spin or two with every woman in his path, light on his feet even in alligator boots. The ladies threw back their heads and laughed at his cleverness, and when he bowed and returned them to their husbands, the men nodded, respect and admiration on their faces.

Flint Fairchild two-stepped his way toward Dusty and Jack, a handshake here, a peck on a cheek there, and sidled up to Dusty as the song from the band came to a close. "Say, Dusty, think you could find me a tall glass of iced tea? I'm drier than a gulch in the desert after those barbecued ribs."

Before she could answer, Jack dropped his hand from her waist and said, "Allow me, Mr. Fairchild." He spun on the heels of his own Tony Lama's and disappeared under the awning where the food and drinks were laid out.

Flint pulled a monogrammed handkerchief from his back pocket and mopped under the brim of his Stetson. "I must say, Dusty. You're pretty as a Texas sunset tonight. And it looks like you and Morgan are getting on all right." His blue eyes drilled into hers.

"He's a swell dancer."

"Good kid from what I gather. Got his CPA the first rattle out of the box." He nodded at Lila May, the banker's wife, who sashayed by with an empty wineglass in one hand and a cigarette dangling from the fingers of the other, her eyes sparkling as she headed to the refreshment area.

A warning knotted Dusty's stomach. She knew what was coming. *He might be a nice fella and smart, Dusty, but you'd better watch your step and remember you're a Fairchild.*

None of the boys she'd dated, and she could count those on one hand, measured up to her daddy's standards. She sucked in a big breath and straightened the string tie under Flint's collar. "You have nothing to worry about. Jack and I are just friends. Besides, you promised. A year at Miss Fontaine's and then we'll look at colleges. A Fairchild always keeps his word."

"You're putting words in my mouth again, missy. Morgan is a fine man. I was only making an observation. You never know when I might need a good financial wizard at Fairchild Oil, if you get my drift. Reckon if he hired on, he'd practically be in the family."

"Jack's not looking for a new job. He just started the one he has." Her dad was right, of course. Jack was smart. A Southern Methodist graduate. Hired on as a loan officer at the bank, but it was a starter job, she knew. College grads didn't stick around Two Forks for long.

"You never know. The right offer comes along and any man worth his salt is interested."

She gritted her teeth. It was enough that she'd bowed to her daddy's wishes about school; he didn't have to meddle with her boyfriend, too. The fact was, no one argued with Flint Fairchild. No one at the ranch. No one at Fairchild Oil. And certainly not his only daughter.

While Little Earl and the band played "Tumbling Tumbleweeds," Dusty's own thoughts tumbled back to the day two months before when her dad had come from an oil symposium at the state capitol and presented her with the brochure to Miss Fontaine's. She'd reminded him that she was hoping to check out the University of Texas geology program.

He'd scoffed. "The only rocks you need to be worried about are those in your head. Girls don't become geologists. You go to Miss Fontaine's, and I bet my next gusher, you'll forget all about such foolishness."

Arguing was futile once her daddy had made up his mind.

The only one who came close to telling Flint Fairchild what to do was Rosalita, their housekeeper, who drew her aside later that day and said, "Mr. Flint's nuttier than a hoot owl for not letting you go to college."

Rosalita had said the same thing about President Kennedy's plan to put a man on the moon, and Dusty figured the two had about equal chances of happening—slim and none.

Rosalita waved a wooden spoon dripping with enchilada sauce at her. "Dusty, you leave it to Rosalita. I tell him how the cow eat the cabbage."

Only the following week, Rosalita had gone to Old Mexico to take care of her ailing mother and left Dusty to handle her dad on her own. Perhaps sending her to charm school was his way of making up for handing her off to Rosalita the day her mama died. She personally thought it would've been better for her dad to throw the money into the West Texas wind, but when he offered to pay the tuition for her cousin Paisley, she'd agreed. Miss Fontaine's it was.

Bo Richards from Dusty's graduating class interrupted her thoughts. "Hey, I thought Paisley was coming." Acne had taken up permanent residence on Bo's face, and his eyes shone beneath his straw hat. He had it bad for her California cousin.

"She couldn't make it. Her bus broke down."

"What bus? Don't Trailways have a spare they can send?"

"Not Trailways. Tour bus." In her side vision, Dusty caught her dad flaring his nostrils. She swiveled a half-turn away and lowered her voice. Her dad had taken the call and had a few choice words on the subject of Aunt Edith and her vagabond ways.

"Her mom's new boyfriend is in a band, traveling around the country. They were going to drop Paisley off. Looks like now she'll just meet us in Alborghetti at the finishing school."

"Dang it. The only reason I came to your party was to see her."

Bo might not have the smoothest line in the book, but at least he was honest. She smiled. "I'll tell Paisley you asked about her."

He shuffled off as Jack returned with an iced tea for her dad and a lemonade for her.

"Thanks, son." Her dad took a long drink and nodded at someone across the lawn. "Dusty, there's a fellow over there I need to talk to, and I think I might need a little financial guidance from Morgan here. You go on and mingle with your guests."

Jack shrugged and followed after Flint Fairchild like a puppy. Onstage, Little Earl warbled "On the Wings of a Dove" as the sun gave a final nod and dipped below the horizon. So much for moonlight kisses and come-hither looks. Maybe going to Miss Fontaine's would be a good thing.

❧

The letter had been explicit about the arrival time. One o'clock. The gold Bulova on her wrist winked up, tiny diamonds encircling its face. Twenty after. Dusty swallowed the irritation that rose in her chest and glanced at her dad. With his hand on the steering wheel, he tapped to the beat of LeRoy Van Dyke's crooning on the car radio.

She clutched the brochure in her hand.

Poise and charm: the secrets to being a gracious Southern woman.

It was on good stock with a nice sheen. On the front, a woman held a cocktail glass in one hand and a silver cake server in the other. The curlicue letters looked French.

*The Rosebriar, home to Miss Fontaine's Finishing School for
Girls, borders a scenic bayou in the quaint town of Alborghetti,
Texas. The historic mansion is the perfect stepping-stone into the
finest social circles of the South.*

She knew it all by heart.

*Pastry techniques taught by a professional chef.
French lessons thrice weekly to enliven your conversations.
Practical steps in planning perfect parties.*

That was the one that made her laugh. With all those *p*'s, she'd be
lucky if she didn't wet her pants. *Charm school?* In 1962? It sounded
ridiculously Victorian. And stuffy.

She craned her neck looking for the turnoff, and when she spotted it, her heart lodged in her throat as her dad wheeled into the
circle drive. Two limos and a Rolls-Royce loomed before them.

Her dad pulled in behind the Rolls and whistled. "I've not seen
this many swanky cars since the governor's inauguration. Makes my
humble little Lincoln Continental here look like a sad sack." He
laughed and thumped her on the arm. There was nothing humble
about Flint Fairchild or his choice of automobiles. "Now scoot on
in there and see if Paisley's here yet. She sure as blue blazes didn't
arrive in one of these vehicles."

A blast of hot swamp air hit Dusty in the face and paralyzed her
lungs when she emerged from the car. It took a moment to get
her equilibrium and smooth the wrinkles from the skirt of her sundress. A ripple of last-minute jitters went through her. Now that
the calendar had flipped over to September were bare shoulders
deemed proper? She glanced at her feet, grateful that she'd remembered to wear her taupe close-toed pumps—suitable for any season
or occasion. Chin up, she marched up the walk and paused out-

side the double leaded-glass doors. At least it was a gorgeous place. She leaned back and admired the matching lace at every opening. Lovely—it just wasn't the University of Texas dorm she'd set her heart on.

The doorbell set off chimes louder than St. Mary's Catholic Church in Two Forks. The door to her right swung open, and a properly dressed housemaid, white apron and all, invited her in. Rosalita would have kittens if Daddy asked her to dress like that.

The maid extended a soft, gnarled hand, liver spots the size of grapes dotting her pale flesh. "I'm Miss Swanson." She stood unblinking, waiting, as Dusty detected the scent of cinnamon and apples. What she wouldn't give to be digging into a bowl of Rosalita's apple cobbler swimming in cream. The tug inside came not from hunger, but from the fact that even if she were back home at the ranch, Rosalita was not.

She shook it off and took Miss Swanson's hand. "Pleased to meet you. I'm Dusty Fairchild."

"The others are waiting in the parlor."

A mass of girls in high heels and frocks, not a bare shoulder in the bunch, turned when she entered the cavernous parlor with ornate furnishings. Their plastic smiles and Aqua Net–secured beehives made her think she'd come to the wrong house, that perhaps she'd stumbled into a photo shoot for *Vogue* magazine. Her own hair, tucked behind her ears to keep it from tangling in her earrings, tickled her shoulders.

An older woman with a spooked starling look—Miss Fontaine, she assumed—stepped from the group. "You must be Miss Fairchild."

Her manner was formal, but her appearance was elf-like with rusty hair wadded up in a bun and cherry tomato cheeks. An image of Mother Goose flashed through her head.

"Yes, I'm Dusty Fairchild. My sincerest apologies for being late.

It took longer than my father estimated." Her voice sounded like someone else, like the type of person Miss Fontaine might be hoping she was. Not some ranch girl from the boondocks.

Relax. You can do this.

Miss Fontaine drew her mouth into a rosebud and eyed the grandfather clock. Dusty was sure she'd just flunked the first test. Her heart pounded in her ears.

"Only a few minutes. And Miss Finch, your cousin, is she with you?"

"I thought she'd already be here. Her mom's dropping her off."

"From California?" Her eyebrows shot up, her eyes catching the light from the chandelier. One blue eye. One brown. "Well, we certainly can't wait to meet your cousin. If she's anything like you, then I'm sure she's a delight. Do you need to freshen up?"

Dusty made a quick trip to the ladies' room at the end of the hall, and the minute she stepped back into the parlor, Miss Fontaine was at her side. "Miss Swanson will direct your father regarding the placement of your luggage. Perhaps he'd like to join the other drivers and family members in the kitchen for a light lunch before he leaves. There are refreshments on the sideboard for you girls. Get some punch and we'll continue with the introductions." She clapped her hands and directed her attention back at the group.

For the next several minutes, her dad's boots echoed in the hallway as he brought in the luggage. Dusty was tempted to step out and ask if there was any sign of Paisley, but the girls were taking turns telling about themselves and any special interests they had. Beauty pageants, raising Pekingese for dog shows, volunteer work for the March of Dimes. Just like the icebreakers at Girls State and church camp meant to help them remember one another, but all Dusty could think about was, *Where is Paisley?* She hoped something hadn't happened.

"Miss Fairchild?" Miss Fontaine's lips twitched.

"I'm sorry. What was the question?"

"Where you're from, your hobbies, something fascinating about you." She emphasized *you* like Dusty was important. Dusty had never felt less so in her life.

"Okay. I'm Dusty Agnes Fairchild from Two Forks, a little town out west. Not too far west, just the other side of Fort Worth. My dad's in the oil business, and I have two miniature schnauzers who will chew your leg off if you don't come to the door armed with dog biscuits." Prattling. How pathetic.

"Lovely." Miss Fontaine tilted her head, the bun bobbling. "Your interests and hobbies?"

"Well, I collect rocks."

"Oh, you mean like the beautiful turquoise stones in your earrings and necklace? Semiprecious stones?"

"Not exactly, although I wouldn't mind going to Old Mexico or Arizona on a mining expedition."

"So you like to travel and collect gemstones?"

"No, what I meant was that I collect phyllite, quartz, fossils, whatever turns up in the creek bed at the ranch. Rocks. All kinds." She slipped her hand into her skirt pocket and curled her fingers around the sandstone she'd remembered to tuck in for good luck. Her thumb rested in its comforting hollow as a dozen pairs of eyes glazed over. Heat crept up her neck as she imagined her face splotching purple.

She cleared her throat. "I have a classification chart back home, and someday I hope to study geology; perhaps travel, as you said, to the bottom of a volcanic crater; and add to my igneous collection. It's a fascinating field."

"Dusty, what on earth?" Her dad's voice boomed from the doorway. "Miss Fontaine, I do apologize. Dusty is nuts about her hobby. I'm hoping you can steer her into a more domestic direction." He laughed and rubbed his shoulder. "Feels like she packed a few of those rocks in her luggage."

Miss Fontaine slid across the ancient oak floor like it was a sheet of ice and clasped his hands. "You must be Flint Fairchild. Please, you can call me Birdie. Your daughter is charming. As are you. I'm certain she will be a lovely addition to our group. Variety is the spice of life, you know!"

A rumble came from the drive out front, followed by a loud backfire. Dusty knew without looking it had to be Paisley. Girls clicked on their sling-back pumps over to the window and parted the lace curtains. In the commotion, Dusty slipped past Miss Fontaine, who was still clinging to her daddy's hand, and flung open the front door.

An old school bus, rusted and painted over in shades of lime green, orange, and blue, sat in the drive beside the Rolls-Royce. Letters painted on the side said The Asterisks. The bus door screeched open, and in the driver's seat, with her long dark hair tumbling from beneath a baseball cap, sat Paisley wearing cutoff blue jeans and a T-shirt.

Behind Dusty, air hissed from Miss Fontaine's mouth. Her dad let out a chortle and a "Glory be!"

Dusty stepped onto the porch and hollered at Paisley. Halfway down the sidewalk, she glanced back at the house. Miss Fontaine was leaning against the doorframe, mouth agape like a catfish thrown up on the riverbank. Dusty raced to her cousin for an embrace. "What took you so long? And why are you driving the bus?"

Paisley looked at the junk heap with loud paint and shrugged. "I've never driven a bus before." She leaned in and whispered, "I'll tell you later." Although her lips trembled, Paisley blinked hard and smiled. "I'm so glad to see you. What's it like here?" She stepped back, taking in the exterior of Miss Fontaine's, her eyes round. "Oh, it's gorgeous! We're going to have a blast. So cool.

Oh, there's Uncle Flint." She shot up the sidewalk, leaving Dusty in her wake.

Some things never change. Getting Paisley to be still long enough to have a French lesson or roll out a piecrust would be a miracle.

Passengers descending from the bus caught Dusty's attention. When Paisley had told Dusty that Aunt Edith was dating someone in a folk band, she pictured the Kingston Trio with their standing bass fiddle and crooning sweet harmonies. Crisp, striped shirts. Flattops.

The first Asterisk off the bus had a Falstaff in his hand, shirttail hanging out, buttons undone. No flattop. Head shaved with bushy sideburns like Brillo pads. The roadie perhaps? One by one, three others staggered off and squinted at the sunlight, two with shoulder-length hair, one with a tattoo peeking from the rolled-up sleeve of his T-shirt. They nodded, then congregated behind the bus, checking something on the undercarriage.

The last one out was Aunt Edith. She stopped at the last step and adjusted her pump, which had at least a four-inch heel. Gold hoops dangled from her ears, her platinum hair in the latest bouffant. She wore skintight pants in a black-and-white harlequin pattern and a halter top in hot pink that showed off every curve of her shapely figure.

"Aunt Edith!" The familiar thrill of seeing her aunt zipped through Dusty. She embodied everything Dusty was not. Free-spirited. Unpretentious. Not afraid to stare down Flint Fairchild and come away laughing.

"Oh, for the love of Mike, please call me Edie." The kiss she brushed on Dusty's cheek smelled of onions and stale cigarette smoke.

Paisley sailed up. "She won't let me call her Mother any more either. It's not hip."

Aunt Edith—Edie now—wagged a manicured finger at Paisley.

"I can't help it if I want to stay young." She waved at one of the band members. "Sloan, could you get the boys to take Paisley's things in?"

Sloan? Dusty was dying to know which one was Edie's new boyfriend, but her dad sauntered down the sidewalk to join them before she could ask. "Well, Edith, good to see you finally made it. Your chariot there gave the sweet little headmistress the vapors."

Edie glared at him. "Hello to you, too. My chariot? Aren't you the clever one?" She puckered her lips and left a lipstick smudge on her brother's cheek. "You'd be surprised how plush the tour bus is inside. Fixed up real cute and sleeps six comfortably. I'd give you a tour, but I know the girls are anxious to get on with..." She surveyed the house, the grounds, and then sniffed. "It's so formal. So establishmentarian. Whatever possessed you—"

"Nothing *possessed* me. You're always so dadgum dramatic. I only thought our girls should be schooled in some of the finer points of etiquette, that's all. You and me, sis, we've not exactly been sterling examples."

"Speak for yourself. I've given Paisley a life of adventure. You can't put a price tag on that." Her eyes clouded with tears. When the tears beaded up and spilled onto her cheeks, she wiped them away, leaving a smudge of mascara. "I've tried to talk Paisley out of this. A whole school year will be a long time without my little girl."

Dusty's dad removed his Stetson and wiped his forehead with a handkerchief. "The girls are eighteen—I'd hardly call that little anymore, and it looks like you've taken up with a band of gypsies."

"They're musicians with a hit record on the pop charts, but I'm sure you've not heard of them, stuck as you are up to your eyeballs in sagebrush and cockleburs."

With his hat still in his hand, he did a mocking bow. "Whatever you say, little sister. And as I was saying, this'll be good for Paisley—

reckon it might be the longest stretch she's ever had the same address."

Dusty sucked in a breath. Sparks flew whenever her dad and his only sister got within a country mile of one another. Why couldn't they just shake hands and forget about their differences?

Paisley had disappeared momentarily but then emerged from the bus with the one named Sloan. He had a beat-up suitcase in one hand and Paisley's beloved guitar in the other. The guy with the tattoo had two cardboard boxes, his biceps bulging from the effort. He looked more like a roustabout than a folksinger. Aunt Edie called him "darling," and with her penchant for bulky Mr. America types, Dusty thought this one must be her boyfriend.

Paisley hooked arms with Aunt Edie. "That's it. I think I got everything. I know you need to get on the road if you're going to make Austin tonight."

More tears tracked black streaks down Edie's cheeks. "It's not too late to change your mind."

"Edie, we've been over this a million times. You're going to be busy with the band. I'll just be in the way."

Edie sniffed. "I know you're right, baby, but I'm going to miss you like the dickens." She kissed Paisley on the cheek, then pulled Dusty into a hug. "You think I might find the little girls' room before we leave?"

Paisley ran ahead to see about her things, so Dusty led Edie up the walk and into the front hall. She nodded at Miss Swanson with her dour face, her posture erect as if standing sentry. "It's all right, Miss Swanson, I'm showing my aunt the ladies' room. Just take a sec."

As they passed the parlor door, Dusty caught a glimpse of Miss Fontaine, apparently over the vapors and back at her station among the girls. The room grew silent for a moment as if Dusty might pop in and introduce her aunt. When she didn't, the chatter resumed, a low-thrumming buzz, like a swarm of gnats. Paisley's arrival had, at the very least, added a little spice to the day.

While she stood outside the ladies' room waiting for her aunt, she made a decision. She would make the effort to like it at Miss Fontaine's. Success here could only increase her chances of going to college. With her jaw set, she determined not to be intimidated by a group of girls who already regarded her as if she were a two-headed calf in a sideshow. She might not belong to a country club or an elite clique, but she was proud of who she was and where she came from.

When her aunt emerged with cheeks free of mascara and her mouth sporting fresh lipstick, Dusty clasped her hand.

"Here you go, Edie. Why don't we stop in the parlor and let me introduce you? Besides, it would be a shame for you to come all this way and not have a cup of punch."

CHAPTER 2

"What? Why are you looking at me like that?" Paisley locked eyes with her cousin, and it was Dusty who looked away first, her cheeks pink.

Dusty leaned in and whispered, "I sent you the information with the dress code."

Paisley shrugged. "I must've lost it somewhere between San Fran and here. I didn't know it was written in stone. So you don't like what I'm wearing?" She planted a fist on her hip and struck a pose. She'd just spent every last cent of her tip money from waiting tables at the Penny Loafer on new clothes for this lark Dusty insisted she come on. Apparently her leotards and smocked top that landed just shy of her kneecaps weren't regarded as high fashion in Texas. She could only imagine the reaction the gauzy skirts and colorful beads she'd bought at Izzy John's Boutique would get. Uncle Flint already thought they were a band of gypsies, and nothing in the suitcase Sloan deposited at the top of the stairs would prove otherwise.

A twinge of regret went through her, though. Dusty was the best friend she'd ever had, the only real friend if you wanted to get down to it. Paisley didn't deserve to walk on the same ground with someone whose heart bled kindness the way Dusty's did. She was so pure and innocent it stunk. If the girls gathered here with their paper doll smiles and snickers meant anything, Dusty didn't belong here, either. They were doomed.

Dusty sighed. "You hair is cute. Updos are all the rage."

Paisley laughed. "This was the best I could do in the few minutes I had to change with that woman upstairs hurrying me along. Have you seen her? A maid of some sort, I'd guess. She looks like she leapt from the pages of *Gone with the Wind*. For a minute there, I coulda sworn I was on a bad trip."

Dusty shushed her and nodded toward a shrewish woman with a ruffled collar and rouged cheeks coming toward them.

"I must say, Miss Finch, you have an interesting choice in style, not at all what I expect from the young ladies here, but I know you were rushed in dressing for the afternoon. I'm sure you'll acquire more suitable tastes once you've been here a few days."

Ouch! So charming to lay it out there.

Miss Fontaine continued to eye her. "Please tell us where you're from and what your interests are."

It wasn't a good start. There was no use blaming her mother; Paisley had given that up long ago. Edie Horton had her own problems, not the least of which was her current infatuation with *finding herself*. Oh, brother. Paisley didn't think the answer for her mom was on a psychedelic bus or in the dives where the Asterisks played. And as quaint and almost creepy as Miss Fontaine's was, Paisley didn't regret her decision to come here. Sloan was getting tiresome with all his smarmy remarks and pulling her onto his lap in the back of the bus. It was time to cut loose. A shiver crept over Paisley's bare arms, and a warm glow that felt like happiness bubbled under her rib cage.

Dusty slid beside her and took her hand, giving it a squeeze. Paisley squeezed back and answered Miss Fontaine, "Gee, I don't know where to start. Getting here was a real trip, but I'm grateful to my uncle for making it all possible. And to you, of course, for accepting my application."

One of the girls held her hand over her mouth as if to cover a laugh. Paisley locked gazes with her, keeping her own face calm, serene. The girl swallowed, erasing the smirk. Paisley could spot a ringleader a mile away. She liked to think of it as one of her special gifts that had been refined as a result of attending eight schools in twelve years.

"You asked about me. I lived in San Francisco before I went on the road with my mother and the band. I play the guitar and collect unusual photographs of people and places. Just a few days ago, I snapped one of the Asterisks onstage at the Coliseum in Lubbock. Davis and Sloan stood on the same spot as Elvis did back in 1956. You just never know when you're going to have a brush with fame. And—"

"Most interesting, to be sure, Miss Finch, but I'm afraid time is getting away from us. We must keep to the schedule if we are to get the orientation done this afternoon." Miss Fontaine still had that pinched, waspish look about her. Paisley wanted to tell her to chill but smiled instead.

"Yes, ma'am. I was just going to add that I'm looking forward to taking photographs while I'm here. I think this might be one of those historic turns in our lives."

Miss Fontaine's lips twitched at the corners. "Historic, indeed. Which does bring up the subject of Rosebriar's history." She straightened up and addressed the group. "You will note on the plaque outside the entry that the home was established in 1836. It's of the Federal revival style and built by Folsom Petry, a noted horticulturalist who became a general for the Confederacy. The acreage in the back was once part of a small plantation that grew alfalfa, cotton, and sugarcane. My grandfather married General Petry's daughter, Noralee, and through the years, the property has come to me. For almost one hundred years, Fontaines have lived here."

She paused and let her eyes scan the room, seeming to rest on the dentil molding at the ceiling, then on the furnishings one by one. They were evidently of some value by the looks of the detailed carving and brocade upholstery. Miss Fontaine's expression changed to one of reverence when her gaze landed on a six-foot-tall painting in an elaborate gold frame. The decorated soldier with a musket in his hands had funny-colored eyes, like the artist ran out of blue and had to paint the other one brown. Paisley looked closer at Miss Fontaine and realized she'd inherited the odd trait, and for a moment, she wondered if Miss Fontaine had other peculiarities.

Paisley shuddered as the general's eyes pinpointed her. She looked away but had the feeling the eyes were following her every move, examining her, sizing up her suitability for a place like Miss Fontaine's. She was sure if the general could speak, he'd tell her she didn't belong. No surprise there. Fact was, she didn't know where she belonged. This house was cool, though. Inwardly, she saluted the general in the painting. Paisley's war wounds might not win her any medals, but in her life with Edie Horton, there had been plenty of battles.

She looked sidelong at Dusty. Somehow, she did fit in with her cute dress, her long wavy hair the color of the California sun, and her stylish pointed-toe pumps. Her eyes, though, had a faraway look like she'd rather be somewhere else.

Then the pitch of Miss Fontaine's voice shifted. "Mercy. Oh my goodness." She rustled the papers in her hands, adjusted her reading glasses, and blinked like she was tripping out. "I had hoped to give you your assignments next, but I seem to have misplaced the list. Let's take a short break while I retrieve it from my quarters. Feel free to use this informal time to get to know one another."

The room burst to life the minute Miss Fontaine left. One of the girls, a chunky brunette in a suit reminiscent of Jackie Kennedy, beelined for Paisley and Dusty. "Isn't this just the coolest place? So countrified." Her chocolate-colored eyes gleamed round and luminous behind her pale blue cat-eye glasses. Cute in a way, and she reminded Paisley of someone, but she couldn't quite figure out who.

Paisley nodded. "Yeah, the happening place. But cool, like you said. Sorry, I didn't catch your name."

"Alexandria. But call me Xan. It drives my mother bonkers that my friends call me Xan, and I do hope we're going to be friends."

"Sure, no sweat."

"I'm from Houston. You know, I think I even saw some horses when we drove up. I wonder if we can sign up for riding lessons. Wouldn't that just be the niftiest?" She turned to Dusty. "And you live on a ranch, so I bet you know all about that cowgirl stuff."

Dusty and Paisley exchanged glances. *Who was this girl?*

Dusty shrugged. "I'm not exactly a cowgirl. Paisley and I ride sometimes on the ranch, but she's better than I am in the saddle."

"I wouldn't say I was better. I just whisper sweet nothings in the horse's ears."

The brunette who had smirked at Paisley earlier brushed past, stopping long enough to whisper something to Xan, which made Xan's face flush crimson.

Paisley said, "What was that all about?"

"Nothing." Xan smirked. "Actually, it's just Sharon Kay and her ways. Acting like she's God's gift to the universe. Lord, I hope I don't end up being her roommate because we're from the same town."

Dusty thumbed toward Miss Fontaine who had appeared in the parlor doorway. "Guess we'll find out soon enough."

Xan stepped back to give Birdie Fontaine room. When their headmistress whisked past, her eyes sparkled, and Paisley caught the whiff of something fruity and sweet. She held back a chuckle. She was certain it was alcohol and not mouthwash on Miss Fontaine's breath. Sometimes she just knew these things. And the way this little soiree had gone, it was no wonder Miss Fontaine needed to take a nip.

Miss Fontaine read from a small pamphlet the list of rules, quite a long list actually, that included curfews, study times, and use of automobiles (no private cars allowed until the second semester). The school station wagon was available for trips to town—driven by Miss Swanson only. Miss Fontaine made eye contact with Paisley as she spelled out the dress code and the smoking rules. Because of Miss Fontaine's allergy, the upstairs sitting room was the only room in the house where smoking was allowed. Paisley's head was spinning. That's the thing about living out of a suitcase—it meant a simple life. She hoped she'd be able to keep it all straight.

Dusty gave her an *I'm sorry* look, but it didn't sound so bad. Not really. At least here she was in a real house. A mansion at that. Decorated like something in a magazine. A bathroom that didn't have a grunge ring in the toilet.

Another part of her trembled. Sharon Kay and the girls on either side of her laughed as if they were sharing a private joke. When Paisley looked at them, their faces gave them away, like they wanted her to know the joke was about her.

Paisley averted her gaze and stared at the toes of her boots, wondering if she'd packed the shoe polish. What an odd thing to think of. Her neck prickled with regret that she hadn't paid more attention to the dress code. Rule number one: blend in. Not that it had helped diddly in the past, but maybe this time would be different. Paisley eyed the outfits of the other girls. She'd blown it already.

Miss Fontaine shuffled her papers and put on her reading glasses. "Two of our girls, of course, live right here in Alborghetti and will be day students. They will be able to help you with questions about shopping and what to do on the weekend. You may, of course, ride with them if Miss Swanson can't accommodate you with the station wagon." She glanced at the paperwork in her hands. "Here we are. In the Daffodil Room, Carmel Zanick and Stacia Pruitt." Paisley held her breath as Miss Fontaine went down the list, assigning girls to the Iris, Peony, and Violet Rooms. "In the Rosebud Room, Sharon Kay Blanchard and Dusty Fairchild."

Beside her, Paisley felt Dusty straighten and suck in a quick breath.

"Bringing us to the last two girls. In the Honeysuckle Room will be Alexandria Bennett and Paisley Finch." She looked directly at Paisley like she might have something to add but brightened her face instead. "I'm sure we're off to a wonderful start, and I think you will find the amenities here as charming as each of you are. You're dismissed until dinner to settle in and begin unpacking."

Dusty leaned in and whispered, "Congratulations. You're the answer to Xan's prayers."

"What a crummy deal. Not that Xan isn't cool and all that, I just thought we'd be together."

"Yeah. Me, too. Guess we're not here to think."

Paisley swallowed her disappointment and braced herself. Xan was dancing toward her, her face aglow.

CHAPTER 3

Dusty's room at the end of the hall overlooked the back of the property—a neat garden with mums and late-blooming roses close to the house, a meadow beyond, and to her far right, an attached carriage house. Two horses grazed, one a swaybacked dapple, the other a chestnut with a blaze of white above its eyes, ending between black ears that even from the distance looked velvety soft. To the left was the bayou, and in the violet hush of evening, the shifting shadows gave it a mysterious presence. Dusty's pulse hitched up a notch at the thought of exploring its banks.

She arranged a small collection of rocks she'd tucked in her suitcase on the marble windowsill. It was chilly to the touch, like the reception she'd gotten from her roommate when Miss Fontaine announced the assignments. Dusty felt it was a slap in the face since she'd requested Paisley on her application. Instead she was paired with Sharon Kay who had let it be known she was the daughter of Judge Blanchard, like that was supposed to mean something. Dusty was nearly certain Sharon Kay was just as disappointed.

"You're not seriously thinking of leaving those rocks in the window?" Sharon Kay's voice startled Dusty as she hadn't heard her come in.

"If you're okay with it, I am. Touch of home and all that." Her fingers lingered on one of her favorites—a geode with a deep purple center and delicate white crystals. Rosalita had given it to her for Christmas when she was sixteen, purchased from a roadside souvenir shop on her annual visit to Mexico.

"If you ask me, it's rather strange."

At least Sharon Kay was honest. Dusty's dad always said he'd rather deal with a pompous honest man than a sneaky son of a buck any day of the week. "Probably. Daddy's tried to get me interested in stamp and coin collecting, but there's something satisfying about unearthing treasures like these."

"You can leave the rocks. Just so you know, I used more than half of the closet. I didn't suppose you'd have that many clothes since I saw you only had two pieces of luggage."

"These are the only two I brought into the room before supper. The others are still out in the sitting area, but it's not a problem. We'll work it out." She closed her suitcase on the floor and pushed it out of the way. "Paisley and I are going for a walk. You wanna come?"

"What does it look like?" She pointed to the bed where clothes and lingerie spilled from an open leather suitcase. "I still have to set my hair when I'm finished here. Providing I find room for everything." She brushed past holding a stack of twinsets and put them on a closet shelf.

"Why don't you take one of the drawers in my dresser? I'm sure I won't need them all."

"It would be nice under the circumstances. I guess people in Two Forks aren't quite into fashion the way we are in the city."

"I guess not. I just didn't see the point in overdoing it."

"I'd hardly call this overdoing it. I told Mother I'd send her a list of everything I forgot. She'll be coming for the Mother/Daughter Tea in three weeks. Your mother will be here then, I presume."

"Not exactly. It's just Daddy and me at the ranch. One of my brothers is married and lives close, but Susan—that's his wife—is nearly seven months along so I doubt she'd want to come."

Sharon Kay raised her eyebrows, a flicker in her eyes that had a mocking look—like maybe Dusty's mother had run off with a traveling salesman or a gambler. Or the circus after the fiasco with the painted bus.

Dusty shrugged. "My mother died when I was three and a half. Automobile accident."

"Oh, sorry. Guess we won't be seeing her then."

Dusty grabbed the Levi's and T-shirt she'd laid aside and began changing. "It sure will be nice to meet your mom, though. And just so you know, I didn't mean that you were overdoing it. Just that I don't have that many occasions to wear fancy clothes. Not much going on in Two Forks, you know."

Sharon Kay shuddered. "I can only imagine. Must be quite the affair when you have your debutante season. What are there? Three? Four girls every year?"

The temptation to ask her who put a hitch in her britches surfaced, but Dusty took a deep breath and smiled instead. "You never know. Depends how many single girls show up for the hog calling and square dance at the Burroughs County Fair."

"That's disgusting."

"Don't knock it till you've tried it." She dropped her sundress on top of her suitcase and slipped on her Keds. "Sure you don't want to join us?"

"No thanks."

❦

Dusty inhaled the scent of freedom, escaping from the walls of Rosebriar. She and Paisley half ran, half skipped toward the pillars and circle drive that marked the entrance to Miss Fontaine's. At the end of the sidewalk, they read the plaque bolted to the brick pillars: "Miss Fontaine's Finishing School, Estab. 1948." To the left was the town of Alborghetti. To the right, a flagstone walk led to a wide lawn on the east side of the house. They chose the flagstones and followed them to a fountain where a giant fish with coppery-green scales projected a spray of water from its gaping mouth.

They sat on the low brick wall of the fountain with their backs to the house, the bayou before them shrouded in twilight. The smell of rotting pine needles and late-blooming honeysuckle made a strange combination that captured the way Dusty felt—at odds with this place and uncertain why her dad thought this was a good idea. Paisley dug in her pink suede purse with long fringe swinging from the bottom and pulled out a pack of Salem cigarettes. She offered one to Dusty.

"No thanks."

Paisley shrugged and ripped a match from a matchbook, lit up, then stretched her legs out in front of her. "Man, you don't know how good it feels to be here and off that stupid bus."

"I'm glad you made it. You never said why you were driving."

"Because Sloan is a moron. He couldn't even read the map. We ended up somewhere in Louisiana this morning." She took a long drag and shook her head. "We wouldn't have made it at all if I hadn't jumped in the driver's seat when he stopped at that last filling station. I told you I'd be here. And here we are."

Yeah, here we are. "So I take it this group your mom is with isn't the all-American folk group?"

"Not even close." Paisley puffed on the cigarette and stared into the distance. "That's behind me, though. I've been over the moon about getting here and hearing about the big party at the ranch. So tell me, how was it?"

"Good. Daddy always puts on a big doin's, you know that. Bo Richards asked about you."

"Poor Bo. Such a sweet guy. Not really what I'm looking for, though."

"What are you looking for?"

She shrugged. "I'd say it's more like what I'm not looking for. Not the kind of jerks Edie is attracted to." Dusty recognized the tone, the edge that sometimes crept into Paisley's voice. The one that said, *Back off, I'm not going to talk about it.*

Dusty thought perhaps they should. "Has something happened? Something you need to tell me."

Paisley ground out the cigarette and tossed it into the grass. "What do you want to hear about first? Sloan, the groper, or fun with Dick and Mary Jane?"

"Mary Jane?"

"You know, reefers. Pot." She sucked in a big breath. "Edie's still trying to find herself." Her laugh was harsh but sad. "Like it's going to be on a psychedelic bus." She pulled the bobby pins from her hair and shook her head, letting her dark hair fall in tangles around her shoulders.

Silence fell between them. Dusty wished she hadn't pushed the point. Their worlds were so different if Paisley was to be believed. Her cousin's penchant for embellishing the truth gave her a mysterious air that people were drawn to. Dusty envied that about her, but deep down, she wasn't sure she wanted to know the whole truth about Paisley. Or Aunt Edie.

Paisley punched her on the arm playfully. "So tell me, was this groovy new guy you're seeing at the party? He works at the bank, right? I mean, for real, is this serious? Has he kissed you? What rotten luck that you find the guy of your dreams and then have to split. Are you sad?"

Dusty threw up her hands. "Gee, I don't know which question to answer first. I'll start with the last. I am sad, though not for the reason you might think. Going to charm school wasn't my first choice."

"Uncle Flint's cool. Not too sure yet about this place, though. Your dad probably didn't want you going off and joining a sorority and ending up in trouble like your brother did at Tech. I mean, crud, blowing up the boys' bathroom in the frat house."

"Patrick hasn't changed all that much. Still drifting around. Daddy put him on an oil rig over the summer, though. Said it's time he quit spending money like it blew in off the sagebrush and earned some of his own." A queasy feeling sloshed in her gut. She had to prove to her dad she could succeed at Miss Fontaine's—then he'd have to agree to her going to college. She would not be a disappointment to him like her brothers had been. "Enough about them. How was your roommate? Xan, isn't that her name?"

"Bubbly. Like a bottle of champagne. Sweet, really. She's sorry for what she said about Sharon Kay since you ended up with her."

"I think I can handle her. I'm not getting bent just because she took three-quarters of the closet and half my dresser drawers."

"You're kidding."

"Not kidding. I'm just glad you're here."

A banana moon was cradled in a high branch over the bayou, the air warm and still. Peaceful in its own way. Behind her the fountain bubbled, and for a fraction of a second, Dusty could almost imagine that it was the creek on the ranch. That she and Paisley were ten again and enjoying the wild, carefree days of summer. Like the summer after fourth grade when Aunt Edith had dumped Paisley so she could go on her honeymoon. They tramped through the creek beds by day. At night they would lay under the stars, whispering and giggling as they made their dream list.

"You first," Paisley had said back then as they squinted at the stars above them. "What's the number one thing you want to do before next summer?"

"Learn the periodic table."

"You goose! I meant adventurous things. Something dangerous

and exciting." She'd leapt to her feet, her dark hair wild as it floated in the breeze.

"Like what?"

"Have you ever kissed a boy?"

"No. They're gross. Look at my brothers if you don't believe me."

"Not your brothers, silly. I kissed a sixth grader, and it wasn't gross. But what I really want to do is learn to play the guitar. Leonard said he would buy me one when he and Mother get back from Old Mexico."

"That doesn't sound dangerous."

"If you learn that goofy rocks and elements thing, then I'll play the guitar. What else?"

That summer they'd put skinny-dipping, getting their ears pierced, and smoking a cigarette on their list. Paisley instigated it all. Snitching cigarettes from Dusty's brothers. Begging Rosalita to numb their earlobes with ice cubes and poke red-hot needles through them. Paisley sneaked kisses from the stable hands and double-dog dared Dusty to try it. She didn't...couldn't bring herself to be so forward, but even then Dusty was enchanted with Paisley and her crazy mother and their vagabond life.

Maybe coming to Miss Fontaine's was just another caper for Paisley. Then, as if she read Dusty's mind, Paisley said, "We have to make a list. Things we're going to do at Miss Fontaine's."

"Sure. You go first."

Paisley nodded toward the bayou. "You always like to explore. How about if we put hunt alligators on our list?"

Dusty laughed. "Oh yeah, that shouldn't be too hard. Matter of fact, I already know where one is." She thumbed toward the house. "And I guess I'd better boot scoot on up there and see if she's sleeping in my bed."

It felt like old times being together; time stretched out before them like a distant horizon. Which was fine when they were ten. Now nine months at Miss Fontaine's felt like an eternity.

They linked arms and walked in silence back the way they'd come. The house rose like a shadow before them. Dark. Imposing.

A chill, like a gauzy cape, draped itself around Dusty's shoulders.

CHAPTER 4

"P atsy. Patsy Cline. That's who you remind me of," Paisley said.

Xan threw a towel around her just-shampooed hair. "Really?"

"Yep. My mom knew Patsy's mom when we lived in Virginia."

"Really?"

"Really. And stop saying really. It wasn't that big a deal. I was in the third grade and grew about a foot that year. We didn't have money for new dresses, so my mom hired Mrs. Hensley to let down the hems in my old ones. My mom said it was serendipity that she found her." They hadn't seen Patsy's mom since they left Virginia, but a Christmas card or two was enough for Edie to think that since Patsy had become such a big star, she and Paisley were famous by association. Edie was like that, still holding out on being *discovered*.

"So you met her then? Patsy?" Xan batted her eyelashes and got this dreamy look that made Paisley sorry she'd brought it up.

"Yeah. I have a picture of her somewhere. Edie pasted it in a scrapbook. It's in one of these boxes."

The scrapbook had a cheap red cover and gray pages and was her mother's attempt to give Paisley roots by pasting pictures in it of the places they'd lived, like that was supposed to give her some sense of who she was and where she was from.

The truth was she was from Two Forks just like her cousin, Dusty, but her mother's rocky relationship with Uncle Flint was one of two topics she was forbidden to discuss. The other was Paisley's dad. Justus Finch gave Paisley his name and his emerald eyes. Beyond that, she knew nothing. And there were no pictures of him or Uncle Flint in the scrapbook.

Xan persisted. "Find it. I want to see. How did you meet her? Was it before she was famous?"

"She was singing then but not a star like she is today. Her mother still made her outfits, and she'd come over to pick one up when Edie and I were there." Paisley remembered the picture—sort of fuzzy and it made Patsy look plump, which is why it reminded her of Xan. She moved a box that was on top of the one she wanted and undid the flaps.

She found her collection of 45s—Patsy, of course, and Roy Orbison; Bobby Darin; and a new group, Peter, Paul and Mary. Paisley wasn't sure why she'd brought them since her mom had sold the hi-fi to pay the light bill two months before. Under the records were spiral notebooks from literature class and bundles of letters she'd gotten from Dusty over the years. But no scrapbook.

"It's not here. I know I packed it. It would be so like Edie to dig in my stuff and take it."

"You keep saying Edie. Is that your mom?"

She nodded. "She wants people to think we're hip."

"Your mom was original. I liked that about her."

Paisley pretended she didn't hear and put everything back in the box. "Guess it's not here. I can't find the camera, either. And I was planning on taking lots of pictures this year." She kicked the box, then grabbed her guitar and dropped to the floor, back against one of the twin beds. "So tell me. Why did you come to Miss Fontaine's?"

Xan sat on the edge of her bed, untangling her wet hair with a wide-toothed comb. "Why I wanted to come or why my mother wanted me to come?"

Paisley cradled the guitar close. She strummed and listened, adjusting the tuning pegs. "Guess that means they're not the same?"

"Not hardly. Mother wanted me to come so I could learn how to run a house and not embarrass her when I marry Prentice Robbins."

"So you're engaged?"

"Basically. Daddy thinks he's pulled off the coup of the century, merging his little manufacturing business with Robbins Fabrication."

"You've got to be kidding. Your parents have picked out your husband? Not sure if you've noticed or not, but this isn't the Dark Ages." At least Edie had told Paisley she should play the field before picking out a husband.

"Mother would flip her lid if she heard me. Forget I said anything. I don't have a ring, so it's not official, not yet anyway." Xan yanked at a snarl and let out a long breath. "Swear you won't say anything when my mom comes for that Mother/Daughter Tea thing. She says chubby girls—that's what she calls me when no one's around—chubby. She says we have to take what we can get and I should just be thankful Prentice is nearsighted."

"Your mom sounds as charming as mine." Paisley played the intro to "Crazy" and smiled. "So what's the reason you wanted to come to Miss Fontaine's?"

"Get a little space from my family. And—" She giggled like a naughty two-year-old. "I want to turn into a thin beautiful blonde. At least if I were skinny, I'd look good in my wedding gown."

Paisley hummed to clear her throat and began singing. *Crazy.*

Xan's eyes lit up and she swayed to the beat; then she held her hairbrush like a microphone and mimed while Paisley sang. Xan clapped when she'd finished. "Holy moly. That was sweeter than a root beer float with two scoops of ice cream."

She laid the guitar aside. "Which you won't be eating if you're serious about the skinny thing."

"Oh, I am. Will you help me?"

"Sure. We'll put it on the dream list."

"Cool. Or should I say groovy?"

They laughed and spent the next half hour straightening up their room, stuffing things wherever they could find a spot. Xan put a ruffled cap over the brush rollers she put in her hair, then changed into baby-doll pajamas and yawned. She set the alarm on her clock radio and crawled into her bed. "I hope I can sleep. Tomorrow's a big day."

"First day of the rest of our lives. Sweet dreams."

Paisley gathered her shampoo and the long T-shirt she slept in and slipped out into the dark hall toward the bath where she'd changed earlier. It had a double sink, swan-shaped soap dishes, and an armoire supplied with fluffy towels. It sure beat the pants off of the truck stops and lounge dressing rooms she'd been using the last two weeks.

She stood under the showerhead, the water turned as hot as she could stand it and scrubbed her skin until it tingled. Like Xan, she hoped to find a new groove. Somehow she didn't think this was the place, but another day on that bus and she would've gone bananas.

Xan was already breathing deep when Paisley tiptoed into her room and slipped between the sheets. They were cool and soft, the feather pillow like a cloud. As she drifted off, she realized she could still smell the grime of the bus—man sweat, her mother's loud perfume, and stale beer. It saturated her nightclothes and probably everything she'd brought. She'd ask Miss Fontaine about the laundry facilities in the morning.

She dreamed she was in a Laundromat. While she plugged dimes into the machines, a man sat in the corner and watched her. She turned her back but felt his gaze following her every move. She threw in a load and sprinkled Tide crystals atop her clothes, and when she closed the lid, a hand clamped around her wrist. She pulled back, but his grasp was stronger as he guided her toward his dark corner. The man—Sloan, she now realized—lowered himself to the floor, his back to the wall, and patted the floor for her to sit down. She rubbed her wrist where he'd grabbed her, unable to turn and run as she wanted, her legs stringy like a puppet as she plopped beside him. Then she saw the others.

Edie with a beer in one hand, a roach clip in the other. Davis, the guitar player from the band, had his arm draped around her. Edie raised the joint to Davis's lips and laughed, her voice tinny, but she paid no attention to Paisley. Sloan offered the joint to Paisley and teased her, telling her they'd have some real fun later. She got that clammy feeling that comes before you throw up and faked a drag, but Sloan caught her and said she'd get the hang of it. She called out to Edie, but Edie was laughing and busy unbuttoning Davis's shirt. She looked around for someone to help her, but everyone had glassy eyes and clown smiles. And clown faces. She stood up to run away, but Sloan's clown shoes tripped her and she lay on the floor and pounded her fists as soap bubbles from the washing machines spilled over and came at her like ocean waves.

She thrashed and shook her head, but Sloan put his hand on her shoulder and shook it. Hard. Paisley opened her eyes, and it was Xan's face she saw, Xan's hand on her shoulder. Somewhere—off to her right, it seemed—the Everly Brothers were singing "Cathy's Clown."

"Wake up, sleepyhead."

Paisley couldn't remember what day it was. Why was Xan on the bus? Where were the clowns? She closed her eyes and took a big breath. She wasn't on the bus or in a Laundromat. Edie wasn't here. Nor was Sloan. The Everly Brothers were singing on the radio. Relief washed over her, but she still had a clammy feeling as she propped herself up on one elbow. "Hey, who you calling sleepy-head? And is that bacon I smell? Man, I'm starved."

It was only a nightmare. But it felt so real.

CHAPTER 5

Miss Fontaine approached the podium at one end of a long oak table where they'd gathered for the first day of class. Dusty believed the room had once been a solarium since it stretched the width of the back side of the manor house. Windows wrapped three sides of the room giving a sweeping view of the cypress and pine trees of the bayou. A gentle breeze made it look as if the trees themselves were breathing. Or sighing.

Miss Fontaine clapped her hands to begin the first official day. "Young ladies, the greatest asset that a man or woman or even a child can have is charm. The moment you step into a room or open the door to greet a guest, it's best foot forward." Her eyes took on a starry quality as she chirped about the essence of proper etiquette and its eternal effects on society. Dusty smothered a smile as Rosalita's rules to live by danced across her brain.

"If you sass your daddy or Rosalita catch you picking your nose, you no get sopapillas for a week." She was pretty sure Rosalita had never been to charm school, but Dusty had somehow, through the process of osmosis, learned to be polite, say "yes, ma'am" and "no, sir," and extend her hand to give a firm shake.

Miss Fontaine paused and glanced her way.

She gave herself a mental slap on the wrist and focused on Miss Fontaine.

"First impressions are of the utmost importance, so today we'll be going over the basic introductions that you, as genteel ladies, might be called upon to make in the course of your life."

She reminded Dusty of a turtledove with her rising inflection, honeyed words. "It's easy as pie for any woman to acquire a charming bow. Just incline your head and smile as if you thought, *Why there you are! How glad I am to see you.*"

Bows? Really? They proceeded into the mastery portion of introductions after Miss Fontaine concluded her lecture. Dusty was grouped with Sharon Kay—no surprise there—and Stacia Pruitt, a girl from Dallas whose mother was president of the Junior League.

Stacia was all giggles showing Sharon Kay the diamond that twinkled on her left hand. When Dusty admired it, Stacia's fingers fluttered, her pale pink nails like rose petals around the sparkling stone.

Her cheeks matched her nails. "I can't decide if I'm more in love with Michael or the ring." She gushed about him starting medical school at Baylor and couldn't wait for everybody to meet him. "Oh, just listen to me going on and on. Tell me, are y'all pinned or seeing anyone?"

Sharon Kay shook her head. "I'm playing the field, hoping to meet some of the guys from Miller College. My friend who came here last year said they hang out at the movies on weekends. Guess where I'll be this Saturday?"

Miss Fontaine walked by and made a clucking noise with her tongue. "Remember, ladies, you're supposed to be practicing your introductions, not socializing."

"Yes, ma'am," they said in unison and opened the pamphlets that had the skills checklist. Unit One: Introductions. Dusty flipped to the back. Twenty-four units. *Oh. My.*

When Miss Fontaine was out of earshot, Stacia nudged her. "How about you, Dusty? Do you have a boyfriend?"

She shrugged, the question throwing her off guard. "Sort of... not a steady or anything. Just a guy I dated over the summer." Warmth crept up her neck. Paisley had asked about Jack, and she really hadn't told her anything. Now she felt like a traitor telling two strangers, both of whom were waiting for details.

"It's nothing, really. Just someone to dance with. Daddy's always throwing parties for this or that..." *Jack*. Had it only been five days since the send-off party at the ranch?

Sharon Kay nudged her. "Would that be like a square dance?" Her tone was light, but Dusty knew her intent was not.

She ignored the comment, still thinking about Jack and the way he'd come back just as the party was breaking up. They'd walked around to the back of the house, away from the cleanup crew, and stood under the canopy of oaks. Being with Jack had stirred something in her she'd never felt before and hadn't even known she wanted. At the same time, she kept waiting for him to discover that she was a fraud, just a tomboy who'd learned to be comfortable in a skirt and high heels. Either way, her stomach was a fluttery mess.

Dusty ran her tongue over her lips, the memory of Jack's kisses lingering. Maybe the less said about Jack, the better.

Miss Fontaine returned to score them on their proficiency at introductions, rescuing Dusty from having to talk anymore about Jack. All three perfect scores. "Well done, young ladies. You're excused until this afternoon. Sulee serves lunch at twelve thirty."

She bobbled off to the next group while Sharon Kay left with Stacia to go look at bridal magazines. Dusty flipped through the skills book to see what was on for the next few weeks and groaned. It was enough to give her palpitations, but one date jumped out: Mother/Daughter Tea—October 3.

Rosalita would have been a nice choice, but that was out. Maybe

Aunt Edith. She and Paisley could share a mom. She scanned the room and found Paisley perched on the wide ledge of the window, her knees drawn up, her back against the thick plaster encasement. The gauzy fabric of her long skirt draped her legs as she looked outside.

"Hey."

Paisley turned and hopped down. "Wanna go down to the swamp?"

Dusty checked her wristwatch. "Maybe just a short trek before lunch."

As they headed for the classroom door, Carmel Zanick, a petite blonde, ran over and joined them. "Don't y'all just love it here? I am expanding my horizons and becoming a woman of the world, just like Momma said I would. Oh, my gracious goodness, I'm dying to hear about the ranch you live on, Dusty. And Paisley, I'd give my liver to be tall like you and wear those dreamy clothes." She drew out every syllable, the vowels all rounded and sweet, like Carmel herself.

"Miss Fontaine looked at me like I'd plucked them off the rack at the Salvation Army. Inappropriate, I think she said."

"You can't be serious. Why, they're divine. And I love your boots."

Paisley lifted the edge of her skirt and did a curtsy. The ankle boots were scuffed a bit, but honestly, with her filmy skirt and ropy beads, Paisley had a style all her own.

❦

Outside, Dusty kicked off her flats and wiggled her toes, the grass spongy and cool. "I'm sorry Miss Fontaine didn't like your outfit. You're free to raid my closet if you'd like."

"Thanks, but I'll pass. Miss Fontaine already has me pegged, so I'll just be myself and try not to let her intimidate me."

"As long as you can handle it, I'm fine with that."

"I'll let you know if I change my mind." Paisley looked at her, her eyes crinkling at the corners. She'd pulled her dark hair up into a French twist and put on some blush. Not that she needed makeup. Her skin was flawless, her eyes the color of peridots, so green it looked as if an artist had taken a brush and painted them.

Paisley sidestepped a wet spot in the grass. "The poor little rich girl thing doesn't really suit me like it does you."

Dusty bristled. "I hope you don't mean that. I'm nothing like those girls in there. And you…you're like the sister I never had. What's mine is yours, you know that."

"I'm not a charity case."

"I didn't say you were. You're family. There's a difference. We can go shopping in town if you'd rather. Providing you want to stay. You seem a little unsure."

"It's not that at all. I'd really like a chance to prove I'm not the gypsy your daddy makes me out to be. I just want to do it in my own way."

"Daddy just says that to get Aunt Edith's goat. But seriously, if you don't like it here, I can call Daddy and tell him we changed our minds."

"Sure, that would go over like a lead balloon. Besides, you wouldn't want to disappoint him."

"It is true that I want to stick it out here to prove I'm ready to go to college, but it's also not quite clear to me what finishing school has to do in the eternal perspective, you know. So say the word, and I'll call Daddy." Even as Dusty spoke, her stomach twisted. She'd rather eat glass than confront her dad, and what would be her excuse? Her roommate was a spoiled brat? He'd want to know if she had an alternative plan, and of course, she didn't. It was too late to get into college now, and he'd disown her if she said they'd decided to go on tour with the Asterisks.

"If you ran back home, you could be with Miles or Mack, whatever your bank dude's name is."

"Jack. His name is Jack. And I wasn't thinking that at all." And yet, now that it had come up, the thought warmed her. Maybe a little too much.

"You never did tell me about him."

She gave her the facts. Jack. Last name Morgan. Hometown: Houston. Accounting degree from SMU.

"What do his parents do?"

"His dad's a state senator, just got elected. Not sure about his mom. We don't talk about things like that."

"So what do you talk about?"

"Movies. Music. Nothing much." It sounded vague, and she realized she didn't know all that much about Jack Morgan. Except that he was a great dancer and kissed liked a dream. "Why so many questions?"

Paisley shrugged. "Just curious."

"What about you? Any guys in San Francisco waiting for you?"

"Yeah, dozens of them. Just can't keep up with all the boys lined up outside the apartment, waiting for me to come out and eeny-meeny-miney-mo for the one I'm going to grace with my presence." A harsh laugh bleated from her throat.

"Sorry. You've always been the one with boyfriends, not me. Is that what has you bent out of shape?"

"I'm not bent out of shape. I'm just curious. Are you dating-dating or is it a casual thing? Has he kissed you?"

Dusty chewed her bottom lip. "What do you think?"

"I think there's a lot you're not telling me. Spill it. How could you have kept this from me? We tell each other everything. Man, I knew I should've come to the ranch this summer. How tall? Blue eyes or green? When can I meet him? Does your daddy like him?"

"Stop! You're driving me nuts! That's a perfect example of why

I didn't tell you, sweet cousin. You always make everything into a production. Jack is nice. Really nice. And brown eyes."

They'd come to the trees that lined the bayou. The rich scent of mud and decaying leaves came like steam rising from a pot of Rosalita's chili. The thought of ditching lunch and the afternoon class was tempting. Dusty inhaled until she thought her lungs would burst, then gave a lingering look at the trees and told Paisley they should head back.

Paisley linked arms with her. "Just for the record, I think we should stay. This place is growing on me. Besides, I need to help Xan with a little project."

"Really. What's that?"

"Come on. I'll tell you about it on the way."

CHAPTER 6

The first two weeks breezed by in a blur. Paisley could hardly believe how many topics on etiquette and manners there were. Writing bread and butter notes. Short correspondence. Long correspondence. And the posture lessons. What a trip, all of them walking around with books on their heads while Miss Fontaine stood on the sidelines and coached them about keeping their chins up and sucking in their stomachs for inner control.

And then there was learning which spoon to eat soup with and how many inches to the right of the bread and butter plate to put the water glass. Paisley was sure it was all useful, but the day she caught herself daydreaming of marrying someone like Prentice Robbins, who ran an important business by day and greeted Paisley like she was a princess at six o'clock, she knew she'd flipped her wig. She asked to be excused and marched out the front door and sat on the steps.

It took four Salems before she came to her senses and remembered that girls like her didn't grow up to live in picturesque neighborhoods and chat with other housewives over backyard fences about whether or not it was appropriate to serve clam chowder in the summer or what happened on their soaps that day. She had a better chance of being asked to man a rocket ship than she did of living the kind of life Miss Fontaine's girls were destined for.

When she got her wits back, she returned to class and doodled on her notebook while Miss Fontaine stood poised at the podium and said, "Learning the art of good conversation will give you the foundation you need to be charming in any situation."

Her voice lilted up and down like a seesaw on the playground as she lectured on the travesty of butchering the English language. Paisley cringed. She'd been doing it all of her eighteen years and didn't even know it. Bouquet was *boo-kay*. Garage, gar-*razhe*. And amateur wasn't *amachure* but *am-a-ter*.

Paisley thought Miss Fontaine's eyes rested on her a tad too long when she said, "You know she is a lady as soon as she opens her mouth. Enunciate clearly and learn proper breathing techniques to properly refine your voice."

If Miss Fontaine ever sat in on one of the Asterisks jam sessions, she would have a stroke. Paisley shifted in her seat, pushing that part of her life out of her mind and trying to concentrate.

Miss Fontaine had perfect diction and had moved on to talking about French. "Dropping French words into your conversations to prove you are clever or superior is a strict no-no. However, beginning on Monday, you will have the honor and privilege to begin French lessons. I'm sure you will find my dear friend and distant relative, Adrian Simon, a delight. It's a plus for any proper Southern woman to be well-rounded in many subjects."

Since Miss Fontaine took dinner in her quarters and didn't join them in the evenings, the girls at the table that night had a free-for-all speculating what Adrian Simon would be like.

"Fat and bald most likely." Xan twirled her spaghetti and glanced at Paisley. Translation: like Prentice Robbins.

"Or pigeon-toed and knock-kneed." This from June Little from Jackson. "Like my French teacher from high school."

"You don't suppose he's single?" June's roommate, Roberta Lee, gave a coquettish look and batted her eyelashes. "I'm hoping suave *and* available. We need a little excitement, if you ask me."

Dusty shook her head. "You don't think Miss Fontaine would bring her cousin or nephew or whatever he is around here if he was good-looking and single. You know how she adheres to propriety."

Sulee, the cook, swished in with a tray holding individual serving cups of banana pudding. She glided around the table, her head bobbing on her neck as she distributed the desserts. She reminded Paisley of the spindly man on Fisherman's Wharf who tossed bread crumbs to the seagulls and sometimes pulled a harmonica from his pocket, nodding his head when people dropped nickels and dimes into his bowler hat. She half expected Sulee to do a little soft-shoe when she'd finished, but she slipped back to the kitchen without a word. Paisley winked at Xan who had pushed her dessert aside without touching it.

When Sulee was out of earshot, Sharon Kay put her palms on the table and leaned in.

"Say what you will. I know what he's like." She smiled, then leaned back and crossed her arms.

Paisley bit back a smile of her own. The world could only stand so many Sharon Kays who threw out tempting morsels, then waited for the girls, like seagulls on the wharf, to swoop in, begging.

Questions flew like confetti. *Tell us, what's he like? Have you met him? Please, don't leave us hanging.*

Sharon Kay shrugged. "Oh, all right. Since you're dying to know. Babs Murphy came here last year and is one of the top debs in Houston this year. She said..." She looked toward the door, which led to the kitchen, then motioned for them to draw closer. "She said our dear Mr. Simon has been known to give a little extra credit on your grades if you participate in extracurricular sessions."

She took a sip of sweet tea before she continued, "A little tête-à-tête, if you know what I mean."

Xan, up until this point, had been lapping it up. She squinched her eyes and shook her head. "Babs Murphy? Really? I played tennis with her last summer. She didn't say anything to me, and she knew I was coming to Miss Fontaine's. Not only that, she spent the whole time flirting with the pro at the club, trying to arrange a little tête-à-tête, like you said."

Sharon Kay snapped her head toward Xan. "Babs is one of my best friends, not yours. Why would she confide in you? And you have a lot of gall suggesting—"

Xan shrugged. "I just call it like I see it. More than likely she threw herself at Mr. Simon who—since you brought it up—I'm simply dying to meet, aren't y'all?" She looked around for approval and got a few nods. "I bet Babs flirted with Mr. Simon, and he gave her the cold shoulder."

Sharon Kay threw her napkin on the table. "You're wrong. Dead wrong."

Sulee pushed through the swinging door. "Sorry, misses. I forgot to ask if any of you would like coffee with your dessert."

Sharon Kay straightened up and clasped her hands together, her expression turning at once into one of angelic proportions. "Oh, no, ma'am, we're all doing fine. Just fine." She shoveled the last of her pudding in her mouth, and when Sulee was gone, eyed every girl at the table. "Don't say I didn't warn you."

⌘

Mr. Simon was nothing like Dusty imagined, and she was sure some of her classmates must've shared her disappointment after their speculations…and hopes that he would have movie star looks and irresistible charm. Dusty found him ordinary in every way. Medium build, neither tall nor short, plain brown hair in the same shade as his tweed jacket and trousers. The only hint of color was a red stripe in the olive tie knotted at his neck. His fawn-colored eyes matched, unlike those of Miss Fontaine and the general in the parlor painting.

Miss Fontaine introduced him with a flourish and blushed when Mr. Simon kissed her on the cheek and said something in what Dusty assumed was French. The words had a melody to them, poetic and charming. Dusty's estimation of him grew, although it was possible Mr. Simon was merely asking Miss Fontaine to do his laundry or bring him a cup of tea.

Miss Fontaine excused herself, her heels clicking on the wide-planked floor as she went. Mr. Simon surveyed the class and spoke with native East Texas warmth. "I see Miss Fontaine's choice of students is as lovely as ever, and I'm looking forward to the few short months we'll have together. This will be a practical course, focusing on vocabulary, sentence construction, and learning how to order from a French menu or make purchases. I suspect many of you will travel to *gay à Paris* in the future, so to understand the basic nuances of the French language and to be understood will be our goals."

Simple, straightforward. He passed out mimeographed sheets of paper with two columns of words. "You will note that these words are in French. Some may look familiar. They are the root words from which much of our own English is derived." This was their homework for which they would use their French-to-English dictionaries with the first test on Friday.

The two hours flew by as Mr. Simon moved on to simple greetings and how to ask basic questions. Dusty was mesmerized. After the tiresome etiquette lessons, this was like a real class, one she might have been taking on a tree-lined college campus if not for the detour to Rosebriar and Miss Fontaine.

The class after lunch was Preparing for the Formal Afternoon Tea. Fresh air wafted through an open window, but even with that,

Dusty's mind wandered as Miss Fontaine explained the difference between a coffee and a tea, who might be included on the guest list for each of them, who pours the tea, and the appropriate foods to serve. To keep from nodding off, Dusty drew out the placement of the cups, saucers, and napkins, making *x*'s and *o*'s with arrows and labeling each one. She sighed. It looked like the plays her basketball coach in high school had drawn on the chalkboard. She was sure she'd never keep it straight. Maybe she'd come down with a case of poison ivy or get tonsillitis and escape the torture.

At the end of the session, Miss Fontaine passed out linen card stock on which they were to write invitations to their mothers using the proper wording they'd gone over. Miss Fontaine glanced at Dusty and Paisley and amended her charge. "Because some of your mothers may have other obligations or be unavailable, you are at liberty to invite someone else. You will be planning and conducting the tea completely on your own and scored on your individual contributions. It's always a popular and lively event."

Dusty nudged Paisley and mouthed, "Edie?" She pointed to the card.

Paisley quirked her mouth and drew her eyebrows in like she was impatient with Dusty for even thinking it. When they were dismissed, Dusty pursued it.

Paisley shrugged. "The Asterisks' tour won't be over by then."

"Maybe they'll be in the neighborhood. You said they had a lot of bookings in Texas."

"Sorry. I don't know their schedule. Besides, this sort of thing isn't exactly the happening scene Edie's used to, you know that."

"That's not true. Aunt Edith—Edie—lights up the room when she walks in, and besides, she seemed sad when she left you here. I know she misses you."

Paisley waved away the comment, then took the blank invitation, ripped it in half, and dropped it in the wastebasket.

Miffed at Paisley's flippant attitude, Dusty slipped away and checked her mail slot in the walnut cubbyholes above a desk in the hall. As she pulled out a letter, a tiny noose lassoed her heart. *Jack.* She pocketed it, then ran upstairs and changed, transferring the letter to the pocket of her Levi's.

She grabbed her easy translator dictionary and the French vocabulary sheets and went outside. The fountain bubbled from the fish mouth as she sat on the ground with her back to the brick wall. It was soothing in its own way, and the solitude suited her.

Dusty knew she was being petty, but she was growing more weary by the hour of the giggles and innuendos among the other girls. Even Paisley had tittered with the girls as they'd discussed teacups and silver service and the polishing thereof. She wished she were half as slick as Paisley at taking any situation and turning it into the *groovy* thing to do. She just didn't have to be so cavalier about Aunt Edith.

Dusty wasn't sure why it chafed that she wouldn't have a mother to invite. Rosalita had taken care of cookie and cake duty whenever she'd needed birthday treats or home-baked concession stand items. Rosalita's tamales sold out at every football game, sometimes before halftime. She had been more than a housekeeper, guiding Dusty through the tricky miseries of adolescence, and she had no inhibitions whatsoever about telling Dusty when she needed to straighten up and fly right.

A pang wrapped around her heart. Maybe it wasn't not having a mother that bothered her, but being worried about Rosalita. Aunt Edith would be a nice consolation. What would it hurt if she sent her an invitation? She had the San Francisco address, and surely her aunt had made arrangements for having her mail forwarded. Or not. It was hard to tell with Aunt Edith, but at least she would know she'd been welcome to come.

Dusty couldn't decide which to do first—French vocabulary or read Jack's letter. Because she'd be in deep Dutch if she didn't do her homework, she tackled the list first. She'd do the first page and save Jack's letter as a reward.

The words were grouped in categories, places first.

Maison—House; *Marché*—Market; *École*—School; *Université*—University; *Théâtre*—Theater; *Restaurant*—Restaurant; *Église*—Church.

It surprised her how similar the two languages were. Pronunciation might be tricky, but she hurried on to the next group: colors.

Bleu—Blue; *Vert*—Green; *Jaune*—Yellow; *Rouge*—Red; *Noir*—Black; *Blanc*—White; *Orange*—Orange; *Brun*—Brown.

Then things in nature:

Ciel—Sky; *Terre*—Earth; *Arbres*—Trees; *Fleurs*—Flowers; *Eau*—Water; *Soleil*—Sun; *Nuages*—Clouds; *Pluie*—Rain.

She liked the rhythm of looking up the words, letting the new words trip off her tongue—no doubt hacking the French language. She found it interesting and similar to poring over a book classifying rock samples. With the first page done, she set her French homework aside and pulled Jack's letter from her pocket.

Her fingers trembled as she ran her nail under the flap and pulled out a single sheet of bank stationery, the sort of note where she imagined Jack might scribble estimates for customers about how much the bank would loan them.

Dear Dusty,
 I hope you're enjoying your stay in East Texas. I couldn't remember exactly what you were doing there, but when I had lunch with

your dad at the Cattleman's Café, he filled me in about your taking lessons in etiquette. My sister went to a place back East and came home with a Boston accent. Her training has come in handy a few times as I'm sure yours will. I must say, though, you have a certain charm of your own.

I enjoyed our time this summer. Maybe we can get together over the holidays.

Sincerely,
Jack Morgan

Sincerely? The breeze over the water in the fountain brought a chill to the air. He *had* written. And paid her a nice compliment. He wanted to see her again. But he'd also seen her dad. Had they bumped into each other or was it an arranged meeting? And did he, along with her dad, think she was just an object that needed to be trained? Like a puppy?

She stuffed the letter back in the envelope and shoved it in her pocket. No use in getting worked up. Jack probably thought he was being considerate by writing. And he thought she was charming. That was something. Her inexperience in the dating department left her unsure of what she should be feeling at this point in their relationship. Was it even a relationship?

The flutter in her chest when she thought of him made her think it was. She liked him. A lot. He was intelligent and kind, comfortable to be with, and she fit perfectly in his arms when they were slow dancing. She felt warmth rise from her chest at the thought.

Thanksgiving wasn't that far away. She'd write and let Jack know she missed him and couldn't wait to see him over the holidays. In the meantime...

She picked up her dictionary and flipped to the back for the English-to-French version, looking up her own words.

Letter—*Lettre*. Boyfriend—*Petit ami*.

A tiny prick of disappointment went through her. *Petit* sounded like something small, not Jack's strong arms that twirled her on the dance floor. She wished she hadn't looked up the words, hadn't hoped for something more exotic.

CHAPTER 7

Paisley could only think of one word to describe Mrs. Pellerin. Robust. Miss Fontaine maintained her usual formal tone when she introduced her as an accomplished pastry chef, one of the finest in the South. Mrs. Pellerin was anything but chef-like. Or formal. She wore a pinafore apron with a ruffle at the bottom and was more like a plump granny whose arms jiggled along with her rosy cheeks when she laughed. After Mr. Simon, who'd turned out to be dead dull and uninspiring, Paisley liked her in an instant.

They gathered in the kitchen around a large island with a wood surface where bowls and spoons and canisters were strung out over the length of it. Mrs. Pellerin had a smudge of flour on her chin before they even started. She got right down to business.

"Don't believe that nonsense about me being a pastry chef. I've been a friend of Birdie Fontaine's since we were children. My mama cooked for the Fontaines, and when I married big old Buster, that strappin' Cajun from across the border, I put what I learned in this here kitchen to work straight away. I've been running the Pie Barn outside of Crowfoot, Louisiana, for twenty-six years. Now let's get started."

She had laid out the ingredients to make lemon bars, and working in groups of three, they were to follow her lead through the steps.

"The secret to Southern cooking is real butter. Fresh if you have it, but since you darlings are probably from the city, more'n likely you don't know fresh butter from a poke in the eye. Just remember, you use that oleomargarine you buy down at Piggly Wiggly, and you'll never get a flaky piecrust or a pound cake worth beans. So the first thing we're doing is making the crust."

She scooped heaping teaspoons from a box labeled Confectioners' Sugar into a cup, used a knife to level it, and dumped it in the mixing bowl, sending up little white bursts with each action. She wiped her hands on her apron, then added butter and held up two forks. "Cut the butter into the powdered sugar until you get pea-sized lumps."

Next to Paisley, Xan concentrated on the forks in her hands while Paisley measured the flour and salt for the next step.

"Your mixture should be crumbly like this." She tipped the bowl to demonstrate. She offered bits of encouragement here and there, then opened the oven door of the cast iron stove and let the girls file by and insert their baking dishes. "Nice job." "Lovely dress, miss."

And to Paisley, she said, "Aren't you a vision today? Voile is a fabric we should use more of, in my opinion. And that purple color, oh, my, such a lovely hue. And quite a history, too. Lydia in the New Testament was a seller of purple, and I've no doubt, your skirt would bring a smile to her lips."

Paisley thanked her, secretly pleased that this was the skirt Miss Fontaine had suggested was inappropriate.

While they waited on the crust to bake, Mrs. Pellerin showed them how to beat the eggs for the filling and put Sharon Kay to work with the cut glass lemon juicer. "Put a little oomph into it, darling."

Sharon Kay looked as if she'd just sucked on a lemon as she

jammed the halved lemon on the center of the juicer and twisted it halfheartedly. Stacia gave her a hip shove and took over while Sharon Kay ran to the sink to wash her hands.

Across the table, Paisley saw Dusty bite her lip to keep from laughing. At least the kitchen was one area where she and Dusty had an edge on the other girls. Dusty grew up at Rosalita's feet and could whip up a cobbler or a pan of enchiladas in nothing flat. In her own house if Paisley hadn't learned how to scramble eggs and make tuna casserole, she and Edie would've starved.

They poured the filling over the hot crust, and while they waited for it to bake, Mrs. Pellerin said, "Let's clean this mess up and talk about what you want to serve at your mamas' tea party. It's coming up just around the corner."

When they'd finished and Mrs. Pellerin sailed out the door with promises that she'd turn each of them into Betty Crocker, Sulee announced that it was lunchtime. She'd laid out cold chicken salad and fruit cups on the glass-topped tables in the flower garden.

The air was festive, the sun warm as the girls buzzed with their assigned duties for the upcoming tea. Paisley was pleased she'd be making custard tarts and lemon squares. At least she wouldn't screw that up, *and* she could hide out in the kitchen if things started going south.

Paisley elbowed Dusty. "What are you doing for the tea?"

"Table arrangement and polishing silver." She gave a two thumbs-up.

Sharon Kay, sitting at the next table, said, "It's perfect for you, Dusty. You're really talented at lining things up. Maybe you could use some of your gorgeous rocks as centerpieces."

Dusty shrugged. "You never know. I might have the ladies from the Two Forks Methodist women's circle send one of their cow patty centerpieces. They sell them every year at the fall bazaar. With gold spray paint and little sprigs of holly, they look quite fancy."

Sharon Kay glared at her. "That sounds disgusting."

Stacia laughed. "I heard Lady Bird Johnson took one to the White House. Poor Jackie nearly passed out."

Dusty laughed. "I think it's a rumor the bazaar ladies started to sell their artwork. Not the best idea for our tea party and your sweet mamas."

Talk turned to floral arrangements, which was the afternoon class topic. When Sulee brought out a platter of lemon bars from their morning cooking lesson, Xan nearly drooled but passed them without taking one.

"None for me," Stacia said. "I just saw the mailman drive by out front. I'm going to see if there's a letter from Michael." She dashed off and came back moments later, shoulders drooping. "Nothing." She sniffled and passed an envelope to Paisley. "You got something, though."

Paisley inhaled and choked on the powdered sugar from her lemon bar. Only one person knew she was here, and it wasn't like Edie to write her a letter unless something had happened.

"Go on. Open it."

The writing on the front was clearly not Edie's. Voices from around the tables continued. "Hey, you didn't tell us you had a boyfriend." "Come on. Don't keep us in suspense."

She took her knife and slit it open. A photograph fell from the folded note. She recognized it as the one she'd taken of the band onstage in Lubbock. Edie *had* kept the camera and gotten the film developed, but why send her the picture? The note quivered in her trembling fingers, the dining room quiet as the girls around the table stared and waited.

She lifted her chin and smiled. "Edie got the pictures I was telling you about developed. Here's the band standing on the spot where Elvis did." She handed the photo to Dusty and said, "They were always clowning around."

She tucked the letter in her lap as the photo went from table to table. Overhead, the sky darkened as an angry cloud passed over the sun. Reading it was the last thing she wanted. Seeing the signature was enough.

For old time's sake.

Love, Sloan.

She wanted to puke.

❦

Dusty found the photograph of the Asterisks on the flagstone of the garden patio after the others went to freshen up for the afternoon class. She pocketed the photo and lingered behind to soak up every bit of outside air that time would allow.

The solarium classroom felt airless and cloying when she entered, but the floral scent was nice, and she remembered this was the class on arranging garden flowers. Clusters of roses, zinnias, gerbera daisies, and coneflowers stood upright in pitchers of water on the oak table, along with a supply of baby's breath and ferns with a florist emblem on the paper wrapped loosely around them.

Miss Fontaine twittered away about choosing blossoms with petals that weren't fully opened so they could be at their maximum beauty when guests arrived. She demonstrated how to remove the barbs from thorny stems and how to cup the fingers around a bundle of stems before placing them in vases or decorative urns.

As they made their own arrangements, Miss Fontaine was helping Stacia add a spray of baby's breath to her pink roses when Sulee came in, her eyes wide, her chest heaving as if she'd been running. She put a bony hand around Miss Fontaine's arm, pulled her aside, and whispered to her. Miss Fontaine's face drained of color as she nodded and spoke in low tones.

She discharged Sulee and faced the group, her voice gravelly. "You will have to continue without me. A matter of some urgency has come up." She sauntered off, her steps wobbly.

"Wonder what that was about," Xan said. "Sulee looked like she'd seen a ghost."

As they speculated about every possibility from Mrs. Pellerin having a car accident on her way back to the Pie Barn to a crisis in the kitchen, the station wagon backfired, followed by the sound of tires peeling out on the gravel.

One by one, they looked at Sharon Kay until she blurted out, "What? Why are you looking at me?"

"Because you're the only one who has inside information—Babs Murphy from last year, remember?" Xan cocked her head. "Maybe she told you Miss Fontaine is in love with a riverboat gambler or belongs to a secret clan like the Ku Kluxers, and they had an emergency meeting, and they're going to hang one of Sulee's relatives."

Sharon Kay sniffed. "My, my, don't you have the imagination? The only love affair I know about is the one our dear headmistress has with her sherry bottle. She likes a little afternoon toddy, you know."

"That wouldn't explain the sick look she got on her face." Carmel knitted her eyebrows together. "And Sulee seemed frightened, too. I hope it's nothing serious."

No one really had her heart in finishing up the flower arranging, so after poking the flowers into vases and calling it good, they cleaned up the debris and left. Dusty looked around for Paisley, who'd been distracted and contemplative since lunch. She wasn't on the porch taking a smoke break nor was she in the garden where Dusty thought she might have gone to retrieve her photograph. She hoped her cousin was all right.

Of course she would be. Paisley could brush off disappointment in one breath and be laughing in the next. She would find Paisley later. She sat for a moment wondering what had pulled Miss Fontaine away, but nothing came to mind. Her sight drifted to the edge of the garden next to Rosebriar's carriage house. A wrought iron fence separated the garden from a footpath—the one she'd seen Sulee walking down of an evening after she'd cleaned the kitchen. Dusty walked over and found the gate in the ironwork. When she lifted the latch, it swung open noiselessly. She turned left and walked the way she'd seen Sulee going. There wasn't a breath of air, the sky layered with steel-colored clouds that pressed in and gave Dusty a sense of foreboding. She dismissed it as Miss Fontaine's unknown emergency.

The path was well-worn and mowed along the fence, and when the iron fence from the garden stopped, a board fence like the ones in the horse pastures at the ranch began. Miss Fontaine had said this was a plantation at one time, and Dusty wondered if Miss Fontaine had kept all of it or only the house and grounds. Workers came several times a week for trimming, mowing, and tending the garden. Did they maintain the area along the footpath, too?

Thoughts of Rosebriar carried her along the trail as she enjoyed the day. After a while, Dusty propped her elbows on the fence's top rail and scanned the pasture for a glimpse of the horses she'd seen from her upstairs room. Finally she spotted them in a far corner, grazing near a grove of trees. Beyond that, she couldn't see anything but forest, maybe a crook in the bayou that ran alongside the back edge of the property.

She felt the wind pick up and looked overhead. The clouds churned now, and she could smell rain. The first sprinkles were heavy, as large as lemon drops on her arms. She turned to go back and didn't realize she'd come so far. She lifted her face to the sky, the clouds growing darker by the minute, and decided she needed to hightail it. The sprinkles quickly turned into a heavy shower, then fell in sheets, soaking her skirt and blouse so they clung to her back and legs. She tried to go faster, but her flats slipped on the muddy path. She stopped long enough to remove them and raced like the wind in the downpour.

As she passed the carriage house, she got a short respite from the pelting rain but hurried on and ran to the back door. This way was quicker, and she hoped there would be a towel in the room she knew was a service entrance for deliveries. Besides, she'd hate to track mud into the front hall.

She stood on an old rug inside the door, her wet hair matted against her face. She brushed it away and looked up hoping to find something to dry off with. She came face-to-face with Delia, the upstairs maid, with hands on her hips and a glare that made Dusty want to charge back out into the rain.

"What in the Sam Hill you doing out there in that mess? Look at you."

Dusty didn't have to look. She knew she looked like a drowned rat. "I'm sorry. Got caught...didn't realize it was fixin' to rain. Is there a towel I can use?"

Delia shoved one at her. "The bigger question be, why was you tramping about in the first place? I seen you coming up from the horse pen. Ain't you ever learned to pay mind to No Trespassing signs when they're right there in plain sight for all the Lord's creation to see?"

"I didn't...no, ma'am...I—"

"You be getting yourself sick with a chest cold gallivanting in the rain. And where you got no business being either, missy."

"I said I'm sorry." She ran the towel over her arms and bent to dry her legs and feet, her clothes dripping water as fast as she dried it off, and answered Delia's questions. "I didn't see any sign like you're talking about. I went out through the garden gate, and I guess I wasn't paying attention."

Delia crossed her arms and shook her head. "You best be thanking your lucky stars Missy Fontaine is gone, or she be dressing you down like you never seen before."

"So Miss Fontaine is still gone?"

Delia's face softened. "Far as I know."

"I hope everything's all right. Do you know what happened?"

"None of my affair. Or yours."

"Sorry." She held out the soggy towel. "Could I have another towel? I'd hate to track up the house."

Delia traded the wet one for a dry one and handed Dusty a raincoat that was hanging on a peg. Dusty now saw that they were in a fairly large space that doubled as a utility room with a washer and dryer humming along the far wall. Delia pointed to a door next to the machines. "There's a half bath in there. Get out of your wet clothes and cover up with this raincoat. Just leave your wet things here, and I'll wash them before Miss Fontaine sees what you've been up to. Now, scoot! And mind what I told you."

"Yes, ma'am. And thank you."

After slinking upstairs in the raincoat, she took a hot shower and shampooed her hair, which felt like heaven. It was while in the shower that she remembered Paisley's photograph which she'd shoved in her pocket. Ruined by now, no doubt, and too late to retrieve it as Delia was probably already washing her clothes. She also didn't relish another run-in with the maid. She was always pleasant enough, doing her cleaning while they were in class. She guessed most people were until you stepped across the line. And the off-limits line was one she would have to try and remember.

At dinner, Dusty told Paisley about the photo, that she feared it was ruined.

Paisley shrugged. "It's not that big a deal."

"It was nice that your mom sent it."

"I guess." She turned in the direction of the stairs, then paused. "She could have told me she was keeping the camera. She knew I wanted it, and it's not like she'll ever use it."

"If it's the camera you're worried about, I'll have Daddy send the one I got for graduation. It's one of those nifty new thirty-five-millimeter types. I just didn't think to bring it."

"What happened to your Brownie?"

"I gave it to Rosalita to take to Old Mexico. What else did your mom have to say?"

"Not much. Still on tour." Paisley's nonchalance meant she wasn't ready to talk about it.

"Well, it was still nice that she thought of you."

Paisley didn't answer, just gave a lopsided grin and said she needed to do her French homework.

By early evening, Miss Fontaine still hadn't returned. They were supposed to get Miss Fontaine's permission to make long-distance phone calls, but in her absence, Dusty decided just to call collect.

She got the long-distance operator and gave her the number.

Her dad answered on the first ring and accepted the charges. "Glory be. Got your letter the other day. Sounds like you're getting along all right there."

"Not too bad. The etiquette lessons are what you would call horse sense, but I think the French is going to be quite a challenge." She told him how much she liked Mrs. Pellerin and hoped to be an accomplished pie maker by the time she got home for Thanksgiving.

"Can't wait to see you, sugar. And Paisley, too. Hope you two aren't getting into too much mischief."

"No, just doing what I'm supposed to." Innocent trespassing and getting caught in a gully washer was hardly mischief. "I need to ask you a favor."

"Shoot."

"Can you send the camera the Byerleys gave me for graduation? I didn't think to pack it, and Aunt Edith took Paisley's by mistake."

"Nothing that woman does is ever by mistake."

"Maybe. All I know is Paisley would really like to have a camera to take pictures and commemorate our time here."

"So I'm guessing that means there's something there to commemorate." His tone had a hint of *I told you so*, but his voice was warm, and Dusty was glad she'd called.

"It's not college like I wanted, but yeah, it's okay."

"How's your money holding out?"

"Fine. Miss Swanson takes us into town whenever we want to go, and she shuttles us all to church on Sunday."

"Be sure and leave a little something in the offering, you hear?"

"I will, Daddy. And I do need to go shopping this Saturday for a new pair of flats. Mine got wet in the rain today."

"Good gravy. You took more shoes than there are fleas on those pups of yours."

"Yes, I know. These were my favorites, though."

"Well, go ahead. Get what you need. And Paisley, too. I know Edith didn't leave her with any mad money."

"Thanks. And you're right. Paisley might want a new outfit for the ladies' tea we're having. I'll let you know if I need more money." She was grateful that even with his stubbornness her daddy was generous.

Ice clinked in a glass in the background. Dusty imagined her dad in his dark paneled study swiveling in his leather chair to the whiskey cabinet he kept behind his desk, the aluminum ice bucket handy. She asked about Lamb Chop and Juanita—her pups, as her dad called them. Hers and Rosalita's. They'd each named one when her dad brought them home from one of his clients. A twinge went through her. With her and Rosalita both gone, they were probably lost.

"They're fine. Terrorizing the joint as usual."

She asked about Rosalita and her brothers.

"Haven't heard beans from Rosalita. Figger she'll just show up and want her job back one of these days. Never mind that I'm left to do all my own cooking." He paused and she recognized the small sigh that he let out after taking a drink.

"She'll be back." Her stomach pinched with worry. "Daddy, I can come home if you want."

"Hell's bells, it's the first time in a coon's age I've had the house to myself. Besides, I like sardines and crackers. You'll stay put right where you are. No fussin' about me."

Dusty let out a breath. She had to ask, but she felt a small release when he said no. Now that the first days of settling in were behind her, she didn't want to leave. Mrs. Pellerin was fun, and like she told her dad, French was a challenge. She had that in common with Flint Fairchild—they both liked a challenge. When she hung up, a tiny flicker of homesickness went through her. Maybe that's what Paisley felt when she got the letter from her mom. A home was where those you loved were. For Dusty, it was the ranch. For Paisley, she couldn't tell. She'd acted weird about her mother, but Dusty had always heard that even though moms and their girls went at each other like fighting chickens, the bond between them was sure and strong.

Dusty didn't know anything about that.

What she did know was that her daddy's voice had a tone she'd never heard before. Flint Fairchild was lonely. And alone.

CHAPTER 8

When Paisley aimed the viewfinder at Dusty, her cousin brandished the knife she was polishing and gave her a cheesy grin. The blade, glistening and smooth, caught the light from the teardrop chandelier in the dining room. Paisley focused the lens on the Canon 35mm and clicked, then snapped a shot of the table all set for the Mother/Daughter Tea.

Dusty put down the knife and lined it up with the others. "It's no wonder Rosalita always took a day off after one of Daddy's doin's. There's a lot more work to this than I thought."

Stacia flicked a linen napkin, then twirled it like magic in her fingers and came up with a perfect four-point tulip, which she set in the center of the last Wedgwood china dessert plate. "There you go, sweet cakes." She curtsied and stood back, the three of them admiring their handiwork. *Click.*

Dusty shook her head. "I think I'll run up and get another roll of film. The way you're taking pictures, we'll need more for when the moms get here. Anything I can get for you?"

"I'm good. Just want to get a couple more of the flowers that Xan and Carmel did." She went into the parlor where Xan paced the floor. "Mother is going to have a cow over my hair." She twirled a golden strand and bit her lip. They'd bleached and dyed Xan's hair three times as part of her scheme to reinvent herself.

"It looks great. I think we got the color right this time. It looks very natural and becoming."

"She'll be in orbit over it, I know. She probably won't even notice that I've lost weight. Six pounds already."

"Don't sweat it. You're following your dream."

And just that moment, Bobby Darin came on the radio singing "Dream Lover." They laughed and did a twirl on the rose-patterned rug in the middle of the parlor.

Miss Fontaine came in and switched off the radio. "A time and place for everything. My, but you two look lovely." She had a sparkle about her that Paisley thought was pride at how well they'd done. Whatever crisis she'd had passed without mention, and the conjecture about what might have happened had died down.

Paisley thanked her for the compliment, but felt silly in the Bobbie Brooks outfit Dusty had insisted on buying for her in one of Alborghetti's dress shops. Xan had shown her how to stand the back of the collar up and loaned her a see-through scarf to knot at the neck, telling her she looked very cosmopolitan, which made Paisley laugh. The navy pumps they'd bought the same day pinched her toes, but in an odd sort of way, she felt chic. Paisley almost wished Edie was coming, but deeper down, her gut rumbled at the thought. Being the official photographer with Dusty's camera would be drama enough.

Girls began drifting in the parlor, giggling, bringing with them a swirl of perfume and hair spray scents. Paisley snuck out and looked in the hall mirror to make sure her updo was still plastered in place. The bobby pins itched her scalp, and she was tempted to yank them out and wear her hair down. She probably even had time to dash upstairs and change into one of her own outfits. *Too late.* Miss Swanson had just opened the door for the first guests. Two ladies in almost identical pillbox hats, except for the netting on one, introduced themselves as being from Jackson. June and Roberta Lee swooped into the hallway and hugged their moms.

Paisley positioned herself under the painting of the general and took mental photos of the reunions, the hugs, the way the moms gave their daughters approving looks and relayed kisses from their dads and families back home. Sharon Kay, who'd told everyone her mom couldn't wait to meet them, stood by the window, her hand quivering as she drew back the lace and craned her neck. She then backed away and toyed with one of the Hummel figurines atop a piecrust table.

Xan, who stood with Dusty near the fireplace, fidgeted, and when Miss Swanson announced the arrival of Mrs. Bennett, Xan stumbled forward, her high heel catching on the edge of the rug. Dusty kept her from toppling and went forward with her to meet her mother.

"Oh, forevermore, Alexandria Lucille Bennett. What on earth has happened to your hair?" Mrs. Bennett's face turned red as she turned to Dusty. "You. Who are you? Are you the one responsible for ruining Alexandria's hair?"

"No, ma'am." Dusty extended her gloved hand. "I'm Dusty Fairchild. Pleased to make your acquaintance."

Xan looked as if she might cry, but she lifted her chin and turned around slowly, letting her mother get a good look. "I was hoping you'd like it, Mother."

Paisley knew she was hoping her mom would notice how she'd slimmed down. With her dark eyes and cute outfit, she could be a ringer for Sandra Dee.

Mrs. Bennett lowered her voice, but even from across the room, her words were loud and clear. "I don't. You look like a tramp, certainly not like the fiancée of Prentice Robbins."

Mrs. Bennett wagged a finger in Xan's face, lowering her voice, but the skin on her face was stretched taut, her lips pinched, her eyes like fiery darts.

Paisley wanted to slap Mrs. Bennett. Instead, she clutched the camera and strolled across the room. Dusty muttered something about checking on things in the kitchen and slipped away.

"Okay, Xan, you and your mom give me a smile." Paisley aimed the camera. Mrs. Bennett's lip curled back, her attempt at a smile making it look as if she'd just eaten two-day-old fish.

Click.

Xan took her hand. "Mama, I want you to meet my roommate. Remember me telling you about Paisley? Here she is."

Mrs. Bennett's eyes scanned Paisley from head to toe. "Paisley? Wherever did your mother come up with that?"

"I thought it was beautiful. Like my baby." Edie Horton stepped into their midst.

"Mother? What...where...how did you know about the tea?" The room swirled around Paisley as she tried to catch her breath.

"How about a hug?" Edie opened her arms and without waiting for Paisley to comply pulled her into an embrace. "You know me. I just have these instincts, and when I found the packet of information you left on the bus, I read about the tea. So here I am." She smiled, her eyes tearing up as she gripped Paisley's shoulders and held her at arm's length. "Oh, gracious, look at you. You don't even look like the baby girl I dropped off."

Paisley tried to gulp in a breath, but her lungs were frozen. Visions of the psychedelic bus in the driveway and the Asterisks hanging around the entry gate gave her gooseflesh. She crossed her arms and rubbed the sleeves of her Bobbie Brooks blouse.

"Mama...I...I'm surprised to see you. I'm glad you like my outfit. Dusty and I did a little shopping."

"I didn't say I liked it, although I suppose you're just doing what you've always done, trying to be something you're not. Where did I go wrong?"

Mrs. Bennett nudged Edie. "That's just what I was thinking. You devote your entire life to your children, and they throw it in your face."

Xan's eyes turned stormy, and Paisley felt her own face flaming with what Edie implied. Edie was chafed because Paisley was dressed like the other girls. Paisley wasn't thrilled about it herself, but when a bitter taste came in her mouth, she realized she didn't want to be like Edie, either. Headstrong. Rebellious. Pathetic. Look what it had gotten Edie: a lifetime of living in a string of dank apartments and hanging out in smoke-filled clubs from sea to shining sea. Edie's arrival had stirred up a boatload of memories Paisley had tried hard to forget. Perhaps if she closed her eyes and opened them, Edie would be gone.

She looked away and counted to ten silently, then looked at her mother. "Edie, you look nice." That, at least, was the truth. Edie had on an off-white shirtwaist dress with a cinched belt that made her waist look tiny. With her spiked heels, platinum hair, and full red lips, she had a sultry but breathtaking beauty that none of the other moms had with their sensible boxy suits and perfectly coiffed beauty parlor hair.

"Oh my goodness. Aunt Edith!" Dusty ran across the hallway and embraced her aunt. "You got my invitation? I was so afraid you wouldn't get it, but here you are." She turned to Paisley. "Sorry, can we share your mom?"

Paisley frowned. "You invited her?" She opened her mouth to say more and bit her lip instead.

Edie looked from one to the other. "No, I didn't get an invitation. I found the information on the bus."

Dusty kept her arm around Edie's shoulders. "It doesn't matter how you found out. You're here. And you know, you look just like

Marilyn Monroe in that yummy dress. Come on, I want to introduce you."

And just like that, Dusty escorted Edie off into the crowd squeezed into Rosebriar's parlor.

Paisley raised the Canon and snapped a photo of Dusty and Edie with their heads touching. Not a profile exactly, but the two blonde heads together made them look like mother and daughter. Friends. Smiling. Sharing a laugh.

It made a nice illusion. And that's all it was. Edie hadn't come out of the goodness of her heart—she was after something.

Click.

Only time would tell.

❦

Dusty nibbled on a custard tart. "Yum. These are marvy, Paisley. Even better than the ones we made with Mrs. Pellerin."

Edie polished hers off and rose from the needlepoint cushioned chair, one of three they'd pulled into a circle in the parlor. "I'm going to have another chicken salad cream puff. Can I get you two anything?"

Dusty and Paisley answered together, "Nothing for me."

Paisley waited until her mom was in the dining room, then leaned in. "Has she said what she really came for?"

"What do you mean? She said she came to see you. You are so paranoid. Relax already. Look around. Everyone's having a grand time." She did a quick survey of the guests. Mothers sat erect with ankles crossed, legs tucked neatly to the side. Their daughters, younger versions of almost all of them, chattered away, sipping from cut-glass cups.

"I am relaxed. I just have a bad vibe about Edie. She's too happy, and did you notice how she toned down her getup to fit in? Trust me, this is not the Edie I know."

"She probably feels bad because of the impression she left the first day. And you gotta admit, you've changed a little yourself. Here you are, poised and proper, lifting your pinkie while you sip tea." Dusty gave an exaggerated demonstration. "Personally, I'd just as soon slip on my Keds and take a walk, but then I'd miss the entertainment."

Paisley pursed her lips together. "I wish I hadn't agreed to play the guitar. Edie will get all swoony and try to talk me into going back on the road—"

Dusty cut her off. "Shhh."

Edie took her seat and crossed her legs. "Miss Fontaine's darling, isn't she? She thanked me for coming. And I thanked her for being so clever to hire that nice Adrian Simon. What a charmer."

Dusty and Paisley exchanged wide-eyed looks, but Paisley hissed, "Are you talking about the French teacher? Our Mr. Simon?"

"What other Mr. Simon would I be talking about? He came to my rescue earlier today."

Paisley stiffened. "Come again."

"How did you think I got here?" She took a bite of cream puff, a stray crumb of chicken stuck in the corner of her mouth. She dabbed it away with a napkin and laughed. "I get it. You thought I'd come with the Asterisks, didn't you?"

"Well, it did cross my mind, since that's what you were doing the last I heard." Paisley's cheeks pinked up, an edge in her voice.

"Well, I'm not with them now and thank my lucky stars for that. We…um…we parted ways in Houston." She took a deep breath. "I'll tell you the whole story later. For now, let's just enjoy this lovely party."

Dusty lifted her cup in a toast. "To the party." Around them, laughter sparked the air, and in the midst of it all, Miss Fontaine bobbled about, spending time with each little circle, being the perfect hostess. Oddly enough, she reminded Dusty of her dad as he played host over his kingdom when he threw a bash at the ranch.

The only thing missing was the smell of barbecue and sagebrush in the air.

Dusty had the nagging feeling that something else was missing, but it wouldn't quite come to her. She finally decided she was just on edge with Aunt Edie's surprise arrival, and it wasn't until Carmel tapped a spoon on a crystal glass and asked for everyone's attention that it hit her. Sharon Kay's mother hadn't come.

Carmel's voice sparkled as she spoke. "Thank you all for coming. And thank you, Mama, for bringing Aunt Pearl's pralines." She looked at the crowd and smiled. "Don't worry, girls, she brought enough to share with all y'all. But now, we've come to the best part of the afternoon—our entertainment. First up, June Little from my hometown of Jackson will be playing the flute." She set down the glass and spoon and clapped as June went forward and began playing "Flight of the Bumblebee."

Dusty chewed her lip and looked around for Sharon Kay and spotted her sitting alone by the window, arms crossed, staring into space. Dusty hoped her mother hadn't had car trouble or taken ill. Even though Sharon Kay was a pain in the patootie most of the time, Dusty had looked forward to meeting the wonder woman her roommate talked about all the time.

Click.

Paisley took a shot of June, then handed the camera to Dusty.

Dusty mouthed, "You're next." Paisley slipped away as June finished playing and bowed to the round of applause.

Aunt Edie leaned in. "Where did Paisley go?"

Dusty pretended not to hear. She hoped Paisley had gone to get her guitar, but after her earlier comment, it was possible she'd skipped out and was halfway to the bayou by now. Her fear was unwarranted for as soon as Carmel made the introduction, Paisley stepped forward and thanked Carmel, made a couple of minor adjustments on the tuning pegs of her guitar, and strummed softly.

Her fingers trembled and she frowned momentarily, which made Dusty think she was nervous. Paisley took in a deep breath, looked out over the audience, and played the intro. When she began singing, her voice was strong with just enough twang to give the McGuire Sisters' smash hit "Sugartime" a Southern flavor. Mothers and daughters swayed and nodded their heads to the beat and burst into applause when she'd sung the final chorus.

Beside Dusty, Edie sniffled and ran the back of her hand across a tear-filled eye, leaving a mascara smudge on her cheek. Dusty handed her a napkin and said, "Aren't you glad you came?"

"Oh, you know it, sugar." She blinked back the tears, her eyes now flashing. "I just love that my baby girl breaks my heart every chance she gets."

"What? I don't follow."

Edie pursed her full red lips making the age lines around her mouth more pronounced. "She sang that song deliberately since she knows I utterly despise it."

"She didn't even know you were coming. Besides, who doesn't love an upbeat song like 'Sugartime'?"

"Me, that's who. That was our song—me and Merlin Rogers—until the day he beat the tar out of me. I snapped the record in half and told Paisley I never wanted to hear it again. She sang it on purpose."

"Aunt Edith, I'm so sorry. I didn't know about your…uh… troubles. How awful! But I don't think Paisley sang it to hurt you."

The applause had died down, the room growing quiet as a dozen pairs of eyes were on them. Dusty took her aunt's hand and whispered, "It's all right. Look, Paisley is going to sing again. Maybe this will be one you like."

Edie fumbled for her purse and rose. "I need a smoke. You can find me outside when the party breaks up. I need to talk to you alone, okay, sugar?"

She marched out as Paisley played a few chords and launched into Patsy Cline's "Crazy," her pure, sweet voice once again filling the room. Dusty and Paisley had played the record a million times after they'd seen Patsy onstage. Patsy wore a gold lamé outfit with a wide belt that night and winked and flirted with the audience, reeling them in so that it felt like you'd known her forever.

Goose bumps popped out on Dusty's arms. Paisley's voice was an almost perfect imitation of Patsy's. Dusty lifted the Canon from her lap and found her cousin in the viewfinder. The blurry image could have been any of the girls at Miss Fontaine's. Beehive hairdo. Pert outfit and pumps that matched. Another perfect imitation.

She shuddered and focused the lens. *Click.*

Paisley looked beautiful, but a shadow crept into Dusty's thoughts. She shouldn't have insisted on buying Paisley that outfit. It was all wrong on her and made her look stiff. She missed the old Paisley, the one who wore purple and orange together and wove flowers in her hair and painted her fingernails lime green. The daring Paisley who French-kissed stable hands and ran back to the house breathless, covered in hay. The Paisley who drove Dusty's T-Bird a hundred miles an hour, her hair flying through the open window.

It wasn't Paisley's fault. She'd invited her here, thinking only of herself and making it through the year so she could prove something to her dad. All she'd proved was that she and Paisley were both a couple of frauds. Aunt Edie breezing in hadn't helped a bit. And now she wanted to talk to Dusty alone. What in the world? Something crazy was going on all right.

❧

Dusty found Edie in the rose garden, having a glass of iced tea, puffing on a Salem. Her aunt told her a nice maid had brought her the tea and invited her to stay for dinner. "Of course, I accepted. Out of courtesy."

They chatted awhile, and Dusty found out that Aunt Edie had arrived in Alborghetti on the bus, that her luggage was in a locker at the bus station. In Houston, she'd gone into a truck stop restroom to dress for the evening show while Sloan stocked up on beer at the nearby package store. When she came out, the bus was gone, her things piled next to a fire hydrant.

Dusty draped her arm around her aunt's shoulders and offered her condolences, but Edie pulled back. "Good thing I tucked the packet Paisley left on the bus in my purse. It had the time and date of the tea." She gave a soft snort. "I also had the proceeds from the joint where the boys played the night before—it must've slipped their ever-lovin' minds that we hadn't divvied up the money yet. At least it got me a bus ticket here and a cheap motel."

Muttering another "I'm sorry," Dusty really didn't know what to say. Aunt Edie had agreed to having dinner at Rosebriar. Did she plan on bunking here, too? She could only imagine Miss Fontaine's response. Before she could come up with anything, Edie cupped Dusty's chin in her hand.

"Listen, sweetie. That's why I wanted to talk to you. Paisley will think it was her fault the band busted up with me. I see now that Sloan was a disturbed man and wanted Paisley for his own needs. And Davis didn't exactly turn out to be the prince I thought he was, either." She brushed a strand of hair from her face. "What's done is done, but I need...well...I hate to even ask..." Her eyes filled with tears. "I was hoping you might loan me enough money to get back to San Francisco."

A chill crept over Dusty. What did she mean about Sloan wanting Paisley? Why wasn't she protecting Paisley? Wasn't that what mothers did?

She had the money; that wasn't the problem. She'd been by the bank when she went with Xan to pick up a special order from the florist on Thursday afternoon. Mad money as her dad would say. And something for the church offering.

Aunt Edie flashed her a look. "If you don't want to, just say so."

She swallowed hard. "No, it isn't that at all. I can help you out. I was just thinking that since you're sort of in between right now, you should go over to the ranch and stay with Daddy, be with family awhile. Fall is always the best time with all the leaves turning and the geese flying over."

"Oh, baby doll, that's simply out of the question. That's what I've always loved about you. You take people in and try to fix their problems—the way you always have with Paisley. Just loving on her. It's nothing short of miraculous, really, bein's how Flint Fairchild is your daddy. He would no more welcome me than he would a rattlesnake."

"You never know. He's out there alone. Rosalita is still in Mexico, and my brothers are busy. You'd be good company for one another."

Aunt Edie looked off in the distance, her voice just above a whisper. "There are some things that can't be fixed. Your daddy and me for one. Some scars are written on the heart. You might not be able to see them, but they're there."

"What are you talking about?"

"Nothing." She shook her head and shuddered as if flicking off a memory. "I said too much. Besides I've already called an agent in San Francisco. He's expecting me in a couple of days."

Several of the girls and their moms had drifted into the rose garden, taking a tour of the grounds, Dusty suspected. She looked at Aunt Edie. "It's all right. I'll give you enough to get back to California."

Edie threw her arms around her. "Oh, sweetie. You are a lifesaver."

"On one condition."

"What? Anything you say."

"You have to tell me how you met Mr. Simon."

Edie threw back her head and laughed. "Oh, my stars! You see, it's like this. I had all morning with nothing but time to kill so I went in all the darling shops downtown. One of them had whatnots up front and little sachets that you put in your panty drawers. In the back, there were a few antiques and mirrors and such. I was just looking over all the bric-a-brac, waiting until I could find a taxi-cab, when a gentleman asked if he could be of assistance. We started chatting, and the next thing you know, I was telling him about my baby girl being one of Miss Fontaine's students. Of course, I didn't know he was your French teacher at the time; I thought he was just the store owner. We sure had a laugh about that, and then he had the nicest things to say about you and Paisley."

She winked at me. "He says you're his star pupil. Just a really nice fellow, you know. He asked if I wanted a sandwich, so we went to the malt shop next door, and then he drove me out here."

During the whole telling of the story, Dusty could picture the way Edie probably patted Mr. Simon's hand or paid him little com-pliments.

Aunt Edie lifted her chin and smiled. "Oh, look, there's Paisley now. I think I'll see if she can show me her room."

The garden patio was empty then and Dusty wanted to give Paisley time alone with Aunt Edie, so she sat down. Edie had left her pack of Salems on the table. Dusty picked it up to return it to her aunt later and saw there was only one cigarette left. A match-book was tucked in the cellophane wrapper. It said Shady Acres Lounge on the front. She fished the cigarette from the packet and tore a match from the booklet. It took three tries before she got it lit, the first puff contracting her throat. She swallowed and took an-other drag. Better, but she blew the smoke out quickly, then leaned back in the chair and looked out at the rose garden and pasture beyond.

Dusk had come, shadows from the bayou slanting toward Rose-briar. She puffed on the cigarette and thought over the day and all of its surprises: Aunt Edie coming. Mr. Simon being a shop owner. Sharon Kay's mother noticeably absent. The words to "Sugartime" wafted through her head. There was a lot about Aunt Edie she didn't know—mysteries that surrounded her and Paisley. She'd always been attracted to their freedom and lack of convention. Was there a price that came with that? One that money couldn't fix?

She took another drag, then threw the cigarette on the flagstone and ground it out with the toe of her pump. A sour taste lingered in her mouth that she didn't think came from the foul flavor of tobacco.

CHAPTER 9

Sulee served vegetable soup and Southern corn bread to the three of them—Paisley, Dusty, and Edie. Everything from the afternoon tea had been cleared away, the dining room returned to normal. Some of the girls had gone to the country club to eat with their moms, and Miss Swanson had taken the remaining ones in the station wagon to the Palisades theater in town where Elvis was starring in *Kid Galahad*.

"Delicious soup," Edie said to Sulee when she came to ask if they needed anything else. "And this corn bread, oh my gracious, it's divine." She held up a chunk. "Is that real corn and jalapeños in there?"

"Yes, ma'am. My mama's recipe."

"Smart woman, your mama. Does she live around here?"

"No, ma'am. She's passed."

Edie held out a hand. "Oh, you must be heartbroken."

"Yes, ma'am." She backed toward the door to the kitchen.

Paisley shook her head. "Don't mind my mother, Sulee. And thank you for fixing our dinner. We can manage all right from here." She looked at Edie as Sulee scooted back to the kitchen. "More soup?"

"No thanks. And what do you mean by 'don't mind my mother'?

I was only being courteous. That's all the rage you know, treating the colored people equal and all."

"Edie. How rude. For one thing, they're called Negroes, not colored people. And Sulee is equal—an employee, part of the staff, just like Mr. Simon and Mrs. Pellerin and the others who work here."

"Well, excuuuuse me. Guess that now that you're so learned you won't have any use for your poor mama."

Paisley refused to dignify that with a reply. It would only lead to no good. They ate in silence, the only sounds the scraping of their spoons on the earthenware bowls as they finished. Edie dotted her mouth with a napkin and looked at her watch. "Gracious, I need to scoot. Dusty, if I could trouble you for the little matter we talked about?"

Paisley snapped her head toward Dusty, but Dusty had already risen from the table and left the dining room.

Edie rolled a shoulder and waited until Dusty was gone. "Davis didn't bother to give me enough money to get home. I've called Ollie in San Francisco. He offered to wire me the money, but I told him I'd figure something out. Dusty was kind enough to offer me bus fare."

"Ollie Winesap?"

"Yes, you remember him. The talent scout."

"I remember." Paisley wanted to puke but remembered what else her mother said. "You asked Dusty for money?"

Edie pulled a compact from her oversized purse and powdered her nose, then bared her teeth, probably checking for corn or jalapeño particles stuck between them. Finally, she snapped the compact shut and sniffed. "You don't have to make it sound so pathetic—"

"But it is. Admit it, Edie. It's just like all the other times. You get yourself in these messes and then take off like a butterfly, looking for another spot to land."

Her mother's chin quivered, but her blue eyes turned to ice. "I'm not asking you to understand. I'm not even asking you to join me, although I nursed that hope when I set out from the bus station today. Your underwhelming delight at seeing me laid that to rest. I'll be fine. And as soon as Ollie comes through with what he's lined up and I get some cash, I'll send Dusty the money."

"And what's Ollie got lined up?" She had to ask. Sure, he said he was a talent scout when he hung out at the Penny Loafer and threw out the names of record labels and people in showbiz. He would give Paisley a friendly pat on the rear or run his finger up and down her arm and compliment her on her singing if she'd been onstage that night. Skeptical didn't begin to describe the way she felt about Ollie Winesap.

"He didn't really say. I was the one who called him, so he's doing some checking."

"And where will you stay when you get back?"

"It's really none of your concern now, is it? That's just it, sugar. You're always sweating the details. I've been a total failure at teaching you that getting wherever you're going is half of the fun. *Que sera sera.*"

"Yeah, you got that right. Maybe I'm tired of living life that way. I like having a plan and knowing what's going to happen tomorrow and the day after that."

"I knew it was only a matter of time until my darling brother poisoned your mind. I'm surprised it took this long."

"Uncle Flint? What does he have to do with any of it?"

"Luring you away with his money, his big plans for finishing school. I don't believe for a minute he didn't have this planned."

"Mother." Paisley's voice was sharper than she meant it to be. "You are so wrong. Uncle Flint had no idea you were fixing to go on the road. I was fine with staying right where I was, waiting tables at the Penny Loafer until I saved up enough to take classes at the junior college. Why can't you see it? We have nothing. At least coming here showed me that a different life is possible." Her insides shook like she'd come down with a fever, but she was determined not to let on. "And by the way, where's my camera?"

Edie jerked her head up. "In Timbuktu for all I know. I haven't seen it since Sloan took it to get the pictures developed. Who knows? Maybe he's planning to swing by here on the way to their next gig and drop it off. Knowing how Sloan liked you, it wouldn't surprise me even a tiny bit."

Paisley didn't know whether to spit or thank her lucky stars that Edie was finished with the Asterisks.

Her mother rose from the table. "I need to see what's keeping Dusty." She marched off, leaving Paisley as wrung out as a wet rag.

❧

Before Edie stepped into the cab they'd called for her, she touched Paisley's cheek. "I'll write you, baby doll. You two be good now, okay?"

Paisley was relieved and sorry at the same time to see her go. She wanted to run after her and tell her to be careful with Ollie. To tell her she was sorry she hadn't been happier to see her. To dip her head into her mother's neck and inhale her scent one more time. Instead, she stood on Rosebriar's porch and watched as the taillights of the taxi grew smaller and smaller, then disappeared.

"Hey, are you all right?" Dusty nudged her.

"Peachy."

"Guess we have the house to ourselves. Any ideas?"

"If you mean other than raid Miss Fontaine's liquor cabinet or make prank phone calls, then no."

"You're no fun." They headed up the stairs to change from their party clothes. There was an eerie quiet—no radios blasting from the other girls' rooms or anyone hollering about hogging the bathroom mirror.

Dusty turned toward the Rosebud Room. "See you in a jiff."

Paisley turned on the radio to fill the silence and hummed along with Peter, Paul and Mary singing "Lemon Tree." A few minutes later, Dusty knocked and came in before Paisley could get across the room. She had one hand behind her back and two decks of cards in the other. "Wanna play double sol?"

"Why not? We haven't done that in ages. Here, we can play on my bed." Paisley swooped her clothes off onto the floor and straightened the bedspread. "What else you got?"

Dusty bit her lower lip, then took a deep breath and handed Paisley her red scrapbook. The one she'd accused Edie of taking.

Paisley's hands went clammy and her chest tightened. "What? Where did you find it?"

"I didn't. Aunt Edie gave it to me."

"You. Why you?"

Dusty shrugged. "I think she didn't want to argue with you about it. She brought it with her this afternoon and stuck it behind the table in the entryway. When I came down with the money, she asked to see my room and gave it to me. She said she was sorry she took it from your things."

Hot tears stung Paisley's eyes. "It's just a dumb scrapbook."

"No, it's not. This has all your memories in it. Yours and Aunt Edie's. Yours and mine."

Snapshots of her gypsy life with her mother flashed through her head. Not just the ones with Patsy Cline, but the one of her climbing the steps of the school bus on her first day of school, the one with her two front teeth missing, the one of her wearing her first bikini at Pismo Beach. The tears now ran down her face. "I should've been nicer to her today."

Dusty wrapped an arm around her shoulders. "You want to look at it now?"

"No." She spat out the word. She didn't want the reminders of the life that took them hither and yon. The past was best forgotten. She hugged the scrapbook to her chest for a minute, its cover tattered—like her relationship with Edie. She would look at it, just not now. She tucked it under her pillow. "Let's play cards."

Dusty was ahead by fourteen points, and they'd just finished a hand when Xan came storming in and threw her purse on the bed.

Paisley gave her a hooded look. "Hello to you, too."

Xan hiked up her skirt and unhooked a nylon stocking from her garter belt. "Yeah. Hello." She did the same with the other stocking, then plopped down on the edge of the bed, removed the nylons, and threw them in the corner by the sink. "Thank goodness, she's gone."

Dusty and Paisley gave each other a questioning look. Dusty said, "Sorry. Anything you want to talk about?"

Xan pulled her dress over her head and threw it on top of the stockings. "Prentice told Mother to go ahead and plan an engagement party at the club over Thanksgiving. He wants to make our engagement official." She grabbed her fuzzy robe with covered buttons, jammed her arms through the sleeves, and pulled it tight around her.

Paisley sorted the cards, tallied the score, and told Dusty, "You're still ahead. But only by three points." She turned to Xan. "The big question is, why is he talking to your parents about this instead of you?"

"He does talk about it in his letters. 'When we marry.' 'When we have children.' This and that. Mother went on forever about what a wonderful wife I'm going to be to Prentice…when my hair is returned to the natural color, of course." She propped her pillow against the oak headboard and flopped on the bed against it.

Dusty shuffled her cards and counted out the cards for her draw pile. "Xan, if you don't want to marry Prentice, then you have to speak up. Write him a letter if you don't want to face him. People write Dear John letters all the time."

"The truth is, I do want to marry him. Prentice is swell, really. It's my mother who drives me nuts." She flipped onto her stomach and watched as Dusty and Paisley played another round of double sol.

Paisley hit a hot streak, slapping cards in the middle at lightning speed until her draw pile was gone. "Out! Let's see who's ahead now." She wrinkled her nose and did a two thumbs-up.

Dusty said, "I give up. You want to play, Xan?"

"Nope. But I just had this crazy thought. Why don't you two come home with me for Thanksgiving?"

Paisley laughed. "I'm sure your parents would love that."

"No, listen. Hear me out. I'll tell them I want you there for my big weekend. And maybe with y'all there, my mother won't be so overbearing."

Dusty wound a rubber band around the cards. "I don't know. Daddy's expecting us. Susan and Greg's baby will be here by then, the first Fairchild grandbaby. I don't want to miss being there for that. And other stuff."

Paisley couldn't resist. "Stuff like Jack, you mean."

Dusty stuck out her tongue. "He did mention we might get together when I heard from him, and besides, I thought you wanted to meet Jack."

"It's not that long until Christmas. We should go to Xan's. Come on, Dusty. It'll be a blast. We'll go to the country club and the engagement party."

Dusty shook her head. "I didn't say *you* shouldn't go. And you're right, you'll be at the ranch at Christmas." She narrowed her eyes at Xan. "I'm just warning you…Paisley might put goldfish in the punch bowl or pull the fire alarm. She likes to keep things lively."

Paisley threw the pencil she'd been keeping score with at Dusty who threw it back and hollered at Xan to pass her a throw pillow. Xan tossed one of the honeysuckle-patterned pillows to Dusty and another one at Paisley. Back and forth, the three of them pummeled each other until they were all giggling. Xan grabbed the pillow from behind Paisley and tossed it, then snapped her head back toward Paisley's bed.

"Hey, what is this?" Xan grabbed the scrapbook.

Paisley reached for it. "Nothing. Just that old scrapbook I told you about."

"I thought you couldn't find it."

"Edie brought it. Hand it over."

"What's wrong? Something in here you don't want me to see?" She was already flipping through the pages. "Look. Oh, you were adorable. And is that Dusty? What are you guys wearing? Cowgirl outfits?"

Paisley felt sick to her stomach as her life flashed through her head. She tried to pry the scrapbook from Xan's hands, but Xan held on. "No way. Not until I see every picture. You all know everything about my pitiful life. Now I'm going to learn about yours." She squinted and pulled the scrapbook up close, peering over the top of her glasses. "Who's this?"

Paisley swallowed the frog in her throat and looked at the spot where Xan pointed. "That would be Leonard, Edie's third husband. The one who gave me my first guitar."

"What happened to him?"

"He left." The all-too-familiar feeling of being pinched on the inside took her breath momentarily as she remembered the police car that arrived, the click of the cuffs the officer snapped on

Leonard's wrists. Edie's explanation that Leonard had stolen money from his boss. She blocked out the memory as Xan flipped through the pages and babbled, asking a million questions. It was all there in black and white. The stepdad in Arizona who took her to the Grand Canyon and drank himself to an early grave. One of her and Edie on the jungle boat ride at Disneyland when she was fourteen, the year they'd moved to California. Riding horses with Dusty at the ranch. Another of them on the swinging bridge that spanned the creek Dusty loved so much. A grainy picture of Patsy Cline on stage in Fort Worth, but alongside it, a shiny postcard of Patsy with rosy cheeks and wearing the fringed outfit that made her famous.

The more Xan chirped about how cute they all were, the darker Paisley's thoughts became. Too bad the pictures didn't show the roaches on the floors of the places they'd lived or the springs poking up from holes in the divan.

Edie hadn't brought the scrapbook out of the sweetness of her heart. She wanted Paisley to feel bad, to see all the fun she'd provided as a mom. Edie was probably scheming for a way right now to show up at the ranch for Thanksgiving. She'd cry about how much she missed her baby girl and try to convince her to come back to California.

Paisley was done falling for her mother's crocodile tears and listening to her talk about how they'd be in high cotton once they were discovered. What a crock.

Paisley was eighteen and capable of making her own decisions. This time she held all the cards. Houston it would be. Dining at the country club. Hanging out with the in crowd.

Paisley picked up her guitar and strummed softly, picking out a new melody. One with a catchy rhythm and all the bright notes she could find.

CHAPTER 10

M r. Simon stood close enough that the tweed of his jacket brushed against Dusty's arm as she sat at the classroom's oak table. He ran a hand whisper soft down the back of her hair, letting it come to rest on her shoulder.

The hairs on her neck prickled from his familiarity, and warmth crept into her cheeks. She tried not to stiffen at his unexpected touch, but his lemony scent mixed with pipe tobacco made it hard not to notice his proximity.

Mr. Simon's tone, however, was casual as he said good morning and mentioned meeting Aunt Edith. "Such a charming woman. As are you and Paisley. Now that I've met her I can see the resemblance to both of you, although in different ways."

Dusty tilted her head to see his face. "She is nice, and it was kind of you to help her out, wasn't it, Paisley?" Dusty turned to her cousin, who was chatting with Carmel.

Paisley swiveled and blinked up at Mr. Simon. "What?"

Mr. Simon's hand fell idly to his side. "Your mother. Such a beautiful woman. I trust you enjoyed her visit. She sure went on about the two of you."

Paisley flashed a smile at him. "She loved your shop. What a tease you are, not telling us about it."

"It never occurred to me. I don't like to take advantage of my position here by drumming up business, but Miss Fontaine's girls usually find out anyway." He chuckled and nodded at Dusty, his brown eyes more gray, like the day outside where moisture seeped from the sky in a thin drizzle. "Alborghetti's not that big a place. Now that the cat's out of the bag, why don't you pay me a visit? I have a nice selection of antique jewelry and some one-of-a-kind gift items. Your lovely mother had her eye on a fetching jewelry box. If you get a chance some Saturday, the two of you should drop in."

Paisley looped a strand of her dark hair around her finger and dipped her chin like she was flirting. "Oh, we'd love that, wouldn't we, Dusty?"

Later, when they were alone in the Honeysuckle Room, Paisley laughed. "Dirty old man. A nice little visit. Ha! Like my mother has use for a jewelry box. What a line." She lowered her voice an octave and mimicked Mr. Simon. "I have some lovely gifts that might interest you. Of course, they're in the back of the shop. And after we do a little hanky-panky, I'll see what I can do about your French grade."

"You don't think Sharon Kay was serious about that, do you?"

"Only one way to find out. We'll take him up on his offer and visit his shop."

"No. That's just courting trouble."

"It beats hanging around here being bored out of our ever-lovin' minds. Besides, you told me earlier that if I wanted to go shopping for new clothes, you'd take me. I can't show up at Xan's country club looking like a gypsy. Someone might mistake me for a fortune-teller."

"I thought you liked dressing that way."

"I do, but it's Xan's big weekend. I don't want to embarrass her or her *so-ci-e-ty* mother. So when do you want to go shopping?"

"I'll agree to the shopping but not going to Mr. Simon's shop. That's just too creepy."

"You never want to have fun."

Paisley was right. Dusty would much rather be running down to the bayou than flirting with Mr. Simon. Something about him, though, felt dangerous in a fluttery sort of way, and it bothered her that she was intrigued and repelled by him at the same time. And maybe that's why, when they did go shopping two weeks later, she let Paisley drag her into Simple Pleasures.

When they entered, a bell tinkled overhead. It was a cute shop, just like Aunt Edie had described, with the pleasant scent of lavender and vanilla, which came from the display of drawer sachets. A jewelry counter on the right had glass display cases with items laid out on black velvet. Shelves behind that were lined with china-faced dolls and a variety of inlaid wood jewelry boxes, which is what must have caught Aunt Edie's eyes.

Dusty looked at Paisley and whispered, "Where do you think he is?" She peered toward the back of the store where wardrobes, an assortment of small tables, and a display of mirrors were.

She'd just barely come out with the question when a velvet curtain next to an intricately carved coat tree parted, and Sharon Kay Blanchard stepped out with Mr. Simon right behind her. Dusty's mouth flew open, but she caught herself and clamped her lips tight.

Sharon Kay blinked once, then again, before flashing a smile. "Hey there, fancy meeting you girls here. I was just telling Mr. Simon about your beautiful rock on the windowsill, Dusty—the one that's cracked open and has the purple crystals in the center."

Mr. Simon nodded. "Sounds like a geode. I've seen them in catalogs but haven't ever carried them here in the shop. I didn't realize you were interested in rock specimens, Dusty."

Her throat felt dry and scratchy, her shock at seeing her roommate emerge from Mr. Simon's back room still ricocheting through her brain like a bullet. "It's a hobby."

Paisley jumped in. "So what brings you here, Sharon Kay?"

Sharon Kay exchanged looks with Mr. Simon, then flicked a stray curl from her face. "My ring, the one with the emerald setting that my grandmother gave me. The setting was loose, and I was hoping Mr. Simon could fix it. Unfortunately, he doesn't do repairs here, so we were looking up the address of a jeweler in Houston to send it to." She turned to Mr. Simon and extended her hand. "Thanks for helping me out. I'd feel dreadful if something happened to my grandmother's ring."

She marched to the front of the store but turned before she left. "Toodles. Y'all have fun shopping." The bell dinged as she went out.

Mr. Simon held out his hand, and when Dusty shook it, his palm was moist and cool, his grip as limp as a salamander. Not what she expected. "How might I be of service to you lovely girls?"

Paisley picked up a china vase and tilted it like she was looking for the price on the bottom. "I don't know, what did you have in mind?"

"Excuse me?" He walked, a little too fast it seemed to Dusty, to a spot behind the jewelry counter.

Paisley set down the vase and trailed after him, stopping short of the glass case. "Well, you asked us to pop in, and here we are."

Mr. Simon reached behind him and took a jewelry box from the shelf. "This is the one your mother liked." He ran a finger over the top and pointed out the mother-of-pearl design in the shape of a lotus flower. He clicked the gold latch, lifted the lid, and held it for them to see. "It has a beautiful satin lining and a tiny hidden compartment that's rather unique. What occasion are you shopping for?"

"Actually, I'm not...we're not. Dusty and I just came into town and wanted to see your shop."

"Christmas is just around the corner. I could put this on layaway for you."

"Not today. What I really need is a hostess gift. Something to give someone for letting me stay at their house."

Mr. Simon returned the jewelry box to the shelf, and whatever awkwardness was there in the beginning passed. He showed them around the shop, and Paisley finally chose a pair of embroidered hankies to take to Mrs. Bennett. Mr. Simon gift wrapped them and held the door when they left.

A light rain had started so they stayed under the store awnings as they made their way to Miss Belle's dress shop. Paisley found a green silk dress to wear to Xan's engagement party. It had a wide belt that showed off her slim figure and matched her eyes perfectly. The sales-clerk talked her into getting shoes dyed to match that they would have to return for later. Paisley argued that it was too much, but Dusty insisted and also talked her into getting two other outfits—a black sweater with a gray tweed skirt and a tennis outfit "just in case."

They piled the dress boxes around them as they sat on swivel stools at the soda fountain in the drugstore and ordered chocolate shakes while they waited for Miss Swanson to pick them up.

Paisley took a noisy slurp and eyed Dusty. "You wanna talk about it?"

"What?"

"You know. What we saw?"

Dusty bit her lip to keep from laughing. "We didn't actually *see* anything."

"Yeah. And I'm as stupid as I am blind."

"You're the one who wanted to go in there. I think you wanted him—" Dusty looked around to see if anyone was listening, but the soda jerk was the only other one in the store and had already re-treated to the other end of the counter where he had his nose in a *Green Lantern* comic book. "You wanted something to happen. I know you. It's all about the thrill of doing something off-limits."

"Well, I struck out. I was sorta hoping for a proposition."

"Shhh. You don't know who's listening."

"Like I care. I mean, really, what did we come here for if not for a few laughs?"

Dusty held the cherry from her drink by the stem and twirled it around. "Sometimes you sound just like Aunt Edie."

"At least he offered to buy *her* a sandwich."

"Maybe he was just being nice. Lady in distress and all that."

"He's not even her type. Too refined and not enough muscle. Or flash."

"And he's *your* type?"

"Hey, I'm always looking for opportunities." She toed the boxes at her feet. "There's the evidence right there. Maybe Prentice Robbins has a rich playboy friend who's just been waiting for the right girl to come along."

"I hope you do find someone. Someone nice."

"I'm just going to go with the flow."

Green Lantern boy looked up. "Y'all need anything?"

Paisley waved him away. "No. We're peachy keen, jelly bean."

When Miss Swanson pulled up in the station wagon, Dusty put a dime tip on the counter and the two of them juggled the boxes and made a dash for the station wagon.

⁂

Dusty wasn't surprised when Sharon Kay never mentioned going to Simple Pleasures, but after that Saturday, her roommate did seem more congenial. As in not hogging the sink in their room and asking her if her slip showed. She even let Dusty listen to the country-western station on the radio instead of rolling her eyes and turning the dial to the one that played her favorite rock-and-roll tunes. It was almost as if they had an unspoken agreement. As long as Dusty kept her trap shut about Mr. Simon, Sharon Kay granted her the privilege of peace.

Their lessons kept them busy during the day. Miss Fontaine had covered most of the basic elements of etiquette and had moved on to planning special events. Baby showers, the formal dance (which they would have right before Christmas), and for the spring semester, planning a perfect wedding. Stacia already had her head in the clouds over her engagement, and Xan was so excited about her engagement party she was about to burst.

The rain that began the Saturday of the shopping trip continued day after day. Sometimes a drizzle, but more often a steady curtain that kept them all confined to Rosebriar. In the evenings, they did their daily ten minutes of posture practice walking around with books balanced on their heads. Some of the girls played canasta like they were training for the Olympics, or sometimes they popped corn in Sulee's cast-iron skillet in the kitchen or hung out in the upstairs lounge where they could smoke and watch TV.

When the clouds rolled away for a few hours one Saturday, Dusty fled to the bayou. The water had risen so that many of the cypress roots, which she learned were called knees because of their bald, knobby appearance, were underwater. She found a place where the bank sloped gently to the water's edge, but the earth was saturated, muddying her shoes. She retreated to higher ground and meandered through the trees along the spongy forest floor, her eyes always on the lookout for unusual pieces of wood or rocks.

With her eyes on the ground, she didn't really pay attention to where she was going as she knew if she got lost, she could follow the bayou back the way she came. She spotted what she thought at first was a cypress knee, but on closer examination, saw that it was a chunk of petrified wood. She used the small screwdriver she carried with her as a lever to lift it from the earth.

It had a honey color she'd not seen before with a nice sheen and darker striations running through it. While she admired it, the wind rustled through the trees, and for an instant, she thought she heard laughter. She looked around and realized she was deeper into the bayou than she'd been before.

Again, a noise like a human voice rode the wind on the leaves. Her armpits dampened as she remembered the day she'd walked on the path and been chewed out by Delia for trespassing. Laughter floated toward her again. Curious, she walked softly on the cushioned earth. Ahead of her, the trees thinned, and a little meadow, hidden from the world, it seemed, appeared. From the high branch of a tree on the far side, a swing went back and forth. A girl of ten or twelve—it was hard to tell from such a distance—gripped the ropes. As a man pushed her higher and higher, the child's braids flew out like wings when the swing went forward and folded back down on the descent.

Shafts of sunlight slanted from a stubborn cloud and bathed the scene in a fairy-tale glow. Something about the man seemed familiar yet out of place. Dusty had seen only a handful of men since coming to Rosebriar, and most of them were taxi drivers or on the lawn crew that kept the grass clipped and the gardens tended. Like the one pushing the swing, a number of them were black men, and she had to admit, she had difficulty telling them apart. The one thing she knew was that the child was definitely not black, but the two of them looked like they belonged together somehow.

She longed to call out and ask them how they were enjoying the sunshine, but guilt, like a heavy blanket, descended on her. She'd already been warned once to stay on the Rosebriar property, and she wasn't really sure where she was at the moment. She watched a few more minutes, then slipped away, following the banks of the bayou, head down, eyes peeled and focused on the forest floor in a never-ending quest for rocks. But her mind was back in the meadow with the young girl. She had a joy about her that Dusty had forgotten existed. Suddenly she couldn't wait for Thanksgiving and going home.

❦

The Saturday before Thanksgiving, Dusty took her French homework out to the patio while most of the girls lounged around, watching television in their pajamas. They were all planning a trip to town later and were going to see *The Manchurian Candidate* that evening, but Dusty itched to be outside. Frank Sinatra was dreamy, but a movie about Communists didn't sound that appealing.

She pulled out the passage from *The Scarlet Pimpernel* that Mr. Simon gave them to translate. He'd given them a brief summary of the story set during the Reign of Terror in France where the main character is a spy. Dullard by day, an engaging member of society by night, he and other members of a secret brotherhood carry out daring acts. Mr. Simon made it sound adventurous and told them it would be good practice to work on their French skills.

Dusty found Mr. Simon's choice interesting and wondered if it had a cryptic personal meaning about his unsubstantiated but clandestine meeting with Sharon Kay or girls from the past in mind. A secret life. It made her wonder, especially since Sharon Kay had made As on every test since that day. Paisley, scamp that she was, always positioned herself so she could take a gander at Sharon Kay's papers when they were handed out. Dusty thought it curious but didn't want to make a federal case out of it. There was no doubt, though, that Rosebriar had secrets.

Miss Fontaine often disappeared of an evening, sometimes in her

Cadillac, other times just out for "a breath of fresh air," she would say. And no matter how she turned it over in her mind, Dusty hadn't been able to get the picture of the young girl on the swing out of her head. She wished she'd taken a picture with the 35mm, because as she thought back, she realized the girl had to be old enough for junior high. And the man with her—was he her father? Perhaps a child from a mixed marriage that would be shunned from society.

The newspapers and television ran news all the time about the situation in the South, and if this wasn't the South, it was within spitting distance.

A flock of geese flew over in a V formation, honking as they descended behind the trees, landing, she supposed, in the murky water of the bayou. Or the meadow where the young girl with the laughter of an angel had swung. It was no use. Dusty tucked her French homework in her notebook, deciding to tackle it later while the others went to the picture show.

And at just that moment, Xan hollered from the upstairs window. "Dusty! Telephone! It's a man's voice."

Her daddy's voice came through the receiver when she answered. "Hey, sugar. We got us a little wrangler!"

"Susan had the baby? Great. A boy, huh? How big?"

"Seven pounder. Heckuva kid. Red as a beet and squalling to beat all."

Dusty had never heard her dad this excited. Her own heart pounded as she asked for the details about her nephew.

"Zachary Flint. Fine name for a Fairchild. And I'd bet my ostrich leather boots he's got the Fairchild nose."

Dusty tried to picture it—a nose with a bump in the middle on a tiny infant face. She laughed and wondered if her dad had said that about her since she'd gotten a version of the famous nose herself.

"I can't wait to see him. And you."

"Likewise. And I'm supposed to give you a message from Vera down at the church. They're having a baby shower the Saturday after Thanksgiving. Planned it that way so you and Paisley could be there."

Uh-oh. She hadn't told him Paisley was going home with Xan. "It'll just be me, I'm afraid."

"Don't tell me Edith's talked Paisley into leaving."

"No, nothing like that. She's going to Houston with her roommate so she can attend Xan's engagement party."

"You had me going there for a minute. I'll miss ole Stringbean, but I'll be glad to have you to myself if you really want to know."

"I know. I can't wait to see you. This coming Tuesday. I wrote and told you the day."

"Got it right here." The line crackled like the connection was going bad, so they both hollered good-bye and hung up.

❦

Three days later, the halls echoed with laughter, and all those swanky cars her dad whistled at the first day of class appeared in the circle drive. Luggage thumped down the stairs, and Miss Swanson manned the door, announcing the arrival of drivers and parents. Since her dad had a long drive, he wouldn't arrive until after lunch. Dusty had asked Jill, one of the town girls, to pick her up and run her into town to buy a gift for baby Zachary. She stopped by Paisley's room, hugged Paisley, and told her to have a blast in Houston. In the entry hall, Roberta waved good-bye and handed one of her brothers a suitcase. Two guys she hadn't seen before were talking to Miss Fontaine, who pointed them toward the dining room. The taller of the two flashed Dusty a smile as she sailed out the door to Jill's powder-blue Corvair waiting in the drive.

Paisley wound her hair into a French twist and secured it with an S-shaped rhinestone barrette. She'd decided at the last minute to wear her hair up for the ride to Houston since Xan had told her they'd be going to the country club when they arrived. She smiled at her reflection. Who was she kidding? She'd never be able to pull off the debutante gig, but she could at least carry on conversations about all the places she'd traveled. Just the mention of San Francisco and people went all goggle-eyed asking questions about people jumping off the Golden Gate Bridge or riding the trolley. She checked her teeth for lipstick, then ran to her room, slipped on her navy pumps, and grabbed the suitcase she'd borrowed from Xan. No sense in giving Mrs. Bennett reason for a conniption about the junker she called luggage.

"Have fun!" Carmel yelled from the other end of the hall. Stacia, her roommate, looked over her shoulder. "If you see Michael, tell him I'm almost ready."

"How will I know if it's Michael or not?"

"You'll know. Dark hair. So handsome it'll make you swoon."

"Yeah. I'm a swooner all right."

She shifted the suitcase to her left hand, and with her purse dangling from her right wrist, used the stair rail to descend the steps. Crud. She'd be the only one at the country club who couldn't walk in heels and chew gum at the same time.

The downstairs buzzed like a street fair on Fisherman's Wharf. As Paisley neared the bottom step, sunlight streamed through the front door, half blinding her. She misjudged the number of steps and toppled forward, losing her balance and landing on one knee atop the suitcase. Heat rushed to her face as she hoped like mad she hadn't dented it too badly. She shook her head, embarrassed and woozy at the same time.

A strong hand under her upper arm tried to pull her up. "You okay?" The voice, a man's, was deep, and even with just two words, she could tell he was a Texan.

She grabbed the stair rail and worked at untangling her legs and retrieving the suitcase at the same time, muttering, "Yeah. Fine." Her purse slammed into a blue jean–clad thigh. "Oh, crud. Sorry. Didn't mean to do that. Are you okay?"

"Couldn't be better." He hovered next to her, his hand over hers. "Here, let me help you with that."

He picked up the suitcase and handed it to her, their hands touching once again. Warm. Strong but soft and supple, like the leather of Xan's luggage.

She ventured a look and stood eye to eye with the most gorgeous man she'd ever seen. The light made funny ripples in his hair. *Dark*, she thought, *like his eyes*, and even though she was no longer touching him, a warmth vibrated in the air between them. He smelled of something woodsy, not those alcohol-laced aftershaves the Asterisks splashed on to cover up four days on the road without a shower.

Her knees felt like rubber bands, her brain awash with a million clever one-liners, none of which made it out of her mouth. That was merciful since it was obvious this was Stacia's fiancé, Michael, and Paisley had done the very thing she never dreamed she'd do— she'd swooned like a born and bred Southern belle. Holy Toledo. What an ignoramus she was.

"Thanks. I'm not usually so clumsy."

His eyes peered into hers like she was a wood nymph and had him under a spell. He blinked and smiled, a tiny gap between his two front teeth. Their hands grazed one another, sending tiny impulses racing up her spine like a flamenco melody. Finally getting her wits about her, Paisley took a firm grasp of the luggage handle and stepped away. Her laugh, meant to be casual, came out breathy.

She coughed and said, "Someone upstairs is going to be very happy to see you. Take care now, you hear?"

She marched toward the sunshine and was greeted by Mrs. Bennett. "There you are. I was afraid you changed your mind."

"No, all ready. And so lovely to see you." She did a tiny curtsy that would have made Miss Fontaine proud. "Thank you for inviting me."

"Hmmph. As I recall, it was Alexandria who issued the invitation and informed me of it later. But never mind. I can use an extra pair of hands setting up the club on Saturday." She turned to Xan. "You ready?"

"Yes, Mother. Whenever you are."

"Alexandria, please sit in the front seat with me. We have a lot to discuss on the drive over. Your friend can have the back."

Paisley's first thought was to change her mind and say, "See you later," but she'd promised Xan, and even though she might have a million flaws, running out on a friend was not one of them. She did as she was directed and climbed into the cavernous backseat of the Imperial that had tail fins as big as surfboards. She glanced back at Rosebriar hoping to catch another glimpse of Stacia's fiancé. Some girls had all the luck. She held the back of her hand to her nose and sniffed, hoping the scent of him remained, but the only fragrance in the car was that of Estée Lauder's Youth Dew. Mrs. Bennett wore the same perfume as Edie.

It figured.

D usty bought a pair of soft pajamas for Zachary at the baby shop in Alborghetti, but she'd hoped to find something he could use and not outgrow in two months. Jill suggested they try Simple Pleasures since "you just never know what kind of loot Simon will have." Not Mr. Simon, just Simon.

When asked to explain, Jill said, "Half the people in town call him Adrian, but since Adrian Simon is two first names, no one can remember which is which, so I call him Simon and try to tack on the Mr. when we're in class."

"You've known him awhile then?"

"For a while. He's nice—not like those rumors Sharon Kay's been spreading."

Dusty was relieved and at the same time wary. Sharon Kay and the incident of her coming from behind the curtain was an image she'd tried to erase to no avail.

Mr. Simon was out of the store, and a lady with chin-length silver hair named Opal waited on them. Dusty chose a box of sachets and the matching honeysuckle body lotion for Susan and asked about baby items.

"We have some lovely silver baby cups. We could have one engraved by the first of next week."

"Actually, I need something today. I was thinking more like a quilt or a stroller."

Opal clapped her hands. "Oh, darling, this is your lucky day. You should see what came on the Mistletoe truck last week."

They followed her to a display near the front window, and Dusty knew without Opal pointing it out that it was perfect—an old-fashioned pram with thin wheels nearly as big as bicycle tires and a bonnet that folded back so Zachary could have his very own convertible. She was almost afraid to ask how much, but Opal assured her they didn't make them like this anymore and that at any price it was a bargain. Dusty ran her hand over the burgundy leather and could tell it was top-notch.

She wrote out a check for the total; then Opal showed her how to fold it so it would fit in Jill's car. Dusty thanked Jill for suggesting the Simple Pleasures shop, and as they turned into Miss Fontaine's drive, she looked for her daddy's Lincoln.

A pinch of disappointment went through her when she didn't spot the car. She squinted and thought she was seeing things. A black Starfire that looked exactly like Jack's sat at an angle in front of a cherry-red Cadillac. Dusty knew at once the Caddy belonged to Carmel as she'd told them how she had to sit on a pillow to see while she wheeled around Jackson, Mississippi. Sure enough, it had Mississippi tags. But Jack's car? Why would it be here?

Her nerves went into overdrive, but first she had to get the pram from the backseat and her other packages. Jill, bless her heart, helped her lift the buggy out and pile the packages on top. She popped the carriage up and wheeled it up the sidewalk. The front hall was empty, but Carmel came from the parlor the minute she got there.

"Hey there! I was just telling your boyfriend what a dandy time we've been having."

"Hello, Dusty." Jack had made his way across the floor and

draped an arm around her shoulders. "Surprise." His lips grazed the soft spot of her neck right below her ear.

Her chest felt like it had been squeezed in a branding chute. "Surprise is right. Why are you here? Where's Daddy?"

"Hey, I thought you'd be happy to see me."

"Happy? Yes, of course, I'm thrilled." She knew she didn't sound it. Being surprised ranked right up there with stepping on a toad while running barefoot through the grass. She liked to know what was going on, what was going to happen. Not that surprises weren't nice sometimes, but they just flummoxed her and made her feel all squishy inside, scrambling her thoughts so she felt like she was plucking words out of the air.

Carmel saved the day. "Jack was telling me he had to go to a bank meeting over in Nacogdoches yesterday and had to bribe your daddy so he could come over here and drive you home. I think that's the sweetest thing I've ever heard."

Dusty smiled at Carmel, then pecked Jack on the cheek. "It is sweet. Thanks. I'm still just a little shocky, that's all. Did you happen to get here in time to meet my cousin, Paisley?"

Jack held up his hands. "How would I know? There were women and girls and suitcases all over the place. For a minute there, I thought I'd taken a wrong turn and ended up in Union Station in Dallas. What does she look like?"

"Long dark hair. Pretty."

"That would describe half the girls I saw. The other half were short and blonde like your friend Carmel here."

Dusty relaxed a little. "And cute. Don't forget cute."

Carmel wiggled her hips. "You better watch it." She turned to Jack. "Nice meeting you. Sorry to rush out, but Miss Fontaine's showing my mother and Nini, my grandmother, around. I'd better rescue Miss Fontaine. Y'all have a great Thanksgiving, and don't forget the grits."

"What did she mean about the grits?" Jack had his hand draped over the back of the seat and rubbed his fingers lightly on the nape of her neck. They'd been on the road half an hour or so, the conversation light, an awkward sort of dance between them after the rocky beginning.

"Paisley and I were the only ones who'd never eaten grits, so Mrs. Pellerin, our cooking instructor, devoted a whole day to the art of fixing grits. Like a dozen different ways. They're really not bad if you use enough cream and real butter and douse them with maple syrup."

"Our housekeeper makes cheese grits. Or at least she did. She's gone to help my sister with her kids now that Mom and Dad have moved to Austin."

It was the most personal thing he'd ever shared with Dusty, and she inched a little closer. "Nieces or nephews?"

"One of each. Sonny and Melissa."

"And your sister?"

"Betty. She's married to a lawyer in San Antonio."

"What does your sister do?"

He had a crooked grin and raised one eyebrow in a quick glance across the car. "What do all women do? She's on committees, goes to the garden club, raises money for the city library, and plays a mean game of tennis. She was singles champ at her club last year."

"What do all women do?" Maybe women who've been to finishing school, like Jack's sister, Betty. Boston at that. Apparently it was a rite of passage for girls with "good breeding and money," as Miss Fontaine would say. Dusty thought she must've been living under a rock all these years as she'd never heard of finishing school until her daddy had sprung the idea on her. At least she'd have that in common with Betty.

"She sounds great. What about you? It must seem strange living in Two Forks after being a city boy all your life."

"Whoa, where did you hear that? I grew up on a ranch fifty miles outside of Houston. My dad and my uncle have a pretty nice spread. Run about five hundred head of cattle. When my dad ran for the state Senate, he tried commuting back and forth to Austin, but my mom got a hankering to live in town, so they moved there last year. Best thing in the world for both of them."

"What about you? Didn't you want to run the ranch?"

"No, I liked growing up in the country and small-town life, but I'm not cut out to raise cattle. I like my cowboy boots free of manure." He said it in a joking tone, but Dusty had the feeling there was more to it than that. Maybe every human struggled with finding their own place in the world.

"Did your dad want you to run the ranch?"

"At first. Said I could get my finance degree, that it would be an asset for running a successful business or going to law school. He was fixin' to run for office about then, so a couple of my cousins took over the ranch. Turns out it don't matter to them what they step in—they're made to be ranchers."

They entered the outskirts of a small town and had to wait on a funeral procession to go by. In reverence, they sat in silence, and when they started back up, the conversation had lost some of its momentum.

Jack turned on the radio, and Ray Charles sang in a rich dreamy voice "You Don't Know Me." She relaxed into her seat and wondered what there was left to learn about Jack Morgan.

"I'm really glad you came to get me. There's never much chance to talk at the ranch. You're coming for dinner on Thanksgiving, I hope."

He shot a side-glance at her but didn't say anything.

She stumbled on. "I don't know what Daddy's got planned.

I hope he doesn't think I've turned into Betty Crocker or something..." That was dumb since Jack's sister was named Betty, but from the sound of it, she didn't know her way around the kitchen, either. "Anyway, we'll have dinner, I'm sure. Can you come?"

He tilted his head toward her. "Actually, no. That's one reason I came over today. I have to work at the bank tomorrow, and then I'm driving to Austin tomorrow night to have Thanksgiving with my parents."

She felt stupid that she hadn't thought of it—that he'd want to be with his family.

Dusty patted his leg. "No problem." She let her hand rest on his Levi's, hoping he would take her hand. "You might not want to eat my cooking anyway. Will you be gone the whole weekend?" Gee, she sounded pathetic, like she was begging, and when he didn't get the hint about holding hands, she removed her hand and shifted ever so slightly in the seat, putting a couple more inches of space between them.

He nodded. "We're all going to Dallas for the SMU–Baylor game on Saturday. Season tickets and all. SMU's got a new coach this year—Hayden Fry. You've heard of him, I'm sure."

She knew the look on her face gave her away. Hayden Fry could've been from another planet, and she would've never known.

They stopped at the Dairy Queen and got ice cream outside of Fort Worth. Jack must've sensed her disappointment that they wouldn't be together, for when he opened the door for her to get back in the car, he cupped her chin in his hand and leaned in for a sweet, strawberry-flavored kiss. His eyes studied her face, crinkling at the corners when he smiled.

"I wish I had the whole weekend to spend with you. Maybe tonight—"

He didn't get to finish. A car pulled into the spot next to them, and two rowdy boys jumped out and practically plowed into them. Dusty ducked into her seat in the car and took another slurp of her strawberry shake.

"Maybe tonight."

The tires of Jack's sleek black car hummed on the highway as they headed toward the ranch. Toward home.

CHAPTER 12

Houston had a familiar feel to it, like Paisley had been there before. As Mrs. Bennett wheeled the Imperial along the freeway, the landscape waved back: Miles of telephone and electric poles. A church steeple Paisley was sure she'd seen before. The skyline of downtown rose like fat fingers reaching for the clouds. Familiar and yet not.

A yearning she didn't expect gnawed at her. Belonging somewhere. To someone. The house with the mythical white picket fence teased from a corner of her brain.

Xan's voice interrupted. "Yoo-hoo! Paisley!"

"Sorry, I was just taking in the scenery." Paisley looked out across a lawn the size of a football field and a house with Roman columns marching across the front like soldiers. "This is where you live? Oh my gosh."

"No, you doofus. This is the country club. Man, you must be in another world."

"I've been told that before."

At the entrance with its gleaming white double doors, Mrs. Bennett squared her shoulders and pinned Paisley with a look of steel. "You may wait in the lobby. I can't imagine what earthly good it would be for you to sit in on the meeting. And don't wander off. It wouldn't do to have you disturbing the members."

Xan opened her mouth to say something and closed it just as fast. She gave Paisley a weak smile and followed her mother across the marble floor.

So much for dressing up and fixing her hair. She took a seat, but she was itching to look around. What could it hurt? She got up and meandered until she found a set of French doors leading to the pool area. Being the end of November, the pool was empty, but Paisley sat in one of the deck chairs anyway and watched a couple on the tennis court adjacent to the pool. A sandy-haired guy with bronze legs coached a woman old enough to be his mother, and when he raised his arms, Paisley imagined the muscles rippling beneath his shirt.

It was hypnotizing in a way, and with the angle of the sun, Paisley couldn't make out the man's features, but in her mind she saw the guy who'd rescued her at the bottom of the stairs when she'd tripped. She could still remember the texture of his blue jeans and the muscled legs beneath. She knew if she smelled his aftershave again, she'd swoon as she had that morning.

What a stupid waste of time to be pining after someone who was already engaged.

The couple on the tennis court finished and came through a gate in the wire fence. They waved at her like she belonged there, and for a moment, she relished the thought.

Then Mrs. Bennett emerged from the French doors. "Gracious, I didn't know we'd have to hunt you down. Let's go."

The Bennett home, while not sporting columns like the country club, was still a sight to take in. It was two and a half stories with dormers on the top floor and shaded by giant oaks. Whatever manufacturing business Xan's dad was in must be doing all right.

As they took their things in, Paisley noted that paint flaked from the shutters and the doorframe. Perhaps Mr. Bennett was, as Xan had hinted, in financial trouble and needed the merger with Prentice's company for monetary reasons.

Further evidence of their state of affairs came when Mrs. Bennett apologized for having to let their cook go. "We've kept the house-keeper, of course. I would spend every waking minute cleaning and not have time for the library council or my Thursday bridge club."

Which left Xan and Paisley to make Thanksgiving dinner. They made rhubarb and pumpkin pies on Wednesday. Sliced and diced vegetables for the dressing and relish trays. Mrs. Bennett passed through the kitchen every once in a while to offer her advice. "You know your father doesn't like his rhubarb pie too sweet." Or "Before I forget, my mother's crystal needs washing. We want everything to be perfect when Mr. Robbins comes for dinner."

"His name is Prentice, Mother."

Prentice was occupied that evening and called saying he would be late on Thanksgiving as he had to go to the retirement center and feed his father.

When Xan relayed the message, Mrs. Bennett said, "Dear Prentice. His poor father doesn't make a lick of sense anymore and can't even feed himself since that stroke. I hope you let him know we'd accommodate his schedule."

"Yes, Mother. I told him we'd have dinner at six. Cocktails at five."

By a quarter after five the next day, Prentice hadn't arrived. Mr. Bennett strolled to the bar at the end of the living room and asked what everyone was having.

Paisley swallowed hard. Was it expected that she'd order a martini and be like one of those society women in magazines milling with the crowd, cocktail in hand? Her stomach knotted as she thought of Sloan's sour breath when he'd had a few and staggered around.

She lifted her chin and said, "Coca-Cola for me, if you have it."

"Coming right up." Mr. Bennett popped the cap off a bottle and poured it over ice.

Mrs. Bennett asked for a glass of Chablis and told Xan to freshen her lipstick. "You want to look your best when Prentice walks in that door."

When Xan returned, Mr. Bennett, a calm giant of a man with jowls that rested on his starched collar, lifted a glass with an amber liquid. "To better days ahead."

Paisley lifted her Coke glass in a toast, but Mrs. Bennett checked her watch and paced, taking long sips from her goblet, which she held out for a refill a few minutes later. She'd nearly worn a hole in the Oriental rug by the time the doorbell rang. She steadied herself on the back of a wing chair. "Xan, shoo now and see if that's our beloved Robin Prince."

Xan shot an apologetic look to Paisley and said to her mother, "You mean Prentice Robbins. Mother, maybe you should sit down."

Mrs. Bennett squared her shoulders. "I'm fine. Just nervous, that's all."

Xan came in, her fingers laced in Prentice's, and made the introductions. Prentice, not nearly as paunchy as Xan had let on, was pleasant and apologized for being late. Mr. Bennett offered him a drink.

Mrs. Bennett asked for another Chablis and turned to Paisley. "It smells like something might be burning. Perhaps you could go check on the turkey while we visit with Prentice."

"Yes, ma'am." She nodded at Prentice. "Nice to meet you." She quick stepped into the kitchen, chagrined at Mrs. Bennett but also relieved to escape. It was a dream kitchen bigger than some of the apartments she'd lived in. She pushed up her sleeves and went to work, pulling things from the oven and carrying them to the dining room. She fanned away the heat, sorry she'd worn the new wool sweater Dusty insisted she buy. When she had it all on the table, she joined the group and announced that dinner was served.

Xan gave her a quick hug and mouthed, "Thank you."

Once they were all seated, Mrs. Bennett passed the corn bread dressing to Prentice, her words slurry as she spoke. "I must say, you're a saint, keeping an eye on your father and being so concerned about his health. I trust you had a good visit with him today."

Prentice assured her he had, then looked at Paisley. "Alexandria told me you play the guitar. That's some talent." He had a bit of a nasal twang and an overbite, which didn't really go with the square look he had about him. Solid. Crew cut. Dress pants and a sweater vest with a tie that bit into his Adam's apple.

Paisley shrugged. "Not sure about the talented part, but I do play. Say, I love that sweater you're wearing. It's a great color on you." She leaned forward and bumped her water glass, thankful it only made the ice cubes tinkle and didn't spill.

Prentice blinked behind his horn-rims. "Thank you. What a kind thing to say. Have you performed onstage?"

"Not much."

Xan bugged her eyes out. "You didn't tell me you'd played for an audience."

Mrs. Bennett cleared her throat. "I'm sure we'd all love to hear about your little hobby, darling, but perhaps we should think of our guest." She smiled at Prentice and passed a silver basket filled with yeast rolls.

"Don't make an exception for me, Mrs. Bennett. I'm interested in Alexandria's friends."

Paisley took a sip of water, being more careful this time, then ran her finger around the top of her scratchy sweater, aware that all eyes were on her.

Mrs. Bennett tilted her mouth into a fake smile. "She and

Alexandria met at finishing school. Of course, we were delighted to help out and have her for Thanksgiving since her mother lives in California, and the distance just didn't make it feasible—"

The heat started in Paisley's chest and traveled quickly to her face. "What Mrs. Bennett means to say is that I'm not really one of you all. You know, refined and loaded with money." She took a breath. "My mother has to work for a living, and I've never laid eyes on my father. That's a dark side to my history that I'm sure is of no interest." In her side vision, Paisley saw Mrs. Bennett tilt her wineglass and chugalug.

Prentice chuckled. "Guess we've all got a few skeletons in our closets." He took Xan's hand. "Which Alexandria will learn about no doubt, eh, sugar?"

Xan wrinkled her nose and told him he was such a tease, then said to Paisley, "Tell us where you played onstage."

"It's just a little coffeehouse called the Penny Loafer in North Beach."

Prentice asked, "San Francisco area, right?"

Paisley nodded. "They have poetry readings and singers sometimes. Folk groups and beatniks mostly."

Prentice widened his eyes. "Beatniks, huh? Well, that must be fascinating."

Mrs. Bennett glared at Paisley like she expected a goatee to sprout on her chin.

Paisley said, "It's all right. Edie—that's my mother—likes it, but actually, I was born in Texas. Over in Burroughs County Hospital." She waved her hand and knocked the ladle from the gravy boat, sending a dollop onto the linen tablecloth. "Oh, crud, I should be more careful." She blotted the spot with her napkin and gave a little wave to Mrs. Bennett. "Sorry."

Mrs. Bennett pinched her lips, but before she could say anything, Xan's dad said, "So you're a Texas girl, then?"

"Yes, sir. Born and bred. Till my mama took off, and we've been traipsing around the country ever since."

Xan, who'd stayed busy jerking her head to look at Paisley, then Prentice, jumped in. "Yes, Daddy, you know I told you Paisley is at Miss Fontaine's with her cousin, Dusty. I invited them both to come, but Dusty went to be with her dad at their ranch."

Mr. Bennett nodded. "Some nice ranches up in Burroughs County. Must be your uncle then that has a ranch?"

"Yes, sir. Only my cousin, Greg, runs it. Uncle Flint's too busy with all his oil wells. You might've heard of it—Fairchild Oil."

Prentice arched an eyebrow. "Your uncle owns Fairchild Oil? Flint Fairchild?"

Mr. Bennett said, "Everyone in Texas knows Flint Fairchild. Self-made millionaire. Goes to show what an ounce of luck and a pound of hard work will do. Bunny, would you pass me another roll?"

Bunny? Paisley held her napkin to her mouth to stop the giggle she knew was coming. *Bunny?* There wasn't a single thing warm and fuzzy about Bunny Bennett.

Mrs. Bennett waved a fork in the air. "We have gotten completely off track of wherever this conversation was going. Skeletons. Beatniks. Honestly." She huffed out a breath. "Prentice, why don't you tell us what you and Alexandria have planned for this weekend?"

She was about as subtle as a brick thrown through a picture window.

Prentice reached for Xan's hand. "There's the party, of course, and..."

The phone on a pedestal table in the corner rang, the jangle so loud that everyone at the table jumped. Mrs. Bennett tossed her napkin on her plate. "Forevermore, I wonder who's calling on Thanksgiving." She shoved away from the table and answered it, her face clouding as she listened to the caller. She held out the receiver. "Prentice, it's for you. Sheridan Oaks Manor."

She wobbled back to the table and collapsed into her chair. "The woman sounded grave. Said it was an emergency."

Paisley swallowed the fear that crept into her throat for the news Prentice might be receiving. She reached under the table and took Xan's clammy hand in hers. Xan clenched Paisley's fingers, her eyes riveted on Prentice's back as he nodded and slipped the phone receiver back onto the cradle.

He turned, his voice shaky as he said, "I beg your pardon, Mrs. Bennett." His eyes wandered to Xan's dad. "And yours, sir. My dad's taken a bad turn, and I have to go."

Paisley nudged Xan, who'd turned so pale she had a greenish cast to her skin. Xan rose and followed Prentice from the room.

When they were out of earshot, Bunny Bennett huffed out a breath and looked at her empty wineglass. "I wanted everything to be perfect, but nothing about this weekend has gone as I envisioned." She lifted her chin and glared at Paisley like it was all her fault.

CHAPTER 13

Dusty tossed Lamb Chop and Juanita each a sliver of the cheese she'd grated for the top of the enchiladas, then checked the pecan pie in the oven. It was her dad's favorite, and the crust was one that would've made Rosalita proud. She still had to toss the salad, but Thanksgiving dinner was almost ready. Not a turkey and the trimmings, but there was little point since it was only her and her dad. Her little schnauzers danced at her feet, acting like they still couldn't believe she was home.

She heard tires crunching on the gravel outside. Daddy. Just in time.

"Something smells good." Flint Fairchild stepped in the kitchen and hung his Stetson on the hat rack by the door. He kissed her on the cheek. "For a minute there, I almost imagined Rosalita had come back. Guess I haven't smelled home cooking in a month of Sundays."

"Well, it is Rosalita's recipe, and speaking of her, I cleaned in her room today—" She nodded toward the quarters behind the kitchen. "She left most of her things like she didn't plan on being gone forever. Have you heard from her?"

"Not a word. Reckon the old girl's gone for good."

Dusty's stomach dropped at the thought. "Don't say that. Maybe we should try and get ahold of her. You think any of the grooms over at the horse barns know anything? Have you asked them?"

"They'd of said if they heard. I know you miss her, but I figgered getting you off to charm school would take your mind off Rosalita."

"Is that why you sent me? You could've let me go to college and accomplished the same thing."

"I could've, but I didn't." He got a cup from the cupboard and poured coffee from the percolator. His tone told her that he was still the parent and she was the child. The one who hadn't matured enough to make her own decisions.

Dusty bit her lower lip. She was home and nothing had changed. And yet, she'd changed. Not in ways that her dad would notice or ways that she could define herself. It was as if a thin layer had been peeled back from her sheltered life and she saw things in a new light: A different side to Aunt Edie. That Paisley and her antics were a cover-up for things she didn't want to talk about. That sometimes pretty girls like Sharon Kay could be cruel. Mostly, though, Dusty had acquired a taste for independence, and with that, the desire to go to college burned within her stronger than ever.

There was no use pushing the point. Rosalita's voice danced in her head. *"You no sass your daddy."*

Dusty sucked in a big breath and spread the cheese over the top of the enchiladas, tossing another bit to the pups. Her dad leaned back in a kitchen chair and nursed his coffee. She took a seat at the table and changed the subject. "Well, then, how about Aunt Edie? Have you heard anything from her?"

"Who?" He grunted. "Oh, you mean Edith. Crazy coot going around calling herself Edie like she's something special."

"You didn't answer the question. Have you heard from her?"

"Can't say as I have. Some reason you're asking?"

"Actually, there is. When Aunt Edie came to our Mother/

Daughter Tea, I suggested she come here instead of going back to California."

"Whatever for?"

"I had the feeling she was having a hard time. Sort of between jobs—"

"Between husbands, you mean."

"No, she wasn't married to the one in the band."

"Lucky fellow."

Dusty's insides roiled. "What's with you two? You're always at each other's throats. You're brother and sister. I thought it would be good for both of you. And while we're on the subject, why did Aunt Edie leave here in the first place?"

"That's something you ought to ask her yourself."

"Maybe I will."

"You won't like the answer, trust me." He drained the coffee cup and pushed back from the table. "And what's *good for me* is not something you need to worry your pretty little head about. What time are we going to eat this fine dinner?"

"As soon as the enchiladas get done. I've set the table with crystal and china…because you thought it would be *good for me* to go to Miss Fontaine's and learn to be proper."

"Touché. I'll be in the front room watching television. Holler when the food's ready."

She couldn't believe he'd let her get by with that. Maybe he missed Rosalita more than he let on—the bantering back and forth. Someone to argue with.

She was still glad to be home even though it would feel more like a holiday with other people around. Her brother Patrick had plans, and Greg was just getting Susan and Zachary home from the hospital, so they weren't up for visiting.

Zachary, at least, had been a highlight of the trip. Dusty had picked up flowers at Bluebonnet Floral in Two Forks and taken them to the hospital, along with the lotion she'd bought for Susan at Simple Pleasures. She and Susan walked arm in arm to the nursery and peered at the baby through the glass. He was wrapped in a blanket like a little burrito with heart-shaped lips and clear eyelashes. When she squinted, Dusty could almost make out the Fairchild bump on his nose. She was glad she'd gone and promised Susan she'd be at the shower on Saturday.

Dusty checked the enchiladas and was getting ice for the glasses when the back door burst open and Patrick stomped in.

"Patrick! Hey, I wasn't expecting you." He had a wild look about him, hair curling around his ears under his hunting cap and mud on his boots.

"Where's Dad?"

"Hello to you, too."

"Hey, Daddy!" He marched past her into the den, his voice loud and clear. "There was a blowout on the Perkins Forty-two. Fire shooting sky high! We gotta go! You got eight guys on that rig."

A well on fire—her dad's dreaded nightmare. Goose bumps broke out on Dusty's arms as she followed Patrick through the door to the den, but he turned and smacked into her, already coming back through. "Out of the way, sis."

Her dad grabbed his jacket and asked which foreman was in charge, cursing when Patrick said it was Beggs Hardesty, their least experienced guy. When he kicked off his everyday boots, Dusty handed him the work boots she found on the back porch, and while he pulled them on, she filled a thermos with coffee.

"Thanks, kiddo," he said and started for the door. "Don't know how long I'll be. Don't wait dinner."

She reached out to touch him, to tell him to be careful, but they were gone. She stood on the back steps and waved as Patrick's pickup peeled out on the gravel. *Dear God, help them. Don't let them be hurt.*

A north wind had come up, but the chill she felt wasn't from the temperature. She looked out over the horizon, wondering where number forty-two was. It could be on the other side of the county or even a hundred miles away. The Fairchild kingdom had a far reach, and Dusty chastised herself for not paying more attention when her dad described the lease locations. She'd listened many an hour while her dad talked about blowouts, fires that could burn for days, even weeks sometimes. She'd once asked him why he wanted to work in such a dangerous business.

He'd looked her in the eyes. "When something's in your blood, nothing else matters."

Funny. She'd forgotten that.

Dusk settled around her, the rolling grass and scrub oak of the land as familiar as the Fairchild bump on her nose. It was the land that had always beckoned her to learn more of its surface and what lay beneath the crusty layers. Even the oil. Where it came from, the rich blackness that spewed like molten lava when its veins were pierced. The yearning cramped her insides. She was more of a Fairchild than her daddy realized.

She squinted, thinking she smelled smoke, but nothing glowed on the horizon. No fiery ball or boiling clouds. The smell grew stronger and wrapped her in its stench.

The enchiladas! She'd forgotten all about them. She raced into the house, grabbed a pot holder, and opened the oven. Black smoke and the stink of burned cheese gagged her. She pulled the pan out and put it on the stovetop, then opened the window above the sink to clear the air.

Her heart pounded as she slumped into a kitchen chair and wiped sweat from her forehead. She hoped it was only Thanksgiving dinner that was burned and not one of the men at her daddy's well.

CHAPTER 14

Paisley rolled down the passenger window of Xan's Chevy Bel Air and let the wind blow her hair. The fresh air was a relief after the past two days under Mrs. Bennett's watchful eye. There'd been no word from Prentice about his dad, so everyone assumed the ominous phone call had been only a minor emergency and ended well.

While they were having breakfast on the back veranda Friday morning, Mrs. Bennett mentioned that the guest list for the engagement party needed to be delivered to the country club. Xan jumped at the chance.

As they sailed along oak-lined streets past houses the size of hotels, Xan sang along off-key to the radio while Paisley took in the scenery and wondered who lived in these mansions and what their lives were like.

"So does Prentice live around here?"

Xan shook her head. "He comes from old money and lives in the swanky part of town. Sharon Kay lives a couple of streets over from him."

"These are pretty ritzy, if you ask me. So when you say old money, what do you mean?"

"Prentice's family did something in shipping. Prentice manages one of the midsized companies and sits on the board of a bunch of others. Some of the early Houstonites were bankers and financiers from back East. Sharon Kay's always rubbing our noses in the fact that her dad owned a bank before he became a judge."

"That would explain a lot. So guess you'll be moving to the *swanky* family mansion when you and Prentice get married?"

Xan stopped at a red light and shrugged. "We haven't even set a date for the wedding, so I have no earthly idea. It just didn't cross my mind."

But it certainly crossed Bunny Bennett's, Paisley was sure of it. It was hard to believe that Xan with her cavalier innocence was even related to Mrs. Bennett.

After they'd dropped off the list at the country club, Xan suggested they go uptown and look around. Xan zipped into a parking space and fed the meter, then led the way. They strolled past bakeries, children's shops, and furniture stores with glass display windows. Paisley caught her reflection in one of them, and for a moment, she could almost imagine herself as a housewife, picking out a dinette or a new set of towels for her house behind the picket fence. Not a fancy place, just one with ivy curling around the windows and a tire swing in the yard. Simple yet settled.

Xan pulled her along, and a couple of blocks up the street, they stopped for a Coke at Ruby Dell's Café. The waitress showed them to a table by the window where sunlight filtered in through streaked glass. Xan ordered a piece of coconut cream pie, and when it came, the meringue was two inches tall and the perfect shade of tan. Mrs. Pellerin would have given it an A plus.

"Man, I know this isn't on my diet, but I've missed coconut pie more than anything. And this is divine." She took another bite, closed her eyes, and looked like she had tripped out. "You sure you don't want something?"

"I'm still stuffed from breakfast. And just for the record, you've done great on your diet, I doubt one piece of pie is going to ruin it. Do you think Prentice noticed your cute new figure?"

Xan twirled her fork. "He was too busy looking at you, chatting about your uncle's ranch and you singing in beatnik clubs."

"He wasn't looking at me. I was only answering his questions. Your dad asked a few, too, if I remember."

"Mother thought Prentice was flirting with you."

Paisley's face grew hot as she tried to remember exactly what was said. She wasn't flirting. Absolutely not. "Is that what you thought, too?"

"I admit, I'm always a little jealous of you. You're so talented and cute, and I'm such a plain Jane."

"That's ridiculous! I'm a nobody, and Prentice kept looking at you like he couldn't wait to get you alone. And besides, what kind of friend would I be to come and impose on your family and then try to steal your boyfriend?"

Xan pushed the half-eaten pie away. "You'd be surprised at what some of my so-called friends have done."

"Well, you have nothing to worry about. You and Prentice are a perfect couple."

"I just get nervous, that's all. And you are the best friend I've ever had."

Paisley had never lived in one place long enough to have a true-blue friend. She didn't think Dusty counted since they were related, but now she looked across at Xan and it was cool. Two people hanging out, shopping, and just talking.

She gave Xan a two thumbs-up while Xan continued to ramble. "Mother gets her nose out of joint over every little thing, and it's been worse lately."

"Why's that?"

"Her best friend moved to North Carolina, and then Daddy's

business partner ran up a bunch of debts, which is why their company's not doing so hot. I think she's afraid they're going to lose their club membership and be embarrassed in front of her remaining friends."

"I'm sorry."

"Listen to me, here I am carrying on like there's no tomorrow." She picked up the check, threw a couple of bills on the table, and then arm in arm, they walked back to the Bel Air.

When they returned, Mrs. Bennett met them at the door, her eyes flashing. "Where have you been?" Her words were directed at Xan, but the slightly raised eyebrows and steely gaze were aimed at Paisley as if she'd taken Xan hostage to go joyriding. Before either of them had time to respond, Mrs. Bennett continued, "I've been beside myself. The receptionist at the club said you left two hours ago, so here I've been pacing and wringing my hands."

"I'm sorry, Mother. Was there something else you needed me to do?"

"I don't even know where to begin. We have to start making lists and phone calls immediately."

Xan stood openmouthed. "Why? What's going on?"

Mrs. Bennett's lips drew into a straight line, her eyes glistening. "Prentice called. His father passed this morning. The engagement party is canceled."

❧

"Got you a stubborn one there, don't you?" Mr. Bennett looked over at Paisley who had both hands around a mean-looking weed in the flower bed.

She bent her knee and put some gusto in it and landed on her behind when the soil finally relented. "Got it!" She waved the plant with a hairy root at least a foot long in the air like a trophy.

"Milkweed. Blasted thing must've been growing since last summer." Mr. Bennett wore an open neck shirt with short sleeves and had welcomed Paisley when she came from the house on Saturday morning and asked if she could help. For two hours, they'd been pulling weeds in Bunny's formal garden that had "gone to hell in a handbasket," according to Mr. Bennett. He didn't offer an apology about letting his yardman go as his wife had done about the cook.

Refreshing after the drama of the past two days. Poor Mr. Robbins. His death left everything scrambled, and Mrs. Bennett had been giving Xan directions nonstop since the minute they walked in from shopping the day before. There were more than a hundred people who had to be called, and when Xan looked like she was about to blow a gasket, Paisley offered to help. Xan waved her away, saying her mother insisted she do the calling. Saturday morning had dawned with Bunny handing Xan a new list of things to do.

Helping Mr. Bennett was a welcome escape. Xan's dad didn't have much to say, just went about his business, telling her which plants were weeds and which ones perennials. Paisley scooped up the last bundle of crabgrass and put it in the metal trash container. Sweat ran from her armpits, and she knew her hair was a mess. Her cutoffs would've been a better choice for yard work than her good slacks, but gardening hadn't exactly been on the agenda when they left Miss Fontaine's.

Mr. Bennett leaned on a leaf rake and looked around. "Sure looks a sight better than when we started." He paused as if gathering his thoughts. "I'm sorry this wasn't the weekend you'd counted on."

"No prob. At least I know milkweed from lantana now. Actually, I had a fab time." Paisley had never lived in a house with a garden, formal or otherwise, and now having worked in her first one, she was surprised at how much she enjoyed it.

"One other thing—" He jerked his head toward the house. "I

hope you don't get the idea Bunny's always wound up like she's been this weekend."

"Hey, I've got a mom. I get it. Honest."

"She's got a lot on her mind."

"My being here hasn't helped." Being rude at the Thanksgiving table wasn't cool, either. She swallowed, trying to decide if she should say something. Her behavior was inexcusable. Guests don't insult their hostesses.

Just say you're sorry.

"Uh, Mr. Bennett."

"Please, call me Forrest."

"Forrest. I shouldn't have acted the way I did on Thanksgiving. I have this tendency to set people off, and...I was trying to fit in and be cultured like you all. What I said to your wife just slipped out."

"No need to apologize—"

"Yes, there is. I acted stupid. And I'm sorry."

"We all do things we're not proud of. It takes a strong person to admit it."

She didn't feel strong. Her muscles quivered and her eyes moistened. Edie's voice rang in her head. *"Laugh it off. You screw up and learn from it. There's no use bawling about it."*

Edie was wrong. Sometimes Paisley felt like crying, but that wasn't Edie's way. Maybe Edie was wrong about other things, too. People like the Bennetts. So they'd had a little downturn in their fortune. They didn't pack up and move across the country, looking for the next big thing.

She leaned over and picked up a weed they'd missed. "I was thinking that now that we're done here, maybe we could wash the windows. You know, stay out of the way."

Forrest Bennett laughed. "You're on. And for the record, having you here's been like a breath of fresh air." He looked toward the peak of the house. "I'll see if I can scrounge up a ladder and some buckets and sponges."

"I'll run in and get us some iced tea."

When she slipped in the back door, piano music wafted from a distant room. Soft and melodic, but in a minor key. Paisley tiptoed in the direction of the music until she got to the parlor. She leaned against the doorway and watched as Bunny sat at the baby grand, her fingers sliding gracefully up and down the keys. Bunny's shoulders moved rhythmically to the beat as she played a segue into "Moon River," a song all the radio stations were playing. It was hard to believe Bunny was capable of evoking something with such grace and ease.

Paisley wiped her hands on her slacks and inched closer. Bunny turned her head and twitched. Startled, it seemed. She looked away quickly, the strain she was playing lost.

"That was beautiful."

Bunny fumbled at the keys, then dropped her wrists into a discordant thud. "Sometimes I have to get away, escape for a minute." She rose and flicked a hair from her face, distancing herself from Paisley.

"I know. Trust me, I know." The room was thick with emotion, and Paisley had the urge to reach out and hug Bunny. Her gut told her not to get carried away. Instead she rocked back on her heels and said, "I just came in to get some iced tea, and uh...to say I'm sorry for being rude to you at dinner on Thanksgiving. I really appreciated you letting me come, and I'll try not to be a pest the rest of the time I'm here."

Bunny blinked and opened her mouth to speak, then stopped. She let out a sigh, then said crisply, "That's something we'll have to figure out. How to get you back to school. Xan, of course, will have to stay here to support Prentice and attend the service. I'll speak to Forrest about it."

"I could take the bus if that would be better."

She fluttered her hand in dismissal. "No, we'll work something out."

What they worked out was for Mr. Bennett to take Paisley back to Rosebriar early on Sunday so he could return for Mr. Robbins's viewing at the funeral parlor that evening. Xan helped carry her things to Mr. Bennett's older model Cadillac and then hugged Paisley. Her eyes brimmed with fresh tears. "Tell everyone I said hi and that I'll be back before you know it."

"Give Prentice my condolences and take good care of him, you hear?"

Xan nodded and stood in the driveway waving as Mr. Bennett eased the Caddy into the street and turned onto the main thoroughfare. Paisley relaxed into the seat and smiled at Mr. Bennett.

He put his hand on the radio dial and said, "What'll it be? Country-western or the Sunday morning gospel hour?"

"You choose."

He fiddled with the tuner until "I'll Fly Away" in four-part harmony came loud and clear through the speakers. The Caddy zoomed toward Miss Fontaine's like it was carried on the wings of a dove.

CHAPTER 15

Although her dad hadn't returned from the fire by Saturday, Dusty went to the baby shower for Zachary. Susan clapped her hand over her mouth when Dusty brought in the pram and told her it was perfect. While everyone tried to stay upbeat, talk about the rig fire overshadowed the afternoon. Luckily no one was killed, but Beggs Hardesty and one of the hands had been burned bad enough that they'd been sent to Parkland Hospital in Dallas for treatment. Everyone seemed to have heard also how Flint Fairchild refused to leave the well that continued burning. An oil fire specialist from Houston came and told them it could be anywhere from a day or two to a few weeks. Maybe months. He ordered everyone away, but Dusty's dad insisted on camping out next to the firefighters' trailer and refused to leave.

He sent word with Patrick Saturday evening that Dusty needed to find another way back to Miss Fontaine's. "The stubborn old coot's going to stay out there till kingdom come, but he wants you back where you belong."

Dusty gritted her teeth. "I belong at the ranch. Who's going to watch the dogs and take meals out to Daddy? He has to eat something."

Patrick told her he'd watch the dogs and their daddy wouldn't starve. He added that he was fixin' to move back into the ranch house now that he was working for their dad. Dusty was glad they'd patched up their differences. Better yet that Patrick had decided to settle down.

Jack didn't plan to return to Two Forks until Sunday evening, so Neva Harris from the Methodist Church drove Dusty over to Miss Fontaine's after church. Neva had been at the shower and offered to help any way she could, so Dusty had called her.

When they pulled into the Rosebriar drive, Neva said, "Oh my lands, such a fancy place. Your daddy done all right by you."

"It's all right for now." Dusty fidgeted in her seat. Neva might not say it, but this was highfalutin for people from Two Forks. Dusty hated when people put on airs, so she just acted like it was no big deal to be at finishing school and asked Neva if she wanted to look around. Neva patted her on the knee and said she needed to be getting back.

Just as the first day she'd come, Dusty felt pulled to be somewhere else. She hauled in her luggage just as Paisley was bounding down the stairs.

Her cousin opened her arms for a hug and said, "Is Uncle Flint here? I should go out and say hello."

Dusty handed Paisley one of her suitcases. "No, one of his wells caught fire. Help me with my stuff, and I'll tell you all about it. Where's Xan? Did you have fun?"

"It's a long story." Paisley told her about Mr. Robbins's death and that Xan's dad had brought her back early Sunday morning so Xan could stay for the funeral.

Thirty minutes later they were still talking when Sharon Kay came in and set two suitcases on the floor. "Be right back. I have another load to bring up."

Dusty jumped up. "I'll help."

"No need. It's just my hanging stuff. Wait till you see the formal I'm wearing to the Christmas dance. Neiman Marcus." She raised her eyebrows as if expecting them to be impressed.

Dusty smiled. "Sounds great. I'm wearing one from senior year."

Paisley made a face. "I have nothing. Are you sure it's formal, like could I get by with just wearing the green dress I didn't get to wear for Xan's engagement party?"

Sharon Kay snorted. "What do you think? Too bad about Xan, though. Everybody was talking about it at the club on Saturday night. Why didn't y'all come?"

"Mrs. Bennett didn't think it was appropriate with old Mr. Robbins just passing."

Sharon Kay started for the door. "Y'all missed a groovy band. Lots of college guys home for the holidays. You might've found someone you could ask to the Christmas dance."

"Rats. Guess I'm just unlucky. Since I don't even have a dress, maybe Miss Fontaine will let me work the lights or something."

"Yeah, like when you were a roadie with your mom's band."

"Hey, I wasn't a roadie."

"So you say." Sharon Kay sashayed out the door and hollered to someone asking about her vacation. Rosebriar was starting to pulse with giggles and life once again.

That evening, Miss Fontaine joined them for dinner. "Alexandria, as some of you may have heard, has had a death to someone close to the family. She won't be back for a few days. I trust that the rest of you had a lovely holiday." She went around the table, asking questions, her cheeks flushed as she nodded and smiled and gave encouraging little remarks. It was almost as if she was gathering her chicks back into the nest after letting them try their wings.

When they'd finished the main course, Sulee came in with blackberry cobbler swimming in fresh cream. A collective groan went around the table with grumbles about fitting into their dresses for the Christmas dance.

Miss Fontaine chirped, "Speaking of the dance, tomorrow we'll begin planning for your first formal occasion." She smiled at Dusty and nodded. "By the end of the week, I'll need to know how many of you will need dates with the Miller College boys."

Dusty could hardly get enthused about the dance when her mind was still on a patch of prairie where orange flames licked the air and men in fireproof suits worked to snuff the blowout. She pictured her daddy pacing against a smoke-filled sky. Helpless, dependent on someone else to fix the problem. She knew he must be half-mad with worry and frustration. The dance seemed a world away. Which is where she must've been as Paisley elbowed her.

Dusty blinked, all eyes on her. "What? Sorry. I was thinking of something else."

Miss Fontaine spoke kindly. "The dance. Will you be asking a beau from your hometown or would you like me to add your name to the list for the fraternity boys?"

"I'm not sure. I suppose I could ask Jack..." Of course she should. She hadn't even thought about it. And she would love to show him off, dance with him. She nodded. "I'll have to call him this week and let you know."

She waited until Wednesday and called Jack at work. "Is this a good time? You're not with a customer or something?"

"No, it's always a perfect time to talk to you. What's on your mind?"

She told him about the dance, that it would be on the last Saturday night before school let out for Christmas, and asked if he'd be her date.

"I'd love it. I haven't been to a sorority party in way too long."

"It's not a sorority party, but I guess it's about the same thing. It's at the country club, so a rather formal affair."

"Sounds terrific. See you in a few weeks, then."

"Wait. One other thing. Have you heard anything about the fire at Daddy's well? Patrick said he'd call and let me know, but I haven't heard."

"Still burning as of a few hours ago, but they're hopeful they'll get it capped by the weekend. Sure hope so. Rumors going around that your dad's aged ten years overnight."

"That's what I'm afraid of, that he'll let this gnaw on him and forget to take care of himself."

"He'll be all right. There's a lot to admire about a man who puts the welfare of others ahead of his own." He cleared his throat. "Not sure I should mention it, but Patrick came in with instructions from your dad to use his personal account to take care of the families of the two guys who were burned. Hotels for the families. Any hospital bills not covered by the insurance. You don't find many people who would do that."

A lump grew in Dusty's throat. "Seems kind of silly to be talking about a dance when stuff like this is going on."

"Not at all. Bad stuff happens, but life goes on, and your dad would want you to have a good time."

Her emotions swirled together when she hung up. Her dad was stubborn and self-sufficient. And impossible. Aunt Edie and Dusty's brothers could testify to that. Not to mention his making the decision to send her to Miss Fontaine's without consulting her. But…that was just it. He also did the right thing when it counted.

She wiped a tear from the corner of her eye and went to give Paisley the update.

CHAPTER 16

"What's going on?" Paisley's first thought at seeing Delia, the upstairs maid, rifling through Xan's chest of drawers the following Monday afternoon was that she was looking for something. A piece of jewelry or something she could steal. Then she saw a suitcase open on the bed and two cardboard boxes on the floor loaded with Xan's clothes.

Delia straightened and turned around. "Sorry, miss. Just packing up Miss Bennett's things."

"Why?"

"She's not coming back to Rosebriar."

"Are you sure? No one said a word to me." Her gut twisted. Something wasn't right. But what? Xan wasn't coming back? When did that happen? Had Mrs. Bennett decided that Paisley was a bad influence on her daughter? Paisley thought when she left they were on better terms. Mrs. Bennett had even been gracious when Paisley gave her the hostess gift. Maybe Prentice changed his mind about marrying Xan, and now the Bennetts couldn't afford the expense. Prentice was nice, though, and seemed crazy about Xan.

Delia carried a stack of folded clothes and piled them in the suitcase. "Just doing my job."

"Did Miss Fontaine say why Xan wasn't coming back?"

"Not my place to ask."

"Well, that's not good enough. How do you know what's hers and what's mine?"

That brought a chuckle from Delia. "Lord a mercy. It don't take a rocket scientist to figure that out. You two are like Mutt and Jeff. I don't think I'll be mixing up what's what."

"Just see that you don't." Realizing in her frustration she'd sounded like Sharon Kay, she added, "Please."

Paisley spun on the heels of the navy pumps she'd worn to survey the digs when Miss Fontaine had taken them all to the country club that morning. She hollered down the hall for Dusty who stuck her head out the door of her room.

Paisley said, "Xan's not coming back. I need you to come with me and see what's going on." She told Dusty what happened on the way down the stairs. They went to the off-limits hallway accessed by a door in the far end of the parlor and knocked on Miss Fontaine's door.

Miss Fontaine peeked out. "Yes?"

Paisley asked if they could come in.

"I don't entertain girls in my quarters. What do you need?"

Paisley gritted her teeth. "We came for some answers. And I think it would be better in the privacy of your room." She stepped forward, throwing Miss Fontaine off guard. The door swung open, and she and Dusty entered.

The room was surprisingly large, not a cluster of rooms like Paisley expected. Having lived so many places, Paisley was good at taking stock of the amenities in a hurry. On the left, a sitting area had a boxy sofa with a faded magnolia pattern and a rocking chair with a knitting basket beside it. On the other side of the space was a small kitchen table with chrome legs and a red Formica top. Everything in one room.

Against the wall in the middle was a plain wooden desk with a straight chair, and off to the right, a bed with a white chenille bed-spread, a small table beside it. Two doors on that end probably led to a closet or the bathroom.

Miss Fontaine clasped her hands before her. "You had a question?"

"Xan. Why didn't you tell me she was leaving?"

"Miss Bennett. I see." She looked at the floor, then off to the corner of the room where a plug-in teapot and hot plate sat on a cupboard beside the kitchen table.

"You see what?"

"I only found out myself this morning."

"You were with us at the country club. Why didn't you mention it?"

"It wasn't an appropriate time. Delia will have her things cleared out soon."

"What I want to know is why?"

"I'm not at liberty to divulge private matters of my students."

"Oh, get real. You could at least tell me the reason. You don't have to give me the nitty-gritty."

"That tone will get you nowhere."

Dusty, who had been pacing and acting like she wanted to be somewhere else, shook her head. "Maybe we should just go now. We can call Xan and ask her."

Miss Fontaine clipped across the wooden floor and plugged in the teapot. "Suit yourself. It does bring up another matter. Sharon Kay originally requested a private room. For financial reasons, I need to fill as many spots as I can, so it's not an option I usually offer. With this new turn of events, I'd like to honor her request. Would you girls like to be roommates?"

Dusty wandered off by the desk, a puzzled expression on her face. She'd been weird ever since coming back from Thanksgiving, and Paisley thought she might be worrying about her dad.

"Dusty, what do you think?"

"As long as it's all right with Miss Fontaine, I don't see why not. But only if you'll let me keep my rock collection on the windowsill."

The teakettle whistled, sending Miss Fontaine scurrying into her kitchen corner. She looked back over her shoulder. "Tea?"

Paisley shook her head. "I thought you didn't entertain students in your quarters."

Miss Fontaine shrugged. "It's always proper to be gracious. Thank you for stopping by."

They scooted out, closing the door behind them. When they got to the upstairs landing, Paisley asked, "What was Miss Fontaine thinking? That we would forget about Xan if she offered to let us move in together? I'm telling you, Dusty, there's something wrong with that woman. She's so stiff I'd swear she has starch in her underwear."

Dusty shook her head. "There's something strange about her, I agree. I'm not sure if you noticed or not, but there were some photographs on the nightstand. I kept trying to get a closer look. One was of a man in uniform. Not like the general that hangs in the parlor. More recent, but still old. Korea or World War II maybe. The other was of a group sitting on a picnic blanket. Maybe a family. I couldn't tell much, but here's the spooky part…I've seen that place."

"Where?"

Dusty told her about the day she saw the girl on the swing.

"How do you know it was even the same spot?"

"I'm not positive, but there was a swing in the picture on her nightstand."

"So, they're neighbors. Or maybe related. Like Simon."

"Probably. It's just odd, that's all."

"Maybe tomorrow we should check out the place. It's supposed to be a nice day."

Dusty shook her head. "Something about it felt private. Sacred almost."

Paisley shuddered. "You're giving me the heebie-jeebies. You never turn down an opportunity to go exploring."

"Guess there's always a first time."

❦

When Patrick called later that day, he got right to the point. "They got the fire out."

Dusty's knees buckled as she sank into the chair by the phone. "Thank God. How's Daddy?"

"He'll be all right after he's cleaned up and slept twelve hours. You oughta be glad you weren't here when he came in. Ten days without a bath or a shave—he looked like something the hound dogs dragged in."

Dusty smiled. Her suave, easy-on-his-feet dad had a tough side. She knew he'd be okay. "Tell me everything. How did they get it out?"

"It wasn't that hard once they got the melted platform cleared away and set everything up. A couple shots with dynamite blew it out."

"Wasn't it dangerous to use dynamite?"

"Everything about this business is dangerous. It's half the thrill."

That's what it was for Patrick. A thrill. Maybe he hadn't changed. Her mind skipped back to the day the police called and said Patrick was in custody for putting a cherry bomb in the men's toilet. A prank, he'd told their dad. Maybe he just liked danger. She bit her tongue to keep from popping a joke about his pyrotechnic tendencies. No use riling her brother, and obviously the blowout at the well wasn't the result of a reckless college kid.

She said, "I'd think dynamite might cause another explosion."

"Nope. It takes away the oxygen, so I'm told, and snuffs out the fire. I'm still learning the technical jargon."

"What happens now?"

"They'll get it up and running soon. Daddy's putting his best men out there. Says this might be his biggest well ever."

She heard something in Patrick's voice she hadn't heard before. Excitement. Relief. Maybe even a bit of tenderness toward their dad. Something stirred in her, too. Patrick and her dad didn't know it yet, but when she went home for Christmas, she was going to put on a hard hat and boots and visit one of her dad's wells. She had to. She was a Fairchild.

⁂

Dusty hoped that sharing a room with Paisley would be like old times, but Paisley was in a funk and called Xan's house three or four times a day. Nothing. No answer. She was convinced they'd packed up and moved away. Dusty could understand Paisley thinking that. What Dusty had always considered Edie and Paisley's adventurous life was, she now realized, just Edie's way of avoiding reality.

When the other girls found out Xan wasn't coming back, rumors flew like poisoned darts. The most popular was that she was pregnant. Paisley assured them that was impossible, that Xan's mother hovered over her like a mother bear every time Prentice was within a country mile.

"It stinks, that's what." Paisley remained crabby for days and stayed in their room playing the guitar any time they weren't in class. She got lost in her melodies the way Dusty did walking the creek banks back home. Only now, Paisley wasn't playing fun, up-beat country songs, but aimless tunes in a minor key.

The rest of the girls were in a flurry getting ready for the Christmas ball. There would be a mixer at Rosebriar before the limousines took them to the country club for dinner and the dance. Which meant Rosebriar had to be decorated. On the evening the tree was to be delivered, Miss Swanson cleared the spot in the parlor and had the girls carry boxes of lights and decorations from the storage closet. Carmel brought down her hi-fi and put on Christmas records, and some of the girls made hot chocolate and snacks in the kitchen.

Brenda Lee was belting out "Rockin' Around the Christmas Tree" on the hi-fi when the deliveryman came with the tree and set it up in the parlor. It was a beauty, full and bursting with a sweet pine scent. The man who brought it looked familiar, probably one of the men who tended the shrubbery and lawn.

Miss Fontaine eyed the tree. "Looks straight to me. Thanks, Winston. You always find one that's perfect."

"My pleasure, Miz Fontaine. I'll leave the cut greenery for the wreaths on the lawn. Anything else?" He pulled work gloves from his jacket pockets and nodded to the girls in general. "Merry Christmas."

Miss Fontaine followed him out, presumably to pay him, and by the time she'd come back, bubble lights rested on the tree's branches, adding a glow to the room.

Paisley came down from her room, and Carmel waved her over to where she and Dusty were stringing cranberries on fishing line. "Isn't this great? An old-fashioned tree-trimming party. Here, I'll get another needle and thread, and you can help with the garland."

Laughter floated in the air as they sang along to "Deck the Halls" and "I Saw Mommy Kissing Santa Claus." When the tree couldn't hold another ornament and a rich-toned nativity, complete with crèche, graced the mantel, Miss Fontaine called them into the dining room for refreshments. While they sipped hot apple cider and nibbled iced sugar cookies in the shapes of reindeer and snowmen, Miss Fontaine tapped a spoon on a glass.

"The arrangements have been finalized with Miller College. It's always a delight to have such bright young men escorting my girls. I need to know your evening gown colors so that the wrist corsages coordinate."

She passed around a clipboard for them to write down their dress colors.

Paisley stepped forward. "I'll have to get back to you on the dress color since I'm not shopping until Saturday."

Miss Fontaine tilted her head, the omnipresent bun bobbling. "Your lack of planning is disturbing, but I know you've had a lot on your mind."

"Oh, my dress will be a knockout." Her eyes sparkled. "Trust me."

Miss Fontaine bit her lip. "I can hardly wait."

Dusty sighed. Paisley was back to her old self.

Or pretending to be, at least.

⁂

"Hey, what do you think of this one?" Dusty held up a dark rose dress for Paisley's approval.

"Too frilly." Since the clerk at Miss Gray's Dress Shoppe stood quietly at the side, Paisley didn't say what she really thought. All it needed was a pair of glass slippers and a pumpkin coach, and it would be perfect.

Dusty went through the rack again. "You've said no to all of them. How about this one with the empire waist. It's elegant."

The clerk looked over the top of her half-glasses and nodded. "The velvet on the top is quite the fashion this year. These are the latest styles from Fifth Avenue."

"I'll try it." Paisley liked the velvet, although the taffeta skirt would be so noisy it would sound like she was wearing a paper bag. Still, they were down to the wire, and Miss Fontaine expected her to have a formal gown. As she followed the clerk to the dressing room, a freestanding rack with long dresses caught her eye. "What about these? Are they already sold?"

The woman flicked her hand in dismissal. "You wouldn't want any of these." She lowered her voice. "They're used. We allow some of our customers to bring in their old evening wear for a small discount on new dresses. They appreciate getting more closet space."

"What do you do with them?"

"Send them to a rummage sale generally."

Paisley ran her fingers down one the color of pale champagne. She handed the clerk the Fifth Avenue dress and removed the rummage sale one from the rack. It had a shimmering strapless bodice with iridescent sequins that cascaded below the waist on a simple netting fabric. When she held it next to her, the silk underskirt had a rich, fluid feel without any crackling sounds. Simple, but breathtaking.

Paisley handed it to the clerk. "Can you tell me the size?"

"Surely you don't want to wear something so outdated. It must be eight or ten years old." She inspected the tag and raised her eyebrows. "It is a Dior and just happens to be your size. It's unfortunate, though, that there are stains here on the skirt. When they're not cleaned properly, they can be almost impossible to get out."

"I'd like to try it on anyway."

"Very well." She set her mouth in a line, and her expression hadn't changed even by the time Dusty got out her checkbook and paid for the "old rag," as the clerk had taken to calling it. Even though they'd added a strapless bra, a nylon slip, and a pair of ecru over-the-elbow gloves, the clerk still had her nose out of joint when they left.

One thing about her and Edie—they'd shopped rummage sales for years and had elevated spot removal to an art. Edie's philosophy was "If lemon juice won't fix it, add a pretty bow."

Dusty waved at someone coming their way. Sharon Kay. She had on a tweed coat and wool slacks, a beret on her head, and came from the direction of Simple Pleasures.

When they got closer, Sharon Kay eyed the dress box. "So you did find something at the last minute."

"Lucky me. A House of Dior that will make you swoon."

Sharon Kay blinked. "Really? I didn't know any place in town carried that label."

"This is one of a kind, I think."

Dusty shook her head at Paisley, then flicked an errant strand of hair from her cheek. "So, Sharon Kay, anything interesting in town today?"

Sharon Kay held up her hand. "Mr. Simon got my ring back from the repair shop. And get this, he told me he's coming to the dance. A chaperone, I think. Won't it be fun to see his moves on the dance floor?"

Paisley said, "Groovy. Hey, there's Miss Swanson. You want to ride back to Rosebriar with us?"

"Sorry. I'm having a manicure at three o'clock."

They hopped in the backseat of the station wagon. Miss Swanson turned around before pulling from the curb. "All set?" The poor thing was so short she could barely see over the steering wheel, and she was fond of hitting the brakes and honking at anything that might possibly get in the way. They careened through town amid beeps and jerks.

When they pulled into the circle drive, Paisley hopped out, tucked the dress box under her arm, and sailed up the walk. Carmel met them at the door.

"Hey, you're back. Xan just called and wants you to call her. Here's the number."

Paisley's heart lurched. "Is she all right? Did she say why she didn't come back?" She looked at the number but didn't recognize it.

"No. She sounded like herself, though. Perky. Said she only wanted to talk to you."

Paisley took the steps two at a time, tossed the dress box on the lounge sofa, and dialed the strange number.

Xan answered on the first ring and accepted the charges. "Paisley?"

Paisley gripped the phone. "Are you all right? Where have you been? And what's going on?"

"Man, you don't know how good it is to hear your voice. Prentice was just telling me this morning that I should give you a call."

"Why haven't you called before now?" *Prentice? Is that what she said?*

"It's a long story. First, there was that business with Mr. Robbins and the funeral."

"And..."

"I've been dying to tell you, but everything has happened so fast. Are you sitting down?"

"Yes. I'm in the lounge. Putting my feet up on the coffee table as we speak."

"Prentice and I are married."

The room swam before her. "No. Impossible. How could you? You said you wanted a big wedding with all the trimmings."

"Oh, I said a lot of things." She giggled. "I should probably start at the beginning." Her voice, like piano keys tinkling, went up and down. Prentice had asked her to stay until the weekend after the funeral, to give him a few days to take care of the business end of dying. He'd taken Paisley to Galveston on Saturday and presented her with the diamond his dad had given his mother—a rock the size of Montana, according to Xan. He didn't want an elaborate wedding and all the fuss, so he'd asked her if she'd like to go to New Orleans the next weekend and get married in Jackson Square in a simple outdoor ceremony.

"What about your mother? Wasn't she devastated?"

"No, just the opposite. She'd been after Daddy to take her to New Orleans for years, so she jumped on the chance."

"Your parents went with you? Please don't tell me they went on your honeymoon, too."

"Only for a couple of days. Daddy had to get back—get this—to talk to someone at NASA about a big contract. It's huge, and you know what everyone's saying—all eyes are on Houston for putting a man on the moon."

"Did he get the contract?"

"Signed. Sealed. And delivered."

"So you married Prentice for nothing."

"How could you say that? I love him. This is the best thing to happen to me since I won Little Miss Rosebud in the second grade."

"Sorry. I didn't mean to imply…okay, so I guess I did. I'm just ripped because I've been worried sick about you for three weeks and come to find out you've gotten married and moved to the swanky mansion on the hill."

"It's not a mansion. Not exactly. And I'm sorry I didn't tell you sooner. Ever since we got back from New Orleans, I've been working with a decorator, picking out paint and new furniture. We won't have the house redone by Christmas, but I was hoping that maybe you could come spring break."

"Hmm. Not sure. Hey, I just got back from a little shopping trip of my own, and Dusty's waiting for me. I'll tell everyone your good news."

Xan giggled. "You can tell them Mrs. Prentice Robbins called."

"Yeah, sure. I'll do that."

Paisley dropped the receiver on the hook and pulled her knees to her chest.

Best wishes, my friend.

CHAPTER 17

Dusty checked her lipstick in the mirror and looked at Paisley's reflection as she stood behind her. Her cousin had no idea how elegant she was. Her narrow shoulders and graceful neck rose above the strapless gown that looked like it had been custom sewn for her. The stain the saleslady had such a hissy about came out in nothing flat, and Paisley had added a wide emerald velvet ribbon at the waist. Bobby pins with rhinestone tips in her updo added just a touch of sparkle to her mahogany hair.

Paisley caught her staring and held up her hands. "What? Are you afraid I'll embarrass you in front of Jack in my ragtag dress?"

Dusty turned around. "You know that's the last thing I'm worried about. You look stupendous. Every Miller College guy waiting downstairs will be hoping you're his date." She pulled on her eight-button gloves that went with her short but fancy dress with a navy lace bodice and matching tulle over a cream underskirt. It might be last year's style, but Jack had never seen her in it, and she knew the skirt would swing easily when they danced. Her excitement rose as she tucked her lipstick in a silver evening bag.

She opened the door a crack to see if it was time. Miss Fontaine was to give them a signal to begin the processional. Each girl would descend the staircase when her name was called and take the arm of her date.

Paisley asked, "See anything?"

"She just gave the sign. Oh, there's Jill. She's wearing red satin and looks fabulous." Butterflies jitterbugged in her stomach. Just a couple minutes and she would see Jack. She turned back to Paisley. "Showtime."

They filed into the hall out of sight from their escorts waiting at the foot of the stairs. Sharon Kay brushed by, head high, and began her descent. She wore a stunning black-and-cream gown that was strapless on one side and had a rhinestone-studded clasp that gathered sheer chiffon on the other shoulder. The fabric showed her every curve as she glided down the steps.

Paisley clutched Dusty's arm. "You'll let me have one dance with Jack, won't you?"

"You'll have so many guys after you, he'll have to wait in line."

Miss Fontaine's voice filtered up the stairs. "Miss Paisley Finch escorted tonight by Chuck Brooks."

Paisley stepped onto the landing and curtsied. Dusty couldn't resist. She peeked around the corner, anxious to see what Paisley's date was like. At the foot of the stairs, Jack and a tall, sandy-haired guy, who looked like he might be a basketball player, waited. Jack's eyes were on Paisley, an odd, quizzical look on his face. Shock, Dusty imagined. Her cousin looked like a goddess.

Paisley nodded at Jack, then took the arm of Chuck and slid to the other side of the foyer with the other couples.

When her name was called, Dusty, too, did a little curtsy and walked slowly down the steps as they'd rehearsed.

Jack smiled and took her arm. He whispered, "They saved the best for last." The words might have been whispered in her ear, but when she looked at him, Jack's eyes weren't on her. They were on Paisley.

Paisley wanted to throw up. She could barely nibble on the hors d'oeuvres without waves of nausea slapping her insides.

Jack. The stranger who'd helped her when she'd tripped and fallen on the suitcase. Not Stacia's fiancé, as she thought. How could she not have known? Dusty could have at least shown her a picture of him. Had the momentary flash in his eyes been recognition or confusion?

"More punch?" Chuck, her date, had fair hair that accented his vivid blue eyes. Perfect teeth. Minty fresh breath. There wasn't a flaw that she could see, except one. He wasn't Jack.

"No, thanks. I'm still half-full." She held up her cup, being careful not to look around, to betray what was in her soul. It was an act she was able to pull off all the way to the country club. Her stomach churned with the knowledge that she and Dusty and Carmel had finagled it so they would be seated at the same round table for the dinner. Her only hope was that she knew Jack's place was across the table and not next to her.

Strains of "Chestnuts Roasting on an Open Fire" filtered over the loudspeaker system in the grand ballroom. Light rose from the fan-shaped sconces on the walls, casting a buttery glow. Each of the tables, set with white linen cloths and topped with greenery and poinsettia blossoms, had a single column candle flickering, beckoning. The effect was regal yet warm. High class, the way she imagined Xan's engagement party might have been if old Mr. Robbins hadn't breathed his last.

They found their seats and waited for the soup to be served. The girls, at least, hadn't been responsible for the food preparation; planning an event such as a ball meant consulting with caterers, doing taste tests, and choosing foods that didn't contradict on the palate. Like she would know.

Paisley made it through the soup, a thin consommé with bits of parsley floating in it. While waiting for the salads to be served, she turned to her date. "So, Scott, what's your major?" The words came out loud and brassy.

"Chuck. The name's Chuck, not Scott."

"I knew that. Silly of me. We've all been so nervous with making all the preparations and just dying to see who our dates were, and…well, here we are." She laid a hand lightly on his arm. "Love the tux."

"Thanks, I think."

Carmel's date, Hal, who sat to the left of Paisley, gave her a nudge. "When we signed up for this gig, we didn't know we'd have to wear penguin suits. Sure hope we get to take off these bow ties when the dancing starts."

Chuck ran a finger around his collar. "I hear you, man."

Paisley laughed. "I was thinking the same thing about my high heels."

Chuck dug into the salad the waiter had placed in front of him. Talking around the lettuce, he looked at Dusty on his right, then Paisley. "Where y'all from?"

Paisley said, "California," at the same time Dusty said, "Two Forks."

"Two Forks? You're kidding? We beat y'all in basketball regionals my senior year."

"What school?"

"Bassville Bulldogs."

"I was there. Were you the one who hit that shot at the buzzer to win the game?"

Chuck did a thumbs-up. "That was me."

While Dusty and Chuck bantered about basketball and Carmel and Hal got better acquainted, Paisley ventured a quick look at Jack. The candle between them flickered, the air fuzzy with the heat of the flame, but Jack's eyes didn't falter. They were focused clearly on her, his lips puckered ever so slightly. His eyebrows rose as the gaze between them locked. The wings of a thousand fairies flapped in Paisley's abdomen. Madly. Furiously. Prickles danced up her spine warning her to keep her cool.

Dusty leaned across to Jack and whispered in his ear, breaking the spell. Jack draped his arm across Dusty's shoulders and whispered something back, his lips grazing her ear. They were a stunning couple. A perfect contrast with Dusty's fair hair and Jack's deep brown hair and eyes. Paisley gave herself a mental slap. Nothing on this earth was worth risking the love of her cousin. Not even Jack. Their chance meeting might've made her heart somersault, but he was probably racking his brain wondering where he'd seen her.

Paisley turned to Chuck and asked who his favorite singer was.

"That's a tough one. Toss-up between Buck Owens and Marty Robbins, but guess I'm partial to ole Marty since he came out with 'Devil Woman.'"

Paisley gave him her most seductive look. "Guess we'll see who's a devil woman out on the dance floor."

"You're on."

The stage band from Miller College, who had promised a mix of country-western and rock and roll, started off with "Peggy Sue," a tribute to the late, great Buddy Holly. Chuck guided Paisley onto the dance floor and was surprisingly agile and smooth as he held her hands and led her through the jitterbug. He twirled her at the end and pulled her close.

"The devil woman don't have nothin' on you." His laughing blue eyes peered into hers.

"That's a line and a half." She kept her tone light and straightened his bow tie as the band started the intro to "Louisiana Man," and she moved her shoulders to the beat.

Other couples swept by, a rainbow of colors, a blur of faces.

A slow number followed, and Chuck's arm felt sure and strong around her waist. She kept her eyes on his face, willing herself to concentrate and fall for this guy. If not forever, at least for an evening. Chuck pulled her hand in close and hummed along to the music. Paisley relaxed into him and glided across the floor. Chuck couldn't carry a tune or a conversation, so they stuck with dancing.

The band had just switched keys and rhythms and begun singing "Bimbombey" when one of the Miller College boys tapped Chuck on the shoulder. "Mind if I cut?"

Chuck grumbled good-naturedly and handed her off. The newcomer introduced himself as Ben, took her hands, and showed her how to two-step. He had a funky rhythm that made them both laugh. Just as she was getting the hang of it, someone else cut in. The room spun with one new face after another until she lost count. Finally, the band broke for intermission and told them they'd be back with a few more favorites.

Across the way, Chuck stood under one of the fan-shaped sconces mesmerized, it seemed, by Sharon Kay. Amusing in a way, but knowing she wouldn't be missed, Paisley grabbed her evening bag from the table and headed to the ladies' room. What she really wanted was a smoke, but the dinky purse didn't have room for more than a lipstick and a pack of Dentyne.

Dusty met her coming out as she went in and gave her a hug. "Man, what did I tell you? Everyone is talking about you. No one knew you could dance like that."

"Like what? I'm barely able to walk a straight line in these heels, and I think I have a blister on my little toe." Dusty followed her back into the lounge. Paisley flopped on the settee and took off her shoe to massage her toe. "You don't happen to have a corn pad or something, do you?"

"No. Do you want me to ask around?"

"Nope. I'm ditching the pumps. I can sit out the rest of the dance."

"Oh no, you don't. Chuck won't let you do that. So, what do you think? You like him?"

Paisley hiked up her dress and unsnapped her nylons. "He's groovy. Actually one of the better dancers out there. And he smells nice." She peeled the stockings from her legs and stuffed them in the toes of her shoes.

"What are you doing? You can't dance barefoot."

"Wanna bet?"

Dusty shook her head and scooted out.

Paisley fixed a strand of hair that had come loose, freshened her lipstick, and waited until she heard the music start back up. A girl singer, it sounded like.

The lights were lower than they'd been, apparently setting a more romantic mood. She carried her shoes to the empty table and kicked them out of sight, then sat down. The singer had a curvy figure and reminded Paisley of Patsy Cline and not just because she sang "She's Got You." The song choice made a ripple in Paisley's stomach, but the singer had a natural beauty and ease on the stage, something Paisley had worked on but couldn't accomplish. Edie's words rang in her ears. *"You have to relax, baby doll, and have fun with it."*

That was it. As much as she cherished playing the guitar, Paisley didn't like the spotlight. She'd much rather be behind a camera, taking shots of other people. Like tonight. She would have loved to capture the look on Stacia's face as she looked up with adoration at Michael—the real Michael, who, with a stethoscope hanging from his neck, could pass for Dr. Ben Casey. She spotted Chuck dancing with Sharon Kay. Where was Sharon Kay's date?

"Why so sad?" The words were whispered close to her ear, but she knew the voice.

She turned. "Hey, Mr. Simon. Who says I'm sad? I'm just waiting on the right guy to come along and ask me to dance. And here you are."

He led her to the dance floor, his movements graceful. He kept enough distance that he didn't step on her bare toes, but when the song ended, his fingers remained laced in hers. He looked into her eyes and in a velvety voice said something in French.

"English, please. You know I'm your worst student."

His laugh was gentle. "I merely said you are a beautiful, one-of-a-kind girl. One who might benefit from extra French lessons, a little extra credit. I'm sure we could work something out." His lips were close enough, she could feel his breath on her cheek.

She bit her lip to keep from laughing. "I'm flattered. Honest. Truth is, I'm not all that interested. Not in French or in what you proposed." She twisted her fingers from his grasp and flashed him a smile. "You're a keen dancer, though."

She spun and started for the table, her face flaming, the sensation of blood pumping in her ears. Sharon Kay was right. He was perverted but not too bright if he thought she was stupid enough to fall for his flattery, and what in the name of Marie Antoinette was he doing coming on to her at the Christmas ball? She shoved a chair out of the way and pivoted—smack-dab into someone with a glass in each hand.

Cold liquid splashed in her face, temporarily blurring her vision, but she knew without seeing who it was. The room spun as her feet slid on the wet wood floor, and she fell into the arms of Jack Morgan.

❧

Dusty tapped her toe as the girl singer finished "She's Got You" onstage. Jack hadn't been at the table when she'd returned from the ladies' room, so she'd inched over to watch the other couples, wondering if he might have been dragged out to the floor by one of the other girls. Sharon Kay had both her forearms on Chuck's shoulders, her eyes lit on his face. A slow burn started in Dusty's belly. Chuck was perfect for Paisley, and Paisley admitted she was having a great time.

Couples applauded the band and milled around waiting for the next number. The girl on stage was joined by two male singers. The drummer counted, "One, two, three, and go." A rocking doo-wop beat vibrated the stage. Dusty skirted the dance floor in search of Jack, but Mr. Simon stepped in her path and offered his arm.

She sighed and allowed him to lead her to the dance floor. The trio onstage belted out "Blue Moon"—a fast number that had her spinning with a very suave Mr. Simon.

Sharon Kay whizzed by and smiled. "Great moves, Dusty." Before she could answer, Sharon Kay was gone. When the song was over, Dusty thanked Mr. Simon and said she needed to find Jack.

"Looks like he's tied up at the moment." He pointed toward the tables where Jack and Paisley stood close, Jack cupping Paisley's face in his palm.

Dusty squinted to get a clearer picture in the low light. It looked as if Jack had a handkerchief and was patting Paisley's face. Had something happened? Paisley's hair looked mussed, ringlets escaping the updo. Before she'd decided whether to go and see what was wrong, Mr. Simon pulled her into an embrace. *Oh, hunky-dory. A slow song.*

Dusty kept her body erect with a respectable gap between herself and Mr. Simon, even though, on each spin, he pulled her in a little more, his hand more than once moving below her waist. She closed her eyes and tried not to think about it. She liked Mr. Simon, but she didn't trust him. As the song neared the end, Mr. Simon whispered, "Looks like your boyfriend's found a new dance partner."

Jack and Paisley. Even with her hair flying around and no shoes on, Paisley was still gorgeous. An uneasy ripple went through Dusty's belly. She dismissed it as agitation at Mr. Simon. Paisley had, after all, asked if she could have one dance with Jack.

"Here you go, young man." Mr. Simon handed Dusty off to one of the Miller College boys. The next song was more upbeat, one Dusty hadn't heard, and her new partner, a guy with dark glasses and an easy smile, didn't seem to know it, either. They stumbled through together, and Dusty was surprised when he asked for another dance, one a little slower that worked well with the box step. Side. Back. Side. Forward.

He blushed when it was over. "Thanks. Sorry, I'm not a great dancer. I can't seem to get the hang of it."

"Nothing to fret over. I'm Dusty Fairchild. I don't think we've met."

"Ramsey Jones, ma'am. From over at Miller College. Jill was my date, but she turned her ankle and went back early. I'm with the other fellas or I'd a driven her."

"Oh, gracious, I hadn't heard that about Jill. My turn to be sorry. For Jill…and you. Guess you're stuck for the duration."

"Looks like it."

"It was nice to meet you, Ramsey." Dusty didn't see Jack or Paisley so she offered to dance again with him. Something about him was genuine and kind. Not pretentious. "Just relax a little and let the music tell you what to do."

He took a tentative step or two, then relaxed his shoulders and moved more smoothly. She asked where he was from and what year he was in college. Georgetown. Junior year.

"Why did you pick Miller College?"

"For their geology program. It's small, but there's a lot of hands-on experience and a great faculty."

"Geology? You're kidding? It's my dream to become a geologist. So Miller College has a good program?"

"One of the best in the southwest."

She wanted to ask a million questions. How hard was it to get in? What kind of hands-on experience? Before she could ask a single one, Jack sauntered up.

"Pardon me, fella, but they just announced it was the last dance. Dusty, may I?"

Ramsey backed away, but Dusty waved to him and mouthed, "Thank you," before she turned and was swept away in Jack's embrace.

CHAPTER 18

Paisley threw some things in her battered suitcase. "Let me know when Jack has the motor running and is ready to peel out."

Dusty shook her head. "What are you afraid of? You didn't even eat breakfast."

"Miss Fontaine will probably tell me not to bother showing up after the holidays. You saw how she looked at me when we were leaving the dance."

"You worry too much. It wasn't your fault Jack spilled water on you and your hair got messed up."

"I was thinking more about the barefoot dancing. I'm pretty sure I broke every rule in Emily Post *and* Miss Vanderbilt. I should have listened to you."

Dusty didn't answer; then Carmel breezed in their door. "Our ride is waiting. Daddy sent a driver over from the limo service to take me home to Jackson. I can almost smell the muddy Mississippi from here."

Dusty snapped the latches on her suitcase. "It's probably just the fog hanging over the bayou. Thick as pea soup out there this morning."

Paisley hugged Carmel and wished her a merry Christmas.

"Y'all, too. See you next year." She left, then stuck her head back in. "Did I tell you Hal is coming for New Year's? He's prelaw and wants to visit with my dad."

"That was quick," Paisley said when Carmel left.

"You never know. Sometimes it's love at first sight."

"What a bunch of hooey."

"Aren't you the cheery one this morning? After all the nice things I told Jack about you."

Paisley winced. That was the other thing bothering her. Jack. "You didn't have to do that."

"He feels bad about dousing you with water."

"It was my fault. I was making tracks getting away from Mr. Simon."

"You're kidding. I didn't know that part."

Paisley told her about Mr. Simon's offer. She sat down and tied the laces on her boots. She had a déjà vu feeling when she realized she'd put on the same short dress and leotards she'd worn the first day she was at Miss Fontaine's. Fitting. Wearing the same outfit on her first and last day.

She chuckled and gave Dusty a sultry look. "You think I should take Simon up on his offer? It might be fun to learn what Russian hands and Roman fingers are in French."

"You're mad, you know that. That's why I love you." Dusty added more toiletries to her train case. "I know what you mean about the groping, though." She made a face. "I didn't appreciate when he put his hand on my butt, either."

"You think I should go talk to Miss Fontaine?"

"About Mr. Simon?"

"No. About going barefoot. Maybe I should apologize."

"Suit yourself. I'm going down to wait for Jack."

Paisley sighed. She might as well face Miss Fontaine and get it over with. She added Dusty's camera to the suitcase, then grabbed it, her guitar case, and her purse and headed downstairs. She set her things in the hall and went looking for Miss Fontaine.

When she didn't find her in the parlor or dining room, she tried the kitchen. Sulee stood at the sink up to her elbows in dishwater. Paisley wished she'd eaten, but she was afraid of what riding in the car with Jack for five hours would do to her stomach. She snitched a leftover biscuit from the stove and asked Sulee if she'd seen Miss Fontaine.

"Not since breakfast. You want some butter for that?"

"This is fine. Was she in a good humor this morning?"

"Near as I could tell. I heard your doin's last night was a big hit. Mighta even heard your name mentioned."

Paisley groaned. "Anything in particular?"

"Only that you were the belle of the ball. It takes a gal with some gumption to take an old dress and wear it like it was next year's model."

"I never did thank you for giving me the lemon juice for that stain."

"Glad to be of service."

"Thanks for the biscuit. And merry Christmas."

"Likewise."

Paisley took a chance and went to Miss Fontaine's quarters and knocked. As before, the headmistress opened the door just a crack. "Yes?"

"Guess I'll be leaving soon. I came to apologize."

"For what, my dear?"

"My behavior last night. Dancing barefoot. I know it wasn't proper, and I probably gave you and Rosebriar a bad name."

She swung the door open. "Come in, Paisley."

"Are you sure?" *This can't be good.*

She nodded. "I must admit, I was a bit shocked when I saw you last night. No shoes...*and* no stockings."

"I got a blister on my toe."

She steered Paisley by the elbow to the settee, indicating she wanted her to sit. "I have a confession to make. When I first saw you on that fateful day in September, I knew you were going to be a challenge. Most girls who come here have been privileged most of their lives, and all I have to do is polish them up. They go on to become pillars of their communities. Once in a while, a girl like you comes along, and I'm reminded of myself years ago. It's true that this old house has been in my family for generations, but there was a time when I was young and learning my way. Some of my ancestors did things I'm not proud of. Slave owners. Poor treatment of the workers." She took a deep breath. "I'm not sure why I'm telling you this except to say that some traditions are worth saving. Others are best changed. You have a spunky nature that will serve you well if you learn what's important and choose wisely."

"So you're not mad at me?"

"I've had a few blisters on my toes." She laughed. "I wish I'd had the nerve to go barefoot."

"Thanks. I'll try to do better."

"You're going to be fine. Have a merry holiday. And give my regards to Mr. Fairchild."

❧

They stopped in Corsicana for lunch, just down the street from the Collin Street Bakery—home of the world-famous fruitcakes. In the front seat, Dusty and Jack talked about the latest news in Two Forks. At first, Dusty kept turning around and saying, "Isn't that right, Paisley?" or "You remember Eudora down at the bank?" or "What do you think?"

Paisley leaned up. "Don't mind me, you two. Just pretend I'm not even here."

She buried her nose in a movie magazine. On the cover, Natalie Wood lifted the hem of her yellow dress in a playful pose. Paisley flipped to the article, then read stories on how Jackie Kennedy saved her marriage and who Richard Chamberlain's latest heartthrob was. Edie ate this stuff up, always imitating one star or another, quoting things she'd read. Even Paisley knew they made up most of the junk in the magazines.

Still, she missed Edie and wondered which new fad she was chasing now. She could at least have written and told her she made it to California and let her know how things were working out with Ollie. Paisley shuddered and tossed the magazine aside. Before she got too worked up, Jack pulled into a parking spot.

"This okay with you ladies?" He offered each of them an elbow and escorted them to the entrance, then held the door for them. A waitress named Mildred showed them to a booth and told them the day's special was liver and onions. Dusty and Jack slid in opposite Paisley and took the menus Mildred handed them. She returned with their water, pulled a pencil from her beehive, and poised it over her order pad.

They all passed on the special and ordered burgers, making small talk until their order came. Paisley nibbled at her burger, unsure whether her stomach was growling from hunger or because of the chemistry between her and Jack. Even sitting three feet across from him made her think she needed her hands slapped for something. After a few bites, she leaned back and crossed her legs and accidentally brushed against Jack's Levi's.

She jumped, uncrossing her legs as spidery shivers raced up them. Dusty mumbled through her food, "You okay?"

"Fine. Just got a cramp in my leg."

Jack didn't hide his grin or the sparkle that came into his eyes. He whispered to Dusty, "I seem to have this effect on your dear cousin. Every time I'm around, she gets a little skittish."

Paisley shot back, "Who are you calling skittish? If I remember correctly, you're the one who threw water on me."

"Man, I'm never going to hear the end of it, am I? Perhaps you forgot that I was the one who caught you at the bottom of the stairs the first time we met."

Dusty pivoted her head slowly in Jack's direction. "When was this? Did you come by yesterday and not tell me?"

Paisley thumbed toward Jack. "He's the one I mistook for Stacia's fiancé at Thanksgiving."

"You two met at Thanksgiving?" She gave Jack a playful punch on the arm. "You told me you didn't meet Paisley. I asked you."

"I didn't know it was her. She tumbled down the stairs, brushed herself off, and ran out the door before we could exchange names."

"I was in a hurry. Mrs. Bennett was about to have a conniption, and my feet got tangled up. Or maybe I was blinded by the glow on your face because you were so anxious to see Dusty."

Dusty huffed out a sigh. "I can't believe you two met a month ago and nobody knew. That's weird. And sort of funny at the same time."

Jack signaled for the check. "Now that that's settled, I bet you two are ready to get to the ranch." He slid out of the booth and offered Dusty a hand while Paisley helped herself out. Without tripping. Now, if she could just get through the next two weeks without seeing Jack, she'd have it made in the shade. The last thing she wanted was to make trouble.

※

The minute Dusty stepped from the car, she was attacked by Lamb Chop and Juanita. She dropped to her knees and scooped them up, one in each arm, letting them lick her face. "You girls are in serious need of a bath and trim. Monday you are going to Miss Sadie's for the complete works."

Her daddy opened the screen door and waved them in. "Put them mutts down and give your daddy a hug."

Dusty did as she was told and said, "Something smells good. What'd you do, get one of the ladies from the church to send over a peach cobbler?"

"I've become a man of great resources. Hey, Stringbean, got a hug for your sorry uncle?"

Dusty thought her dad looked pale, a little thin, and told him so.

"Nothing a little home cooking won't fix. Jack, you can drop those suitcases anywhere and let the girls sort them out later." He draped his arm around Dusty's shoulders. "I've got a little surprise for you."

"Really? What?"

He raised his voice. "I said, I have a surprise for you."

Great. Sitting by the oil rig for ten days had not only taken ten pounds off him, but it had also stolen his mind.

"I heard you the first time, Mr. Fairchild. No need to be yelling now."

Dusty's heart nearly burst. "Rosalita!" She ran to her and pulled her into an embrace. "Oh my goodness. You're back from Old Mexico. How's your mo—" Even as she said it, she knew. Rosalita wouldn't have come back unless her mother had passed.

Rosalita ignored the half-formed question and held Dusty at arm's length. "Let me get a good look at you." Tears streamed down the cheeks of them both. Rosalita waved Paisley over to join them while the two scruffy dogs danced at their feet like it was a fiesta.

They had fresh tamales, black beans, and fluffy, yellow rice for supper. Dusty had convinced Jack to stay and eat, and after they'd had bowls of peach cobbler with fresh cream, he went to the den with her dad.

Dusty and Paisley cleared the table and helped Rosalita with the dishes. Dusty offered to wash and squirted dish detergent into the sink and turned on the water.

Rosalita planted her fists on her hips. "Why'd your daddy send you to some fancy school if you're going to come home and not even bother putting on rubber gloves? You want to end up looking like this?" She held up her hands for the girls to see.

Dusty took Rosalita's hands in hers, hands the color of winter leaves and as dry as parchment. She knew the crook in the little finger on Rosalita's right hand was where she got it caught in a barn door when she was a little girl. Dusty knew the exact shape of the fingernail on Rosalita's pointer finger from when she had held it and run it along the words in *Dick and Jane* trying to teach her housekeeper—her substitute mother—to read English. She held the rough, work-worn hands to her cheeks, emotion filling her throat. "I'd trade hands with you in a minute if it meant you were never leaving again."

"Life no give you promises like that. My mama, God bless her soul, needed me." Rosalita looked away for a moment, then back at Dusty and Paisley. "Nothing so sweet on this earth as being beside someone when they step from this world into the next." She brushed away the single tear that tracked down her cheek.

❧

Rosalita wouldn't let Dusty or anyone dwell on the loss of her mother. Not with Christmas three days away and work that needed doing. Dusty looked at her dad with new eyes, too. When they went to church the next morning, she and Paisley sat in the pew next to him instead of in the back row with the youth group the way she'd done since junior high. After the service, they peeked at baby Zachary in Susan's arms, and Paisley said she hoped to hold him after dinner if they were still coming.

"We can only stay for the meal. I still have some Christmas wrapping to do. See you at the ranch."

Dusty turned and almost bumped into Jack. "Have you been here all along? I thought you played hooky this morning."

He quirked his mouth. "Just running a little late. Hope that doesn't ruin my chances of coming for Sunday dinner?"

"Not at all. Rosalita always cooks enough for an army."

"That's what I was hoping to hear." He offered both his elbows. "You ladies need a ride."

Paisley told her to go on and ride with Jack. "I'll wait for Uncle Flint. He said he'd be just a minute—an impromptu meeting of some kind."

Dusty looked at the front of the church where two deacons, the barber, and the school superintendent laughed with her dad. "Yeah, that would be the gun and rifle meeting. They're probably planning their next pheasant hunt. Sure you don't want to ride with us? I need to go ahead and help Rosalita."

"I'll wait."

❧

Dusty's dad took his place at the head of the table where Rosalita had a pot roast and all the fixin's waiting. Dusty knew she'd been up since dawn, going to town for early mass so she could get back and have dinner ready the minute they walked in from church. They all joined hands for the blessing as her dad thanked the Lord for his provision and bringing them all together. He prayed for those not present and those in need. The words of his petition hadn't changed all that much over the years, but Dusty heard a reverence she hadn't noticed before. Maybe her daddy was getting soft.

Greg teased Paisley and asked her if she'd found any stable hands to kiss at finishing school.

"I have better things to do now. I'm the girl to call the next time you and Susan throw a formal ball. Or if you decide to go to France, you'd be wise to take Dusty and me along. We can ask directions and order from a French menu."

"I'll keep that in mind. What do you think, Sooz, want to go to France?"

"I'll pack tomorrow." Susan had a merry laugh, and Dusty thought she'd been good for Greg.

She wondered what a Sunday dinner would be like with Jack's folks. Sports talk more than likely. She turned to him and asked if he needed anything.

He had a blank look on his face like he'd been somewhere else. "Sorry. You were saying?"

"More roast beef?"

"No, thanks."

Patrick stuck his head in the door. "Something smells good." He was dirty, just in from his shift on the rig. He gave his dad an update and said he was starving. Rosalita waved a spatula at him. "You no sit at this table until you take a shower. Rosalita will keep a plate hot for you in the oven."

Dusty relaxed into her chair. *Home.* Rosalita sassing Patrick just like she had when he was twelve. She couldn't wait to corner her brother about taking her out to a rig, knowing he would probably treat her like she was still a buck-toothed kid whose only reason for living was to annoy him. He'd just have to realize she'd grown up.

When Patrick came down, his hair still wet from the shower, Paisley excused herself and said she wanted to go for a walk. Dusty thought she was a little too anxious to get away from the table and wondered if her dad's mentioning those not present had made her think about Aunt Edie.

Her dad asked Rosalita for a coffee refill and thanked her for the apple pie. He pressed his fork against the dessert plate picking up every crumb and then leaned back in his chair. "Nothing like a fine meal. What do you kids have planned for the afternoon?"

Dusty looked at Jack, who said, "I need to go in to the bank and work on those figures we talked about yesterday evening. I've had a couple of ideas and would like to run them past you when I pick up Dusty tonight for the movies." He lifted one eyebrow in her direction. It was the first she'd heard about the movies, but she gave a nod that she'd like that.

"Can't wait to hear what you have to say. Guess Patrick, here, will be catching up on his sleep."

Patrick said he got that right, but his tone was pleasant, not filled with the fireworks that usually flew between him and his dad.

Dusty's dad looked at her. "How about you and Stringbean and me going over to the north forty and cutting down a Christmas tree? It's plenty warm today, and it'll be good to get out of the house."

Jack told them to have fun and that he'd be back to pick her up at six o'clock. Greg thanked Rosalita for the meal and said they'd better be going, too.

⁂

Paisley hollered up the stairs when Jack arrived right on time. When Dusty stepped into the den, Rosalita and Paisley had shoeboxes full of ornaments and lights strung all over the coffee table and floor and were checking for burned-out bulbs.

Jack held up a section. "Here's the problem. Empty socket. Hey there, Dusty. Looks like we're gonna miss decorating the tree." He dug in a box on the table asking where the spare bulbs were.

Rosalita skirted a box of ornaments. "Be careful. Those old things is fragile as hen eggs. No be breaking them now."

Jack said, "Yes, ma'am," then stepped over and gave Dusty a hug.

"Are you sure Rosalita and Stringbean can be trusted to get this tree done right?"

A shoebox lid sailed across the room and hit Jack in the shoulder. "Who you calling Stringbean?" Paisley had her hands on her hips and a playful ring in her voice.

Jack sent the lid flying back Frisbee-style, but it fell short and plunked on Lamb Chop, who yapped and started running in circles. Her feet got tangled in the light string, and while she was scampering, she plowed into a box of ornaments.

Dusty sucked in a breath to yell, "Be careful," but the words stuck in her throat as ornaments vaulted from their partitioned spaces and rolled across the oak floor with an unmistakable sound of tinkling glass.

Paisley gasped. "Now look what you've done, Morgan."

Rosalita grabbed Lamb Chop and shook her head. *"Los niños."* She rattled off a string of Spanish wagging her finger at Jack first, then Paisley. When she realized they didn't understand a word, she shook her head. "I'm going after the broom."

Dusty dropped to her knees and began picking up the fine slivers of glass. Her eyes stung as sharp as if one of the slivers had pierced her. *Her mother's ornaments.*

Paisley knelt beside her. "I'm sorry. I hope these weren't anything special."

Dusty chewed her lip. It was childish to be upset over a few broken bits of glass. She willed the tears in her eyes not to fall and continued gathering up the red and green and gold shards. "Nope. Just a few old ornaments. Nothing special."

Paisley stood and punched Jack on the arm. "No one calls me Stringbean but Uncle Flint and lives to tell about it. I let you off light this time, Morgan."

"Did I hear someone cussing me?" Dusty's dad walked in, his cheeks ruddy from being outside.

Paisley batted her eyelashes at him. "Nobody cusses you, Uncle Flint. We were just having a little fun."

"Looks like you need to stop having so much fun and get this place cleaned up." He paused and looked at the broken glass Dusty cradled in her hands. His voice was thick when he said, "Mercy. Those were Aggie's."

CHAPTER 19

Paisley and Dusty crunched through the dry grass along the upper ridge of the creek bank, avoiding the sagebrush and cow
pies that dotted the earth. The water below them was shallow, Paisley knew, hardly more than knee high. They'd gone skinny-dipping
a few times where the only danger of being seen was if one of Uncle
Flint's Herefords came up for a drink of water. Paisley had agreed to
come as a goodwill effort since she felt responsible for the broken
ornaments...and ruining Dusty's evening with Jack.

When the glass was cleaned up, Jack had suggested they stay and
trim the tree. Paisley sensed Dusty's disappointment that she wasn't
going to the picture show with Jack, but when they tuned the radio to a station playing Christmas songs, Dusty brushed it off and
handed Jack ornaments to hang on the high branches.

Paisley kept her wits about her and refrained from making a
snappy comeback when Jack called her Stringbean again. His lopsided grin told her he thought of her as a kid sister. Whatever attraction had passed between them was history. One of those snapshots
in time that was a pleasant memory and nothing more.

Paisley had made a graceful exit as soon as she could to give them
time alone. When she got to the head of the stairs, she took a quick

look back. The lights of the tree twinkled as Jack draped an arm around Dusty. Strains of "Silent Night" floated in the air soft as a feather.

Paisley felt anything but heavenly peace as she slipped into her pajamas. Jack had seen her looking back, and for the briefest of moments, their eyes had locked, a silent longing passing between them. Paisley had turned quickly and sped to her room. Jack belonged to Dusty. They were a perfect couple. Yet as moonlight filtered through the organdy curtains, Paisley had remained awake, afraid of what her dreams might bring.

Now in the brisk morning, a swinging bridge with twisted wire cables for handrails came into view. "Race you to the bridge."

Dusty turned the collar of her jacket up. "You're on."

A cool breeze bit Paisley's face and burned her lungs as they flew across the cow pasture. They'd done it a hundred times, chugging up the hill to the highest point on the ranch. Every step tightened the knot in Paisley's stomach. When she was younger, she'd pretended she wasn't afraid of the bridge, of being suspended twenty feet in the air. Each trip up the hill, though, added another layer of dread, her throat a honeycomb of unspoken fear.

Dusty beat her as she always did and started across the wide boards, releasing creaks into the air. Paisley took the first tentative step, her faith in the structure as thin as the clouds overhead. New gaps had appeared since the last time she'd traversed the bridge. Rotted boards. She clutched the cables on both sides, willing herself not to look through the cracks at the muddy water below. Ahead of her, Dusty was already in the center, her palomino hair flying about in the wind, both hands on a single rail as she surveyed the horizon.

"See over there? That's the well that had the blowout. Daddy said you could see it from here." She pointed to the tower rising from the earth like a Tinkertoy creation, then looked at Paisley. "You doing okay? Not going to throw up like you used to."

"I'll try not to. It's just that heights give me this strange, creepy feeling. When I look down, it's like this urge to throw myself off. Not that I would, but I imagine myself free-falling, landing at the bottom."

"You've never told me that."

"Because it's embarrassing. And dumb, but I can't help it."

"I think it's the only thing in the world you're afraid of. You and Aunt Edie and all of your adventures."

"It's a big show. Edie's just as scared as I am; that's why she runs off every time things start going haywire." Paisley didn't want to think about where her mother might be at the moment. A gust of wind caught her off guard, and she gripped the rails tighter. She tried to keep her eyes from focusing, from looking down. Waves splashed against her rib cage. "Have you brought Jack up here?"

"Once last summer. I showed him how you can see the depressions and pools in the creek bed from here and where the best fossils are." She pointed off to the right. "And the view of the ranch house. Remember when we saw the white dust on the drive, we'd know company was coming?" She squinted her eyes. "Like now. Someone's coming up the drive. Probably Patrick or Daddy, but with the dirt boiling up, I can't tell who."

"Maybe Jack got off early to see you before he leaves for Austin."

"That would be nifty. Should we go?"

"Only if you're ready. I came up here for you."

"I know. And thanks. Daddy doesn't like me coming to the bridge alone, so I appreciate it." She looked again toward the horizon. "I doubt he's going to like me going out to the rig with Patrick, either, but I am."

"The big question is *why*?"

"It would be a shame to live right here with oil wells in my own backyard and go off to study geology without having stepped foot near one."

"What does Jack think about that?"

"What?"

"Your going to college."

"I'm not sure."

"What would you do if you had to choose between him and going to college?"

Dusty frowned. "If he loved me, and I'm not saying he does, then he wouldn't ask me to make the choice. If I loved a guy and he went off to the army or to college, I'd wait for him. So I don't know why it wouldn't work the other way around, too."

"Just curious." Paisley shivered inside her jacket. "I wish I'd brought a scarf or something. I'm cold."

"Let's go back to the house. Shortcut or long way?"

"Shortcut. I'd rather pick the stickies off my pant legs and get there quicker."

Paisley let out a sigh of relief when they were back on solid ground. They followed the ridge back down, then hiked through the pasture's tickle weeds and grasses, distinguishable only by their own shades of winter. The shortcut brought them to the back of the property where a few implements stood idle. The original farmhouse and a well house sat in a grove of trees, and it wasn't until they'd passed them that they came upon the modern additions to the ranch—a Quonset hut and then the sprawling ranch house. Uncle Flint's black F-250 sat in the drive and behind it a white Catalina convertible with whitewall tires and a dark interior.

Paisley brushed off her jeans and pointed to the car. "Anybody you know?"

"Nope." Dusty held the door for Paisley. "Guess we'll find out."

Rosalita stood at the sink in the kitchen scrubbing potatoes. She'd worn the skin down to the flesh on the one in her hand and only acknowledged them with a brief nod.

Dusty asked, "Who's the company?"

Rosalita kept scrubbing. "Supper guests."

"Why the mystery?"

"The only mystery I know is how your daddy can charm the oil out of the ground one minute and then act like a donkey's hind end the next. Go on, Paisley, and say hi to your mama."

Paisley swallowed. *Edie? Here?* She ran into the next room and straight to her mother. Edie's head jerked up. "Oh, baby!" She set her cigarette in the ashtray and stepped around the coffee table with open arms.

Paisley hugged Edie to her chest. "Mother! You're here." And instead of asking why she hadn't written or bothered to let her know she was alive, she closed her eyes and breathed in her mother's scent. A new cologne. Emeraude maybe.

Edie whispered in her ear, "Of course, I came. It's Christmas."

Paisley looked over her mom's shoulder to the sofa. And just as she suspected, Ollie Winesap sat, his lips spread into a grin. His features were set too close together, like someone had drawn a face, then added cheeks and an oversized bald head later. The skin on the top of his skull would be blinding if not for the freckles. And just as she remembered, a fringe of hair like a grass skirt hung past his earlobes. In slow motion, he rose and joined them, draping a stringy arm around Paisley's shoulders as he pecked her on the cheek.

"I must say, darling, you are becoming even in that horrendous getup. Let me guess, you've been out riding the ponies?"

"Hello, Ollie." Paisley dipped a shoulder and freed herself from his grasp. "So what brings you to Texas?"

Uncle Flint snorted from his leather chair. "Your mother has decided to grace us with her presence for Christmas. Not even a phone call warning us they were in the vicinity."

Edie crossed her arms. "I didn't want to spoil the surprise for my baby girl." She gazed into Paisley's face. "You were surprised, weren't you?"

"Shocked...and surprised. In a good way. I'm happy to see you."

"Hello, Aunt Edie." Dusty stepped forward for a hug.

Edie introduced Ollie to Dusty, and then they sat, first Edie starting to say something, then Dusty, then Paisley. Only Uncle Flint sat back and stayed silent.

Rosalita slipped in and offered iced tea to everyone, and when she left, Edie puckered her mouth. "Oh, I hope this won't be too much trouble for your domestic help, having to set extra places at the table."

Uncle Flint's nostrils flared slightly, but enough that Paisley could see he was seething. "You've been gone so long, sis, you don't even remember Rosalita. She's been with us more than twenty years."

Edie's laugh was thin. "That's Rosalita? The pretty young girl who came here from Mexico all those years ago? Oh, my. She's certainly plumped up, hasn't she?"

Uncle Flint shook his head. "We're not getting any younger, either. And it looks like a few pounds would do you some good."

"Now that I'm in show business, I have to keep my girlish figure." She had returned to her spot beside Ollie. He took her hand in one of his and patted it with the other.

Paisley closed her eyes, torn between wanting to pounce on the sofa to shake some sense into Edie and trying to muster up a shred of hope that this was the real deal for her mother. Before she could ask for the details, Dusty did.

Her mother and Ollie exchanged a look like they'd been conspiring on the entire trip from California just how to break the news. Ollie winked at Edie. "You tell them, hon."

"We were going to wait until Christmas dinner, remember?"

Dread wrapped itself around Paisley like a cloak. She hoped they weren't going to say Ollie was her new stepfather.

Uncle Flint put his feet up on the footstool and crossed one boot over the other. "I don't know about y'all, but the suspense is killing me."

Edie took a deep breath and let it out slowly, a grin tilting the corners of her mouth. "Oh, all right. Ollie has landed me an audition for a television show. With my Texas roots, they are seriously considering me as the romantic interest for Ben Cartwright on *Bonanza*." Her voice had inched up a note or two by the time she finished. "Isn't that wonderful? Me playing opposite Lorne Greene. I'm going to come to Virginia City on the stage with my teenage daughter and be the new dressmaker in town."

Edie's eyes widened. "Here's where you come in, baby doll. The producers want you to come and audition for the part of my little girl. Ollie told them all about you and your talent for singing."

Ollie rubbed his hands together. "Matter of fact, they're more than interested. There might even be a chance you'll get a musical number. And depending how the story line goes, you might be a love interest for Hoss, the big, friendly son."

Dusty held her hand over her mouth, her face lit up with excitement. Paisley scowled at her and looked away. Dusty was a sucker for Edie, and even though Paisley had tried to clue her in to Edie's wild notions, she could tell Dusty was secretly cheering for Edie.

Uncle Flint, bless his heart, wasn't so blinded by Edie and her antics. He rubbed his five o'clock shadow and said, "Nothing I like better than catching *Bonanza* of a Sunday evening. It seems to me, though, that the whole idea about parading women across the Ponderosa is to create an illusion of romance, have one of the fellas fall for a pretty gal, and then before they tie the knot, some tragedy strikes. The potential bride dies of a terrible disease or gets in the way of a stray bullet. Sounds like you didn't think this thing through, Edith. You get one, maybe two episodes; then your career is over."

Ollie nodded. "True, true. Only it will be just the beginning of

Edie and Paisley's careers, as once they break in, other offers will commence. More auditions. I predict this is just the beginning of stardom for your lovely sister." He looked at Paisley. "And you, too, darling. Merry Christmas."

One more of those beady-eyed looks from Ollie and Paisley was sure she would puke. It was enough that Edie got herself tangled up with promoters who promised her the moon and the stars, but to involve Paisley was pushing it. Why couldn't her mother see that? Perhaps if they had a signed contract, Paisley would believe it. She shuddered. At least her mother hadn't announced that she was marrying Ollie.

Edie looked at her with raised eyebrows. She wanted Paisley to say something. To be happy with this turn of events and hop in the convertible's backseat and head to the Ponderosa. The fact that her mother had arrived in a convertible instead of a beat-up bus should indicate a step up in class. The truth was nothing had changed. If Paisley didn't say something soon, her mother's face was going to freeze in that expectant pose.

Paisley rolled her tongue around in her mouth, trying to find the words. "Gee, this all happened so fast, I just don't know what to say." *Quit stalling.* "What I mean to say is, I'm looking forward to finishing up at Miss Fontaine's. I promised Dusty. And you didn't exactly ask what I might like to do."

"It's a once-in-a-lifetime opportunity, baby doll. Surely you can see that. It's the chance we've always dreamed of. You and me."

Paisley whispered, her voice papery, "Only one of us has that dream, Edie."

Her mother's eyes narrowed, the right one twitching. Edie wouldn't give up easily. But this time, Paisley wouldn't, either.

❧

The sound of a car door slamming started Lamb Chop and Juanita wagging their tails and doing spins in the air. "Silly pups." Dusty went to the door and opened it before Jack could ring the bell. "Hey there. You're just in time."

"Looks like I'm not the only company."

She held his hand as she introduced him to Edie and Mr. Winesap. "Paisley's mom surprised us by coming for Christmas."

Her dad stood and clapped Jack on the back. "Good to have you, son. Grab a seat if you can find one."

"I'm fine." Jack nodded to Edie. "I saw the California plates on your car. Is that where you're from?"

Edie told him she was and looked at Dusty. "Where in the world have you been keeping this handsome fella, sugar?"

"Jack and I met last summer. He's a CPA at the bank in town."

Her dad said, "Smart as a whip, too. Sure as the sun comes up in the east, this boy's going to make a name for himself."

Dusty's face grew warm at her dad's remark, hoping that Jack wasn't embarrassed by the attention. Edie came over and linked her arm in Jack's. "I want to know all about the boy my niece is dating. Everything." She led him to the sofa. "Scoot over, Ollie, and make room for Jack."

Jack looked over his shoulder and winked. Edie was a charmer, all right. She just hoped Jack didn't mind her fawning over him. But before he'd been sitting a minute, Rosalita announced that supper was ready. Jack took Dusty's hand in one of his and grabbed Paisley's with the other.

"Come on, kiddo." He draped an arm around Paisley's shoulders and gave her a hug. "Proud of me? I didn't call you Stringbean."

She elbowed him and said she needed to wash up. Dusty followed her into the downstairs powder room. "You okay? You seem kind of quiet since your mom's announcement."

Paisley turned on the tap and worked up a lather, keeping her eyes downcast. When she looked up, tears brimmed near the surface. "It's too complicated to put into words."

"Try."

"I'm glad she's here. Honest. It's Ollie. We have a history, and ever since Edie came to the tea at Miss Fontaine's, I've been sick with worry. I know I don't act like I give a flip, but I do." She kept her voice to a whisper. "She doesn't know that Ollie took advantage of me and cornered me in the hallway at the Penny Loafer. You can use your imagination to fill in the blanks for what he was trying to do. Luckily I got away, but if I told Edie, she would just blow it off and say I was exaggerating."

Dusty knew they were waiting supper on them, but it was unlike Paisley to blurt out her feelings. "I'm sorry about Ollie, but you more or less told them you didn't want to go back with them. Once your mom thinks it over, she'll be okay."

"You always think everything will be okay. You are so pure and innocent it stinks. I can see why Jack is crazy about you."

"What does Jack have to do with this?"

"You're just lucky, that's all."

A knock came on the door and Edie's voice. "Hurry up you two and quit primping. I need the potty."

"Coming, Aunt Edie." Dusty put her hands on Paisley's shoulders and whispered, "You'll be fine. And so will she."

Paisley nodded, but her expression had doubt written all over it.

Mr. Winesap was eyeing her daddy's prized sculpture—a Remington bronze of a cowboy on a stallion. He ran his fingers along the horse figure's mane. "These must've set you back a tidy amount. Original?"

Her dad shook his head. "Naw, just a fake. You gotta have money to invest in the real deal. Here, Winesap, have a seat."

Dusty cut a questioning look at her dad. The statue was genuine all right. Her dad winked at her behind Ollie's back. He had gut instincts not only about the oil business, but people in general, and if Paisley was right, Ollie could be a scoundrel.

Ollie picked up the knife beside his plate and looked at Dusty's daddy. "That's funny. Edie gave me the impression you do have that kind of money." He turned the knife in his hand to examine it, and Dusty wished Rosalita hadn't used the good silver.

"Guess you haven't figgered out my sis believes in fairy tales. Like being in a television show. That's a good one. Hey, girls, pull up a chair. Don't leave Morgan manning the other end of the table by his lonesome." Dusty and Paisley sat across from one another at Jack's end of the table.

When Aunt Edie came in wearing fresh lipstick, she sat by Paisley and looked around. "My ears were burning. Were you talking about me?"

"We sure were, sis. We were saying the gravy was going to be cold if you didn't hurry up." Dusty's dad asked the blessing and passed the fried chicken to Ollie after he'd taken a thigh.

"Well, if that's all. I thought maybe you were telling Jack about me auditioning for *Bonanza*."

Jack choked on a drink of water. "The television show?"

"The one and only. The audition is the week after New Year's, and get this—they want Paisley to come out and audition, too. Isn't that just the grandest thing?"

Jack had an odd look on his face as he turned to Paisley. "Really? You're leaving?"

Paisley passed the mashed potatoes to her mother. "They just sprung the idea on me an hour ago. Guess I'm still thinking about it."

Edie took a teaspoon full of potatoes, watching her figure, no doubt. "Chance of a lifetime." Her voice tinkled with excitement.

Dusty turned to Jack, but his eyes were on Paisley, his Adam's apple bobbling as he swallowed. Neither of them spoke, but the look that passed between them didn't need words.

An awkward feeling stayed with Dusty after dinner, and when they retired to the den, Edie told Ollie he better carry their things in before it got too late, that she needed her beauty sleep.

Her dad scowled at Aunt Edie. "I'm happy to share the table with you, but you and your manager here best be getting a room in town. Now that Patrick's moved back in and the girls are here, we're full up. I'll call the Wagon Wheel and tell them you're on your way."

Edie's head snapped up. "I'm sure Paisley won't mind bunking with Dusty. Or she could sleep on the sofa. My gracious, it's every bit as plush as most beds. What do you say, baby doll?"

Before Paisley could answer, Dusty's dad shook his head. "Guess you didn't get my drift. We're not disturbing the arrangements just because you decided to grace us with your presence."

"Then I guess we'll go over to the old house. You still keep it made up for your hunting buddies, I presume. Besides, it'll bring back some good memories of when we were kids." She turned to Ollie. "Our mama had one of those old-fashioned cast-iron stoves. Oh, my, she made the best biscuits you ever sank your teeth into. Not that I'm planning on making you biscuits on Christmas morning, but I'm sure since my *brother* won't even offer his sister a pillow for the night, we'll make do."

Dusty's stomach churned the way it did every time her dad acted so stubborn. She'd hoped to have a nice peaceful holiday and smooth the way for talking to her dad about the future. Not that she was blaming Aunt Edie, but a prick of irritation went through her. She hadn't even called and said she was coming.

Her dad ran his fingers through his hair, a sly grin spreading across his face. "Sounds like a jim-dandy plan to me. I'll get you the key. Just don't pay any mind to the odor. We had a family of skunks take up residence under the house, and we've had a heckuva time rooting them out. Shouldn't be more than a couple still nesting there."

Aunt Edie picked up an ashtray and reared back to throw it, but Ollie caught her hand. "Come on, darling, we'll check into that place in town." He looked at Dusty's dad. "Guess that Southern hospitality you hear about is nothing but a myth."

Jack, who'd stood back during the exchange, nodded toward the kitchen, so Dusty slipped out and joined him.

Rosalita stood at the sink shaking her head. "Those two be killing each other one of these days."

Dusty laughed. "I don't think it's that bad. I do wish they'd stop fussing." She turned to Jack. "Sorry you had to see that."

"Sorry I have to leave and can't see how it turns out, but I have to get on the road early in the morning. I'll give you a call when I get back."

Rosalita pointed to the back door. "Mind your manners and walk your guest out to his car."

God love her. She knew Dusty wanted to be alone with Jack, even if it was just a quick good night kiss. Jack thanked Rosalita for the meal while Dusty grabbed her daddy's shearling jacket from the hook in the utility room.

The sky was black and dotted with a million stars as they walked hand in hand to the pavilion where they'd danced at Dusty's going-away party in September. The bandstand and party tent were gone, leaving just the pergola with its columns that matched those on the porch of the house. They sank onto the glider where Dusty loved to curl up with a book on hot summer days. The metal of the glider, though, was cold even through her slacks as she shrank into the wool of her daddy's jacket.

Jack pulled her close to his chest and kissed her, his lips full and gentle. She closed her eyes and saw the look that had passed between him and Paisley. Had she imagined it? She felt herself pull away from the kiss first.

"You okay?" Jack's breath was warm on her cheek.

"Just tired, I think. And cold." She wanted to grab his neck and kiss him fiercely, but Jack pecked her on the cheek and stood.

"Me, too. And I have a long drive in the morning. I told my mom I'd be there for her Christmas brunch." He shrugged. "Betty and her gang will be there and a few friends. Sort of a tradition."

"Sounds great." She walked him to his car. "Merry Christmas."

He kissed her briefly on the lips and opened the car door. "Same to you. Tell Stringbean to behave herself, okay?"

Dusty stood and watched as he circled the drive and pulled onto the road. A puff of dust roiled up as he sped away.

CHAPTER 20

Going back to California with Edie and Ollie would be the smart thing to do. Edie would be happy, and Paisley would be there to help her mother pick up the pieces when another one of her dreams was shattered. She could handle Ollie if he tried coming onto her. A bitter taste bit her tongue when she remembered the incident at the Penny Loafer. Reliving it in her mind was a waste of time; she would be careful and knee him in the groin again if she had to. Her stepdad Leonard had not only gifted her with her first guitar, but also a few lessons in self-defense.

Jack was another matter. Maybe twelve hundred miles away would be enough that she would forget about the vibes that went through her every time he looked at her. They hadn't even had a decent conversation, and she shuddered to think of what she might do if they were alone together. It was a feeling akin to standing on the top of the swinging bridge and resisting the urge to throw herself off. Two minutes alone with Jack was heavy with the danger that she would fling herself at him and forever ruin her friendship with Dusty.

No man was worth that.

Her resolve remained strong through dinner on Christmas, and several times she almost told Edie that she'd made up her mind. She and Ollie had arrived around eleven with a handful of gifts. They'd insisted Paisley and Dusty open theirs right away. A charm bracelet with a tiny moon and stars dangling from it for Paisley and a coral silk scarf for Dusty. Paisley kicked herself for not getting the jewelry box from Mr. Simon, so now she was empty-handed. She tried to make it up by thanking her mother over and over for the bracelet.

"I'm glad you like it, baby doll. You know I'd give you the moon and the stars if I could. And in a way that's what Ollie's doing." Edie gazed into Ollie's eyes, but Paisley had to look away. If she could avoid the endearments between them, she might be able to stomach the trip back to California.

"I love the scarf, Aunt Edie! It'll be perfect with my navy sweater." Dusty went to the mirror, and while she knotted it at her neck, Greg and Susan came with baby Zachary. While everyone admired the baby, Paisley saw Dusty corner Patrick. She was no doubt talking to him about going out to the rig, and by the look on her face, she wasn't taking no for an answer.

After Uncle Flint asked the blessing, Rosalita brought a basket of dinner rolls. She had to have been up half the night making the turkey and dressing, sweet potatoes with marshmallows puffed and golden on the top, three vegetables, and two Jell-O molds.

While Rosalita was looking for a place to set the rolls, Edie picked up her dinner plate and turned it over to look at the mark on the bottom. "Spode. Gracious, I'd forgotten all about these dishes. They were Aggie's favorites." She whispered to Ollie, "Agnes was my brother's wife, but we all called her Aggie. Sweetest girl you ever saw."

Uncle Flint scowled but raised a glass and kept his eyes on Edie. "To the mother of my children who died tragically and too young."

Rosalita's hand slipped and dinner rolls tumbled out onto Uncle

Flint's plate. She muttered in Spanish as she gathered the rolls. "I'm sorry…you always say for me to use Aggie's dishes for special occasions."

Uncle Flint told her it was okay, and Rosalita hurried from the dining room.

Edie blinked her eyes rapidly and lifted her chin ever so slightly. "We all miss her, don't we?"

Uncle Flint opened his mouth to say something, but Zachary started squalling. Susan jumped up to tend to him, and the subject of Aunt Aggie passed.

After dinner, the men, including Ollie, went outdoors. Dusty asked Paisley if she'd like to hold Zachary. Susan handed him over and placed a cloth diaper on Paisley's shoulder. "For the spit-up," she said.

Paisley couldn't remember ever holding a baby and couldn't take her eyes off his creamy soft face, the cupid mouth that had a little bump in the center of the upper lip.

"From nursing," Susan explained and showed Paisley how to cradle him next to her. Zachary curled up like a kitten and made squeaky noises as he slept.

Susan chatted about feeding schedules and being lucky that Zachary didn't have colic like her sister's baby. "Listen to me. All I've talked about is Zachary this and Zachary that. Tell me, how are you girls doing at finishing school?"

They filled her in on their classes and pastry lessons and skipped over the drama of Mr. Simon, mentioning only that they took French classes.

"What about your friend in Houston, Paisley? Did you have a good time with her?"

Paisley told her about Prentice's father and that Xan ended up eloping and didn't return to school. All the while they were chatting, it occurred to Paisley that Susan was really nice, that she cared about what they did. Edie hadn't asked a single question about school or their friends. Even now as Paisley talked, Edie sat in Uncle Flint's chair and flipped through the movie magazine Paisley had left on the end table.

When Zachary whimpered and stirred in Paisley's arms, she ran the back of her finger along his silky cheek, and he settled down.

Susan smiled. "You're good with him. I wish I'd had the chance to go to finishing school. I'd be a lot better at entertaining the horse owners that come to the ranch. Greg says I do all right, but it would have been nice to learn some of the finer points of etiquette."

Dusty said, "You went to college, though, and that's something."

"I didn't finish, and all I've ever done with my music is give a few piano lessons. Of course, I met Greg in college, so not all was lost. What are y'all going to do when you get finished?"

Paisley laughed, and Susan realized what she'd said. "Not *finished* as in properly finished, but when your next semester is over?"

Without even blinking, Paisley said, "I'd like to take photography classes." It just popped out, and she knew right then, without thinking or analyzing, that the answer had been right below the surface all the time.

Edie ruffled the pages of her magazine and looked up. "Where'd you ever come up with that?"

"You know I've always loved to take pictures." To Susan, she said. "Dusty loaned me her thirty-five millimeter at school, and I'm learning a lot, but I'd like to learn more about lighting and how to adjust the shutter speeds."

Susan said, "Oh, I wish you'd come and take pictures of Zachary. All of mine are blurry or off center. How about later in the week?"

Edie cleared her throat and crossed her arms.

Susan turned to her. "I'm sorry. I should have asked if you'd like to come, too. What day's good for y'all?"

Edie waved her away. "It's not that. We'll be on the road soon."
She made a point of eyeing Paisley. "And if you're planning to come
with us..."

A gap filled the air. The big question. Of course, Susan didn't
know what Edie was referring to and said she didn't realize they'd
planned a trip. "So, where are you going? Skiing or heading down
to the coast?"

Paisley looked at Susan. "She meant to say that she and Ollie
would be on the road by then. I'll be right here, and I'd love to
come over and take pictures of Zachary."

❧

Aunt Edie huffed out to see what Ollie was doing, and after a while,
Dusty asked if she could get Susan and Paisley something to drink.
They both said they'd like a Coke so Dusty went to the kitchen to
fix them.

Ollie and Edie were having a heated discussion in the hall that
led from the utility room to Rosalita's quarters. She heard Ollie ask
what time Paisley would be ready to leave the next morning. "We
need to make tracks so I can do a wrap on the acts I have lined up
for New Year's. We can't be lollygagging in Texas all week."

Aunt Edie hissed, "She's not coming. You'd think buying her that
expensive bracelet and coming all this way to see her would show
her how much I care."

"She's *not* coming? You'll have to do better than that. You know
this deal is dependent on her. I promised them raw, young talent.
You'll make me the laughingstock if I parade you in there and pass
you off as young."

Dusty cringed and got out the glasses for the Cokes.

The day lost its glow, and as night crept on the ranch, Dusty
added a log to the fireplace and chatted with Susan. Zachary was

fussing with his routine being upset for an entire day, but Greg was in the office with her dad talking horses.

Susan asked Dusty to hold Zachary while she went to the powder room, and as Dusty paced in the front hall with him, she saw Paisley and Edie go upstairs. Dusty was glad they were getting to spend some time alone.

Zachary pumped his tiny legs as Dusty held him over her shoulder and patted his back. "Shh. It's all right. Mommy will be back in a minute." He waved his arms like a duckling trying to take off, then burped, a loud, soggy burp. Dusty could feel the wet spit-up in her hair and soaking through her sweater. Sour milk dribbled down Zachary's chin and saturated the soft pajamas Susan had just put on him. Dusty stepped back into the den and grabbed a receiving blanket from the sofa back and wiped Zachary's chin.

"Oh, goodness." Susan took the baby and had just cleaned him up when Greg came and said they oughta get going.

After their good-byes, Dusty went upstairs to change sweaters. The door to Paisley's room was closed, but Edie was talking and clearly distressed.

"It's not like the other times; Ollie's building his clientele."

Paisley's voice was too quiet for Dusty to hear, and she hated that she was even trying to listen. There was a long pause, then Edie again.

"Sometimes you have to make choices, sacrifices if you want to get into show business."

"That's what you don't understand. I don't want to be in show business or sing onstage." Paisley pronounced the words slowly and clearly.

"Here's what *you* don't understand. If I let you stay—"

"You're not *letting* me. It's my decision, not yours."

"Minor point. If you stay, then not only do I lose the best opportunity of my life, but that slimy brother of mine wins. He said he'd get revenge, but I never expected that it would be to lure you away from me."

"Leave Uncle Flint out of this."

"How can I? It's his money that's paying for you to wear fancy new clothes and go to that prissy school that's filling your head with thoughts of becoming a photographer. You could make more from one television show than you'd make in a year taking pictures of babies. And I bet Susan isn't even going to pay you. Fairchilds might have money, but they're cheap when it comes to their own blood."

"You always said money didn't interest you."

"I'd rather see my name on a marquee and live on the street than depend on my brother's money. Now, pack your things. We're leaving."

"You're leaving. Not me."

Dusty tiptoed into her room and closed the door, silently turning the knob. She sank onto her bed and stared at the ceiling, the smell of the curdled milk on her sweater sweet compared to the taste in the back of her throat.

One word was branded in her brain. *Revenge.*

For what? She played each word of their conversation in her head over and over. She knew Edie dreamed of seeing her name in lights. And she'd kept herself up. Kept trying.

Dusty must've drifted off, for when she woke up, the fragments of a dream clouded her thoughts. The moon shone through the curtains, and the house was quiet. It wasn't a dream, but a memory from Thanksgiving that disturbed her. She'd asked her dad why Aunt Edie left, and he'd been evasive, said she had to ask her herself.

Dusty hadn't even thought about it. The clock read 12:30. She'd been asleep four hours at least. Edie and Ollie would already be back at the Wagon Wheel in town. The sour baby smell drifted up. What if they'd left straightaway and were already halfway to New Mexico? She took off the scarf from Aunt Edie and peeled off her sweater and dress slacks. Digging in her chest of drawers, she pulled on an old pair of Levi's and a sweatshirt she'd worn in high school.

Revenge.

The word hit her in the gut. Her dad was strong willed and butted heads with Aunt Edie, but he'd never been spiteful.

Was Aunt Edie delusional? Dusty found it odd that she hadn't inherited the Fairchild money along with her dad, but her dad had always claimed he didn't strike it rich until he married Aggie. Maybe Edie had always thumbed her nose at life on the ranch. Yet Edie talked fondly about growing up in the old house. Dusty thought there was more to it—that something had happened to cause their rift. Whatever it was, Dusty intended to find out.

She slipped downstairs, hoping her dad wouldn't hear the T-Bird when she started the engine. She'd never snuck out in her entire life, except when Paisley had some crazy idea and they'd go down to the creek in the moonlight or ride Dusty's old roan mare over the hill to the stables. Her dad had always laughed and called them scamps. But tonight it didn't feel like childhood mischief.

As she tiptoed across the den, a sliver of light shone under the door that led into the dining room. She paused and listened. Rosalita's voice, muttering softly. She peeked in the door. Rosalita sat at the dining table with all the silver laid out, forks, knives, spoons all in a row.

"Hey, it's kind of late to be polishing the silver. We won't even need it again until next year."

Rosalita raised her head, wrinkles that hadn't been there last Christmas fanning out from the corners of her eyes. She pursed her lips. "Your daddy asked me to count and make sure nothing was missing."

Sadness crept into the corners of Dusty's heart. He didn't like or trust his sister. Or Ollie. "Well?"

"Every piece accounted for. What are you doing up so late?"

"I fell asleep accidentally, but I remembered something I wanted to ask Aunt Edie. I don't want to wait till morning, so I was going to town to talk to her."

"Are you crazy? It's the middle of the night."

"Well, it's important. Like counting silverware after midnight, I guess."

"You go back to bed. Edith and that man with her left. Said they had to get back to California. Everything's just crazy. You walking around in the dead of the night. Your daddy acting like a loony bird. Even me, counting silver when I should be asleep. You ask me, this whole place is crazy, and Rosalita should go back to Old Mexico."

"It is crazy. But I don't want you to leave. Ever." Dusty was relieved in a way that Edie was gone. She took one of the flannel silver holders and started putting knives in the pockets. "Come on, I'll help you so we can both get to bed. And since Aunt Edie is gone, I'll just ask you what I wanted to know. Do you know why she left Two Forks all those years ago."

Rosalita's eyes grew wide, and Dusty knew she knew. "It's none of my business."

"But you know."

"None of your business, either."

"Yes, it is. It affects our family. Paisley. Daddy. Me. And Aunt Edie. You saw how tense everyone was at the dinner table."

"Ask your Daddy."

"I have. He said to ask Aunt Edie."

She clamped her mouth shut and shook her head. Dusty knew Rosalita would never breathe a word. She walked around the table and held Rosalita's head to her waist.

A wrinkled brown hand patted her arm.

CHAPTER 21

Paisley put a fresh roll of film in the Canon while Susan changed Zachary's clothes. She'd already taken an entire roll of him propped on pillows under the Christmas tree and wanted to get some of him and Susan together. She checked the instruction book to refresh her memory on shutter speeds and drew the drapes to cut the glare through the windows.

She had Susan hold the baby under the arms and lift him up so they were nose to nose. Paisley shot a couple of profiles, then had Susan cradle him in her arms. Zachary grabbed Susan's finger, his face focused on Susan's. *Click.*

"That's going to be a good one. I like the natural look you two have."

"You have good instincts. I hope to have an enlargement made and surprise Greg for his birthday. And I should get a couple of Zachary wearing the boots and cowboy hat Greg got him for Christmas."

Paisley had just finished the roll when Zachary started fussing.

"This little guy loves to eat." Susan grabbed a receiving blanket and positioned him for nursing. "Do you mind if I feed him while we chat?"

Paisley shook her head and looked around. The living room of Susan and Greg's house was comfy but not fancy. "So you and Greg met in college?"

"Yes, he was an animal science major at Tech and wanted to be a vet. Truthfully, though, Greg partied a bit too much and didn't have the grades. We were fixin' to get married so he asked his dad if he could come back here and run the horse business."

"Who ran it before?"

"A foreman, but Flint wasn't crazy about him and had his hands full with the oil company, so he gave us this house and a stake in the horse operation."

"Are you glad?"

"Mostly. Since I grew up on a cattle ranch in the Panhandle, I'm used to living out in the sticks, but it took awhile to make new friends."

"I figured you'd have swarms of friends."

She laughed. "Not swarms. Girls from the church, and I've joined the music club in town. Just not a best friend."

"I know what you mean. Dusty's the best friend I've ever had."

Susan shifted her position and changed Zachary to the other side. "Where is she, anyway? I thought she'd come over with you."

"She...she had something she wanted to do so she let me borrow her car."

Susan didn't ask what Dusty was doing, so Paisley didn't elaborate. When Zachary was full and she'd taken him to the nursery for a nap, Susan asked her to stay for lunch—grilled cheese sandwiches and homemade tomato soup.

Halfway through the meal, Susan stirred her soup and looked up. "How about you and Jack? Something going on between the two of you?"

Paisley swallowed, the crust from the grilled cheese sandwich going crosswise in her throat. "What? Why would you think that?"

Her windpipe felt like a knife was lodged in it. She reached for her iced tea, her face hot. *What nerve.*

"Oh, honey, the air was charged with electricity at the dinner table last Sunday. He couldn't keep his eyes off you."

If Susan suspected, was it that obvious? "He's Dusty's boyfriend. I'm shocked that you would even say such a thing."

"It was a bit of a shock to me, that's for sure. Unless I read more into it than was there." She resumed eating like they were talking about the virtues of breast-feeding over bottle-feeding.

"I barely even know Jack. He treats me like a kid sister." The need to defend herself coiled inside her, but she kept her voice light.

"My brother sure didn't look at me that way."

"There's nothing going on." That part was true. Nothing had gone on. Nor would it.

"Whatever you say. Just a word of advice. Be careful. Dusty's the pride and joy of her daddy. And Flint Fairchild can hold a grudge a long time."

"You're not telling me something I don't already know."

"Just some friendly advice."

Paisley wanted to leave right then, but if she did, Susan would think she was guilty. She *was* guilty. Being at the ranch by herself didn't hold any appeal, so she spent the afternoon talking about movies and looking at Greg and Susan's wedding pictures. Safe subjects, and Susan didn't bring Jack up again.

By four o'clock, Zachary had eaten again, and they'd laughed and talked the afternoon away.

Paisley said she needed to get the film to the drugstore. "I'll bring the photos over before Dusty and I leave."

"Sometimes it takes a week, especially with the holidays, so if they're not ready, I can pick them up." Susan excused herself, and when she returned, she pressed a folded bill into Paisley's hand.

"You only owe me for the film."

"I know, but you and Dusty might get the itch to go on a shopping spree. You have to keep up with those debutantes, you know."

"Matter of fact, we're going to stop in Dallas on the way back. Thanks. And thanks for lunch."

"My pleasure."

Paisley didn't look to see how much Susan had given her until she got in Dusty's T-Bird. She fished the bill out of her pocket, expecting five or, at the most, ten dollars, but Susan had given her a fifty. She almost ran in to tell her it was too much, but the clock on the dash said 4:15, and it would take fifteen minutes to drive into Two Forks.

She sped down the dirt road, and by the time she pulled up in front of Gibson's Rexall Drug, her heart was light. She filled out the ticket for the photos at the druggist's counter and asked if she could put Susan's name on it, as well, in case the photos didn't get back in time.

"Of course." The druggist, a balding man in a white coat, looked over the top of his half-glasses. "Paisley Finch. Are you new in town?"

"Sort of. I'm Dusty Fairchild's cousin, and I'm visiting the ranch for the holidays."

"You must be Edith Fairchild's daughter."

"Yes, sir."

"Whatever happened to Edith? She was always raring to get out of Two Forks and become famous."

"She's in California."

"Did she ever make it into the movies?"

"Not yet."

"She had the looks, Edith did. Just here for a visit, huh?"

"Yes, sir. And thank you…for helping me with the film."

"You bet. Tell Edith her old heartthrob was asking about her."

"I'd do that if I knew your name."

"This here's Ritter Gibson, the friendly hometown druggist."

Paisley spun around and looked into Jack Morgan's laughing brown eyes.

She sputtered, "You. How dare you sneak up on me like that."

"I didn't sneak, but since you think I did, I'll make amends by buying you a root beer float."

Mr. Gibson said, "Good to see you, Morgan. Reckon Marylou can help you with that float over at the soda fountain."

Jack's hand in the small of her back was warm as he guided her to the counter and told Marylou they'd like two root beer floats.

Johnny Mathis crooned "Chances Are" over the store's speakers as Jack patted the round vinyl stool for her to sit.

"What makes you think I even like root beer?"

"Just guessing. Am I right?"

Heat rose from her chest, and Paisley was sure her face was red. "It'll do, Morgan." No way would she admit that it was her favorite. "Shouldn't you be at work?"

He swiveled so he was facing her, but she kept her legs straight ahead and turned her head just enough to get a glimpse of Jack. "The bank closes at three, but most days I don't clock out until five."

Marylou set the frosted mugs in front of them. "And we close at five thirty, so drink up." She gave a curious look at Paisley. No doubt everyone in Two Forks would be talking about the new girl Jack was seen with at the soda fountain.

"I was on my way home and saw Dusty's car out front, so I came in to say hi. What did you do, steal her car?"

"That's right. And then drove it down Main Street in her hometown so I'd be caught red-handed. Do you always make criminal assumptions about people?"

Jack let out a long, slow breath and swirled the straw in his float. "Sorry." He spoke quietly, as if to keep Marylou from hearing. "I

can't help it. You just do something to me. Something I can't explain." He studied his drink a while longer, then said, "I took a
psych class in college, and the professor said people make wisecracks
when they're uncomfortable. It's a defense mechanism."

Paisley slurped the creamy root beer. "I'm sorry I make you uncomfortable. I'm not trying to."

"It's not like that. Maybe I feel something that I know shouldn't
be there, and that's what makes me uncomfortable."

"In that case, it's simple to fix. If you get too close to a flame, you
get burned. It doesn't take a fire expert to tell you to stay away." She
took another sip, then pushed the glass away. "Thanks for the float."

CHAPTER 22

Patrick didn't show up until after lunch to take Dusty to the oil rig. She'd almost wished she'd gone with Paisley to see Susan and the baby. In typical fashion, Patrick didn't offer a reason for where he'd been, but he had a hard hat and a pair of steel-toed boots waiting for her in his truck. She was glad Rosalita was having her siesta so she didn't have to explain anything.

Patrick gave her instructions on the drive over. "Since the blowout Thanksgiving, Daddy's been a stickler for keeping only authorized personnel near the rigs. He used to bring me when I was little and let me climb out on the platform."

"Really? I never knew that."

"You were too busy tracking dinosaurs in the creek beds."

Even from a distance, the steel tower was imposing, more like a giant erector set with platforms at different levels and men shouting and moving about like worker ants. Patrick had explained that a special mud was pumped into the hole as the drilling was done, that it washed out the cuttings and debris into the slushpit. He pointed to a large pipe where the thin yellow mush came out.

They stood well back, the motor noise rumbling. Patrick stood close and spoke loudly. "Crew boss, one of the drillers, heading our way."

The man, bundled in a canvas jacket and steel-toed boots, scowled. "Fairchild, you're nuts. You can't bring your girlfriend out here. It's restricted access."

Patrick nodded. "Yes, sir, I know. And this isn't my girlfriend. It's my sis." The roaring noise halted, making conversation easier. "She wanted to see where our daddy's money comes from. Mind if I take her in the doghouse?"

"I figured she thought it came from the bank or grew on trees. That's what my better half thinks." He looked back at the well. "They're making a new connection, so you've got a few minutes before they start drilling if you want to go on up. It's your neck on the line if your daddy finds out."

Patrick said, "I know I can count on you not to tell him."

They talked about how soon they would get to the casing and the depth so far. Someone shouted for Shorty, and the crew boss yelled, "Coming!"

The man stomped off. Patrick turned to her. "Seen enough? Ready to go?"

"What about the doghouse?"

"Just a quick look, okay?" He looked at her and frowned. "I don't even know why I'm doing this. You've always been strange, you know that? Guess that's why Daddy sent you to that school, to charm the tomboy out of you. Apparently, it didn't take."

"I'm not strange, and I outgrew the tomboy stage a long time ago. I just happen to have always been interested in geology. That hasn't changed, and I don't see it happening in the future."

"And just how many girls do you think study geology?"

"I have no idea, but I don't see why a girl shouldn't. It's a science, like nutrition or anatomy, and girls seem to do okay as dieticians and nurses. Why not geologists?"

He glared at her. "Look at those guys. They have muscles in places you can't imagine, and this is grueling, dirty work. Not to mention the language that isn't fit for a kid like you. If Daddy knew I exposed you to this, he'd kill me."

"I don't have to work the oil field to be a geologist. I'm more interested in fossils and rock formations, but oil is part of that. I just wanted to see a rig, that's all."

"Then come on."

She followed Patrick, not as brave as she thought she'd be this close to the well. They climbed up the stairs into the doghouse, a small enclosure six or eight feet off the ground with lockers and bins full of extra tools and gadgets. A desk held a log of some kind and had a corkboard above it.

Patrick pointed to the corkboard. "Permits. Well locations." He riffled through the paperwork on the desk. "This is the driller's log. They fill it out daily with the depth, core samples, and so on." He motioned her toward the door.

"This is the platform, where all the connections are made and that up there—" He pointed to a place halfway up the rig. "That's the crow's nest."

She squinted and pointed to the top where another steel grid was, a worker moving about.

"Most dangerous job is at the top. He's guiding the pipe into the fingerboards, holding it still while they connect. Each piece of pipe is thirty feet long. Three pieces make a drill stand."

At the level where they were, men were moving chains and cranking with metal tools.

A shout went up that they were connected, and the engine noises started again. Dusty shouted and pointed to a cable. "Is that to anchor something or for balance?"

"The one you see over there is the escape hatch—a cable with a harness. If something goes wrong, the roughneck buckles up and shinnies down."

"Like the blowout on Thanksgiving?"

"Exactly. Hardesty was lucky. He got down in time, but not before the flames got him. He'll have scars the rest of his life."

The engine noise grew louder. Patrick shouted, "Come on, let's go. I have a date tonight."

When they reached the ground, Dusty asked, "Anyone I know?"

"Nah. Someone I met over at the college."

"What college?"

"Guess Daddy didn't tell you. I'm taking business management classes at Burroughs County. You don't think I'm gonna work on one of these rigs forever, do you?"

"I never thought about it. I'm glad you're taking some courses, though."

They walked across the dirt, Dusty's eyes on the ground to sidestep the ruts the trucks had made in the soft earth.

Beside her, Patrick stopped and spit out a string of curse words.

She jerked her head up and saw their daddy charging toward them like a rabid animal.

Patrick raised his arm in greeting. "Hey, Pops!" In two strides they were nose to nose. Patrick said, "Thought I'd come out and check on the crew. They tell me they'll be casing it tomorrow. Right on schedule."

"Don't get fresh with me. I ain't blind. What in Sam Hill got into you, boy?"

Dusty's hand went to her hard hat as she bit her bottom lip. "Hi, Daddy."

"Dusty wanted to see a rig up close."

She held her breath, the metallic taste of blood on her tongue. Her dad glared at her, his face almost purple. He grabbed Patrick by his coat collar.

"Simmer down, Daddy. I didn't think—"

"That's just it, you never think, do you? This ain't no place for your sister."

Dusty stepped between them. "It's my fault. I asked him to bring me."

She winced, afraid he would strike her, but she wouldn't back down.

Her dad whirled around. "Get in that truck and don't you ever let me see you doing something like this again. The oil field ain't no place for a woman. Never was and never will be."

"I can explain."

"In. The. Truck. Now." His nostrils flared, anger firing from his eyes.

She started toward the truck, then stopped. This was her fault, not Patrick's.

The noise of the engines crescendoed, blocking out what her dad said to Patrick.

Her brother yelled something back. Then she watched as her dad reared back and plowed a fist onto Patrick's jaw. Patrick stumbled back and lost his footing, planting his behind on the rough ground.

Dusty marched to her dad's side, her heart pounding. "Patrick didn't do anything wrong! It was me!" Her dad looked at her in disgust, grabbed her arm, and pulled her to the truck like she was a toddler. He yanked open the door and shoved her onto the seat.

"I better never see you pulling a stunt like that again. Ever."

He went back and gave Patrick a hand up, said something, which Dusty couldn't hear, then marched toward the rig.

They rode in silence on the way back, blood trickling from the corner of Patrick's mouth. Dusty found a red rag in the cubbyhole that didn't look too crusty and handed it to Patrick to wipe away the blood. As they made the final turn up the drive, Dusty gathered her courage. "I'm sorry. I shouldn't have asked you to take me out there."

No answer.

"If he was mad, he should have hit me."

"You? Get real."

"It was my idea. You took the rap for something that was my fault."

"It's all right. That's what brothers do."

"I couldn't hear what Daddy said. Did he fire you?"

"Not yet." His hands gripped the steering wheel. "Just when I thought things were getting back on track." He lifted a hand and slammed it on the ball of the floor gearshift. Swear words filled the cab. He shook his hand and looked at her. "It's nothing you did. He always gets his nose out of joint when Aunt Edith comes around. I've been expecting him to blow up before now."

"What's with him and Aunt Edie anyway? Everyone tiptoes around the subject like it's dynamite."

"You don't want to know."

"Yes, I do."

"Look what your curiosity got you today. Just go off to your fancy little school and forget about it. Daddy will be all right after he's cooled down."

Subject closed. Dusty took off her boots and put her loafers back on and told Patrick once again she was sorry. Inside she shook like the leaves on a cottonwood.

She would've been fine if Rosalita hadn't met her at the door. The next thing she knew, she was babbling to Rosalita about what happened.

"Why does Daddy have to be so bullheaded? If he was reasonable, I would've asked him to take me himself."

"Listen to you, blubbering like a sick cow. Your daddy loves you. He's protecting you."

"From what?"

"Only thing in this world more precious to your daddy than his oil wells is his little girl. You. If you'd open your eyes, you could see."

"He has a funny way of showing it."

"You go take a shower. Rosalita will make sopapillas. Make you feel better."

While the hot water beat down on her, Dusty remembered Jack was taking her to the movies. Surely he would understand that she wanted to spend time with her family. She didn't relish what would happen if her daddy showed up but going out held no fascination, either.

She dressed, then picked up the phone and dialed Jack's number. She told him she wasn't feeling well and wanted to stay home. "Maybe some other time."

"Sure. I'll give you a call." He sounded rather detached like it wasn't all that important. And maybe it wasn't. She sure didn't want to ruin whatever relationship they had by whining all evening. And she did feel sick.

Paisley was helping Rosalita in the kitchen when Dusty came down and whispered, "Rosalita told me what happened. Poor Patrick."

"It wasn't even his fault." The smell of Rosalita's chili made her stomach rumble. Maybe all she needed was to eat. Rosalita rolled out the sopapillas and fried them in hot grease while they ate. She sprinkled powdered sugar on top and brought them to the table with a jar of honey.

Dusty took their bowls to the sink and said, "I'll do the dishes later. Your favorite television show is fixin' to start. We can have dessert in the den."

Rosalita's eyes lit up as she hummed off-key the theme song to *Rawhide*, and they went to watch TV.

Paisley reached for the last sopapilla during a commercial. "If I eat this, I'll be sick." Powdered sugar, like tiny snowflakes, swirled as she raised it to her lips and took a bite. She mumbled with her mouth full. "You think Mrs. Pellerin will let us make these when we get back?"

"I don't see why not. She said to bring recipes for the ethnic unit we're doing in January."

"Shhh. You girls be quiet. I missed ole Rowdy when I was in Chihuahua with my poor mama."

Rowdy Yates, *Rawhide*'s handsome drover.

Paisley laughed. "If Ollie got me a part playing opposite Clint Eastwood, I might've jumped. What a pistol."

Rosalita dabbed at her eyes the way she always did at the end of the show. She'd made a valiant effort all evening to make Dusty feel better. Dusty kept waiting for the back door to open and her daddy to come strolling in, and when Rosalita saw her eyeing it, she said, "Don't worry. Your daddy came home while you take a shower. He grabbed his Stetson and said he had a meeting tonight, that he'd be late.

Route 66 came on next, but Rosalita said she was tired and needed to wash the dishes.

"Absolutely not. I told you I'd do them. You go on to bed."

Rosalita didn't argue and trudged back to her quarters.

She and Paisley watched *Route 66*, and during commercials talked about their day. Every other sentence out of Paisley's mouth was something about Susan or the baby.

"I'm glad you had a good time. We'll have to take the film to the drugstore tomorrow."

"I already did. Hey, I forgot to tell you, I ran into Jack there. He saw your car and thought it was you."

"What all did he have to say?"

"I didn't talk to him all that long. They were fixin' to close, and I wanted to get back since I'd been gone all day. You know, Susan is checking on photography classes at the junior college. Wouldn't it be groovy if I could come back here and take some classes?"

"What about your mom?"

"What about her? Ever since I realized that photography was

what I wanted to do, I can't stop thinking about it. I think I dig how you feel about geology now. Unless the trip to the rig ruined it for you."

"I haven't had time to think about it. It was louder and dirtier than I thought it would be. I feel terrible about Daddy and Patrick, but I'm still glad I went. I have a new appreciation for what Daddy does and the responsibility of running an oil company. Who knows? After I get my degree, I might even go to work for Fairchild Oil."

"I thought you wanted to visit volcanoes and hunt for rocks?"

"That, too. I have a lot of catching up to do before I've had nearly as many adventures as you."

Paisley made a face. "Not that again."

Dusty had stewed over the conversation she'd overheard between Paisley and her mom and then Rosalita clamming up when she asked about Aunt Edie. "Can I ask you something?"

"Fire away."

"First, I have a confession to make. I heard you and Aunt Edie arguing in your room the night she left. I understand why you didn't want to go with Ollie. He sort of creeped me out, too. I'm glad you're staying and going back to Miss Fontaine's. What I can't figure out is what your mom meant when she said my dad threatened to get revenge on her. Do you know why?"

Paisley pulled her knees to her chest and stared straight ahead. "Not exactly. I think my mom did something to get kicked out of the family."

"Like what? Our grandparents kicked her out? What would be so awful that they would do that?"

"Could be because she wasn't married to my dad. Maybe they wanted her to give me away, and she defied them and stayed in Two Forks with an illegitimate kid—me. All I know is the name on my birth certificate isn't Finch. She just always told people that to make it look good."

"But you all did leave when you were little."

"She wanted to make a name for herself, and Two Forks isn't exactly the center of anything."

"Well, it is the center of the oil field. But that doesn't explain why my dad would want to get revenge."

Paisley shrugged. "I have a feeling I know, but I don't think I can tell you."

"Why?"

"It's just a theory, and I'm certain you wouldn't like what I had to say. I love you too much to hurt you."

No amount of pleading would get Paisley to say any more. Just like everyone else, her cousin treated her like she was a piece of porcelain and might break.

CHAPTER 23

Paisley bought a new suitcase on clearance at Otasco in Two Forks with part of the money from Susan. With the rest, she bought a neck strap for the camera, a dozen rolls of film, and a book on beginning photography. For the remainder of Christmas vacation, she took pictures at the ranch—Rosalita making tortillas, Uncle Flint with his chin on his chest taking an afternoon nap, Dusty sitting on the front porch with Lamb Chop and Juanita in her arms.

On New Year's Eve, she took half a dozen shots of Jack and Dusty gussied up in their boots and jeans for the western dance at the Veterans of Foreign Wars hall and politely declined their offer for her to tag along.

The next week, Uncle Flint sent them off to Miss Fontaine's and told them to have fun shopping in Dallas. At Sanger-Harris in Dallas, the saleslady showed Paisley how to combine the soft, flowing fabrics she loved with necklines that flattered her small bust and long neck. They each left with two shopping bags full, so many new clothes that Paisley wished she'd bought two new suitcases.

They spent the night with one of Uncle Flint's investors since he didn't think it proper for two single girls to be *carousing around.*

If he only knew the places she and Edie had stayed over the years. Maybe he did, and it was sweet of him to go to the trouble. The older couple took them to dinner at their club and treated them like they were long lost relatives. Paisley almost hated to leave the next morning, but they loaded Dusty's T-Bird and headed east in a drizzly rain. They sang along with Patsy Cline on the radio at the top of their lungs and laughed about the windshield wipers swooshing back and forth to the beat.

When they pulled into Rosebriar's drive, Paisley ran from the car and up the walk. The rest of the day, squeals of laughter shook the walls, and Miss Fontaine welcomed them all. She had a new hairdo, shorter with burnt-orange curls around her face. She gave a knowing nod when Paisley marched in later with her new suitcase. It felt like a fresh start for everyone.

"Hey, Paisley! You've got mail." Carmel handed her a postcard with a picture of the Grand Canyon on the front. She turned it over and read: *Had a marvelous time on the way back. Stopped in L.V. and played the slots. The canyon is grand. Hugs and kisses. Edie.* Across the bottom: *xxooxxoo.*

Her mother was flying high. For now. Adventure was her opium. Paisley hoped Edie's cheerfulness was because she'd hit the jackpot in Las Vegas and not because she was tripping out on something with Ollie. The only difference between Ollie and the Asterisks was that Ollie drove a better car and could read a map. Paisley hugged the postcard to her chest. At least Edie had written.

At the dinner table, everyone talked at once about the movies they'd seen, going to the *Nutcracker* ballet, and their New Year's resolutions.

Everyone laughed when Paisley said her resolution was to give up Salems and be the first woman to land on the moon. "Just kidding about the moon. I'm afraid of heights."

When a lull came in the conversation, June Little, who played the flute like a bird and was as shy as a field mouse, said, "I have an announcement." She held out her left hand to show off a sparkling solitaire diamond. "Reuben Skinner and I are getting married." She drew *married* out into four syllables, her face glowing. "The wedding is June fifteenth at All Saints Church in Jackson, and all y'all are invited!" The rest of the meal was spent on talk of weddings and honeymoons with moans from some of the girls that they would never find the right man. Stacia offered June a stack of *Modern Bride* magazines.

Sulee brought in pound cake with lemon sauce, and long after dessert was finished, the chatter continued. Paisley slipped from the room and came back with the Canon. She stood outside the doorway and framed groups of two or three. She liked the weight of the camera in her hands as she snapped candid, almost playful shots. Girls with longings and dreams not unlike her own. She zoomed in and captured a shot of June's diamond that glittered like a sunburst under the light of the chandelier.

❧

Dusty got a note from Jack three days after she got back to Miss Fontaine's telling her he'd found the earring she'd lost the night of the VFW dance and that he'd bring it when he came for the Valentine party at Miss Fontaine's unless she wanted it mailed. He'd signed the note simply *Jack*.

It would have been just as easy for him to wrap the earring in a napkin and send it to her, but she guessed he hadn't thought of that. She wrote him a thank you and told him she was looking forward to seeing him when he came.

A warm feeling bubbled under her ribs when she thought about the dance. He'd been the same handsome guy she'd been attracted to the summer before, and they'd laughed and danced until they couldn't catch their breath. It had been a good ending to a frustrating holiday.

Miss Fontaine started right in with the units on wedding preparation reminding them that at least six months was needed to plan a proper wedding. Paisley had looked at her and mouthed, "Xan." Ha! She'd accomplished it all in one weekend and saved herself the trouble.

Dusty wanted to be excited about the classes and as perky as Paisley was. She tried to concentrate and picture herself carrying off the most important day of her life, as Miss Fontaine—who had never had the pleasure herself—put it. It sounded tedious, and every time the mother of the bride was mentioned, Dusty winced. Not everyone was destined to have a traditional wedding. And by the time she was ready for that day, she would have forgotten everything Miss Fontaine taught them.

It should have been enough to keep her mind busy, but she couldn't get in the groove, as Paisley would say. Dusty didn't realize she'd been letting her feelings show until the week after they'd returned to class and Mr. Simon asked her to stay after the morning session for a minute. He probably wanted to rake her over the coals for blowing the last test. She barely made a B, and she was lucky to get that.

"Please, have a seat." He sat opposite her, his hands folded before him. "I've noticed you've seemed rather melancholy, Dusty."

"I wouldn't call it melancholy. That sounds morbid."

"Perhaps preoccupied, then?"

"Maybe a little. If this is about my French test..."

He laughed and leaned back in the chair. "It wasn't up to your usual high marks, so I thought something might be bothering you."

"Not really." She wouldn't know where to start. The suffocating feeling that the walls of Rosebriar gave her. Being at odds with her dad, who acted like the incident with Patrick at the rig never happened. *Jack*. She enjoyed being with him and could almost picture him in the wedding lineup that Miss Fontaine was having them do, but that was way in her future. Which was probably why all the talk about weddings had burrowed under her skin like a sand tick.

The corner of Mr. Simon's mouth cocked into a half grin. "I'm a good listener. You wouldn't believe what I hear down at the store, ladies you wouldn't think had a care in the world, pouring their hearts out. I like to think I have an empathetic ear." He did have a genuine look, his pale brown eyes looking intently at her. She thought briefly of the rumors about him, even the Christmas dance when he'd let his hands wander below her waist. She didn't think he meant anything by it, and his eyes spoke kindness and caring.

"There is one thing. I'm interested in geology, as you know. I've heard Miller College has a great program. Do you know anything about it?"

"Miller College is one of the best kept secrets in all of East Texas. I don't know anything specific about geology—not sure they allow females in their program."

She moaned. "Not you, too. That's all I've heard my entire life."

"You didn't let me finish. Perhaps you could take a geology class or two to fulfill your science quota, and if you excelled, they would consider you. Did you do well in the high school sciences?"

"I was valedictorian of my class. I haven't mentioned it to the girls here because they already think I'm from Mars growing up on a ranch. I'd just as soon not be an egghead, too."

"That's one thing I've noticed—you're modest and quiet, almost to a fault. You'll have to cultivate your confidence if you want to be taken seriously in a male-dominated field. Have you thought about that?"

She felt her hackles rise, but she knew what he said was true. She wasn't exactly a doormat, but she might be a kissing cousin to one. "I'm working on that."

"Your academic record is in your favor, so that's a good start. Miller College is quite progressive, and they often host guest lectures. I attend occasionally when someone is talking about French literature. Perhaps you'd like to come with me next time I go and look at the campus. You could pick up an application."

"I'd love to have a look around, but no thanks. I appreciate your asking, though." She pushed her chair back and gathered up her books.

Mr. Simon walked around the table and put a friendly arm around her shoulders. "About your French grade, if there's anything I can do—"

He didn't get to finish as the door creaked open, and Sharon Kay walked in. She raised one eyebrow and said, "Uh, sorry. Didn't mean to interrupt. I forgot something." She clipped over to the reference shelf and pulled out a volume on creative napkin folding. "Carry on."

Dusty didn't know whether to laugh or stomp out and tell Sharon Kay that she had *not* interrupted anything, that she was having an adult conversation about career planning. Somehow she didn't think that her former roommate would be convinced.

The rumors flew like dandelion dust on the West Texas prairie. Dusty found it laughable almost. Mr. Simon was kind and sincere. Not handsome, but interesting looking. He was well traveled and knowledgeable. The way she hoped to be someday. On Friday, he brought a booklet about the Hope diamond, a magnificent violet-blue diamond from India that had once been owned by King Louis XIV of France. It had been cut from its original 112 carats down to the modern-day size of a little over sixty-seven carats. A couple of the girls oohed over the diamond while Mr.

Simon told them about seeing it shortly after it was acquired by the Smithsonian.

"That would be quite a rock to add to my collection."

"The Smithsonian might object to that."

She wasn't flirting with him, just conversing, along with her classmates. Which didn't stop the rumor that they were an item.

Paisley was livid. "You need to say something. I've known girls like Sharon Kay. They get their kicks out of stirring up trouble."

"Why should I? That would make me look pathetic, like I had something to hide."

"I still say, she's out to make your life miserable."

Dusty wouldn't tell Paisley that she was already miserable, stuck until the end of the year. Paisley had become so chummy with all the girls, she couldn't—she wouldn't—spoil it for her. Having intelligent conversations with Mr. Simon made the rest of it bearable.

After her talk with him, she requested a course catalog and the admission requirements from Miller College. The last day of January the packet arrived in the mail. She spent the evening poring over the pages, making up sample schedules. She read the entrance requirements and read every word in the geology section. Nothing about accepting only male students. That night, she dreamed of the tree-lined walks of the campus, hurrying to her next class and waving to the other students.

Sharon Kay was the first one to burst her dream bubble the next morning at breakfast when she whispered in her ear, "Ready for the French test or are you getting a little extra credit?"

Crud. She'd forgotten about the test, and it was on the tricky conjugation of verbs, her weakest area. She smiled at Sharon Kay. "Today? Oh, I forgot. Quick, everyone, let's have a little jam session." Inside, she felt sick. A feeling that only intensified as she stared at her exam paper. The college catalog had mentioned academic references, and she'd hoped to get Mr. Simon to write one for her. That would be down the tubes after she got her test back.

She completed the matching portion, trying to remember how the words looked when they'd gone over them in class. For the translation part, there were two paragraphs in French that were to be written in English. By the time she got to the last paragraph, the other girls had gone. Mr. Simon stood nearby, waiting. She felt like the time in second grade when she panicked over whether *Nancy* was spelled with an *s* or a *c*.

She gave him a weak smile and chewed the end of her pencil. Finally, she took a deep breath and scribbled what she thought was correct, then turned in her test.

"Having a little trouble today?" He glanced at her paper, his face unreadable.

She decided to come clean. "Actually, I didn't study. I got the catalog for Miller College yesterday, and last night that's all I did—looked at it. I'll be glad to retake the test on Monday."

"I like that you're honest about it. That's a trait that will serve you well in getting along with professors. Of course, they won't take the I-forgot-to-study excuse, so hopefully you've gained a little wisdom today. Sometimes that's more important than verb conjugation." He winked at her.

"Thanks, I'll remember that."

At the lunch table, Paisley asked what had taken her so long.

"My mind went blank, and it took me forever to finish."

Sharon Kay leaned across the table and whispered, "Unless you just wanted to stay after class."

"Could be. You all know I have this wild crush on Mr. Simon and just get breathless the minute he's around." She glared at Sharon Kay. "Honestly, I have better things to do than listen to this." She grabbed her plate and flatware, took them to the kitchen, and threw the utensils in the sink.

Sulee stood at the counter spooning rice pudding into parfait dishes. "Some reason you're marching into my kitchen throwing things?"

"Sorry, Sulee, sometimes I let people get the best of me."

"If it's the one I reckon it is, you probably had good reason and then some. You got to turn the other cheek."

"If only it were that easy."

"I seen a lot of girls come and go around here. Seems to me the ones with the acid on their tongues got the most festering inside."

"Are you saying I have a sharp tongue?"

"I ain't pointing fingers. Just giving you something to dwell on."

It didn't hit her until she was halfway up the stairs. Sulee was referring to Sharon Kay as the one with a festering inside. Sulee must be paying more attention than she let on, bringing food in and out. Serving them. What earthly problems could Sharon Kay have? Other than a superiority complex that kept her nose twenty feet in the air. She would dwell on it later.

Dusty threw her books on the desk and grabbed the Miller College catalog. A sketch of an ivy-covered building graced the front. *Thomas A. Jefferson Library*, the caption read. She thumbed through it once again and noticed a section at the back she hadn't read before. Campus organizations. Pep squad. Band. Athletic Club. French Club. Rock Hounds. *Rock Hounds?*

Meets third Saturday each month. Spivey Hall. Room 203.
Fossil Field Trip each semester.
President: Ramsey Jones.

Ramsey? The guy from the Christmas Ball.

Her mind was racing like her heart. She drafted a letter on her best stationery, then dug through the box of Paisley's photographs and found the one Paisley had taken of her with the pups. On the back she wrote: *Remember me?*

She tucked the photo in an envelope with the letter and addressed it to Ramsey Jones in care of the geology department. She grabbed her purse and skipped down the stairs. As she passed the dining room, Sharon Kay hollered, "Gee, Dusty, you on the way to a fire or a little tête-à-tête with someone we know?"

Dusty pulled to a stop and bit the retort on her tongue. She squared her shoulders and walked out the front door into a gray January day.

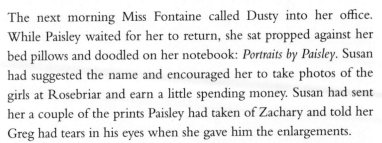

The next morning Miss Fontaine called Dusty into her office. While Paisley waited for her to return, she sat propped against her bed pillows and doodled on her notebook: *Portraits by Paisley*. Susan had suggested the name and encouraged her to take photos of the girls at Rosebriar and earn a little spending money. Susan had sent her a couple of the prints Paisley had taken of Zachary and told her Greg had tears in his eyes when she gave him the enlargements.

Ever since she'd been back, Paisley breezed through the classes, looking for opportunities to capture expressions and the activities of Miss Fontaine's on film. She took the finished rolls to the drugstore on Main Street and picked up the developed ones. She bought a new scrapbook, one with gold leaves embossed on the front, and pasted in her favorites.

One day, Dusty peered over her shoulder as Paisley sorted through a new batch. "These are really good."

"Some of them. Which one of these pictures of Sulee do you like best?"

Dusty studied the four pictures of their cook. "That's tough, but I think this one." She pointed to the one of Sulee sitting at the kitchen table having a cup of coffee, the newspaper crossword beside her cup.

"I agree. When Sulee caught me taking her picture, she grabbed the flyswatter and told me to skedaddle or she'd whack me. Who uses words like *skedaddle*?"

Paisley loved the microscopic view of life she got when she looked through the lens. More than that, it gave her something to occupy every spare minute so she didn't have time to worry over the knots in her stomach.

The ones called Edie and Jack.

She tossed the notebook with her doodling aside and picked up her guitar. She hadn't played much lately, and it felt like an old friend cradled in her arms. She tuned it and strummed lightly, waiting and hoping that Dusty would get back soon from her summons from Miss Fontaine.

Paisley picked out the melody to "Lemon Tree" from her Peter, Paul and Mary single and hummed softly. A lump formed in her throat. She knew why she hadn't played the guitar. It reminded her of the Penny Loafer and Edie. Almost a month since the postcard. She thought she would've heard something by now.

The door inched open and Dusty poked her head around the corner. "Get packed. We're leaving."

"What?"

Dusty broke into a grin. "Gotcha!"

"That is not funny. What did she want?"

"Well, not to give me the Most Promising Debutante award, that's for sure. Let's see." She put a book on her head and stood erect, pinching her lips like Miss Fontaine. "It has come to my attention that you may have acted with impropriety with one of our faculty. Perhaps you weren't aware that fraternization between male faculty and female students is strictly forbidden." Dusty blinked in perfect imitation of Miss Fontaine but couldn't keep a straight face. The book crashed to the floor and Dusty flopped onto Paisley's bed.

"What did you tell her?"

"The truth. That Mr. Simon asked me to stay after because he was concerned about me and that we discussed my college plans for next year. I assured her that except for a down-home Texas hug as I was leaving that Mr. Simon was as pure as the driven snow and that nothing was improper. She gave me a warning. No, wait, she called it a gentle reminder." Dusty sat up. "Crisis over. What are you doing today?"

"Taking pictures of Stacia and June. The camellias between the leaping fish fountain and the house are blooming. Wanna come watch?"

"Maybe later. I'm going to take a walk first."

Paisley grabbed her notebook. "What do you think about this? Five bucks for the sitting fee and five proofs. Fifty cents for each extra proof. Does that sound reasonable?"

Dusty shook her head. "You're like a dog gnawing on a bone. Once you get an idea in your head, you don't give up."

"Look who's talking."

Dusty held up her hands. "Truce. Guess Daddy was right. When something gets in your blood, nothing else matters. My best guess is that you need to charge enough to pay your expenses *and* make a profit. Jack's always talking about balance sheets, assets, and expenditures."

"I don't think I'm quite ready for an accountant. I'm just concerned because I'm not a professional photographer, and these girls are my friends."

"Friends who have money, don't forget that."

"Okay. I should charge at least double my expenses. And I can offer framed enlargements as well. Mr. Simon has some nifty frames down at his store."

Dusty made a face at her.

"Oops. Scratch Mr. Simon." She jumped up and grabbed the camera. "Toodles."

Thin clouds made a perfect canopy for the photo session. The day was cool enough for a sweater but pleasant enough for the last of January. The camellias, the same shade of pink as the heart of a conch shell, bloomed on plants that looked like they'd been there since the Civil War. Paisley had the girls take turns sitting on the stone wall of the fountain, throwing in pennies, then one of June hugging her knees to her chest, her full skirt falling gracefully almost to the ground. She took a dozen with the camellia background, another dozen with the spray from the fish's mouth behind June.

By the time they'd finished, the clouds overhead had darkened, the smell of rain teasing the air. Paisley looked toward the bayou where Dusty had gone and saw her in the distance, the pockets of her sweater sagging. Rocks, no doubt. She waved and met the postman coming up the walk with a fistful of letters.

"I'll take those if you'd like."

He handed them to her and bid her a good afternoon.

Paisley riffled through the mail quickly to see if there was anything from Edie. One addressed to her jumped out at her. Not Edie's writing. Ollie? No return address. She set the mail and the Canon on the hall entry table, then returned to the porch steps and ripped the envelope open. She pulled out the single sheet, her eyes drawn at once to the bottom: *Love, Jack.*

"Hey, it's fixin' to rain." Dusty sailed up the walk.

"Go on in. I'll be there in a minute."

"You okay?"

"Peachy." She scanned the letter quickly, then read it again word by word while raindrops splatted on the sidewalk, but it wasn't rain that wet Paisley's cheeks.

CHAPTER 24

L ord, give me patience just to make it to the end of the school year.

Dusty didn't know if being in church made it easier for God to hear her prayers, but she did feel better when she prayed silently during the petitions and meditations portion of the service. She reached across and squeezed Paisley's hand and said a quick prayer for her and Edie, feeling sort of sheepish that she couldn't remember the last time she'd done that. When she was little and Rosalita knelt with her beside her bed, she'd always remembered them. And her dad and brothers.

The walk she had taken the day before had cleared Dusty's head and given her a plan. Attend her French class as usual. Avoid eye contact with Mr. Simon. Don't give anyone a reason to suspect anything.

She was stupid to buy into the rumor Sharon Kay had started at the beginning of the school about Mr. Simon, for it had colored every thought she had about him. Had she somehow presented herself in such a way that *he* thought she was flirting? Perhaps she should talk to him and tell him what Miss Fontaine said, but that meant having a private conversation with him. She didn't take Miss Fontaine's warning lightly. She had the gut feeling that with her you were guilty until proven innocent.

Although she'd hammed it up with Paisley, Dusty wanted to crawl in a hole. If her dad caught even a whisper of the rumor, she was doomed.

The pastor cleared his throat as the organist played the last strains of "Sweet Hour of Prayer."

"In the book of Romans, we find these words." He held a well-worn Bible and adjusted his glasses as he found the spot he was looking for. "And not only so, but we glory in tribulations also: knowing that tribulation worketh patience."

Great. Maybe she shouldn't have prayed for patience after all. There was something soothing in the pastor's voice, though, as he talked about tribulations perfecting one's faith and drawing his children closer to him. When he asked for an amen, a couple of weak responses came from the congregation. Not much different than the church in Two Forks. Every time the sermon veered into sin and tribulation, people got squirmy. Dusty squirmed, too, as she thought of her Bible in the bottom drawer of her desk, untouched since she'd moved in with Paisley.

While they filed out at the end of the service, Dusty nudged Paisley. "You want to ride over to Miller College with me and look around?"

Paisley grabbed her arm and pulled her around an elderly couple who were dawdling up the aisle.

Dusty whispered, "That was rude. What's your hurry?"

They made it to the T-Bird, and Dusty had just turned the ignition key when someone tapped on the window. Mr. Simon.

She rolled down the window, realizing why Paisley had acted so strangely. "I didn't know you came to services here?"

"On occasion. I just wanted to tell you that I got a new catalog in the store called *Treasures from Mother Earth*. Some nice geodes, fool's gold, things for the rock collector. You're welcome to stop by and have a look sometime." He leaned down and smiled at Paisley.

"You, too, of course. I still have those jewelry boxes your mama had her eye on."

Dusty thanked him, feeling self-conscious as curious churchgoers eyed them on the way to their cars. "Sorry to rush off, but we need to get going." She waited long enough for him to step back before throwing the gearshift into reverse and backing out.

Paisley held one of her pumps in her gloved hand. "These heels are killing me. You think we could just go back to Rosebriar?"

"Sure. I just lost my appetite for adventure."

❦

Paisley didn't have an appetite for anything. Not since Jack's letter the day before. Dusty hadn't noticed what she was reading on the porch steps so Paisley didn't tell her. How could she?

Dear Paisley,

I'm a fool of the worst kind. I can no longer deny that you stir deep feelings in me that I can't explain. Dusty is a swell girl who deserves better than me. I know it would only hurt her and the special bond the two of you have if I came between you, and I fear that's where this is headed. I'm going to break it off with Dusty when I come to the dinner next week. The timing with it being Valentine's is rotten, I know, but I need to look in her eyes and be honest with her.

It will be good-bye for you and me as well. My contract with the bank is up in May, and I will look for another position. Maybe in Alaska. Somewhere far enough away so I can have a chance to forget about what might have been.

Love, Jack

A knife in her heart couldn't have hurt worse. Jack was right, though. Paisley didn't think she could keep up the pretense much longer herself. If it was that obvious to Susan, it was only a matter of time until Dusty realized it, too. Her cousin was no fool, just naive. And the timing *was* the pits with Dusty already on edge because of Mr. Simon.

The one consolation was knowing that not all men were like Sloan and Ollie and the string of stepfathers she'd had. Someday she hoped to find another good man. Maybe she, too, would be able to forget what might have been.

⁂

That week, there was no time to worry about rumors and who was dilly-dallying with whom as they only had five days to get ready for the Valentine sweetheart dinner on Saturday while still taking their regular classes with Mrs. Pellerin and Mr. Simon.

Mrs. Pellerin kept them busy learning how to prepare the ethnic recipes they'd serve at the dinner: French, German, Mexican, Greek, and Cajun. "Something for everyone," she said.

Mr. Simon didn't give a test on Friday but brought a collection of foreign dictionaries and helped them make placards out of card stock with the names of the dishes they were serving. On the back was the English translation in case they got mixed up and put the Moussaka sign next to the cheese enchiladas. Like it would make any difference, but it was a fun class, and they were dismissed half an hour early.

As had become her habit, Dusty avoided eye contact with Mr. Simon as much as possible and didn't see him approach until she felt the warmth of his fingers on her wrist. A screechy violin sensation started in the base of her spine and hissed its way to her neck as she tensed her muscles.

"Sorry, I didn't mean to spook you."

She stepped away and muttered, "No problem."

He closed the gap between them. "I need to ask your opinion about something if you have a minute."

"Can it wait? I promised Paisley I'd meet her upstairs." She clipped the words, her tone rude, she knew.

"It won't take a minute."

The room had a stillness to it that Dusty realized was because all the girls had gone. Her paranoia was getting the best of her. *Tell him you're uncomfortable.*

As if he read her mind, Mr. Simon said, "I'm afraid I've made you uneasy. I apologize for that. The truth is, I find you fascinating. Not like the other girls who only want to talk about what color nail polish to wear with their party outfits and what the chances are that Sandra Dee and Bobby Darin are having marital difficulties."

Dusty narrowed her eyes and chanced a look at Mr. Simon.

He shrugged and smiled. "Yes, I eavesdrop on you girls' conversations."

"I don't see your point. I'm interested in fashion and the movies as much as the rest of the girls. I can't see what that has to do with asking my opinion of anything."

"It doesn't. My comment was only on my observation that you're different from the other girls. I find that refreshing and am nearly certain you have the same regard for me. You've been receptive to my suggestions, haven't you?"

Miller College? Is that what he was talking about?

"You're right. I am uneasy being here with you. People are talking, and Miss Fontaine has already given me a warning."

He laughed. "To watch out for her dear nephew? I'm not concerned about my auntie and you shouldn't be, either. We're adults, right?"

"You said you wanted my opinion about something." She shrank away from him, the heel of her loafer caught on the leg of the table, making her stumble.

Mr. Simon reached out to steady her, and in the awkwardness of nearly falling and trying to run at the same time, they came face-to-face, Mr. Simon's hands on her waist, and not a breath of air between them. His lips grazed hers lightly as he whispered, "This. What do you think?"

"Adrian." Miss Fontaine's voice cut the air. "May we have a word, please?" There was no doubt in her mismatched eyes at what she thought she'd seen. "Run along, Miss Fairchild."

Dusty felt filthy and wanted to spit. This time there was no doubt of his intentions. Excuses filled her mouth, but her tongue was thick, unable to form words. At least Miss Fontaine had seen with her own eyes. She swallowed the elephant in her throat and croaked, "It's not what you think."

She didn't wait for a response, just grabbed her purse and stumbled out of the classroom into the dark hallway.

She ran into the downstairs powder room and locked the door. Her heart pounded as she tried to think what to do. She turned on the hot water, the pipes in the walls groaning. When the water was hot, she cupped her hand and wiped her lips, then rinsed her mouth and spit into the sink. She wished she'd stayed in the shadows and listened to the conversation, but the door had closed behind her. Miss Fontaine's doing most likely.

She sat on the toilet lid and pressed the heel of her hand against her forehead, trying to think but feeling only dirt and shame—shame for staying in the room with Mr. Simon for even a minute. The longer she sat, the more her insides roiled. There was nothing she could do but tell Miss Fontaine the truth of her innocence. She had to believe her. Somehow, though, Dusty didn't think she would. Remembering the cocky tone in Mr. Simon's voice sent another wave of disgust through her.

She couldn't hide in the powder room forever, so she splashed more water on her face and wiped away a mascara smudge, then forced a smile at herself in the mirror. No one would suspect a thing.

Paisley met her on the stairs as Dusty started up. "Where have you been? We're going to start setting up the parlor for the party soon."

"Sorry, I forgot. I sort of got waylaid. Come up to the room and I'll tell you about it."

Dusty shut the door and told her about Mr. Simon, trying to keep her voice from shaking, even as she seethed inside.

Paisley let out a long breath. "Sharon Kay was right. He's a creep." She shuddered. "Trust me, I know exactly how you feel. Filthy, right?"

Another wave of shame washed over Dusty. "You? The thing with Ollie? The reason you've been so worried about Aunt Edie?" How could she have been so callous to think of the incidents as mere bumps in the road of Paisley's colorful life?

Dusty bit her lip. "I'm sorry."

"For what? You did nothing wrong."

"For so many things. For what you've been through and not paying more attention."

Paisley shrugged. "You get over it."

"Will I? If I get the boot, then I go home in disgrace and Daddy will never let me hear the end of it. I don't even want to think about what I'll tell Jack. Whether he thinks I'm innocent or guilty won't matter. He'll always have doubts."

"Miss Fontaine wouldn't dare kick you out."

"I wish I had more confidence in that than you do."

"Look, I know you feel bad. You want me to tell them you have a headache and can't help set up?"

"I do have a headache, but sitting up here won't take my mind off anything. Come on, let's see what's going on in the parlor."

Miss Fontaine came in when they were nearly finished decorating the tables, which they'd draped with colorful cloths and centerpieces depicting various countries—a sombrero, a miniature Parthenon, the Eiffel Tower. Miss Fontaine bobbled about, clucking and making check marks on a list.

Dusty held her breath, weighing the possibilities of approaching her and requesting a meeting in private to catch her off guard or pretending nothing happened. Before she decided, Miss Fontaine pinned her with a stormy look and cocked her head toward her quarters.

Once they'd entered, Miss Fontaine pointed to the love seat. Dusty pulled her arms close to her body and listened as her headmistress talked about degrading the good name of Miss Fontaine's, her unbecoming demeanor, and projecting an image of being a loose woman.

When Dusty had heard enough that she feared she would explode, she said, "Excuse me. I couldn't agree more with what you're saying…if it were true. However, I did nothing wrong. Mr. Simon"—saying his name scalded her mouth—"approached me. I tried to tell him I couldn't talk, but he said it would only take a minute. He rambled about finding me attractive, and when I tried to leave, I tripped. He caught me and tried to kiss me."

Miss Fontaine shifted in her seat like she had a cocklebur in her underpants. "Miss Fairchild, the particulars are of no interest to me. It is entirely in the woman's realm to control situations such as these. You have perhaps lured him with your previous conversations or the way you looked at him. Men have an innate ability to pick up on signals from women, so whether you kissed him or he kissed you is completely irrelevant." Her gaze drifted toward the window, her words unconvincing.

"It's relevant to me and my reputation."

"Which I value as well. And in light of your upbringing without a mother, I'm of the opinion you would benefit from completing your course here. I've come up with a workable solution. Since Adrian will be my dinner companion tomorrow evening, I don't want to cause you untoward distress. I believe that you have come down with a stomach virus and should remain in your room for a day or two." Her eyelids fluttered, but when she turned her head in Dusty's direction, her gaze was on the wall above her.

The words of Dusty's dad came to her: *"You can always tell a lying son-of-a-buck when he won't look you in the eye."*

As much as she wanted to lash out at Miss Fontaine for her screwy philosophy and the solution to the immediate problem, she knew it would only make matters worse. Mr. Simon was too self-assured when he spoke of Miss Fontaine. He had a hold on her somehow. Whether it was personal or had something to do with Rosebriar she might never know. She looked squarely at Miss Fontaine. "Yes, ma'am. I'll be sick all right, but it won't be from a stomach virus."

"I thought you would understand. I see no need to speak of this incident again. Upholding one's honor isn't always easy, but it is worth the effort. I hope you feel better soon."

CHAPTER 25

Paisley was the one who felt sick. Dusty had tried to call Jack and tell him not to come, but the bank was already closed and she couldn't get him at his home phone.

Dusty said, "You'll have to be the one to talk to Jack when he comes. He mentioned getting together with a college buddy in Palestine on the way over."

Being alone with Jack scared the pants off Paisley. "Surely you could talk to him for a few minutes."

They'd gone back and forth on what Dusty should do about Jack and the whole situation with Mr. Simon. On whether she should tell her dad. And what about French class? Wouldn't the other girls suspect if she didn't show up?

Paisley wanted to blurt out that Jack was history as far as both of them were concerned, but she couldn't. Not now. Besides, it was Jack's place to do that. He might've even changed his mind about breaking up with Dusty. And yet, her gut burned knowing she should confess her attraction to Jack.

Even after they'd turned out the lights, Paisley stared at the ceiling and thought about Jack. She didn't believe in love at first sight. Still, she couldn't deny that Jack made her heart beat the rhythm of a new song, and when he made her laugh, it was like soaring on a wind current.

The sting of betrayal, though, was greater than all the music and laughter. The fact that she had flipped over Jack before she even knew his name was little comfort. Bitterness filled her mouth, and as she tried to find sleep, her pillow was wet with silent tears.

❧

At noon, she brought Dusty a bowl of chicken soup from Sulee and handed over a pocketful of cookies she'd snitched when no one was looking. "You have to keep up your strength, you know." They giggled and dreamed up ways to get back at Mr. Simon.

Paisley said, "I could put a rose on his plate at the dinner tonight with a note that says it's from his secret admirer, then watch him squirm."

"No fair, I wouldn't be there to see it."

"He might really squirm if I bumped into him and accidentally poured itching powder down his neck."

Dusty snorted soup through her nose. "And you just happen to have itching powder handy?"

Paisley batted her eyelashes. "You never know."

Dusty shook her head. "You're a mess, dear cuz. He wins no matter what." She pushed away the unfinished soup. "So what's the name of the Miller College guy you've got a blind date with?"

"Harvey, maybe Harry, I can't remember. All I know is he's on the student council and a junior. Jill said he's pretty cute, so it oughta be a blast. I hope he doesn't mind that I'm also taking the photographs."

"Drat. I was hoping for one of me and Jack."

"Sorry." *In so many ways.* "I have kitchen duty from one to three. Holler if you need anything."

Five minutes later she was back up the stairs waving a letter at Dusty. "Something to cheer you up. Mail call. A letter from Miller College."

Dusty ripped open the envelope and read the letter, then smiled. "The Rock Hounds meet next Saturday, and get this, they're planning their spring field trip to Dinosaur Valley on the Paluxy River. You remember it? Daddy took us once. It's over by Glen Rose, not all that far from the ranch."

"That's when you became obsessed with finding the remains of a T.rex in the creek on your ranch."

"Hey, it could happen. Sauropod, theropod, and carnosaur bones have all been identified along the Paluxy."

"Like I would know the difference."

"Trust me, the guys in the Rock Hound Club will know." Dusty hugged the letter to her chest and laughed. "Let's just hope I'm recovered by then."

⬧

Jack arrived at six o'clock. He hadn't called that he was in town, but Paisley, armed with the Canon, was taking the final pictures of the tables before the dinner when she heard Jack's voice and then Mrs. Swanson asking him to have a seat.

Chill out. You can do this.

Paisley lifted the camera and stuck her head around the corner. "Smile!"

Jack's eyes widened, the bouquet of pink carnations on his lap nearly falling. *Click.*

"Paisley. What in the devil are you doing?"

"I'm the official photographer."

He scowled and looked around. "I came early. Nerves, I guess."

"That's as good a reason as any." *Keep it light. Don't think.*

"You think Dusty's ready? I brought her something." He held up the flowers, half a dozen ruffled blooms in florist paper.

"Pretty. I'll take them to her. She tried to call you, but guess I get to give you the message instead."

"You...you didn't tell her, did you?"

Paisley shook her head. "It's not my place. Look, maybe we should walk outside."

He followed her, his fingers light as a hummingbird wing on her waist as she led him to the fountain and perched on the edge of the wall. Shadows came from the bayou in the east, but an orange glow from the sinking sun divided the sky into separate worlds. Paisley looked toward the light.

"I got your letter."

"You didn't write back."

"No need. What you said was partially true. Dusty deserves to hear how you feel face-to-face. That's between the two of you. The rest of it, you know, it's sort of crazy. I had this buzzy feeling the day we met, which I guess you took to mean I was interested in you. You're a super guy and all, but you were wrong about the rest of it. Whatever attraction you thought was there was just your imagination."

Jack took in a quick breath like he'd been punched. Paisley forced herself to look him in the eye, to not allow tears to well up in her own. She was onstage now giving the performance of her life.

Jack grinned, giving her heart a stutter. "Guess you won't mind if I call you Stringbean then?"

"It's a free world."

Dusk had come quickly and several sets of headlights approached Rosebriar. A couple of guys she recognized from Miller College stepped out of the first car.

"Your date, by chance?"

"Not yet, but he'll be along soon. Student council. Big man on campus."

"He's a lucky guy."

She remembered Dusty upstairs and turned to Jack. "What I needed to tell you is that Dusty is sick tonight—down with a stomach bug. She wanted me to give you this." She leaned over and kissed his cheek. "Good-bye, Jack." She took the carnations from him and said, "I'll be sure she gets these."

CHAPTER 26

Dusty and Paisley lounged in their pajamas the next morning while Paisley gave her a rundown on the Valentine dinner and her blind date, Harvey, who wasn't as cute as rumored, but he'd asked her to the movies that evening.

And they talked about Jack.

"Did you tell him why I couldn't see him?"

"I'm not a gossip. Besides, I don't know what you want him to know. Maybe he'll call to check on you, and you can tell him." Paisley clipped her words the way she did when she didn't want to talk about something.

Dusty wasn't sure she wanted to discuss it, either. Jack's last letter had been rather sterile, and unlike the old adage that "absence makes the heart grow fonder," she'd begun to doubt it. She didn't know whether it was all the drama with Mr. Simon or the sneaking suspicion that Jack was growing tired of her, but she wasn't as devastated as she thought she might be over not seeing him. Or maybe it was the letter from the Rock Hound Club.

Ramsey Jones had scrawled across the bottom: *Yes, I remember you. RJ.*

That evening, the upstairs was quiet—no radios blaring or girls hollering from room to room. Paisley had gone out with Harvey, and she'd heard the other girls making plans for the movies, too. Dusty took a shower and thought about going downstairs to raid the kitchen. Sulee usually worked on Sunday evenings planning the week's meals and might need a taste tester. She'd just pulled on her Levi's when the phone in the lounge rang.

After three rings, she assumed no one was answering so she ran down the hall to do so.

"Rosebriar. Girls' Lounge."

"Dusty Fairchild, please."

"Daddy! It's me." A sudden panic seized her. Her dad never called.

"It's not my way to beat around the bush, so I'll come right to the point. What in the name of thunder is going on there?"

"Nothing at the moment. I'm here alone."

"I had a phone call. That battle-ax, who calls herself a headmistress, called to inform me that my daughter has been carrying on with a faculty member, some foreigner."

"He's not a foreigner. He teaches French."

"So it's true. You admit it."

"No! Of course, it's not true. You raised me to know better."

"Not according to that woman. She said there had been certain *missteps* where you didn't conduct yourself properly. I told her to give it to me straight. Seduction of a teacher? What did you do, show him your legs or . . ." He cleared his throat, obviously catching himself from saying something rank to his daughter.

"Will you listen to me?"

He ignored her. "Sending you to that place was supposed to refine you, not turn you into a tramp like your aunt Edith. Lord knows, I've dreaded this day and should've seen it coming after the stunt you pulled going out to the rig at Christmas. It's bad enough you're the spitting image of Edith, now you're hell-bent on acting like her, too."

Dusty's head spun with his accusations. The best response was to let him finish. She'd seen the rants with her brothers over speeding tickets and blowing money. She'd done her dead-level best to never give her dad a reason to lash out at her. She pinched her lips between her teeth and said nothing.

Which was just as well because he wasn't finished and threatened to come and yank her and Paisley both out of Miss Fontaine's. "If this is what finishing school teaches, then you're done. I'll send you to junior college and let you get a secretary degree so I can keep an eye on you."

She remained silent, boiling inside. Maybe she should do something rash and wild, like join the carnival or hop in her T-Bird and cruise to California to be with Aunt Edie.

"Are you there? Have you heard a blasted word I've said?"

"I'm here, Daddy."

"Then speak up."

She took a deep breath, willing her voice to be strong. "I didn't do what Miss Fontaine said, but Mr. Simon did make advances toward me."

"I'll kill that—"

"Stop it, Daddy. Let me finish. I thought Mr. Simon was nice, but I misjudged him. That's what I'm guilty of. Miss Fontaine chose to believe him over me, and you can believe whatever you'd like, but that's the truth."

"If I find out otherwise, I'll be there faster than greased lightning."

The temptation to tell him she'd like nothing better than to leave was on the tip of her tongue, but she wasn't a quitter. And neither was Paisley. All she said was, "Yes, sir, I know you will, but we'd both like to finish the semester. No more incidents."

"I hope not."

"Can I ask you something?"

"Shoot."

"What did Aunt Edie do to make you despise her?"

The line went dead. Or so she thought. She expected him to say it was none of her business or to ask Aunt Edie.

He didn't, though, and she could hear his breaths in and out before he said, "It was her fault Aggie died. Because of her, you don't have a mother." He slammed the receiver in her ear.

Dusty felt like she'd been punched in the belly.

No! It's not true. She must have misunderstood. Heard wrong. It wasn't true.

Breathe in.

Breathe out.

Aunt Edie killed her mother? How? Was Aunt Edie driving when her car hit the cattle truck? She'd always heard her mother was alone in the car. Is that why Aunt Edie stayed away? Why else would her dad have such a venomous attitude toward her?

The walls closed in on her, the air wavy and thin. She ran to her room. She had to get out, go somewhere. Anywhere. Just away from this house. This nightmare. She grabbed the first sweater she saw and ran down the servant stairs that came out next to the carriage house. She stuffed her hands in her pockets and realized they were full of rocks from the last time she'd worn it. She cupped one in each hand and walked in circles trying to think.

No wonder no one would tell her anything about Aunt Edie. Did Paisley know? Somehow, Dusty thought she knew or suspected. Patrick. Rosalita. Greg. They all knew but her. Why hadn't they told her? For someone who built a life on dealing honestly with people, her dad had just blown it! And he'd told her on the phone, not looking her in the eye when he said it.

Dusty walked faster, trying not to think at all. She wanted to scream and lash out, but settled for letting her feet bruise the dirt as she stamped one foot in front of the other. Cold moist air seeped into her bones, whether from the night air or her own misery, she didn't know. Or care. She looked up, a fog blanketing her, and yelled at God, "Thanks a lot for helping me learn to be patient. Any other things you want to dump on me now?"

The heavens didn't answer.

The fog thickened and she could no longer see the road or anything at all. She wasn't even sure which direction she was going. She slowed her pace, wondering if she would end up walking into the bayou and drowning. She laughed. At least she knew trees bordered the bayou. She was more likely to bump into a tree and be knocked unconscious.

Whack! Her knee slammed into something and she toppled forward, fire shooting through the spot she'd hit. She landed on all fours, dead grass and nettles biting her palms. She felt around in the dark, her fingers coming in contact with what she'd fallen over. A stump, sawed off, the bark coarse and rough. She hauled herself up and sat on the stump, rubbing her knee.

Tears trickled from her eyes at first, then came like someone had turned on a faucet. She wrapped her sweater tighter around her middle and rocked back and forth. Groaning. Crying.

This is stupid! What good did crying ever do? Not only that, if she didn't get her wits about her, she'd end up really lost and miss curfew. And this time she would be guilty.

It sort of startled Dusty that she even cared after the past two days. She looked around her, the fog not quite as thick as she'd thought. She could make out the merest light off to her left. She wiped the wet spots from her cheeks and started toward the glow, hoping it wasn't her mind playing tricks on her. A tiny bungalow came into view. She hurried up two wooden steps onto the porch and knocked.

A gentleman opened the door partway, creamy light pouring from inside. His dark eyes registered surprise followed immediately by a scowl. Behind him a young girl with a round face and hair the color of honey clapped and chattered, "Company. Please, come in." Her voice had a singsong nature to it, and her curious, almond-shaped eyes peered at Dusty.

Dusty smiled. "I'm sorry. I'm one of the girls from Rosebriar. I was taking a walk and didn't see the fog come in. Could you tell me how to get back?"

The man waved the girl back and stepped onto the porch, closing the door behind him. As his tall, thin frame towered over her, something about him was familiar—his dark skin, the salt-and-pepper hair that kinked close to his scalp.

"Rosebriar? What did you say yo' name was?"

"I didn't, but it's Dusty Fairchild. I'm one of Miss Fontaine's students."

"Lost, hey? Reckon you best be getting back as quick as you can. Just follow the same trail you got here on." He pointed a calloused finger.

Dusty squinted in the direction he pointed. The fog had thinned, and she could make out a rail fence in front of the house and a dark ribbon of a trail to the left. She turned back to thank him and knew where she'd seen him. He'd brought the Christmas tree into the parlor. He'd been courteous to Miss Fontaine but casual, too, like an old friend. It was more than that, though. She'd seen him before in the meadow with the girl, only her hair had been in pigtails.

"If you know what's good for you, you best not be coming this way again." He spun on his heels, went back in, and started to close the door.

An odd sensation brought goose bumps to Dusty's arms. She rubbed them, the air chilly and moist, the smell of hay from the pasture tickling her nose. Why was the man so abrupt, so intent on getting rid of her? The warning tone in his voice was so unlike the pleasant scene she'd seen when the child pumped her legs and flew through the air on the tree swing. Another memory popped to the surface. The day she'd been caught in the rain and Delia had lectured her about trespassing.

A secret lurked in the cottage.

She turned suddenly, catching the man off guard, and stepped forward into the house before he could close the door completely. She found herself in a small living room with tasteful furniture. It was well kept, but it wasn't the furnishings that interested her; it was the girl with almond eyes.

"I don't mean to be rude..."

And yet she was, stepping into a place where she'd not been invited. The man looked down at her, black eyes unmoving as were his lips.

"I just remembered where I'd seen you. You brought the tree to the house at Christmas."

"Yes, that would be me." His voice was mellow but guarded.

The child, who wasn't a child at all but a young woman, smiled. "Santa gave me a teddy bear at Christmas. Wanna see?"

"I'd like that very much."

She disappeared into an adjoining room.

The man extended his hand, which easily made two of Dusty's. "Winston Guilford. And you are Dusty, I believe you said. I've heard my wife speak of you."

"Your wife?"

"Sulee to you, miss. Guess you didn't know her last name."

"No, sir, I don't believe I did. I've seen her walking the path that leads by the horse pasture before. Is your home part of the Rosebriar property?"

"Indeed it be. The old caretaker's cottage."

The girl returned with a fluffy tan bear with button eyes and jointed arms and legs. "This, Buddy." She held it up, then hugged it to her chest.

The girl-woman had an innocence and unsuspecting nature that tugged at Dusty. She should just leave and forget she'd happened upon this oddly matched pair. The man clearly wasn't her father, not with the child's fair skin. Dusty itched to know more, but her sense of propriety was stronger.

She reached in her pocket and pulled out one of the quartz-flecked stones she found along the bayou. "Do you like rocks?"

The girl smiled and looked at the man, who nodded that it was all right to take the stone. The girl cupped it in her palm. "Robin like rocks."

"So do I. They're my favorite thing to look for when I go for walks." Dusty lifted her chin. "I should be going. I'm sorry for the intrusion."

The front door opened and Sulee walked in. The eyes of Rosebriar's cook grew round; her head lurched forward. "Dusty! What...how?" She made fish-mouth moves with her lips, but no words came out. Her head jerked toward the man. "Winston. What is the meaning of this?"

Winston chuckled. "It's all right. Dusty got herself lost in the fog and this here's where she ended up."

Sulee scowled at Winston, then Dusty, as Robin came and wrapped one arm around Sulee. The child looked up. "Mommy come?"

"She'll be along after a while."

Dusty was sorry for the awkwardness she'd caused and surprised at what Sulee said next.

"Winston, did you offer our guest a cup of tea?"

"She just got here."

Winston turned on the television for Robin, then nodded toward a door that led to a kitchen with a dining alcove. He put the kettle on and nodded toward a red vinyl chair for Dusty to be seated. Sulee hung her sweater on a hook and sat opposite.

No one spoke until the tea was poured, and even then, it was Dusty who spoke first. "Thank you for the tea." She looked toward the front room. "Robin asked about her mother. You must be watching her until her mother comes?"

Sulee folded her hands neatly on the table and gathered her words carefully, it seemed. "Winston and I are her caretakers. Have been so since she was an infant."

The events of the past days swirled in Dusty's head. Her dad and Edie. Miss Fontaine and her unbending notion that Dusty had played the vixen with Mr. Simon. Now this strange encounter. It made sense that Sulee would live on the property since she worked there. But who was Robin? More importantly, who were her parents? Dusty huddled inside her sweater, a chill going deep into her bones. "Look. You don't have to tell me anything, but I am curious. Is Robin's mother or father someone I know?"

A hooded look passed between Sulee and Winston.

Dusty chewed her lower lip and waited until Winston cleared his throat. "The child is Miss Fontaine's. Born right here in this cottage."

"Oh, dear." Two sets of black eyes pierced her. "I didn't know, but gracious, why does she stay here? Why doesn't she live at Rosebriar?"

Sulee shook her head. "'Twouldn't be proper. People wagging their tongues and whatnot might scare away some of the girls coming. Best for everyone if Robin stays here. And she's happy."

Winston interrupted. "That's the main thing. Better than the institution that doctor in Houston suggested when he told Birdie that Robin had Down syndrome. Like to broke poor Birdie's heart. This is best."

"What about her father?"

Again, Sulee and Winston exchanged looks of caution, but this time, Sulee folded her hands on the table and thrust her head forward, her lips tight. "He died in France. In the war."

Tears sprung to the surface of Dusty's eyes. "I'm so sorry. How sad for all of them."

Dusty could piece it together without them giving her the details. The man in the picture in Miss Fontaine's quarters was probably Robin's father. She still went by her maiden name, so more than likely, they were planning to marry after the war. Robin was an unplanned surprise perhaps.

While Dusty processed the possibilities, she realized she'd stumbled on something that was none of her affair. Miss Fontaine was entitled to her privacy. And yet the incident with Mr. Simon took on a new light. Was Miss Fontaine protecting Dusty from getting into a similar compromising situation? Or did Mr. Simon know about Robin and hold it over her?

Dusty had to ask. "Do other people know about Robin? Townspeople? The staff?"

Sulee sipped the last of her tea, the lines in her face deep. "A doctor in town. Robin suffers from asthma, you see. She had a fierce attack awhile back, the day I fetched Birdie from the classroom."

Dusty told her she remembered.

Sulee continued, "The staff, they know. They're loyal and trustworthy."

"Except for one." Disgust roiled through her as Dusty remembered the cockiness in Mr. Simon's voice when he spoke of Miss Fontaine.

Sulee nodded. "Yes, a pity. I'm sorry about your troubles. We only told you because we didn't want you asking others about it. Now that you know, we implore you not to speak of this. For Robin's sake."

Giggles came from the tiny living room. Dusty recognized the voice of Allen Funt on *Candid Camera*. Whether Robin understood why the show was funny or only laughed because the people on the television did, Dusty didn't know.

Dusty sighed. "You have my word."

CHAPTER 27

The lights were out and Dusty already in bed when Paisley came home from the movies. She moved around in the dark, finding her nightshirt and toiletries and going to the hall bathroom to get ready for bed, puzzled that Dusty didn't wait up for her. They had been up half the night on Saturday so maybe she was just tired.

Paisley slipped into bed and yawned, then curled into a comfortable position, weary herself.

"I had a phone call."

Dusty's voice startled her, and at first Paisley thought she'd dreamed it. Heaven knows, she'd been dreading when Jack did call Dusty to break it off with her. Paisley mumbled an "oh" and waited. Perhaps Dusty was just talking in her sleep.

"Why do people keep secrets?"

Paisley's stomach clenched. *Jack.* Oh, crud. They must've talked about her, how somehow, without meaning to, Jack had been drawn to Paisley. She needed to say something, but what? "Different reasons I suppose." That was evasive enough.

"Do they do it to protect themselves or to protect other people?"

Dusty had figured out something, but Paisley was afraid to say too much. "I guess it depends on the secret."

"What do you know about my mother's death?"

Paisley bolted upright. "What are you talking about?"

"My mother. She died, remember? Of course, you don't. I don't either. But I think you know something about the circumstances around the accident."

"What, may I ask, brought this on?" Paisley was afraid Dusty had gone mad.

"Something Daddy said."

"When?"

"When he called."

"Tonight?"

"Earlier."

"How much earlier? Last week? When?"

"Earlier this evening. Don't avoid the question."

Paisley's skin dampened with perspiration. "I don't even know what the question is. What exactly did your dad say?"

"He told me I was turning into a tramp like Aunt Edie." Her voice was flat, without emotion.

"Why were you talking about my mother?"

"Miss Fontaine called him, told him about the stuff with Mr. Simon."

"That has nothing to do with Edie."

"He said I look like her, but I don't."

"Have you ever looked in the mirror?"

"I'm plain, gawky."

"But you have the same hair, the same nose, the same smile. And you are anything but plain."

"I always thought I looked like Daddy."

"You're a Fairchild. You all look alike. Except Patrick. He's more like your mother, I think."

"Do you remember her?"

"No, of course not. I've just seen her picture, and that's what Edie says."

"What else does Aunt Edie say?"

"She says a lot of things. Why? Why are we even having this conversation?"

"Because I've asked Daddy, Rosalita, Patrick, and you about why Edie left. No one will tell me. Tonight I asked Daddy, and he said your mother was the reason I don't have a mother."

Paisley let out a long, slow breath.

Dusty continued, still in that monotone voice, "I thought she was alone in the accident. Was Aunt Edie driving?"

"No, I don't think so. It's all kind of fuzzy. Is that what your dad said?"

"No, he hung up as soon as he said it. Later I got to thinking about why people keep secrets. I don't need to be protected from the truth."

Paisley tried to piece together the remnants of the conversation with her mother. It was the night she came home to the flat in San Francisco, and Edie and Davis were sitting on the carpet—it was gray and smelled of mildew and stale beer. They laughed while passing a joint around the room. The Asterisks were all there. Including Sloan. Paisley felt sick, but Edie told her to sit down, that she had a funny story to tell. Only it wasn't funny.

Paisley debated whether to tell Dusty the story.

Dusty sat up and turned on the lamp beside her bed. Her eyes were puffy, like she'd been crying, and she had a haunted look on her face. "The truth can't be any worse than not knowing."

Maybe it was time to tell her.

"One night, when she was high on pot, Edie told us—the Asterisks and me—her daddy had disowned her and her brother hated her. She had this crazy laugh and said all she and Aggie wanted to do was go shopping in Fort Worth and then hear a band at the Armory. Uncle Flint pitched a fit and wouldn't let your mother go. Your mother said she was going whether he liked it or not. She left, but before she met up with Edie, the accident happened. Uncle Flint blamed my mother for putting foolish ideas in her head."

Dusty had a dazed look on her face. "Why wouldn't Daddy let her go? Didn't he trust her?"

"I don't know. Edie said your mother was a knockout in the looks department, so maybe your dad was afraid of losing her."

"How could a shopping trip be that big a deal? My mother was a grown woman and could surely make her own choices. And it doesn't sound like the accident was Edie's fault."

"That's what Edie said, but from other things she's said over the years, your dad worshipped the ground your mother walked on. When she died, he needed to blame someone, so it was Edie."

"Daddy never talks about my mother. It's like he locks that up and keeps it to himself."

"And I think it's why he wouldn't tell you. Because it's still painful for him. And he wants to protect you."

"From what? Living?"

Paisley had no answer.

Dusty lay back and crossed her legs at her ankles. "Do you really think your mother was disowned?"

"That's what she said."

"Why would someone do that?"

"I always thought it was because she wasn't married to my father. Maybe they wanted her to give me up and she refused."

"Your mother did the right thing, keeping you. That took courage."

Edie was a lot of things—vain, careless, and headstrong—so keeping an illegitimate kid probably took a certain amount of courage. If that was even the reason she'd been disowned. "She has a good heart and good intentions, I suppose. And so does your dad. Who knows, maybe someday we'll have kids and we'll be ogres, too."

Dusty chuckled. "Who knows?" She leaned over, clicked off the lamp, and said good night.

Even after Dusty was breathing soft and even, Paisley lay awake thinking of Edie, wondering where she was and what she might be doing. But mostly she thought of her own black heart—that she'd abandoned Edie and betrayed Dusty.

CHAPTER 28

On Monday morning, Miss Fontaine greeted Dusty as if nothing had ever happened. No wayward encounter with Mr. Simon. No phone call to her dad. Dusty held her breath, watching for a flicker of something in Miss Fontaine's eye that communicated their shared knowledge of Robin and the caretaker's cottage. Nothing.

Just a twitchy smile when Miss Fontaine drew her aside in the dining room before class and told her that, after careful consideration, she was assigning her a research paper in lieu of attending French class.

"We have a lovely library in town, and since you have your own transportation, you are excused to work on a project of your choice."

"Anything?"

"Perhaps something to do with gemstones since you have an interest in geology."

So be it. Miss Fontaine had hidden her secret this long, and Dusty had given her vow of silence to Winston and Sulee. She would play the game.

Besides, the research paper was like being handed the keys to the kingdom. Dusty thanked her, and from ten to twelve on the days Mr. Simon came, she hopped in the T-Bird and went to the library in town. By Friday, she'd chosen what she wanted to research and checked out a stack of books.

Paisley eyed them warily. "What's your project about?"

"Fossils of the Cretaceous period in the Glen Rose formation. You know, gastropods, clams, echinoids, things like that."

"Sorry I asked."

"I want to be up to snuff when I go on the field trip with the Rock Hounds."

"You think they'll let you go with them?"

"I'll find out at the meeting tomorrow. You want to ride over to Miller College with me? You could look around or meet Walter for a Coke or something."

"Harvey, not Walter, but no thanks. I'm doing a photo shoot for Roberta at the gazebo in the town square, and we have a double date later with Harvey and one of his buddies."

"So you like Harvey?"

"Sure. What's not to like? I figure he's good for a few kicks."

Dusty was envious that Paisley could be so casual about dating, and truthfully, she still got a guilty pang for not thinking more about Jack. Then again, maybe Jack thought their dating had just been for a few kicks.

❧

Miller College was considered part of the town of Alborghetti but was situated on the outskirts on its own expansive, wooded acreage. Dusty allowed extra time so she could find Spivey Hall which she knew, from studying the campus map ahead of time, would be on the right.

Eight members of the Rock Hound Club showed up for the

meeting. Ramsey Jones, dressed in olive dungarees, a short-sleeved plaid shirt, and tan suede Chukka boots, waved her in and asked her to introduce herself.

She told the group she was interested in studying geology when she finished at Miss Fontaine's. "I live about forty miles from Glen Rose, but I've found heart clams, crab claws, and pieces of coral in the creek beds on our ranch."

Ramsey, who wasn't nearly as nervous as he'd been at the Christmas ball, raised his eyebrows. "You'd be welcome to join us for the daytime excavation exercises if you'd like. Since it's a college-sponsored trip, I'm not sure you could go as a full-fledged member. Anyone have any objections to Dusty joining us part of the time?"

"Not me." A girl with short dark hair waved across the room. "I'd love to have another girl along."

The meeting flew by with a lot of bantering back and forth about driving arrangements, camping gear, terrain maps, and the schedule. While they talked, Dusty gazed around the room, a classroom obviously with maps on the walls showing cutaways of the different formation periods, and along one side of the room, glass display cases like the jewelry case in Simple Pleasures. Instead of jewelry, though, the cases were filled with rock samples, fossils, and what looked like the hip socket of a dinosaur or some other creature.

After the meeting, she was glancing over the labeled items in the case when the girl who'd spoken earlier came up to her. "I'm Dana. A bunch of us are going over to the Huddle for a burger. You wanna come?"

The Huddle was a tiny little diner between the girls' and boys' dorms. Elvis was singing "Good Luck Charm" on the jukebox when they went in, and Ramsey asked if he could get her a burger. "It's the least I can do for stepping on your feet at the dance."

"You weren't that bad." She told him what she wanted and that she'd be in the booth with Dana and a guy they'd introduced as Wayne.

When Wayne and Dana asked how she and Ramsey knew each other, Ramsey got a sheepish grin on his face and said, "The guys on my floor dared me—said if I went to Miss Fontaine's dance, they'd do my laundry for a month. The girl I went with turned her ankle and had to go home, so Dusty took pity on me and danced with me."

His eyes were kind, and he was much cuter than Dusty remembered. No pretense. No expectation.

Dusty asked a million questions about the college and where they were from. Johnny Horton and Patsy Cline and Burl Ives and Johnny Tillotson sang through the jukebox, and when the last French fry had been gobbled up and they'd ordered chocolate milk shakes all around, the sun had gone down on the most perfect day Dusty could ever remember.

Her room was dark when she returned. She flipped on the light and flopped on her bed, letting the day's events wash over her. She'd been there awhile when she realized something was poking at her neck. She reached up to feel what it was and pulled out a letter. Jack's handwriting on the front.

Guilt nagged at her. She hadn't thought about Jack all day. For several days in fact. She went to her desk for a nail file to open the envelope, then read Jack's letter.

Dear Dusty,

I'm a coward of the worst kind, and I hope you'll forgive me. I wanted to talk to you when I came last week, but in reality, I was relieved that you were ill. Telling you face-to-face would be more dignified, but I seem to be running low on dignity at the moment.

I think perhaps...No, I know for certain that I've led you on

*and pretended that I cared for you. I do care for you, but I don't
think we have a future together. You're a wonderful gal and a great
dancer, but...*

*This is the hard part. I think (and this part is not for certain) that
I love someone else. I've been attracted to her in a way that I can't
describe since the moment I met her. I don't deserve her or you because
of my cowardice in not being honest with both of you. As you may
have guessed, the girl I'm speaking of is your cousin, Paisley.*

*I'd give anything if these weren't my feelings, but they are. I hope
you will forgive me and that we can remain friends.*

Cordially,
Jack Morgan

The paper fluttered from her fingers to the floor. *Paisley.* Her own
cousin?

She picked it up and read it again. It wasn't unexpected that he
would break up with her. She'd felt it coming, knew in her heart
that Jack might not be the one. She'd seen the looks between him
and Paisley. How stupid of her to not figure it out. What felt like a
knife to her flesh was that Paisley hadn't told her.

Nothing. Not. One. Word.

❧

By intermission of the movie *Lawrence of Arabia*, Paisley groaned to
herself. Two hours already, another hour and a half to go. All she'd
thought of since mail call that afternoon was the envelope addressed
to Dusty in Jack's handwriting. She'd stuffed it in her pocket to give
to Dusty personally along with an explanation. Only Dusty hadn't
returned from her visit to the Rock Hounds before Paisley's date
arrived. When Roberta hollered that the boys were waiting, Paisley

tucked it halfway under Dusty's pillow and sailed off for her date with Harvey.

An evening that lasted an eternity, it seemed.

Dusty's T-Bird was in the drive when the boys dropped Paisley and Roberta off near midnight, close enough to curfew that they didn't have to invite them in. Paisley said good night to Roberta and climbed the stairs on legs that felt like they had sandbags tied to them.

Dusty sat cross-legged on the bed and lifted her chin when Paisley entered the room. "How was the picture show and your *date* with Harvey?"

"Not as exciting as you might think. Three and a half hours of camels and horses and men with towels draped around their heads didn't do much for me. The guys thought they'd died and gone to heaven." Paisley tossed her purse on the bed and kept her voice light. "How were the Rock Hounds?"

"Fine." Dusty lifted a sheet of paper from her lap. It didn't take the brains of a gnat to know that it was Jack's letter.

Paisley raised her eyebrows. "I see you got Jack's letter."

Dusty lifted her chin. "You know what's in this letter, don't you? How could you?" Her tone was clipped, red with anger. And hurt.

Paisley flinched. "It's not what you think."

"How do you know what I think? Did you open the letter and reseal it?"

"No. Please believe me…I don't know what it says for sure, but I have an idea."

"An idea? You fell in love with my boyfriend and never said a word about it."

"I didn't mean to fall for him. Honest, you have to believe me. I told him there could never be anything between us, that it was wrong."

"So you've talked to Jack? On the phone? In letters? What?"

"He wrote me."

"And you forgot to tell me."

Paisley kicked off her shoes and sank onto the bed. She'd never wanted a smoke as bad as she did at that moment. "I've been sick over how to tell you. He wrote before the Valentine party. Told me he was going to talk to you then. That he knew what he felt was wrong while dating you."

"So what was he going to do? Wait a week or two and then start calling you?"

"No. No! He said whatever we might have had was over."

"But you liked him? Loved him?" Dusty's face was flushed, her eyes brimming with tears.

"I don't know about love, but liked, yes. It was torture not telling you, and I told him we couldn't see each other."

"Have you kissed him?"

Paisley closed her eyes. "No kisses. Unless you count when I kissed him on the cheek at Valentine's and told him good-bye. And we talked at the drugstore in Two Forks the day I took in Susan's film. I told you I saw him."

"But not that you were discussing your mutual love life."

"Don't twist things around, Dusty. You're hurt by Jack's letter. Devastated, I know. But maybe you were never meant to be."

Dusty turned away, her arms crossed. Paisley wished she'd never come to Miss Fontaine's. Never seen or heard of Jack Morgan.

Dusty rose from the bed, hands on her hips. "I'm not devastated that he broke up with me. I'm crushed that you didn't have the guts to tell me."

Paisley swallowed. "I wanted to, but I just couldn't."

"Because you didn't want to hurt me?" Dusty's voice had a mocking tone. "The way you didn't want to hurt me by telling me about Aunt Edie and my mother?"

"The truth hurts all of us."

"I wouldn't know. No one ever tells me the truth. Not even you." She grabbed her pillow and her robe. "I'm going back to my old room. At least Sharon Kay was honest."

❧

"I don't care whether you want me to sleep here or not. I can't sleep in my room." Dusty shoved her way past Sharon Kay as soon as she opened the door, thinking as she did so that she'd gotten pretty good at butting into unwanted places of late.

"Care to elaborate? Having a spat with your cousin? Don't tell me, she's sick of your rocks on her windowsill now?"

"Nothing like that." Dusty threw her pillow on the bed she once occupied and kicked off her shoes.

"Watch it. I don't want you breaking something." She pointed to the windowsill lined with perfume bottles in every shape and size imaginable. "Some of those are priceless."

"Don't worry. I'm not the kind of person who throws things, so your little baubles are safe."

"Baubles?" Sharon Kay strode to the windowsill, picked up a bottle in the shape of a pyramid with a gold stopper, and held it out. "This…is from Italy. Fourteen-carat gold, in case you were wondering."

"I wasn't. Not really." Dusty didn't want to talk about Paisley either, so she stood at the windowsill and looked at the bottle collection. Shalimar. White Shoulders. Emeraude. Chanel No. 5. Woodhue. Some she didn't recognize.

"They're gorgeous. Where did you get them?"

Sharon Kay cradled the Italian one in her hands. "From my grandmother mostly."

Dusty pointed to a tiny glass globe with a glittery atomizer. "And this one?"

"She bought it for me when we went to France."

"You've been to France?" Sharon Kay never missed an opportunity to lord something over the girls at Miss Fontaine's, so this was unexpected.

"Not that it matters."

"Of course it matters. Going places with your grandmother must be great. Do you have any other trips planned?"

"Not exactly. She died of cancer a couple of months ago."

Dusty winced. "I'm sorry. You never said anything. Did you go to the funeral?"

"Yeah, the day after New Year's."

"How awful. Which grandmother? Mom or dad's side?"

"Daddy's." Her voice quavered. "I'd rather not talk about it."

"I know how that is. You're lucky you knew her, though. I didn't know either of my grandmothers. Or my mom."

"You know what they say. Tough toenails." She set the perfume bottle back on the sill and crossed her arms. "So what did Paisley do that's got you all hot and bothered?"

"Let's just say it's what she didn't do—I'll get over it."

"Like you did with Mr. Simon."

"I'll never get over what that creep did to me." Might as well be honest.

Sharon Kay didn't say anything, and Dusty turned to look at her, but her face was unreadable. When it came, Sharon Kay's voice was a whisper. "I'm sorry."

"For what?"

"For what happened to you. I really didn't think what Babs told me last summer was true. I never thought he'd really...I was just joking around, trying to fit in as well as you, I guess."

Dusty could barely breathe. "You? Why wouldn't you fit in? You're going to be a debutante next year and your daddy is a judge."

"It's not all it's cracked up to be." Sharon Kay shoved her pillow up to the headboard of her bed and sat down.

"I don't even know what to say. You're one of the most popular girls here. And certainly the best dressed."

She shrugged. "Yeah, but you and your corny cousin have more fun. You're free to choose what you want."

"And you're not? I figured you had your life all mapped out. Charm school. Debutante season. Then what? Tour of Europe? That's what debs do, isn't it?"

Sharon Kay let out a harsh laugh. "That's what my parents expect, along with finding the right husband."

"And you, what do you want?"

"You'd laugh."

"No, I wouldn't. Hey, I want to be a geologist—"

"As if I haven't heard that a zillion times. Please, spare me the details."

"I'm just saying, we're all individuals. With different tastes and dreams. I won't laugh."

Sharon Kay knit her brows together. "You got the European tour part right. But I want to do one of those youth hostel trips and tour Europe on a bicycle."

"That's a wonderful idea. You think your parents would go for it?"

"Are you kidding? I've never owned or ridden a bicycle."

"Ever? I mean, like you live in some mansion in Houston and don't have a bike?"

"Ding! You win the prize for the right answer." Sharon Kay made the motion for ringing an imaginary bell.

"I'm sort of in shock. I thought you would say you wanted to be a fashion designer or an anchor girl on television. But I think the hostel idea is fabulous. How did you learn about them?"

"The trip I took with my grandmother. Ever since I've been dying to experience the freedom of traveling with only the items I could carry in a backpack. You know, to places where nobody gives a flying fig if my dad's a hotshot judge or my mother owns three hundred pairs of shoes. You'd think just once they would've asked if I wanted a bicycle for my birthday." She drew her knees up and rested her chin on them. "Half the time they don't even remember I have a birthday."

A bitter tone laced Sharon Kay's voice, the look in her eyes haunting and reminiscent of the way Sharon Kay had looked at the Mother/Daughter Tea when her mom hadn't come. Maybe Sulee had been right when she said that sometimes the ones with the sharpest tongues had the most festering inside. It made Dusty's own misery seem small, but it didn't take the edge off Paisley's betrayal.

Dusty wanted to give Sharon Kay a hug but thought better of it. She still didn't qualify for Miss Congeniality. Instead Dusty said, "I could find information about hostel tours at the library if you'd like."

"Really? You'd do that for me?"

"Sure. After all, you are sharing your room."

When they turned out the light, moonlight cast a creamy glow on the perfume bottles on the windowsill. Sharon Kay switched the radio on low and said she'd clean out one of her drawers for Dusty's things.

"You don't have to do that. I'll just bring a few things down until Paisley and I work things out." Which might be a day. Or never.

Sharon Kay didn't answer, and a few minutes later was breathing deeply. Dusty lay awake, willing sleep to come, and just as she nodded off, Elvis's voice came like velvet through the radio as he sang "Can't Help Falling in Love."

Tears she'd been fighting all evening fell on her pillow. *Can't help falling in love.* Like Jack and Paisley. She hid the sobs in her pillow.

CHAPTER 29

A dozen times, Paisley tried to work up the courage to march down the hall to Sharon Kay's room and beg Dusty to listen to her. And just like the coward she'd been about talking to Dusty about Jack, she couldn't.

Edie's voice played like a stuck record in her head. *"You screw up and move on. There's no sense in crying."*

Paisley hated it when her mother said that, like it was an excuse to do whatever you wanted without consequence. And yet, Edie was a decent mom most of the time. She'd been the one to kiss her skinned knees and take her for ice cream when Paisley had a rough day in a new school. Edie wasn't here now, though, and even if she wanted to, her mother couldn't fix the mess Paisley had made of her life.

Dusty felt betrayed, possibly hated her. Jack was moving to Alaska to avoid any hard feelings. And Uncle Flint would put her on the bus back to California when he found out what she did to Dusty.

Fear coiled around her gut. What if Edie wasn't there? Or what if she was married to Ollie? There was always the Penny Loafer. They might let her wait tables and sleep in the back room, but what kind of life was that? She couldn't even take the camera with her since it belonged to Dusty.

She curled into a ball on her bed and stared into space toward Dusty's bed. Jack's letter lay atop the bedspread where Dusty left it. She hoped he'd been kind. Let Dusty down easy. Of course he had. He wasn't a jerk.

Inch by inch, Paisley uncoiled her arms and legs, feeling like she did when she'd peeked through the keyhole at Edie and one of the men she'd brought home. She sat up, her legs quivery. Perspiration beaded up on her forehead. She leaned over and took the letter, then sat back and read it.

She brushed her fingers across the words *I love someone else.* Love. Did Jack love her? She read it again. And again. Then flopped back onto her pillow holding the letter to her chest. If only.

If only Dusty would listen to her. If only she'd told Dusty the truth. Would she have despised Paisley for that, too? Even though Jack was not part of the future, Dusty was her cousin. And she couldn't bear to let their relationship disintegrate into the acrid feelings of Edie and Uncle Flint. Somehow she thought she'd recover from a broken heart, but not from destroying the love between her and Dusty.

She put the letter back where she found it and opened the door, wincing as it creaked. The oak floor was cool beneath her bare feet as she padded down to the Rosebud room and listened. She had decided if she heard talking, she would knock. She strained her ears, but only a soft hum from the radio came through the door.

Paisley slumped to the floor with her back to the wall. The music was faint, but even in the stillness, there was no mistaking that it was Elvis crooning about falling in love. Tears welled up and trickled down her cheeks.

The next day, Dusty gathered a few of her things and told Paisley she'd be staying in Sharon Kay's room until she had time to sort things out. Dusty didn't even know what she meant when she said it, but a terrible night's sleep and seeing Jack's letter still lying on her bedspread left her on edge. She left the letter and Paisley, and after dumping her things in Sharon Kay's room went to the bayou.

The morning was chilly, but the sun shone a cheery yellow that warred with Dusty's inner thoughts as she hiked along the familiar trail. No more wandering off to places that were off-limits or laced with mystery. Just her and nature. The two things she could count on.

Only her confidence in herself was at a low ebb. Discarded by Jack. Betrayed by Paisley. She knew she should just chalk it up as one of those unfortunate incidents you hope you'll forget about eventually. If only it were so simple.

An egret squawked off to her right. It folded its snowy wings gracefully to its sides as it landed in the shallows on legs as thin as toothpicks. The water shone in ribbons of green and brown with the sun's reflection, calm but for the occasional rippling circle left by a minnow that broke the murky surface. Dusty found a grassy clump and sat cross-legged, absorbing the sun, letting the bayou sounds wash over her.

A pair of blue jays swooped through nearby trees, their bossy chatter intruding.

What if Paisley hadn't fallen into Jack's arms at Thanksgiving and had met him under a different set of circumstances? Would they have still been drawn to each other, as Jack put it in his letter? What did that even mean? Jack and Paisley made choices. Both of them.

She remembered Paisley laughing when they'd talked about love at first sight. Has she already fallen in love with Jack then? And Paisley's questions about Jack and what he thought of Dusty's dream of going to college? Had Paisley been sounding her out? At what point did Paisley intend to tell her she was in love with Jack?

Maybe Paisley was hoping Dusty and Jack would break up for their own reasons—heaven knew Dusty had struggled with the possibility. In which case, Jack would be fair game and no one need know of their earlier attraction. In her gut, Dusty still felt Paisley should have been honest. That's what friends do, especially if they're related by blood.

One of the noisy blue jays dive bombed to the base of a cypress and clutched a berry in its beak. From behind, the other jay plunged and attacked, stealing the morsel. The fight was on as they hopped and swerved, swept and ruffled in a battle over the prize. Back and forth, flashes of blue appeared, then vanished until finally one claimed victory and soared away leaving the loser alone and disheveled.

Dusty wrapped her arms around her knees and stared at nothing until her hips grew numb. She rose and brushed off her pants, then started back the way she'd come, her steps as heavy as the sorrow buried deep in her heart.

❦

Paisley thought of calling Xan to talk about her dilemma, but with her new life as Mrs. Prentice Robbins, she doubted she would understand. And she couldn't figure Dusty out. She was polite, even conversed like old times during meals, but there was a coolness to her, too, that frightened Paisley.

One day when Dusty had come in their room to get more clothes, Paisley asked if they could talk, but Dusty told her she promised Sharon Kay she'd take her into town to look at bicycles.

"Bicycles. Why?"

"She wants to start riding. You know, one of the things on her dream list. Going on a hostel tour through Europe."

No, she didn't know, but when Dusty breezed out the door without an explanation, the room felt as if the energy had been sucked out with her.

Another day Paisley drew Dusty aside at lunch and asked if they could talk.

"Sure, what's on your mind?"

"Could we go for a walk? Maybe out to the fountain?"

"Where you kissed Jack on the cheek?"

"I told him the kiss was from you. Why won't you believe me?"

"Paisley, I do believe you. And somehow I think whatever happened between you and Jack was fate. Or karma. I won't say it was God's will, because I'm not sure what that means. I do know God thinks *honesty* is a good thing."

"I didn't want to hurt you."

"We've been over this before. I'm not hurt, okay? You're free to do whatever you like."

"You say that, but I don't think you're being truthful with me, either. You're still ticked. I don't want to be with Jack if that's what you're implying. I'd rather you and I patched things up and went back to the way things were before."

"You should've thought of that earlier." Dusty turned to go, then stopped. "By the way, Susan called. She's got several people lined up for photo shoots with you over Easter break."

"Really? So you're letting me come home with you?"

"Where else would you go?"

Paisley wanted to spit. Dusty didn't have to be so condescending. And yet, Paisley had nowhere else to go. Xan had mentioned coming to Houston, but then she couldn't take pictures. She hoped that somehow Dusty would accept her apology before that. A month was a long time, but stranger things had happened.

Less than a week later, Paisley woke to Dusty shaking her shoulder. "Wake up!" Dusty turned on the radio between their beds. "Listen!"

Paisley sat up and rubbed her eyes. "What? What's wrong? Why are you in our room and not with Sharon Kay?"

"Dead! She's dead!"

"Who?" *Sharon Kay? Edie? Oh, God, not Edie. Please.*

"Patsy! She died in a plane crash. It's on the radio." Dusty turned up the volume on the Zenith, and as "Crazy" played in the background, they listened to the details from the announcer.

"It has been confirmed that Patsy Cline, her manager, Randy Hughes, and longtime country singers Hankshaw Hawkins and Cowboy Copas died instantly when the private plane they were in went down nose first in the mountains of Tennessee last evening. Patsy had just performed at a benefit in Kansas City along with notable country stars George Jones, Dottie West, and others two days before."

Paisley watched the radio with her mouth open, hoping that the voice in the speaker had gotten it wrong. All wrong. His voice droned on about fog in Kansas City and a last-minute decision to take off when the fog lifted.

Dusty reached over to turn off the radio and Paisley lashed out at her. "No! Leave it on! I have to hear every word. Maybe there's a mistake."

But there wasn't. Paisley sat on the bed hugging a pillow to her chest, frozen, unable to think. The radio announcer called Patsy the "honky-tonk angel" and played another of her songs. Paisley refused to think of her dead and closed her eyes, remembering Patsy alive, reaching out to fans from the stage, laughing, hips swaying as she held the microphone and sang.

Edie. Her mother's face materialized along with the images of Patsy. Edie would be devastated. Was she listening to the same announcer? Why hadn't she called so they could cry together?

Instead, Dusty sat beside her on the bed, her arm around Paisley's shoulder. Dusty handed her tissues, dabbed at her own eyes, and told her everything would be okay.

"It will never be okay for Patsy again, will it?"

Dusty had no answer.

After a while, Paisley looked at Dusty, her throat still clogged from crying. "I don't know what came over me. I'm sorry."

"It's all right. I know you're sad. It was a terrible loss. You met Patsy once upon a time. We saw her together. She will go down in history as one of the greats."

Paisley sighed. "It's just that we'll never see her again."

"No, but we have her music, our memories. And I can tell you right now, Patsy would not want her fans moping around forever."

"I know."

Two days later—on her library day—Dusty came in with an arm-load of newspapers from the drugstore. She handed them to Paisley and said, "You have that new scrapbook, so I thought maybe you could add these articles to it—a small way to remember Patsy."

"Will you help me?"

"That's what I had in mind." She paused, studying Paisley. "I've been thinking, and if it's all right, I'm going to move my stuff back in."

"So, does that mean..." Paisley held up two fingers in a V. "Peace?"

"I'm working on it."

"I really am sorry."

"Me, too." Dusty's voice had a wistful tinge, and Paisley wasn't sure if Dusty was sorry for their fight or sorry about Paisley and Jack. For now, it was a start.

For the next three weeks, they scoured the magazine racks at the drugstore and bought every single one that had Patsy's picture on the cover.

Paisley pasted all the pictures and articles in the scrapbook. "You know, she was always laughing, wasn't she? These articles, though, talk about the troubles she had in her life. You never think about stars having all those worries, do you?"

Dusty agreed. "Goes to show, it's not who you are or how famous, it's what you do with your life. Did you see this one?" She pointed to a picture of Patsy's children, still small and now without a mother. "She was only thirty years old and accomplished what most people don't in a lifetime."

"She was unstoppable, all right. Even when misfortune came her way."

The pictures of Patsy also brought back the yearning Paisley had to know what Edie was doing. She called the Penny Loafer and asked if they'd seen her. No one had since a couple of weeks after Christmas. Paisley whispered prayers for Edie and tried not to worry. Somehow, Edie always managed to make it.

She clung to the hope that once again they both would.

CHAPTER 30

Miss Fontaine handed Dusty the latest report she'd turned in on her special project. "Your research is remarkable. Certainly nothing that captures my fancy, but then I've never had a head for science. History is more my cup of tea."

"Something for everyone, right? That's what I told Paisley."

"Is she doing all right? She's seems rather down lately."

Dusty gazed out the window in the classroom. The horses grazed blissfully in the pasture lush with tender grass. She knew that on the other side of the property, a young woman named Robin most likely watched the same horses. So close together, yet their lives were not to cross.

"Poor kid." Dusty jumped when she said the words, reacting to her own thoughts of Robin and not Miss Fontaine's question about Paisley.

Miss Fontaine raised her eyebrows but said no more. Her head-mistress had been accommodating and pleasant since the incident with Mr. Simon, and yet she seemed afraid of Dusty, too. Like perhaps she knew Dusty had discovered her secret. It was reasonable to assume that Sulee or Winston had told her. Perhaps even Robin herself. Twice now Dusty had slipped a sparkling piece of pyrite into Sulee's palm when she passed through the kitchen. No words were exchanged, only a knowing glance between them. Dusty was certain that Sulee had delivered them to Robin.

Dusty shrugged. "Paisley's going to be fine. We're both looking forward to going to the ranch over Easter. Paisley has appointments to take photos of people in Two Forks—thanks to my sister-in-law spreading the word."

"She's very good. Maybe someday I'll even let her take my photograph."

"She'd love that. Really, what a swell idea."

"I said maybe."

"Thanks for what you said about my paper. I'm filling out college applications and need references from people who know me. Would you be willing to write one for me?"

"I think that could be arranged."

"Thanks. I'll bring you the names and what I need."

Dusty also requested multiple copies of her high school transcript, wanting to have all the applications turned in before she went home for the break. She'd written Jack and thanked him for being honest. He hadn't answered back. She knew in her heart they weren't meant to be, but she was still uneasy about Easter and wondered if it would be awkward to see Jack. Even more, she dreaded what it would be like to see Jack and Paisley together.

The wounds over Paisley were still tender, but Dusty knew she'd done the right thing to move back in and try to get back on track. Secrets did nothing but make people brittle and suspicious. Her dad. Aunt Edie. Not to mention the whole mess with Miss Fontaine and Mr. Simon. Just thinking of him brought a bitter taste to her tongue.

She called her dad the week before Easter to tell him when she and Paisley would be home and to ask how he was doing.

"Fine now that Rosalita's back and makes me bacon and eggs every morning."

"And Patrick, he's still there?"

"Last time I checked. You're not planning any more shenanigans this time, I hope."

"Actually, I want to talk to you about that. And some other things."

"I figured you might. I have an idea I want to run past you, too. Might have some bearing on your future."

Dusty's heart raced. Maybe Miss Fontaine had talked to him and told him about writing the letter of recommendation. "That sounds great, Daddy. By the way, I have some friends that want to come over on Saturday."

"Your friends are always welcome here. Just let Rosalita know how many mouths she needs to feed."

"Thanks, Daddy. See you soon."

School let out on Wednesday, a balmy day that whispered spring. Roses bloomed along the brick entrance to Miss Fontaine's, and Dusty was anxious to get on the road.

Carmel's mom had arrived in the red Cadillac to whisk Carmel to Jackson so her family could board a flight to Acapulco. Hal from Miller College was joining them there. Stacia and June both carried armloads of notebooks bulging with magazine pages and lists as they would be spending Easter break finalizing their summer wedding plans.

Sharon Kay's driver hauled her leather luggage out to the Rolls. She hugged a couple of the girls and stopped as Dusty came up the sidewalk. "Bring back a fossil for me." She made a face. "Just kidding. Have fun, though."

Someone hollered, "Paisley! Telephone!"

Paisley gasped. "Edie? You suppose?" She raced into the house while Dusty loaded the last suitcase and waved at Sharon Kay, who smiled and waved from the front seat of her chauffeur-driven car. Her new Schwinn ten-speed sat in the back.

Five minutes later, Paisley bounced down the steps. "Xan's going to have a baby! We're all going to be aunts."

"Seriously? How did she sound?"

"The same—giddy!"

"You can tell me about it on the way."

"Hang on. I forgot the camera."

She raced upstairs and finally they pulled out of the drive—the last ones to leave.

Paisley chattered about Xan for two hours, how happy she seemed. "You know, we should invite her to graduation."

The closer they got to the ranch, the quieter Paisley became. Dusty suspected she was fretting over Jack. Ten miles from the ranch, Dusty decided to mention it.

"Have you talked to Jack?"

Paisley's eyes grew round. "No. I told you that your friendship means more to me. Besides, he said he was moving to Alaska."

"Alaska? When did you hear this?"

"It's one of the things I wanted to tell you. He said that rather than come between us, he would look for a job somewhere else. He wrote me one letter. That's all. You aren't the only one who got a Dear John letter."

Dusty's face grew warm. She rolled the window halfway down and gulped in buckets of country air. Jack would sacrifice his own happiness for her and Paisley? For both of them? She had underestimated him, caught up as she was with her own feelings. And Paisley was willing to give up any chance with Jack for her.

She turned to Paisley. "Don't you dare let Jack Morgan get

away. If you are meant to be together, then nothing else matters."

Paisley reached over and squeezed Dusty's shoulder. "Thank you," she said quietly, her voice thick.

The scent of sage and bluebonnets swirled together in an intoxicating mix as Dusty turned off the highway onto the drive that led home.

The front door opened the minute the T-Bird stopped. Dusty sailed up the walk and opened her arms for a hug from Rosalita. "Where's Daddy?"

"Fool man's gone off to get himself an airplane. Your daddy and his nutty ideas have worn me plumb out." She reached out and took Paisley's hand. "Rosalita made peach cobbler, and I'm fixin' to put together my famous tamales for that bunch of kids you got coming on Saturday."

Arm in arm, they marched into the house.

⚜

Uncle Flint got home in time for supper and was in high spirits, telling them about his new toy—a Cessna 195 airplane.

Dusty and Paisley looked at each other. Dusty took a deep breath. "Daddy, what do you need an airplane for? Don't you know how dangerous they are?"

"It'll save me a lot of time. I've got crews on location in Midland drilling in the Permian Basin. I can get there in thirty minutes instead of two or three hours."

"But you don't know how to fly. And even if you did, it was just last month Patsy Cline was killed in an airplane crash."

"I know, sugar. And a hundred people a year get attacked by sharks, but that don't keep them from flocking to the sunny beaches. And don't worry, I got a fella giving me instructions and serving as my pilot now. Retired Air Force guy that Jack Morgan introduced me to. Say, why didn't you invite Jack to supper?"

Dusty shrugged. "We're not seeing each other anymore. You want some more iced tea, Daddy?"

Paisley watched, fascinated that Dusty was able to be so matter-of-fact.

"I'm fine, sugar. So what about Morgan? I hope this isn't another fool idea you've come up with."

"No, it was Jack's idea actually. But there is something I want to talk to you about. What we talked about on the phone."

"We'll discuss it later." He nailed Dusty with a look Paisley had seen many times. Not only in her uncle, but also in Edie. The *when I say we'll discuss it* look. Paisley held her breath. She knew Dusty was going to ask him about Edie, and to give him credit, maybe he didn't want to talk about Edie in front of her. Uncle Flint might hold a grudge, but he wasn't heartless.

"All this puts a kink in the news I had for you."

Dusty took a slow drink of iced tea and glanced at Paisley. "What was that?"

"I figured soon as you get done over at Miss Fontaine's, you'd come home and settle down, start seeing Morgan regular, you know. That's why I'm thinking about bringing him on as the tax accountant at Fairchild Oil. Make him part of the family."

Paisley nearly choked on the bite of creamed corn she'd just taken. What would her uncle say when he found out about her and Jack? Of course, maybe she wouldn't have to worry about that since, as far as she knew, Jack planned to move to Alaska.

Dusty lifted her shoulders. "It's your company, Daddy. I've never said a word about who you hire and who you don't. What does Jack say about it?"

"I wanted to surprise him. Word around town is he's looking for a new job when his contract is up at the bank. I made us reservations out at the Elks Lodge for Saturday night—the whole family. I was aiming to give Patrick a promotion, too. He's takin' to the business like a salamander to a mudhole."

"Sounds good to me. Maybe that would be a good time to make my own announcement."

Dusty got up and ran upstairs.

Paisley had no idea what Dusty was doing. It had been a day full of surprises with Dusty's complete turnaround about Jack, so anything was possible.

Her uncle said, "So, Stringbean, you been keeping yourself out of trouble?"

"I haven't short sheeted any beds all semester if that's what you mean."

"I could teach you a few tricks about that."

Ah, the old Fairchild charm.

Paisley chuckled, thankful when Dusty reappeared waving an envelope. She looked at Paisley. "Something that came in the mail today." She removed the letter and handed it to her dad while passing the envelope to Paisley. The Miller College logo was on the return address.

His eyes, curious and laughing at first, scanned the first few lines. His jaw tensed, the blue in his eyes turning icy. He passed the letter back.

"That's nice, sugar. Too bad you'll have to write them and tell them you've changed your mind."

Paisley watched Dusty, who played it as cool as a frosty mug of root beer. She took the letter from her dad. "But I haven't. Unless, of course, another one of the colleges I've applied to makes me a great offer."

"So this is what I'm paying for you to learn at charm school? How to fill out college applications? I could've taught you that for nothing."

"I tried to talk to you about it, but you wouldn't listen. And for the record, I have learned a lot of things there. How to conduct myself when I meet dignitaries. How to plan a formal dinner. How to make hotel reservations. Tipping etiquette for porters, chambermaids, and waiters."

He waved her away. "Okay. Yes, I know, things your old man doesn't know beans about. That's what I have a secretary for—to make my hotel reservations. Actually, I was hoping you might learn the ropes in the office this summer. There's plenty of work to keep two secretaries busy."

Dusty inhaled through her nose, her eyes flashing. "I don't want to be a secretary. Have you not heard a word I've said for eighteen years?" She threw down her napkin and fled the dining room.

The front door slammed while Paisley looked at her uncle.

He threw down his own napkin. "What are you staring at?"

Paisley smiled. "Nothing. Just enjoying the show."

Her uncle leaned back and laughed. "I aim to please."

Rosalita stuck her head in and asked if they needed anything.

Uncle Flint said, "Get in here, Rosie. I know you've been listening to this whole mess standing outside the door. Tell me, what is your opinion? Should Dusty go to college or not?"

Rosalita put her hands on her hips. "You keep up the way you been acting and you be one sorry man. Rosalita knows you think the sun rises and sets in that girl." She held out a cupped hand. "Hold a canary in your fist to keep it from flying away is one thing, but hang on too tight and you be squeezing the life plumb out."

Her uncle's nostrils flared momentarily. He swallowed, his eyes wide and glistening with tears. Paisley knew in that moment Dusty had won. She was just sorry Dusty wasn't there to see it. Or to hear him tell Rosalita, "The next time I want your advice, I'll ask for it."

Rosalita sashayed back to the kitchen.

꧁

CHAPTER 31

Thanks!" Paisley took the twenty-dollar bill from the last of Susan's friends who'd come over to Susan's to have portraits made. She'd done an engagement picture out by the stables of a barrel-racing girl in jeans and a pearl-buttoned shirt. Another of Susan's friends had brought her two preschoolers dressed in their Easter outfits saying she wanted to get a picture of them before they had chocolate bunnies smeared all over their faces and their clothes. Those and two other sittings netted her over a hundred dollars by two in the afternoon.

Susan cut her a brownie hot from the oven while Paisley bounced Zachary, who'd already grown into a twenty-pound butterball, on her knee.

Susan brought the dessert plates to the table. "So, here's what I'm thinking. If you come back for the summer—and I hope you will—then we should turn our empty bunkhouse into a studio for you."

"You'd help me with that?"

"We'd have a blast. And you'll need to get a brochure made up and set up an account at the bank. It's never too soon to be thinking about this from a business angle."

Susan was brimming with ideas, and when Paisley said she'd better get to the bank, Susan took Zachary from her.

Paisley kissed Zachary's cheek and said, "Dusty said she'd be by after she gets her shopping done in town."

"Easter outfit?"

"No, hiking boots and a new Windbreaker for her fossil expedition with the Rock Hounds."

"God love her. She's got a one-track mind, just like her daddy."

"You better not let her hear you say that. She's mad at Uncle Flint at the moment."

"What did he do now?"

"They're arguing about whether or not she can go to college and study geology. I think he's about ready to cave, though."

"Let's hope so." She followed her out the door and waved as Paisley put the T-Bird in gear and started down the drive.

Paisley knew she might run into Jack at the bank. Two Forks only had one bank, after all. If she ran into him, then she would see how it went. While she felt like she had Dusty's blessing, she didn't intend to throw herself at Jack. She'd worn a sleeveless salmon dress with a lightweight sweater since she hadn't known what Susan's friends might be like, but her hair was a mess after Zachary had yanked on it with his pudgy fingers. She put on a fresh coat of lipstick while looking in the T-Bird's rearview mirror as Miss Fontaine's voice chirped in her head, *"You aren't properly dressed until you have a little color on your lips."*

She swung her long legs from the car, then stood tall and walked into the bank like there was a book balanced on her head.

A woman she recognized from the Methodist Church helped her with the new account. As she signed the card, one of the office doors on the far side of the bank opened. Jack stepped out shaking the hand of a man dressed in overalls and work boots. He nodded at her politely, then blinked, like it just hit him who she was.

The account secretary handed her a pad of blank checks and told her she could use them or counter checks locally and that when she knew her permanent address, they would order her personalized checks.

"Thank you." Paisley turned and walked to the double doors to leave. Jack was holding the door for the farmer and telling him they'd know something on his loan request the first of the week. He turned, their eyes meeting. His were cautious, looking to her for some lead.

"Hello, Jack."

"Paisley." He looked behind her and she followed his gaze. The wall clock read straight-up three. "Closing time. You made it just in the nick of time."

"Did I?" Her tongue felt stuck to the roof of her mouth, and that was the only idiotic thing she could think of to say. "Guess I'll scoot on out then."

Jack touched her lightly on the wrist, the warmth of his fingers causing a hitch in her breath. "Could we talk a minute?"

"I didn't come to interrupt your work."

"Hang on." He stepped to the teller and said something she couldn't hear, then returned and held the door for her. "Even lowly loan officers get a break once in a while. Soon as they lock the front doors, all the tellers run to the back room for a smoke, so no one will miss me."

The sky had darkened while she'd been setting up the account. Jack eyed the clouds. "Looks like a storm brewing."

"Which means I oughta get back. I don't want to get Dusty's car stuck on the dirt road."

"I was going to ask if you wanted to go in the drugstore—"

"That's my next stop. I'm dropping off the film I shot today. I'll meet you there in a jiff."

Jack had a root beer float waiting after she'd turned in the film. He took a slurp, elbows on the counter. "Déjà vu?"

"Sort of."

"I heard back from Dusty. I guess she told you I'd written."

"She did."

"You're not making this easy for me, you know."

"What can I say? Sure, we'll just pretend you never had a thing for my cousin, who just happens to be my best friend. I'll bring you over and introduce you as my new boyfriend, and you'll say, 'Hey, I think I used to date you.'"

"I am sensitive to Dusty's feelings. And those of her dad. I've done some work for him and admire his work ethic, his natural ability for running a company. I tried to bring it up with him a couple of times."

"And all he wanted to talk about was his airplane. A Cessna, right?"

"Then I guess he told you all about it."

"That's all he talked about."

"Like I said, I don't want to upset him or Dusty. And most of all you."

"Dusty has some friends coming over on Saturday. They're going fossil hunting down on the creek, and I thought I might take some photos of them, especially if they find a T.rex skull or something. You could come with me if you like, and we'll see how things go with Dusty. Maybe if we're all together, it will just naturally work out."

"I don't want to intrude on her party. Any people I know?"

"No. This is a geology club from the college near Alborghetti. Their version of spring break is to hunt for mummified clams and extinct critters."

"I knew she was interested in geology, just didn't realize it was an obsession." He pushed his empty glass aside. "I'll be over Saturday. Around ten in the morning?"

"Wear old clothes. And boots."

"We'll be really stepping out, huh?"

"Like I said, let's just see what happens."

Dusty spent all day Friday with the Rock Hounds on their field trip to Dinosaur Valley. They scouted out the famed dinosaur footprints in the limestone waters of the Paluxy River, but their best finds were in the exposed layers of a recent roadcut made to access a picnic area. They divided duties throughout the day—digging, chiseling, and sifting the fossil-rich matter in the layers of the cut. They turned up sea urchins, clams, and gastropods. Dana and her team hooted when they found a patch reef made up of rudista. The cone-shaped bivalves were flat on the top with spiked bases, cradled for millions of years in what had once been an ocean-covered land.

Everything was recorded and photos taken of each specimen, both a close-up and then a shot of the area where the discoveries were made. Ramsey was a natural leader at organizing and had a keen eye for hot spots. He took off his shirt during the heat of the day, his upper body muscled with a tuft of dark, curly hair on his chest. He had an outdoors look that Dusty found surprisingly appealing. The other students treated Dusty like one of the crowd, and she was glad for the opportunity to talk to Mr. Williams, the sponsoring professor, who was as enthused as anyone when they found something new.

At dusk, they loaded the shovels, picks, rock hammers, and sifting baskets in the back of the school van and washed up at a spigot in the picnic area. They had blisters on their feet, sunburned faces, and rough hands to show for their day's work. Someone hauled a cooler full of pop and beer from the van while someone else built a fire in a limestone pit. They roasted wieners and ate bags of Oreo cookies and munched on toasted marshmallows while they made plans for the next day.

Dusty pulled a crumpled, damp piece of paper from her pocket and gave it to Mr. Williams. "Here's the directions to the ranch.

Just park anywhere around the house. We can maybe take one of Daddy's old pickups to haul the equipment down to the creek so we don't have to carry it."

Ramsey said, "If we can even move tomorrow."

Dana said, "You're out of shape, Jonesey, but man, I wish I'd put more of that Coppertone on my face. I'm going to be beet red tomorrow."

Ramsey shot back, "At least we'll see you coming with your neon glow." He leaned over and whispered to Dusty, "Thanks for coming. I had a great time."

Dusty sighed. "The best." To the group she said, "Now don't forget, we're eating at the ranch tomorrow night. Rosalita's tamales. World famous."

They dropped her off at their motel in Glen Rose where she'd left her car that morning and told her to be careful going home.

"I'll be all right long as I don't hit a coyote on the highway. See you tomorrow."

She wished her dad had waited up so she could tell him about her day. So that he could see the thrill of exhaustion from doing that which she loved. He'd already turned in, though, and had told Paisley to tell her he'd see her at breakfast.

The alarm rang way too early, but Dusty shot out of bed and pulled on khaki shorts and a striped blouse she knew would be filthy before midday. Her new hiking boots had worked great, and as she was lacing them up, Paisley stumbled into the room still in her sleep shirt.

Dusty said, "You didn't have to get up."

"I forgot to tell you something last night. Jack's coming over today."

Dusty knew she hadn't forgotten, but she also understood. Paisley was being gracious and sparing Dusty's feelings. She gave Paisley two thumbs-up. "Sounds great. What are y'all going to do?"

"Just putter around. I told him I'd like to take some shots of you and the earth diggers in action, so we might come down to the creek later. Just didn't want you to freak out."

"I wouldn't freak out, but thanks. I hope you and Jack have a great day."

"You, too."

Her dad was nursing his second cup of coffee when she came down. "Hey, sleepyhead."

"It's only seven o'clock. You're up early."

"Lots of fish to fry today. New rig going up in the south part of the county."

"I was hoping you'd stay and meet the Rock Hounds. We had a swell time yesterday down on the Paluxy. I hope they're not disappointed in our little creek after all the great finds from yesterday."

Her daddy drained his coffee cup. "Good luck. Maybe this little adventure will get this out of your system."

"Don't count on it."

"That's what I'm afraid of. At least you didn't volunteer to take them on a field trip to one of my rigs."

"That's a great idea."

"Don't even think about it." He put on his work Stetson, the one with oil stains on the brim. "By the way, one of the ranch hands said the old bridge over the creek took a beating in that last storm we had. They're coming over next week to pull it down. You and your rock nuts better steer clear."

"They're Rock Hounds, Daddy. And they're not interested in anything except what's in the creek bed."

He kissed her on the cheek and told her that he'd see her at supper.

Twenty minutes later, the college van pulled into the driveway.

She'd forgotten to ask about borrowing one of her dad's old trucks, but she didn't think he'd mind. She took the key from the rack by the back door and stepped out into the new dawn.

❦

"Play that last part again—the 'crazy for loving you part.'" Jack leaned back in the glider under the pergola, his legs stretched before him, cowboy boots crossed at the ankle.

Paisley elbowed him and said, "How about this instead?" She played a couple of licks and put some twang in her voice as she sang "Just Walk on By."

Jack gave her a lazy grin. "Is that how you serenade all your boyfriends?"

She laid the guitar aside. "Guess that depends on what you mean by *all*."

"The guys you've probably been dating over at charm school."

"Yeah, they're lining up all the way down the drive. How is it that you've made it all this time and not found someone?"

"Just waiting for the right one to come along." He rubbed his chin, and Paisley wondered if he was thinking about Dusty. "Most of the ones my sister picks out have a pedigree a mile long and belong to the country club."

"Country clubs are nice."

"I've been to my share. According to my parents I have underaspired to greatness."

"But you have a degree and your CPA."

"Which, to my dad, should just be a stepping-stone to law school and then politics, like him."

A gentle breeze blew the scent of sagebrush their way. Off in the distance, one of the pump jacks of her uncle Flint's wells bobbed up and down. "And your mom? What does she do?"

"Volunteers at the children's hospital and takes care of my dad. She always wanted to be a nurse but got married, had us kids, and just never got around to it. She understands, I think, that I just want to live a quiet life in a small town like Two Forks."

"Or one in Alaska."

He laughed. "It was the farthest place I could think of when I wrote you that letter. I actually like it just fine in Texas." He draped his arm casually across the back of the glider and twirled a strand of hair on the back of Paisley's neck. "So how about you? Your mom doing okay since Christmas?"

The gentle motion of the glider and the smell of spring toyed with her senses. She'd thought of Edie even more since she and Dusty had been back and still couldn't imagine why her mother ever wanted to leave the ranch and her family. Paisley was tired of playing games, pretending everything was okay.

She said simply, "I haven't heard from her, and truthfully, I don't know that I will."

"You want to talk about it?"

"Yeah, sometime I would. Just not today. Let's walk down to the creek and see how the creek robbers are doing. I'd like to take some pictures for my scrapbook. And if you're nice, I might even take one of you."

He rose and offered her a hand up, then laced his fingers in hers as they went to the house to get the camera.

The walk down to the creek wasn't that long, and before they got there, one of the Rock Hounds hollered, "Got something over here. Anybody know where the shovel is?" Someone answered back, and like worker bees, a swarm of bodies moved toward whatever treasure had been unearthed. Paisley lifted the camera and took some shots from a distance, then turned to Jack. "I think I'd like to get some from the old bridge. You can see the pools and all better from up there."

"Dusty took me up there. Sort of rickety, isn't it?"

"Yeah, but it's been that way forever. We've been going across it since we were in grade school. Or rather Dusty would force me to go with her. Truthfully, it scares the bejeebies out of me. Her brothers used to jump off into the creek after a big rain and there was plenty of water to break their jump."

"I hope you're not planning on doing that today."

"Are you kidding? I'm terrified of heights."

"Then don't go up there."

"I want to take the pictures so Dusty will have them for our scrapbook."

A plane buzzed overhead as they neared the bridge. Paisley pointed. "There's Uncle Flint. Guess he's showing off for Dusty and her friends."

Jack shielded his eyes with his hand and looked up. "Looks like they're circling back."

Paisley took a tentative step on the bridge, then another and another, as the roar of the plane engine filled her ears. She lifted the Canon to get a shot of the plane and thought she heard someone scream. *Click. Wind the film. Click.*

The bridge creaked, the motion more rocking than she remembered.

Another shout. This time from Jack.

A cracking noise splintered the air. Paisley lost her footing and grabbed for the rail. She groped at air as the bridge gave way. Airborne, across the expanse of the creek, she plummeted toward the muddy water below.

CHAPTER 32

Dusty didn't know what was worse—waiting to find out if Paisley would live or facing the wrath of her dad.

"What in the name of thunder were you thinking? I told you not to go on the bridge." His eyes flashed as he stormed up the tiled hall of the Burroughs County Hospital where Dusty waited outside the emergency room with Jack on one side, Ramsey on the other. The events swirled in her head. The ambulance. Shouting. Everyone trying to leave at once. The only one who hadn't been on the scene was her dad who was up in his silly airplane.

"I didn't think—"

"That's just it. You didn't think about anything except running off with a bunch of people who are putting fanciful ideas in your head." He glared at Ramsey and gave him a dismissive look.

"Like Aunt Edie did with my mother?"

He glared at her, his jaw twitching. "It's not the same thing at all."

"What's different about it?"

"My sister is a loony bird, that's what."

"The sister whose daughter is lying on a stretcher fighting for her life?"

"She isn't going to die."

"We don't know that." A wave of terror, like the ones that had come with stomach heaves and heart palpitations ever since the accident, buckled Dusty's knees. She leaned on Ramsey for support and closed her eyes. The image of Paisley flying through the air burned behind her eyelids; her head filled with her cousin's screams and the roar of her daddy's airplane.

Dusty struggled for breath and opened her eyes. The eerie flickering of fluorescent light gave a sallow tinge to her dad's clenched jaws.

Dusty trembled, her breaths fast and shallow. "You're right. If she dies, it *will* be all my fault." She put a tentative hand on her daddy's arm, then clamped his muscled forearm. "My fault. All because of me, Paisley might die. My fault! Do you hear me? All. My. Fault!"

Her shoulders shook as tears built up and fell on her cheeks, and she succumbed to the reality.

Her daddy gathered her in his arms and held her to his chest. His rough hand ran the length of her hair, his fingers catching in the tangles. "I'm sorry, baby."

"I will never…I couldn't…not ever…forgive myself. Ever."

"Shhh. It's all right." He led her away and sat her down; she wasn't sure where. He sat beside her, his arm strong around her as she turned her face to his chest and sobbed.

"Mr. Fairchild?"

Dusty looked up at a man in a green surgical suit. Her dad stood and extended his hand. "I'm Fairchild."

"I'm Dr. Hinds. Is the girl in there your daughter?"

"No sir. My niece. How is she?"

"She's not out of the woods yet. There's a fracture of her right femur, the upper bone in the leg—"

"Yes, I know what a femur is. What else?"

"She's still unconscious, which is not unusual after trauma to the head, but there doesn't seem to be any increased intracranial pressure. We're monitoring that, of course, and have stitched up the laceration on her scalp, as well as several on the right arm. We'll set the leg as soon as we're sure she's stable."

Jack had walked up while the doctor talked. The doctor turned to him.

"Are you her husband?"

Jack shook his head. "A good friend. Can I go in and see her?"

Her dad shot her an odd look, and Dusty whispered that she'd tell him later.

The doctor said, "Not yet. Someone will come and get you when you can go in. I'd like more information about the fall. Do any of you know what happened?"

Dusty's dad said, "She fell from an old bridge over the creek on my ranch. It shoulda been torn down long ago. My fault entirely."

Jack shook his head. "I blame myself. I was with Paisley and shouldn't have let her go. She'd only taken a dozen steps or so when I heard the wood snap." His own voice cracked, and he couldn't finish.

The doctor nodded. "Accidents happen. Does she have other family?"

Dusty's dad said, "Her mother's out in California. I've already taken steps to notify her. She'll be here."

"Steps? What steps?" Dusty asked her dad about it when the doctor had finished.

"Soon as I realized it was Paisley and not you or one of your friends, I put my pilot in charge of finding her. And if I have to charter a Pan Am airplane to get my blasted sister here, I will."

❧

Jack and Dusty remained with Paisley, one on either side. Ramsey had disappeared, or perhaps he'd told her good-bye and she'd been in a fog and didn't hear him.

Paisley remained unconscious. A coma, one of the nurses said. Her vitals were stable, but a pallor remained in her cheeks. Lifeless except for the steady rise and fall of the starched sheet over her chest. Paisley's leg, they'd been told, broke clean and had been set, but was immobilized with a splint and clouds of padding.

"They'll cast it later," the nurse told them. Dusty wondered if it they were waiting to see if she still might die.

The pastor from the Methodist church came and prayed over Paisley as did the priest from Rosalita's little congregation. Hoards of friends filled the waiting room, and the ladies' circle had put the prayer chain into action within thirty minutes of the accident. Dusty hadn't stopped praying, and she knew Jack hadn't either.

Late in the evening, Patrick stuck his head in and signaled for Dusty.

Ramsey waited in the hall, washed up but still wearing his dungarees and hiking boots. "How's she doing?"

"About the same. The doctor came in a while ago and said her deep reflexes were good, which was a positive sign. I thought you all would be long gone by now."

"When I went back out, the others were packing up. Your housekeeper insisted we stay for the tamales she'd made. I think she was glad to have company around. We're on our way back to Glen Rose now. Do you want me to come tomorrow?"

"I'm all right. I'm sure you all have plans."

He fished in his pocket and pulled out a scrap of paper. "Here's my folks' number and the one back at school. Call me."

"Thanks, Ramsey."

She and Jack took turns staying at Paisley's bedside during the night. A nurse brought a pillow and blanket to the waiting room so one could rest while the other kept watch over Paisley.

The smell of fresh coffee woke Dusty. She bolted upright, the first whisper of morning light seeping through the window. She stood at the window and remembered it was Easter. Resurrection Sunday, the pastor always called it. Her heart was as heavy as she knew the followers of Jesus must have been on that long ago morning before the stone was rolled away.

She followed the smell of the coffee and asked a nurse for two cups for her and Jack. She set them on the nightstand and looked at Jack. He leaned over Paisley, the back of his finger gently caressing her cheek. He smiled when he saw her on the other side of the bed, but it wasn't the smile that touched Dusty as much as the look in his eyes. Tenderness. Hope. A love for Paisley.

He stroked the length of Paisley's arm, then gently lifted her fingers and placed them in his palm. He jumped, his eyes widening. "I think she tried to squeeze my hand." He leaned over and whispered to her, "Squeeze my hand if you can hear me." His blinked and waited, then looked up, his face beaming as he said, "Yes. Thank you, God."

⚜

Paisley didn't wake up until eleven that morning. Almost twenty-four hours after she'd plunged into the creek. And when she did wake up, it was her mother, Edie's face, she saw.

"Mother?" Confusion knit Paisley's brows together.

"Yes, baby doll, it's me. Oh, I was hoping and praying you were going to be all right and here you are, like an angel." Aunt Edie leaned over and kissed Paisley's forehead, leaving a lipstick smudge.

Behind her, Dusty's daddy stood, looking weary but happy. He jerked his head toward the door, and Dusty followed him out.

"How did you find her?"

"Colonel MacIntosh, the pilot of that little toy you snubbed your nose at, knows how to ferret people out. At least he knows who to call. They found her in a rooming house in San Francisco. At least she was sober."

"Something about her seems different. Not so flashy."

"She's had a spiritual awakening she says. You ask me, I think she's high on something."

"Daddy, I wish you'd stop. Look, we all know how awful I'd feel if Paisley had died. Did you ever stop to think that maybe Aunt Edie, whether she's guilty or not, might also feel bad about my mother dying. I think it's time to bury the hatchet."

"If Edith's sorry, all she has to do is say so."

Dusty thought it was her weariness that made her hear wrong. She wrinkled her nose and looked at him. "All she has to do is say she's sorry? She hasn't done that?"

"Not that I heard. All she wanted to do was blame me for telling Aggie she couldn't go to Fort Worth with her."

"We were both wrong." They turned to find Aunt Edie had stepped out of Paisley's room behind them. "I apologize. I'm sorry. I wish I'd never asked Aggie to go with me."

Dusty's dad looked at her cautiously. "I'm sorry, too. For a lot of things. Mostly I'm sorry that your daughter is laid up in that hospital bed for something that was my own foolish fault. I've been so busy playing oil tycoon that I haven't taken care of things in my own backyard. Like Dusty. And Stringbean."

Aunt Edie gave him a strange look. "Who's Stringbean?"

"That kid of yours. If you'd come around once in a while during the summers instead of just dropping her off, you'd know that's what I call her."

It was the beginning of a truce. And the beginning of Paisley's recovery.

Jack was ready for a nap and a shower, but before he left, he asked to talk to Dusty in the hall. "Look, I know we've not talked about what transpired between us, but just so you know, I'm sorry I'm a louse…for writing you a Dear John letter."

"You had more guts than I did. I knew we weren't meant to be, but I didn't say anything."

"Will you forgive me?"

"Only if you promise to take good care of my cousin in there. She deserves someone nice. Someone like you, Jack."

He held up his hand. "My honest promise." He took one of her hands and pressed it to his lips. "Thank you."

Paisley clung to her mother's hand, afraid to let go lest it was a vision and she was only dreaming that Edie had come. And yet it was like a dream, Edie dressed in plain slacks and a white blouse, looking like mothers were supposed to look. And when Edie leaned over to kiss her forehead for the tenth time, she smelled different, a soft, powdery scent.

"Tell me again, how did you get here?"

"I flew, sugar. Your uncle Flint sent someone to find me. He's something special, you know that?"

Paisley was sure now she was in a dream. "Uncle Flint?"

"I know it's hard to believe I would say that, but I've had some divine revelations since I last saw you."

"Ollie didn't get you mixed up in some cult, did he?"

"No, I've found something better. The real deal. But we have worlds of time for me to tell you about that. You take a little nap, and then I'll brush your hair and put a little color on your lips. Then I want to hear all about this beau of yours. Dusty whispered something to me earlier about Jack. Said he's crazy over you."

Paisley felt her eyelids fluttering, but she forced them open and looked once again at her mother's face. "Jack's nice. I'm glad you came."

She tried to say, "I love you," but sleep pulled her into a dream of aquamarine skies with camellia blossoms for clouds. Ribbons streamed through the trees as confetti floated in the breeze like sprinkles from heaven.

CHAPTER 33

Rosalita warmed up the leftover tamales and fixed corn salad with onions, pimiento and green peppers, and her special vinegar and oil dressing. Only three of them dined that evening: Dusty, her dad, and Aunt Edie, who had stayed with Paisley until Jack returned. They were all tired and relieved and happy at the same time, but also uncertain about how to rip apart old wounds and stitch them back together.

Aunt Edie started them off. "Flint, I think it's high time you put a fresh coat of paint on these walls. Squirrel gray may have been all the rage when Aggie picked out the color, but I think a lovely lemon color would brighten things up, don't you?"

Dusty's dad stuffed half a tamale in his mouth so he wouldn't have to answer. Aunt Edie looked at Dusty with raised eyebrows.

Dusty said, "Yellow might work, but aqua and coral are quite the fashion now. Trust me, I've looked at enough magazines this year that I can tell you the latest colors for weddings, countertops, luggage, and going-away outfits. And Miss Fontaine said fashion trends seem to mirror home decor."

"A pale aqua, then."

Dusty's dad cleared his throat. "We're not painting the dining room. End of discussion. And we all know you brought it up because you don't want to talk about what happened in the past. I have some things to tell you, but first, Edith, why don't you tell Dusty why you left here in the first place?"

"Well, aren't you the fly in the ointment?" Aunt Edie looked at Dusty. "When I grew up, things weren't like they are now at the ranch. There weren't any oil wells shooting money in the sky, although our daddy kept saying, '*Someday.*' I got tired of waiting and swore I was getting away from Two Forks the first chance I got. Mama died of the flu one winter, and Flint was already dating your mama, Aggie. I got lonesome and started hitching rides with some of the cowboys over to the rodeos in Fort Worth for some fun. Daddy got wind of it and told me he better never catch me in a bar or he'd give me what for. But the Great Depression was squeezing the life right out of me on this ranch. We ate so many cottontails for supper that I checked in the mirror every morning to see if I sprouted fur on my face."

Dusty's dad shook his head. "Enough of the drama, Edith. Just tell her what you did that got you written out of our daddy's will."

Aunt Edie sighed. "I had one of my boyfriends load Daddy's prized mule in his horse trailer and take it to the livestock sale. With the proceeds, I bought me a pair of red high heels, a wind-up phonograph, and a stack of shellac records. I told Daddy I was going to be on the Grand Ole Opry one day. He threw my stuff out the door and told me I better start walking because Nashville was a long ways from Texas."

She told how she hitchhiked her way clear to the Mississippi River and worked as a waitress for a few months. She wrote and lied to her daddy, told him she was fixin' to make a record. He died before she ever made it to Nashville, and when she returned to Texas a month later, she found out her brother had inherited everything, that she'd been disowned. She'd been trying to find her way to stardom ever since.

Dusty was puzzled about the oil wells, but her dad filled her in on that. The first well had come shortly after their dad died. Most of the Fairchild ranch he'd bought a few acres at a time, and luckily one of the pieces was the one where he struck it rich. He and Aggie married, had kids, built the house, and became the wealthiest people in Two Forks.

"What about you, Aunt Edie? Where were you during this time?"

"All over the place, sweetie. But when I wound up expecting without a husband to show for it, I came back to Two Forks. Your daddy didn't exactly roll out the welcome mat, but your mama was sweet as she could be and was helping me get my life in order. The thing your daddy doesn't know because he never asked me is that when Aggie and I went into Fort Worth, I was going to see about enrolling in secretary school. I wanted to make a better life for my baby girl."

Dusty's daddy choked like he had a bone stuck in his throat.

Aunt Edie went on. "When he accused me of killing your mama—"

"I never said you killed her."

"Same as."

"You've always been so busy doing what pleases you; you never look to see what you're doing to others. Maybe I could have gotten over that you were the reason she wanted to go in the first place. But after Aggie died, you lit out of here like you didn't even care about her. Or the kids. Or me."

"Flint, I'm truly sorry for what I did. For the life I gave Paisley and the way things have turned out."

"Ah, your spiritual awakening, I believe you said."

"Sometimes God hits you over the head. Or in my case sends someone like Ollie Winesap to do the work for him. When the audition fell through, we got in an argument. He beat me and left me in the gutter the end of January. A good Samaritan came along and took me into her home. A big old mammy kind of woman nursed my wounds and read to me out of the Psalms. It didn't happen overnight, but I believe there's someone who was watching out for me. Someone who isn't finished with Edie Horton."

Dusty believed her. The same one had been watching out for Paisley. She looked at her dad and saw him weighing it all in his mind. He hollered for Rosalita to bring him a toothpick. When she did, he told her to go get the cedar box off the top of his desk. She returned with it and asked if there was anything else.

"Yes, sit down. You're as much a part of this family as Edith or anyone else. I have something to show you all."

Glances ping-ponged around the table, wondering what her dad was up to.

He pulled out a stack of papers. "These are the oil royalty papers from the original oil well from our daddy. Other than the first couple of years when I used the money to buy land, I've never touched a dime of this. It's all sitting in a bank in Fort Worth. Some of it is for Rosie's retirement. And I was planning to give the rest to Paisley when she turned twenty-five. Instead, I'm giving it to you, Edith."

Aunt Edie gasped, then cried, then hugged her brother's neck. Rosalita dabbed at the corners of her eyes, then got up and brought them all bowls of cherry cobbler.

Aunt Edie licked her spoon and said she thought she'd leave the money there awhile longer. "I thought I might stay here and help Paisley get back on her feet, then look for a job and a little place in town."

Dusty said, "Daddy's looking for another secretary."

He shot her a look and shook his head. "I'm not that desperate." Then he took Aunt Edie's hand. "All you had to do was say 'I'm sorry.'"

Dusty called Miss Fontaine to tell her about the accident. The following Saturday, Dusty returned to Rosebriar by herself, leaving Paisley at the ranch under Rosalita and Aunt Edie's care.

She met Ramsey at the Alborghetti drugstore for a Coke before reporting in at Rosebriar. He'd brought her the two things she'd requested and walked her out to the T-Bird after she'd told him the latest news about Paisley.

Her room had a stale, empty feeling. She set her luggage down and opened the window for some fresh air, but not a breath was stirring. She turned on the radio and rested her arms on the sill as she pondered what she should do first. Aunt Edie's story had made her realize time was too short to waste it holding a grudge or not speaking up. That even when we make mistakes, people are usually more forgiving than you think.

The radio announcer said, "And now, a new song from Patsy Cline recorded only twenty-eight days before she died, 'Sweet Dreams.'" Dusty could scarcely breathe as Patsy's pure, rich voice filled the room. Patsy was gone, but her music would live on. And so would they.

She picked up her suitcases, marched down the hall, and knocked on the door of the Rosebud Room. When Sharon Kay opened the door, Dusty said, "I was wondering. Are you in need of a roommate?"

"Only if you didn't bring those stupid rocks."

Dusty held out one of the boxes she'd gotten from Ramsey. "Just one. And it's for you."

Sharon Kay bit her lip and opened the box. A rock, split open and about the size of a goose egg, sparkled inside with a million crystals. "Is this like a fossil?"

"Not exactly, although they both take eons to form. It's a geode like the one I have. Funny thing is, you never know what's inside until they're broken." She pointed to the one Sharon Kay cradled in her palm. "That one is stunning. Like you."

Sharon Kay sighed and smiled. "Thank you."

Dusty waited until after church on Sunday to deliver the other box. When all the girls were either out for the afternoon or deep into a game of canasta, she slipped into the hall on the far side of the parlor and knocked on Miss Fontaine's door. After a round of polite conversation and repeating what she'd already told her the day before about Paisley, Dusty asked Miss Fontaine to have a seat.

She sat kitty-corner from her on the love seat and handed her the box.

Miss Fontaine's fingers trembled as she removed the top and looked at the geode.

Dusty didn't wait for her to ask questions or say thank you. "It's for Robin. I would like to take it to her myself, but that would be disrespectful of you and the life you've made for your daughter. I would like to ask you, though, to consider what the truth might set free."

"I could never."

"It would be hard, but perhaps no harder than living a lie and letting Mr. Simon control your life. The next girl he approaches might not be so lucky to have you walk in on her."

"No. My reputation would be ruined. My business. The only way I have to provide for Robin."

"I'm not telling you whether you're right or wrong, only that times have changed. People are more open to things than they used to be. And think of the possibilities for Robin. A new set of friends every year. The freedom to run wherever she chooses. A mother who's never more than a room or two away."

Tears fell from Miss Fontaine's eyes, but still she shook her head. "It's too much to think of. I can't."

"I understand. And I honor the vow of silence I gave to Winston and Sulee. I haven't told a soul, and I won't. But I'll be the first in line to hug Robin if you change your mind."

"Why? Why are you so willing to do this after what I did to you?"

"Life is too short to live with shame and regret. We all have dreams, desires that nearly burst our hearts. Have you asked Robin what hers is?"

Miss Fontaine folded her hands around the box and leaned back, gently rocking in her chair.

Dusty slipped quietly out the door.

CHAPTER 34

Graduation, 1963

Fancy cars filled the circle drive of Miss Fontaine's Finishing School, so many that some had to park on the grass between the house and the bayou. Dusty, with Ramsey at her side, watched from behind the lace curtains in the parlor as a red Cadillac with Mississippi plates dispensed Carmel's mother in her pillbox hat and her aunt Pearl resplendent in an ivory suit and wide-brimmed straw hat. Parents, grandparents, and assorted cousins with little boys in short pants and girls in frilly dresses made a steady stream toward Rosebriar, spilling from DeSotos, Galaxies, Buick Rivieras, and even a Corvette.

And then, right on time, her daddy's Continental followed by Jack's Spitfire and Patrick's pickup roared up the drive bringing the whole Fairchild clan. Even Rosalita in a bright poppy-colored dress and her Sunday hat.

The patio was set up with two-dozen tables covered in white linen cloths and riotous bouquets of roses cut from the garden. A canvas canopy covered a makeshift wooden stage with a small podium and two rows of chairs for the charm school graduates.

Miss Fontaine wore a smart new suit with a matching hat and approached the dais. She welcomed everyone and gave a little speech before she handed out the diplomas to her "girls." "You know my motto—a properly trained woman who exudes warmth and charm will always be an asset to Southern society. And there are none finer than the 1963 graduating class."

Dusty's eyes blurred with tears as each girl received her diploma with a white-gloved hand, perfectly poised. They wore frothy dresses of pink and lavender and sky blue. Chiffon and silk, lace and satin. When it was her turn, Dusty smoothed the pencil skirt of her icy-aqua sheath that the saleslady said accentuated her long, slender legs. All she knew was Ramsey's eyes had popped open when he first saw her.

Paisley's name was the last called. She'd insisted she didn't want help with her crutches, so she swung them out in front of her and hoisted herself up. Her red dress with white polka dots and a halter neckline swirled as she gimped her way to the front. Her long gloves covered the healing wounds on her arms, and her white canvas tennis shoes tied with red ribbons helped with her balance.

To Miss Fontaine's credit, she didn't bat an eye and waited patiently while Paisley propped the crutches under her arms and accepted her diploma. Xan, in a navy maternity smock with white piping, rose from a table near the back and cheered, clapping until Prentice tugged on her arm. Paisley blinked back tears, but still they moistened her cheeks.

After Miss Fontaine dismissed them, she strode erect to her place at the head table where Winston held a chair for her between his wife, Sulee, and a young woman whose smile was brighter than a thousand suns. Robin wore a dress of pink lace with a satin sash and cradled a fuzzy yellow bear in one arm.

The air was filled with the clatter of silverware and bubbling voices as waiters in crisp white shirts and black cummerbunds served the garden luncheon. Airy cirrus clouds sailed overhead, the chirp of a nearby warbler bringing birdsong.

Aunt Edie poised a butterflake roll in her fingers and leaned close to Dusty. "I saw the For Sale sign in the window of Simple Pleasures as we came through town. Paisley told me what a gruesome man Mr. Simon turned out to be."

"We're just sorry we didn't get you that jewelry box you liked before he hightailed it out of town."

"Any idea where he went?"

"Paris, we heard."

"Gracious, all the way to France, huh?"

"No. Paris, Texas."

They laughed, and Dusty asked Ramsey if he was enjoying the dinner.

"Nothing to compare to Rosalita's tamales, but tasty all the same." He nodded in the direction of the bayou. "Any chance we might go down there later and do a little rock hunting?"

"Depends on if you play your cards right."

At the next table, Paisley and Jack were like two lovebirds, and they'd squeezed a couple of extra places in for Xan and Prentice to sit with them. Xan giggled when Paisley raised the new Nikon camera Jack bought her for graduation and snapped their picture.

When the waiters took the plates away, Paisley struggled to her feet and tapped a spoon on her water glass. "Listen up, everyone! Jack is going to lug all my stuff out to the fountain so I can take pictures. And he's promised to take a group shot. Just no dancing in the fountain."

Dusty's daddy shook his head and said, "Stringbean's a corker, I'll give her that." He clapped Ramsey on the back. "Now that Dusty's practically got her bags packed for Miller College, you better keep a good eye on her."

"Yes, sir. You can count on that. Miller College is lucky to get her after all the offers she had."

"You got that right." He ambled off and whispered something to Carmel's aunt Pearl. She gave him a dazzling smile when he lifted her hand to his lips and said it was a pleasure meeting her. He worked around the room, chatting and nodding, doing what he did best. Dusty thought her heart would burst.

Then it was time for pictures by the fountain, and Paisley shot four rolls of film. All the girls, their sweethearts, their families. Sharon Kay stood at the edge of the crowd, putting on a brave front, but Dusty knew she was disappointed that neither of her parents had come. They'd gone instead on a Caribbean cruise that had been booked for months and couldn't be changed.

Dusty grabbed Sharon Kay's hand and dragged her into the Fairchild family picture where she stood next to Patrick. He draped a friendly arm around Sharon Kay's shoulders and asked if they could share some lemonade later.

The crowd thinned, and one by one, cars began pulling out of their parking places. When Paisley asked if anyone else wanted a snapshot, Miss Fontaine stepped to the fountain, holding Robin's hand. There, in the shadow of Rosebriar, Miss Fontaine bent down and removed her shoes and told Robin she could as well. The two of them joined hands and ran barefoot through the grass while Paisley aimed the Nikon and clicked picture after picture.

Miss Fontaine's hat bobbled off-center and nobody seemed to notice. Or mind.

1. Who was your closest childhood friend? What kinds of things did you share? Did you talk about your dreams? What was the craziest thing you ever did growing up?

2. Both Dusty and Paisley are like fish out of water when they arrive at Miss Fontaine's. Have you ever been in a situation where you felt you didn't belong? If so, did you try to gain acceptance or were you comfortable being who you were? Discuss the notion of "belonging."

3. Which of the two cousins did you relate to more? What qualities did you admire in Dusty? Paisley?

4. Miss Fontaine was committed to maintaining propriety while harboring her own dark secret from the past. At what point in *Sweet Dreams* did you suspect she was hiding something? What social and moral codes led her to make the decisions she did about Robin? How has that changed today?

5. Flint Fairchild and Edie Horton both let pride and lack of communication stifle their relationship. Discuss the merits of open family communication. Has anyone ever asked you for forgiveness? How did you respond? Have you ever had to ask someone for forgiveness?

6. In the love triangle with Dusty, Jack, and Paisley, what did you hope would happen? Was Paisley justified in staying quiet to spare Dusty's feelings? Were you pleased or surprised at the outcome?

7. How does the tragic death of Patsy Cline bring Dusty and Paisley closer together? Have you ever been emotionally affected by the misfortune or death of a public figure?

8. What social and fashion trends of the 1960s are different today? Name two or three. How would sexual harassment of a student be handled today?

9. Dusty wanted to buck the trend by going into a predominantly male field, while Paisley took the opposite path and wanted a traditional "house with a picket fence" life. Which route describes you more? How do childhood experiences mold people's dreams?

10. What dream have you always had that seems impossible? Today the term *bucket list* is popular. What's on your list?

If you liked *Sweet Dreams,*
you may also enjoy Carla Stewart's
other nostalgic novels.

Stardust

"STARDUST is a smooth, inviting, well told story that will stick with you long after you read the last line and close the book. A worthy read."

—Rachel Hauck, award-winning author
of *Dining with Joy*

When Georgia Peyton is suddenly widowed with two young daughters to care for, she decides to make a new life by taking over the run-down Stardust motel. But the guests who arrive aren't what Georgia expects: her gin-loving mother-in-law, her dead husband's mistress, an attractive drifter, and an aging Vaudeville entertainer with a disturbing link to Georgia's past. Georgia's only hope is to find forgiveness for those who betrayed her, the grace to shelter those who need her, and the moxie to face the future.

Broken Wings

"Set against the backdrop of Tulsa's intriguing jazz culture, Carla Stewart's *Broken Wings* is a captivating intergenerational tale of friendship, love, and music that surpasses the boundaries of age and time."
—Tina Ann Forkner, author of *Ruby Among Us* and *Rose House*

Onstage, the singing duo of Gabe and Mitzi Steiner captured America's heart for more than two decades. Offstage, their own hearts have throbbed as one for sixty years. Only now, Gabe has retreated into the tangles of Alzheimer's, leaving Mitzi to ponder her future alone. Then an accident lands a young woman named Brooke Woodson in the hospital where Mitzi volunteers. Brooke is in a troubled relationship and the two women quickly develop an unlikely friendship. With Mitzi's help, kindness, and insight, Brooke will learn how to pick up the broken pieces of her life.

Chasing Lilacs

Winner of the 2011 Oklahoma Writers Federation, Inc. Fiction Book of the Year

"Coming-of-age stories are a fiction staple, but well-done ones much rarer. This emotionally acute novel is one of the rare ones."
— *Publisher's Weekly,* starred review

The summer of 1958 should be simple and carefree for Sammie Tucker, but Sammie has plenty of questions—about her mother's "nerve" problems. About shock treatments. About whether her mother loves her. As her life careens out of control, Sammie has to choose whom to trust with her deepest fears: her opinionated best friend, the mysterious boy from out-of-town, her round-faced neighbor with gentle advice and strong shoulders to cry on, or the nice elderly widower with his own dark past. Trusting is one thing, but accepting the truth may be the hardest thing Sammie has ever done.